Into the
Mouth
of the Kraken

Pat Cypress

Tellwell Talent
www.tellwell.ca

ISBN
978-1-77302-762-3 (Hardcover)
978-1-77302-761-6 (Paperback)
978-1-77302-763-0 (eBook)

The Big Lie

"If this so-called professor, Kathleen O'Malley, Francis Drake's traveller in time, thinks she can stop either of us from altering history…well, then she is a fool. I, John Stowe, historian, have every right to correct the wrongs of imperial Elizabethan blathering and the stupidity of a woman who thinks she can stop us."

Why should Elizabeth be the only one who controls what is put down for posterity? It is shameful what lies are conjured in order to prevent war, thought John. The bloody Spanish came anyway, and they were thoroughly slaughtered. John made the sign of the cross upon his body then bent over his desk and said a quick prayer to his Lord.

Sir Francis Drake and I, thought Stowe, will see to correcting these abominable lies made up by William Cecil, the late queen's secretary and Francis Walsingham, Elizabeth's manipulating spy maker. Furthermore, our late Queen Elizabeth and her puffing and preening Robert Dudley, the queen's infamous Master of the Horse, will succumb to my truer writings.

Well, I'll simply have to rid the world of their unfortunate alliances. I cannot put up with this virginal image she portrays. There I have said it, and so shall it be.

Elizabeth is, after all, a woman, unable to suppress her need for a man. None of them can. It is only men who are really capable and able to fully understand their own minds and control their desires, thought Stowe.

Now that so-called, great playwright, William Shakespeare has died as well as all the other Elizabethan courtiers. I can see to his historical undoing. What possible merits can he have in the future? Really, an actor, thought Stowe, a writer? What utter nonsense he doth write!

"I, John Stowe, historian of London, have far more intellectual contributory and stimulating facts to divulge than a mere playwright. I shall eliminate all traces of this bard, and my dearly departed friend, Sir Francis Drake, will finally be credited with the full accounting of his voyages of discovery. Nova Albion's true identity will be revealed, and history will finally be recorded properly!"

John paced his rooms. Speaking out loud always helped him to solidify his thoughts so much more clearly than mere writing, especially when it came to recording the past and supposed future.

"This traveller, whom Drake has, unfortunately, chosen in our pursuit of correcting history's misunderstandings, is a useless wench. She calls herself professor. Rubbish! What woman can teach?" he spat out.

So far, he thought, she has produced nothing of consequence, except of course that Spaniard, Carlos, and even then, she cannot remember those events. Saving a Spaniard! Really! What for?

A traveller in time, humph, and still she refuses to believe in the art of transference. Useless! I, however, have not forgotten the emotion of these events. What good can come from the use of her? Be rid of her, I say. Whatever Drake sees in her abilities, I cannot. Another means of persuasion will need to be inflicted upon her soul, something more compelling, something more...

Ah, the love for one's child, and she has several young boys. I think that will be a more riveting means of eliciting compliance.

That slippery so-called professor will be better controlled this time, he thought.

"She can forget about making any more foolish alliances again. Drake and I have plans. They are brilliant, of course. Changing -- no, recording history properly is imperative. We'll bring that conniving traveller to her knees." But then, thought Stowe, Drake and I are so much smarter anyways.

Children are a woman's biggest weakness. I'll set Francis Walsingham and his minions, Owen and the urchins into action against her. In fact I'll set a trap for her if she does not comply soon.

Unfortunately, I'll have to use one of Drake's secretive backers to manipulate this traveller as well. Dudley, that cagey Queen Elizabeth's infamous lover will become useful again, despite how much I did enjoy his passing.

"The art of transference! What a wonderful means of travel. I might even be able to improve upon the soul of Robert Dudley in the process this time. Oh, what a splendid idea. However did that prat garner the right to be made the Master of the Queen's Horses? Although stupid men are so easy to manipulate, especially prancing preening ones.

Owen, of course and his feeble wife Edith, pathetic, silly, stupid woman, I'll be using again. Owen, indecent bastard, useful, though, still a bastard and a Catholic."

Stowe shook his body in revulsion. This is one corrupt sinful Catholic, and hiding his sanctimonious religion by marrying a Protestant, even if she's a rather ungrateful one, she will be useful to our cause, he thought.

"Cecil, I'll need as well. He'll get wind of this traveller, once she returns to our England. He can smell distrust before it appears. Such a decisive individual. Brilliant, mindful of his faith. No, true to his -- our faith.

I was quite sorry to hear of Cecil's passing. Great man, really great man. At least this way I'll have another opportunity of speech with him. There are some benefits of transference I really quite like."

Cadboro Bay

"Nightmares, these bloody nightmares!"

Kathleen O'Malley, professor of history at the University of Victoria grabbed hold of her gym bag and quickly changed into her running gear. Upright and moving quickly was as good a way as any to rid herself of these distressing thoughts. How could she have possibly been part of the Elizabethan world? And yet they had seemed so real, thought Kathleen. She shook her head to rid herself of them.

"Stupid. Idiotic. What kind of person thinks they've been someplace before, especially in the very distant past. Breathe... deeply, run... just run it away."

On the path, Kathleen's body finally started to relax. She felt the ground more clearly beneath her feet. Solid ground was somehow very comforting right now. It was familiar, one foot landing in front of the other, soft soil, crunching leaves and the earthy smell of the woods.

"No bloody privateers, spies or invading Spanish forces in these woods."

Kathleen smirked to herself.

7

"I'll have just enough time to take the long route down towards the sea, zip through the path, past the elementary school and emerge at Cadboro Bay. I'll be showered, refreshed, my mind clear of these needling visions and all before lunch. Excellent."

Kathleen understood the evidence needed to establish Sir Francis Drake's long lost claims of discovery of the northern Pacific shores of Nova Albion were almost impossible to prove. Primary source documents were needed, not just the stories told by the Songhees and other Native tribes along British Columbia's Canadian coastline.

Francis Walsingham, Drake, Elizabeth I, William Cecil, Shakespeare, John Stowe all of them from the Elizabethan era, and all of them messing with her life. "No, I'm not doing this again. I have never been to Elizabethan London before. No, no, no!" Kathleen ran faster, determined to outrun her thoughts.

"But you have, my dear, you have."

Kathleen skidded to a stop, almost crashing into an enormous Douglas fir tree at the sound of that voice again.

"Go away," she yelled out at the abyss of trees.

"Fine. But I'll be back until you get it. You don't have a choice but to listen to me." She could hear him laughing at her, taunting her.

"Nope, I'm not going to listen to you anymore. I'm going to talk to someone about you and rid you from my everyday life. I'll decide, not you, what's real."

Last night was bloody awful, she thought. Was I really being chased down the streets of Old London by men on horseback? Kathleen remembered the sweat on her body after she had woken from the vision, her sheets clinging to her and suffocating the life from her body. But the smells, they had lingered far too long. Horse sweat, man sweat and unwashed bodies. She had gagged at the smell of urine, bad breath and sewage. There was a dampness and a mildewy component to everything around her. And then it was gone, except for the image of blood oozing from the side of her neck when she had looked at her reflection in the mirror. The blood had been running down into her breasts and congealing. It had clung to her for over an hour. Numerous attempts at washing the blood away did little to remove it from her skin. Showering hadn't done anything either. And then it simply vanished, melting away leaving not a trace behind except for the sensation of it running down her body.

Kathleen remembered checking for the cumbersome dress she thought she had been wearing in her dream. She sensed it was somewhere near or least present in her bedroom. And then that memory too dissipated. There was no dress to be found. Nothing in any corner of the room or part of her closet.

Kathleen remembered the sensation, the need to find her sons to make sure they were really tucked up in their beds sleeping. They had to be sleeping, and they were…but something was still niggling at her, despite the fact that she must have walked into their individual bedrooms at least five times, checking, checking and re-checking, just to make sure they really were there.

Kathleen shook her head again. All these jumbled thoughts of mine are getting in the way of my work. Perhaps I should be spending enough time on real events, instead of wondering what the Elizabethans were really up to. She thought about her research. It was the only way to prove unequivocally the likelihood of Drake and his contemporaries having reached British Columbia's shores. Maybe then these nightmares and thoughts would cease and leave her alone.

Current knowledge of Elizabethan history confirmed the obvious. Sources pertinent to Drake having travelled up the Pacific coast of America, past San Francisco were emerging. That book, *The Secret Voyage of Sir Francis Drake*, by Samuel Bawlf had thrown an interesting twist into the mindset of historians everywhere. It purported that Drake had been as far north as southern Alaska, and that he had only stopped his progress northward when impeded by snow and ice in the middle of July.

And then there were the troubling accounts of Drake's missing whereabouts for six months. His records had vanished, except for one map made outside of England and published without Elizabeth I's knowledge by Abraham Ortelious, the Belgium global map-maker of the sixteenth century.

Once again Kathleen shook her head clear of these distressing thoughts.

Facts, that's what I need to prove Drake's whereabouts on his great circumnavigation of the world. I shall contact the Spanish archives in Seville to see if the rumours are true. We'll see what they say about him travelling further north than San Francisco in 1579.

Kathleen recalled telling her students about Drake's impact on Elizabethan life, especially after his return from his great voyage around the world. Queen Elizabeth had seized all of Drake's documents from that excursion, confiscating logbooks, maps, journals and all evidence of his circumnavigation immediately upon his return to London. The impact of Spanish distrust about the English was mounting even before his famed return laden with Spanish ingots, jewels and pride. King Phillip was most displeased, demanding a return of goods pillaged by Drake. Although no acts of war were committed against the inhabitants of the Southern Americas, his outrage was evident enough. Drake needed to be reined in and fast.

Deciphering historical facts from fictional myths is essential; like the contemporary one down in Cadboro Bay about the beast swimming along the shoreline, nicknamed the Cadborosaurus. Cute as it is, that likeness of cement imbedded in the sand, well, myths, truths, facts, it's all simple really but very important. That is, after all, what she taught her students. Evidence is supported by documentation. Supposition was another matter. Facts must be tangible. Beasts and their likeliness in the sand, well, that's just good imagination.

The Voyager and the Traveller

London
June 1576

"Your Majesty, Master Francis Drake's proposal has merit in many ways. We have a limited understanding to date of the activities of His Majesty King Phillip of Spain in the New World. We must consider the prospects of the South Seas. If we set him on this course of discovery, many answers to our concerns dealing with the New World's boundaries can be gleaned first-hand. I propose that we let Drake embark on this mission, with explicit provisions and restrictions."

Elizabeth forced her chair swiftly backwards sweeping the odour absorbing straw beneath the carved legs. Dust billowed slightly and settled again. She glanced at the portrait of her late mother, which hung over the fireplace. Turning quickly she rounded on him. Ann Boleyn's penetratingly black eyes bore down on the scene, from above the fireplace. Cecil looked from the portrait to the fiery black-eyed vibrant, scrutinizing gaze of Elizabeth.

"Cecil, you have yet to express clearly to us the advantages of our letting Master Drake depart on such a dangerous voyage when we have need of him here, upon our shores. He has caused us great consternation and grievous harm to our realm in regards to King Phillip."

"Your Highness, I must interject here. As Master of Your Horses, I too believe this voyage must take place."

"Master Robert Dudley, you take liberties with me. How is it so that you can interrupt my conversation with Cecil and retain that smirk upon your face?"

Elizabeth moved away from her Master of the Horses, picking up her skirts as if to leave them both there in their insolence.

"Your Majesty, I mean no effrontery. I merely mean to state that it would be in the interest of your realm and the interest of your person to invest in this venture. Cecil speaks wisely, as always. However, I am not sure that we should enlighten Walsingham as to your intentions."

Elizabeth spun around and looked sternly into the eyes of Robert, revealing yellowing teeth. Her ice black eyes, hardened on Master Dudley and then softened as she glanced swiftly at Cecil. Her lips parted further as she forced out her implicit question.

"Is not Walsingham concerned, above all else, with the security and prosperity of my realm? Is this not also the interest dearest to your hearts?"

"It is," echoed both voices.

"Then explain your intentions concerning Walsingham and Drake."

"Your Majesty --" replied Robert.

"First of all," said Cecil, interrupting Robert, "I propose that we allow this voyage to begin but with specific revisions to his plans. I think it best that we extend this voyage to include the search for the western end of the east to west Northern Passage. Surely he can find his way through this passage."

"Why, when we have Frobisher looking from the east for a Northwest Passage?" spat out Elizabeth.

"Your Majesty let me explain, Frobisher has yet to find anything useful, and as far as I can tell, he has not searched far enough in terms of a passage to India. It must exist. There are no known impediments, and this is an area of great import to your realm."

"How so, my dearest Cecil?" She glared at him in his perch upon her softest chair.

"Your Majesty, may I remind you of the perils of travel to the east since Pope Gregory divided the world's new land acquisitions in two. This decree of giving the eastern New Worlds to the Portuguese and the western New World's acquisitions to the Spanish and therefore eliminating access to the Silk Route and its riches for any other nation is outrageous, is it not?"

Elizabeth twirled the pearls between the thin, taut fingers of her right hand and moved towards the window overlooking the rampart below. The stench of lasts night's high tide residue wafted through. Dropping the pearls dismissively she gathered her arms about her body and squeezed the new chill running up her spine from enveloping her chest.

In his usual softly spoken voice Cecil began his retort. "These are the prohibitive costs, the perils of pirates, of sultans, of thieves. We must find a quicker, safer way to China and India and gain access to their riches."

"Indeed, Cecil. Indeed we must, even if to thwart that pope's assertions and designs on the proliferation of that Catholic faith," quipped Elizabeth.

"Frobisher has not searched far enough across that Newfoundland's seas, and if he does not succeed, then we must have someone else in this region exploring its possibilities. This is the only alternative we have to Pope Gregory's decree. We need a safe passage to the eastern cities. The Silk Route has become perilous and costly."

"You are usually right, my good friend. However, such an endeavour needs be kept quiet, and we cannot have Phillip know of such a venture."

Elizabeth would consult with many men over the next twenty-seven years to ensure the safety of her realm. Not letting anyone leave her shores without consulting Walsingham, Cecil and her merchant-men would become the norm. Seers, Protestants, philosophers, even witchcraft will be employed in her quest for information and truth. Catholics will be consulted necessarily for their expertise and to keep them from rioting and troubling her streets again. Kat Astley and Elizabeth's father's bastards, Catherine and Henry Carey, will become informants to these rich sources of intrigues and sorcery.

"Your Majesty...pardon my intrusion into your thoughts, but have you also considered the possibility of Drake discovering new lands and treasure which could be of use to England," stated Cecil.

"I have not. And what do you suppose Drake could bring back of use to this realm besides King Phillip's gold and silver?" laughed Elizabeth.

"It has been said that the waters on the Atlantic coast of this New World are stocked full of fish, so much so that they can be caught with a mere hand net. Its lands are full of the finest oak trees. Amongst its native plants, there can be found new animals for our bait rings. The indigenous inhabitants are clothed in the finest of furs."

"And what do you suppose is an impediment to our use of those shores?"

"The impediment my dear Majesty, is a mere trifling consideration and is simply the wild inhabitants. But I am sure that they too can be of use. And if that is indeed true on the east coast of that Newfoundland, then surely the west coast is equally and if not superior to it."

Elizabeth paced the room further. She brooded over the ever-present matters of court life. She had no idea what she was about to set loose

15

on the inhabitants of those far-off lands, plundered for furs, timber and land. The abundant sea would supply armies of men who fought amongst its shores. Its indigenous peoples were yet to suffer the indignities of white man's incursions and the waves of foreign men yet to come.

Plunder seemed to be chiefly on the minds of her seafaring men. She turned back towards her councillors now.

"Why should we believe that, Cecil?"

"Why should we not, Your Majesty?"

"Why? Why? Why? Simply because you say it? Surely not!" snapped Elizabeth. "My dear man, enlighten me!"

"Your Majesty--"

"Cecil, may I remind you of the great concern Drake has caused me of late. Have he and Hawkins not already caused this realm great anxiety?"

"Indeed he has, Your Majesty. But he has also caused greater concern in Phillip's realm than yours?"

"Humph," she sighed. "Cecil. You will make it clear to Drake that he is being reined in!! He has no licence to aggrieve or cause more worries. He is good at creating great interest in himself. He has a countenance that elicits fear and admiration amongst sailors in equal amounts. This alone will cause King Phillip's ears and eyes to open wide. Therefore, no further knowledge shall be leaked of his ventures inside Spanish waters. It is far too dangerous a ploy to play folly."

"Indeed, Your Majesty. But it is folly to believe that we would not look for alternate sources of wealth from these dubiously claimed shores. Why should the pope, the kings of Spain or Portugal enjoy the fruits of this New World? Why should we not enjoy them too?"

"Why, indeed, Cecil. Why, indeed?"

"When should I inform Drake of your wishes for him to begin provisioning his ships for such a voyage?" interjected Robert Dudley.

"Not until we have laid out strict stipulations. Secrecy is paramount. Let us put forth that it is upon pain of death that any such future voyage be revealed beyond these walls. You may join in on these if you like, Robbie, but for now, let it be known to Francis that his voyage to these far western shores is being considered. He must wait with patience for my permission and no one else's."

"Now on another matter Cecil, what have you heard lately about this traveller, who has come upon my shores?"

Cecil raised his brows. "A traveller? There are many. Of which do you speak?"

"Humph, so you have not heard of her return, then. Good."

"Why do you ask about her again, dearest Elizabeth," said Robert. "Surely she would not set foot upon our shores again?"

"My shores, Robbie, not ours."

Robert blushed and turned his face away from Cecil to hide his embarrassment. Cecil stared intently at Elizabeth, scrutinizing her gaze.

Turning, Elizabeth returned Cecil's stare, raising her eyebrow and tipping her head forward. She leaned in closely to his person. "I know she is on the way back, and that you know it as well. There is much talk of late from my dear half-sister and cousin, Catherine."

Robert smirked. "Ah, your half-sister. She has predicted another visitation has she. Shall I impress upon her the importance of her silence in this manner? We wouldn't want another rumour of witches amongst the servants."

"I want this talk of her appearance eliminated. I need no more interference in the operation of my realm."

Cecil ran the tips of his fingers over his chin repeatedly. Elizabeth watched him, searching for any signs of truth that that woman had reappeared in her realm, and was predicting Elizabeth's future. Once was surely enough, however, correctly she had alluded to her and Robert's future prospects.

Robert leaned in towards Cecil now as well. "Do you mean to say that the woman who escaped from the Tower when we were imprisoned there is back?" Robert quickly realizing that his understanding of the traveller meant something quite different than he had first thought.

Cecil's eyes widened, his mouth opened slightly. "She is back, then, is she? The woman who sought you out in the Tower Prison, warning you to reveal nothing of your religious tendencies to Queen Mary?"

"It is just a rumour, I expect, but one that could have great consequences if she is to be caught by someone other than yourself or Robbie." Elizabeth stared intently into Cecil's eyes.

"I understand completely," said Cecil, "I shall listen more carefully to what the speech of our emissaries, courtiers and servants profess. However, I suggest we do not ask directly if she has been spotted. That will only kindle the rumours into flames of panic. She needs to be found, if she really has come ashore once more. Her predictions, however accurate they were last time, could be misconstrued. And our dear friend Walsingham has an uncanny way of eliciting information, does he not? We want our information fresh and unfiltered."

"Indeed we do, Cecil, indeed," whispered Elizabeth.

The feud bubbling between Robert and Drake would complicate matters of future voyaging. Robert knew exactly what Drake wanted. Drake had an insatiable need to pursue King Phillip's gold. The man's distrust of the Spanish was infamous, and Robbie would do everything in his power to goad Drake on in his desire for revenge against King Phillip. Despite Drake's abilities, his manners towards Robert prevented any great formal bond between the two. It was far easier to keep Drake at a distance. Any association between the two must be kept tepid at best. It was an agreement the two men relied on. Their associations of the past would provoke and horrify Elizabeth.

Robert's need for Drake's skills at relieving Spanish coin from the pockets and bowels of his enemy was consistently, reliably profitable. The possible acquisition of plunder and the need of the seafaring life was the way to control such a man as Drake publicly, however much Robert had need of his share of Drake's plundered booty.

Elizabeth's need of that coin was immense, but she would have to temper that need for the moment. There were other ways in which an unmarried queen could obtain foreign wealth. The prospects of engagement with such a queen drew into England's shores enough money to keep her kingdom afloat for numerous months at present. However, perhaps another engagement could be prudent, necessary and useful in the near future as well.

Walsingham would control Drake for now, and he would use those skills to the realm's benefit in securing Irish lands from Catholic control. At some point, though, they would be reliant on Drake to disappear into the beyond, across and down the Atlantic, to where troubles unseen as of yet would remain. Troubles immense enough to engage Phillip of Spain perhaps, in an act of war, far exceeding Elizabeth's expectations of Phillip's hatred for Protestant, heretical lands.

Shaman and Emily Carr

"He has taken my daughter's soul. He has broken his promise. I want her returned, or I will destroy him," snapped the shaman of the Songhees tribe to Emily Carr, squeezing the handle of his paddle.

Emily smiled back at him. "You know she has children by him. Killing him now won't endear your daughter to you."

Shaman turned towards Emily. "I did not know this. When and how many children?"

Emily closed her eyes, breathed deeply, savouring the sounds of the sea sloshing against the rocks below and embracing the splashing sensation, which coursed through her veins. It was a moment to treasure, to feel again, to hear once more and to live within the realm of life ebbing all around them.

"Two possibly three, although I have not felt the youngest one's presence in a while now. This is unfortunate, as it means possibly going further into Elizabeth's realm, a troubling encounter with these white men, which has not been without peril in the past, as you are well aware."

"I must close this portal before he destroys my people's souls. He has taken too much from us already. He pollutes our shores with his interferences. My people have demanded that he be destroyed. They cannot rest."

"Yes, and he will be shut out. We must engage our friend once more in helping us."

Shaman rolled his shoulder blades back, straightened his spine and looked out towards the sea. Gripping his paddle, he thrust it skywards and brought it back down, cracking the fir handle, a large split zippering along its length.

"This means engaging the professor again, does it? She did nothing last time but foretell the future of that queen's realm. What good is she to my cause?"

Shaman raised his hand to silence Emily's response.

"I need to speak to the Spirit Keepers and relive the time of Drake's coming. I must remember every detail of what we agreed on. That is the key to this matter, not that professor."

"I disagree, Shaman. It is not easy to embrace transference as a white woman."

Shaman turned towards Emily and nodded. "I have forgotten how difficult it was for you, and you were a willing participant. So how then can we persuade this professor to do my biding, then?"

"There are numerous ways of convincing someone to embrace changes, to accept their calling, their duty to this world. Everyone has a calling; a soul aching for eternity must always obey its path."

Shaman nodded. His paddle creaked, and the two souls watched as its division mended and became whole once more. Perhaps, thought Shaman and Emily together, that the time really had come for retrieving and saving the lost souls of the Songhees tribe.

"This may be a long process, though," spoke Emily softly. "We cannot guarantee that bringing her back to Drake's realm will return them all. There will have to be many more gatherings. I fear that Drake may have lost more than the souls of our tribe along that journey he made to these shores."

Shaman's eyes darkened, sneering in fury, his face contorting, a boiling redness flushing the cheeks on his face. "This white man has no business in treating my people like..."

"Shaman," snapped Emily.

She smiled at him then. "This will not solve our problem. We must teach the professor that history -- our history matters, that she cannot allow Drake to manipulate our world. She must find another way to appease his pride. But she cannot reveal history to him or that queen. And that will be difficult to get across."

"How many others souls can you feel he has taken then?" He has polluted our world long enough!

Emily looked back out to the sea and the snow-capped Olympic mountain range. She breathed in deeply.

"Too many we fear, and that is not all. He has fathered other children. They all must be repatriated. Your neighbours across this strait have been calling out for their lost ones as well. We must bring them all home."

Nodding his assent, Shaman, looked across the strait towards America.

"Then they must be returned as well. Their souls cannot rest in this place he has taken them to."

The two spirits stared across the strait, both imagining how they would cross this new barrier and close the portal through which Drake reigned over them. Drake was, after all, just a spirit; however, at present a most intrusive and troublesome one, much like the thieving otters who inhabited this shoreline, thieving and opportunistic.

"Carlos," whispered Emily softly.

"Humph, he has done nothing of consequence except his..."

"On the contrary, Shaman. He has done much, if only you would pay attention. Your anger blinds you to much that has happened."

Shaman straightened his spine once more, and Emily reached out and held fast his paddle. She felt the softness of its wood beneath her fingers. Oh, to feel again, she thought.

"He has done much towards our cause, Shaman."

"He works amongst them---these white men, helping them. How can he help us as well?"

"Yes, he does work with these people, as did you once!"

Emily glared at him and then softened her expression.

"He is a therapist, much as you were. He gives advice and solace to the souls of these lands. Eh, Eh…" she held up her hand in protest.

"He is alive in the professor's world, unlike us, in her presence, and he can feel her sorrow. This is very important. And he is bound to her like no other." Shaman turned towards Emily and nodded.

"Once again, Emily you speak with knowledge. You remind me again of my weaknesses. My anger blinds me from the truth. How then is he bound?"

"For that we must relive together the moment of his capture and her willingness to save his soul from white man's hell, a place so unspeakably cruel, a place of unforgiveness and wretched misery. Are you willing to go back there and see this?"

Shaman nodded. And the two of them removed themselves from land and slipped quietly below the surface of the sea. They watched as white man's long boat floated above them. Its hull was long and wide, its stern flattened and extending out behind its bulk, plunging deep into the depths below an angular wide paddle-like blade swam back and forth. To this they took hold and melded into it.

Shaman reached the massive totem embedded in the white man's boat first. He travelled up its length from within its inner core. Emily came next. They emerged, somewhere beyond the nest which clung precariously above the boats deck. Their souls hovering like mists crossing the seas. It was warm up there, and little wind blew, but the scurrying below deck by these white men was well, horrific.

Shaman winced at the blood, which curdled all around these dying men. Shouts of outrage came from below them, whilst flashes of silver blades and daggers plunged deep into the bellies of men. Horror-struck, Shaman closed his eyes.

"Do not close your eyes now, Shaman, or you will miss the best part. She is here, amongst these men. She is in the presence of the one you most despise."

Shaman's body shuddered. He opened his eyes and looked down again once more.

"I have seen enough. There is no woman… ah she protects him. They are advancing."

"Be quiet now, Shaman, and watch."

Below them an enormous voice bellowed. Drake halted his men, forbidding them to slaughter the woman protecting Carlos. He clambered over the bodies of his men and that of the Spanish. Carlos remained the only Spaniard still alive.

"Why do you protect him, wench?" they heard him shouting at her.

"Because," she bellowed back at him, "he speaks our language as well as several others. He is useful. He can translate. He can be persuaded to reason. And," she said more softly, "he can heal the sick."

" I have seen enough," said Shaman. "Let us go back home now. I want no more memories of these cursed men invading my soul. My people do not behave like this towards our neighbours. These men have no real soul that is worthy of respect."

Emily nodded her assent and smiled. She had won his approval. The moment of transference would commence again. It was time to contact

Carlos in the living world, the one in which Shaman had no feelings for, no current memory of. The one in which these white men and women did not still do these horrible things to one another anymore. The bloodletting has stopped on these shores, her shores, finally.

Rules of Transference

July 1604

Stowe looked about his study. Rolling his eyes skyward and making the sign of the cross upon his brow, always made him feel safer. Edith's coffee tray lay where she had left it, its contents beckoning him to eat. He gathered by the noise ensuing from beyond his study that his most beloved grandchildren were about. He knew an audience was approaching. He would begin to tell this tale aloud to them. It would make more logical sense this way. The story could then be used as a mere tale told to small children to keep them safely tucked into their beds at night. This fantastical tale will keep them true to their faith in God and safe from their wandering heretical thoughts.

"This portal that lays waiting to be found by accident or pursuit will confound me, I can see. But I will also alas find it out nonetheless."

He picked up his quill again and dipped its end over and over again into the blackness of ink.

- *The rules of transference, he wrote.*
- *The traveller must keep a portal quay at all times throughout this said journey. The loss of which will cause extreme anxiety, perhaps even death, dismemberment or acute deformity of soul or body.*

26

- *The portal must be entered and exited through separate means. The travellers therefore, may not return in the same way of their coming.*
- *Their destination cannot be compromised upon arrival in any way.*
- *There is to be no sharing of knowledge that alters time or history as such, for this will be revealed as needed.*
- *The loosing of the portal quay will most definitely bring great sorrow and loss of a great kind to the loser of said quay. The portal quay's size and shape will alter with each subsequent use.*
- *It must not be reused, or can it? This detail is somewhat not clear as of yet? Problematic, but solvable, I believe. He smiled at his ingenuity. Dipping his quill in the ink again, he began scratching his notes into the vellum.*
- *The travel forwards and backwards in time will not be easy or necessarily to the same place one comes from. It may alter with the tides of the moon.*
- *It is the traveller's need that will bring transference into being.*
- *There will be no rescue from a horrible death if the portal quay is lost. However, death will continue to re-occur until the goals of the mission are completed. And at that time, and only that time, shall death possibly be averted.*
- *The traveller will remember with great horror the extent and brutality of this death. But re-entry into the same place to change an outcome can and will take place. And this will continue until Drake feels confident that his goal has been met.*

I hope to garner this same ability myself. He smiled. Shakespeare will get his comeuppance at last. I will eliminate him from history. Worthless playwright. He gains infamy without toil and hard work. Unlike myself, he is not so good at writing down the necessary everyday activities of the populous. A true accounting of Elizabethan

England will be told by my quill and not his. Clearing his thoughts of Shakespeare was always a difficult task, but he had to, needed to. The transference of that woman was about to happen again and he, John Stowe, was to play a leading role in it this time as the keeper of the children. He smirked at the thought of it. Only this time they would not reside in the same century as the traveller. She will be able to feel them, sense their presence and maybe even smell them. He laughed out loud then. I will convince her this time of her folly in disobedience. He began writing again.

- *This quay it must not be taken away from the traveller indefinitely. There is a time limit to its holding. If it is lost, then it must be placed back within the hands of the traveller on the eleventh day of said travel in time; otherwise the traveller will be lost in time, as Drake has been.*
- *There are dates in history that will be recorded in the Julian and Gregorian calendars. The dates will reflect the comings and goings of these travellers' means of escape from the realms that they reside in. Going beyond these dates, these eleven days difference in time, will likely bring about the death of such said traveller repeatedly, possibly permanently until Drake's goals are met.*
- *Julian time is England's time, and today is July 4th, 1604. Pope Gregory's calendar or Gregorian time would have the Catholics believe that today's date would be July 15, 1604, a change that is* most blasphemous to Protestants.

Drake had uttered with such confidence that Pope Gregory's interference with the calendar was blasphemous. A pope has no business in altering the goings-on of liturgical dates. Consequently, the Catholics have a much inferior calendar than the Protestant and English one.

Dipping his quill once more into ink, he began scribbling frantically. The children would get there shortly.

- *A traveller may only go where their journey has taken them to before. It does not matter in what era that occurred. He or she cannot travel to some place in time of which he has not travelled to before.*
- *Exposures to the dangers of the era in which they have travelled to are of no consequence to Drake. If they die, he can simply bring them back to complete the task for which they were brought forward to do.*

However, Drake's ability to find these travellers and transport them without consequence has not been that successful. The problem, of course, has been the unwillingness of the current traveller to comply with Drake's demands, even if she can travel to England's shores unencumbered.

- *A traveller who does so travels to these places not travelled to before, will therefore not arrive at the intended destination, even if they have not intended to travel at all. And the accidental traveller will put into peril all those whose intent to travel he or she attaches themselves too.*
- *The traveller will not reveal to lesser societies knowledge, which it has not yet gained. Objects useful in one realm will not reveal themselves as being the same thing.*
- *Any revealing of future knowledge before its discovery in time will result in the death of the said traveller, frequently until taken back.*

"This is folly. Why should Englishmen not enjoy the knowledge gained from other realms, especially if they foil the attempts of Catholics and Spaniards?"

My grandchildren are arriving, he thought. I must put away my writings and recordings of London and place them into hiding so that the knowledge of them, once revealed, will not brand them sons and daughters of a heretical man.

Stowe watched as his grandchildren burst through his study door and spilled out onto the carpeted floor coverings, which kept the cold of stone from entering his bones. He enjoyed this tussling of little souls within the confines of his favourite parlour. His heretical texts were well hidden within the casings of oak. Occasionally whilst telling one of his tales, he enjoyed fingering the leather, which bound them, breathing in the odours of their former owner's dens.

He continued to wait as they settled into their little chairs, lining themselves up in rows in front of him. The littlest ones were always sitting closest to him. He smelt the dust they carried with them and smiled warmly at them. His fondness for children and telling grand tales to them was becoming legendary. Farmers' children from fields away would often wander over to him, begging him to recall the legends of dragons, King Arthur and Good Queen Bess. The one legend most sought after was the story of Drake and his exploits of discovery in far-off lands where shamans, Spirit Keepers, eagles and the great white spirit bear resided.

The spirit bear thrilled his flock especially when Stowe told them of the shaman's ability to train the beasts in killing and eating those Spanish Catholics and defending Drake's lost lands from these heretical, ungodly men.

He knew he could get his thoughts in order for perpetuity if he told these tales. It became his way of remembering all the particulars of what Drake had imparted. His mind was like a great large treasure chest. Each scoop of gold reached for revealed another grander piece of information worth remembering. Today he would reveal to these lovelies the mysteries of Drake's Great Drum.

The children squiggled with anticipation barely able to sit upon their bottoms. Eyes shone brightly with the reflections of ghosts, Spirit Keepers and shamans running deeply within the irises of blue, brown and green. Several held hands tightly and squeezed each other continually. Not even the thought of a bee could be heard outside buzzing towards them to sting.

Last night's cry of pain from the sting of a nest had caught more than one of his lovelies. He had calmed them all down with the promise of more tales to come, and here they were ready to be frightened, cultivated, mystified and delighted again.

The sheer joy of their upturned faces captured his imagination. He reached a little ways into the treasure chest of his brain and plucked out another plum, and thus begun another tall tale perhaps of the legendary Man of the Drum.

"UPON HIS DEATH BED," he roared aloud, pausing until the silence in the room hung impatiently for his next words. He watched as the wriggling suddenly stopped. All eyes glistened upwards desperate for more. Deep breaths were taken, sudden squeezing of clasped hands and toes. White knuckles shone out from their boney protrusions whilst silence encased his lovelies. He always watched for who would lick their lips in anticipation first.

"These words did Sir Francis Drake utter," he began again.

"I shall vow to you that if England was ever in danger someone should beat this here drum." Stowe beat his hands upon the sides of his great chair. Conveniently stowed inside its large pockets he had placed the drum made of deerskin, given to him by Drake for safekeeping.

The sound brought shrieks of joy and tears of wonder to all who heard it. Everyone covered their ears. He waited for silence to ensue...

"My soul will return from heaven to defend our country upon the sound of the beating of this here drum." Again Stowe beat his hands upon the drums. Screams arose, and hands flew to the sides of heads. He noted how several of the adults outside his door had opened his door slightly. He smelt the fear radiating from the other side of its timbers.

"Drake ordered this drum to be taken back to England upon his death. This was done, and it resides now in Buckland Abbey in Plymouth town, far, far from London town. It is said that upon the treasonous writings of that heretical queen, Mary Stuart, that the drums could be heard thumping their tones down the Thames every time she wrote down her heretical machinations." His lovelies squirmed before him, for they knew what was to come next.

"These heretical thoughts brought out the most evil kind of women to mankind. A most horrible, ugly queen I have never before seen. She was a tall, proud Jezebel, and she died defiant and unrepentant."

That heretical queen's head came off after three chops from the axe man's blade. There will be no quick end for those who folly with God's true intent. The blood that spewed its wrath out of her wretched soul was as black as a burning charcoal. I watched her head roll to the ground, as did the Spirit Keepers and this woman they call the traveller.

This traveller is a woman who cavorts with the spirit bear, a great white beast, so large it stands two fathoms tall and 60 stones of weight. She picked up the head and ate it right there. Whereupon she vanished, but before she had disappeared completely, she threw up the head and spit it out of her mouth, where it landed upon the scaffold with a thump."

Drake heard the thump of the servant Edith and the ensuing entourage of men and women picking up the prone servant. He smiled, smirked and then sorrowfully parted his lips." *Perhaps that was too much, he thought.*

"But then the traveller, she returned hours later to gain favour with Good Queen Bess. She returned to retrieve something, which Sir Francis Drake had taken from her.

"What did he take," shouted the children.

"Drake," he said, "took the traveller's children from the spirit world into ours twenty-nine years ago. Long before any of your fathers were born. He took them to justify his revenge against the shaman who holds his soul in perpetuity. He cannot leave their world completely until he returns to them his children by them."

"He has children from a shaman?" whimpered the white face of Phillip.

"Yes, he has descendants from the daughter of the shaman. Indeed he does. Half woman, half shaman, neither whole nor complete. They have the bodies of men encased in the heretical minds of this female shaman. These feral people believe in everlasting sprits and travelling souls. Their souls enter the bodies of great creatures in order to fulfill their final destinies. They come to our shores leaping across seas, wreaking havoc and instilling uncertainty, fear and awe in all who come upon them."

"Are they here amongst us now?" cried out one of his lovelies.

Silence ensued as he watched them re-squeezing each other's hands and wriggling in earnest. Several more lips were worked over in anticipation by ever searching tongues. He waited until all their imaginations were ready for more.

"YES," he replied.

"There is one still amongst us who persists in returning again and again, defiantly, purposely, secretively. But I alone know of her ways, and when she will come to us next. For I have spoken to her and recognize the body in which she arrives.

"You may even breathe her in sometimes when the wind blows across your face violently. She harbours a need to pervert the memory of Sir Francis Drake. Even now she has returned seeking out his children to bring them back to the land of these feral people. She haunts our halls looking for her own children as well, capturing men and the occasional woman and anyone who gets in her way. She takes them with her to her far-off lands and does black things to their souls...very black mystic ritual machinations. She changes their very being and captures their minds with her sorceress ways."

Young Phillip covered both of his ears with his palms, but lifted his left palm slightly, just enough to hear what might be forthcoming.

"Now, let us get back to the story of Sir Francis Drake and how he met this most devious, manipulative woman. Let me tell you of his powers of persuasion and how he became entrapped within the spirit world's spidery web."

He paused then to regain his thoughts. All who watched him did so silently. They leaned their slim little torsos closer to him. The cat at the end of the large room that usually slept through all Stowe's tellings abruptly lifted its mottled white and black head as if sensing the spirits' coming presence. It too looked anxiously towards Stowe gazing transfixed into the distance.

The children sat quietly desperate to read his bowed head and its thoughts. They stared in their eagerness at any slight movement in his hands, which now clasped his long head. His forefingers moved suddenly upwards and then pointed leftwards towards the cat. Every head turned in anticipation towards the cat and gasped.

"Unhhhhhh." Every heart and head instantly recalled the curse of Black Cats. Cicero stared back at them and then shifted his gaze back to his large friend, Stowe. The movement of little and large souls awoke the teller of tales.

Stowe lifted his head and parted dry lips starring out at them as if in a trance.

"It captured Drake's soul, this spirit world, at the moment of his death at sea. The Isthmus of Panama has captured many disturbing elements in its grasp. One of those elements takes the souls of the departed deep into the seas and swallows them up.

"However, not before the soul which is being taken lashes back at its keeper. For a soul who is bound for heaven or hell knows where it is to go. A soul need not have this battle except for the interference of this dark shamanic element.

"Drake had met this element before with less sinister beginnings. A shaman from the jungles of Panama had made markings in red ochre upon his breast and head, a ritual he endured to achieve autonomy and safe passage through the jungles standing before him. His life and that of his men had been spared from the purges of fever and the creatures that flourish there. He met a similar but more potent, evil shaman upon the shores of the land he once called Nova Albion and claimed in perpetuity for England's Good Queen Bess. This shaman of Nova Albion now holds Drake's soul in his grasp and will not let it out until his transgressions have been cleared of its debt."

Stowe shifted the weight of his body back and forth in his chair and stretched his legs.

"Is it not time for all your beds?" he asked as he rose from his chair with a wink.

Shrieks of outrage greeted him now from both child and adult alike. He grinned devilishly and settled back down into his chair with a wide smile of satisfaction. He had captured their interests again.

"What does he owe that shaman," asked the timid Edith, who had once lain prone upon the floor.

Eyes, backs, eyebrows turned quickly to Edith and then Stowe. He sensed their mood and dug in joyfully.

"He wants to own his soul and send Drake to hell."

"Unhhhhhhh, no not hell," gasps and groans bounced around his room.

"Ah, perhaps it is heaven which our Drake must return to if only he can find the quay which will release his soul and bones into heaven. What do you suppose that quay is?" They shook their heads in wonder, open mouthed as they did so.

"He must return to the shores of the shamanic woman of Nova Albion and her heirs with Drake. But more importantly, he must awaken from the dead the lost children he fathered with this most mysterious feral princess. She lay with him and bore him two sons." And a few daughters as well of no consequence, he thought.

"These children have disappeared, and it is feared that they may have perished. So his soul will not rest until it finds its way back to them."

"A feral princess! They have princesses, Grandpa?" squeaked Lily. "OH."

"Yes, my dear little one, and many princes too. It was said to me by Drake that these sons," and daughters, he thought, "he bore by this feral woman became shamans themselves upon their birth."

Many eyebrows shot upwards in awe.

"Drake has fathered two princes." Supposedly, I must find them and return them to their shores. I will have to engage upon the services

36

of this traveller to execute this deed and regain Drake's lost soul, he mused disgusted by the idea of it.

He thought then of his last conversation with Drake. They had discussed Drake remaining in the spirit world to finish things still undone. His intention was to remain there for as long as it took to reverse the course of injustices prevailed upon him by other men and Queen Elizabeth. They had argued about this for several days. In the end, it was necessary to let Drake prevail. But he would be looking out for signs of trouble. Drake he recalled had a way of stirring up more than a country's worth of grief.

He noted the fear displayed upon the brows of his lovelies. "Not to worry...I am safe from harm. The traveller cannot take me."

"I have heard from my dear late friend. Drake resides at present inside a spirit world with his feral princess. He has even suggested that he prefers to reside there forever and forgo ascension into heaven."

"NO, he cannot," yelled out Edith. Two strong men shook her into silence. Their purpose being more than silencing. Edith was known to faint easily.

John Stowe smiled at Edith and looked at her. Edith quickly looked away.

"Drake once spoke of a grand white spirit bear which these shamanic people revealed as possessing a great chieftain's soul. These large white monsters roam amongst the black bears in the forests, which lie next to the sea. They roam about scooping salmon within their paws and tearing their flesh open with one swift swipe, leaving the carcass to rot in the sand and stone and gorging only upon its entrails. They refer to these animals as Moksgmol, but Drake's men called them the white spirit bear. He said the males of these beasts were two fathoms tall and fifty-five stones in weight. Their lighter females bore both white and black cubs and were a mere one fathoms tall and twenty-seven stones in weight. GIANTS," he roared.

He loved how they all reacted to his teasing, but regretted his shouts when he noticed wee Elisa's tears.

"Now, now dear Elisa, all is well. These bears reside far from our shores. You are all safe at present, but there is another beast, which lies close to these spirit bears. It is a great confounding thing, as it possesses two different species. It is a half-white spirit bear and half-white and black whale. A great large beast it is that clambers out of the sea with its hind paws, twisting its great wriggling black and white whales head onto the shore seeking anything to sink its great arm's length teeth into. It is a fearsome beast to be sure, and it is only to be found in the cold north seas of Nova Albion. It is said to have great strength and possesses the souls of the ungrateful dead."

"It is here upon those shores that the traveller comes from, in a world far different to ours. She comes into our world from hers, leaves her presence upon our shores and vanishes again. I must find her and retain her into Drake's service once more."

He reached then into his chair pouch and pulled out a drawing of a woman and the faint drawings of the beasts, which Drake had reproduced. He lifted them up to show all and watched as their eyes protruded and wandered from the drawings upon the velum he held out to them. Lips parted, teeth clenched and heads turned away, but peeped back for a wee glimpse of the looming beasts.

"She's not that old. I have seen her," blurted out Edith.

Every bone in the room went rigid. Every hair stood on end. All eyes glimmered.

"She was here yesterday and today. She was in the garden when the bells rang for compline."

Stowe looked straight at Edith, brought two of his fingers to his mouth, tapped them three times and shook his head at her to indicate no more.

"Now, Edith, come now. It is only today that I show you this drawing. Surely you are mistaken."

Sighs of relief could be heard from all in his parlour. Little William looked disappointed. A few of the adults rolled their eyes at Edith and made the sign of the cross upon their brows and chests. Squiggling little boys chatted quickly and made plans to seek her out. They would find Stowe's traveller and question her themselves.

Edith blushed violently and shook the tremors out from her hands. She coughed and took an enormous gulp of air and slowly nodded her compliant head. She knew that this was a sign from Stowe, that he had plans for her, the traveller and the others again. Her body shook at the memory of Owen, her former husband, the traveller's kindness and the children she so desperately wanted for herself. She closed her eyes, realizing she would have to go back again. Rocking back and forth helped ease the pain of those memories.

Walsingham

June 1576

Francis Walsingham had enlisted many men into his network of intrigues. The one he most preferred, though, was Owen, his childhood companion. Neither of them had enjoyed much parental affection or love. Walsingham, though, had taken a liking to Owen, a younger man by five years. They had conspired together to play overt, secretive games on their parents. Each of them had delighted in the other's company during times of infinite stress. The two boys were forbidden from meeting or talking to each other, a rule imposed upon them by their parents, which only furthered their commitment to one other.

Owen's family was and remained pious Catholic, Bloody Queen Mary supporters and was only barely tolerated at present by the majority of the Protestant populous. Walsingham's parents were devout believers in the conversion to Protestant worship. Their elder son's death at the hands of Bloody Mary still burned memories in their hateful hearts. Walsingham was conflicted by the hatred he harboured at the evil of Catholicism and its flagrant intolerance to logical thinking, especially as he was tortured some days by the prospect of losing his most trusted ally, Owen, a Catholic, and it had crossed his mind of late to betray him to Her Majesty. Owen's cruelty was becoming worrisome.

Walsingham recalled his escape to Paris during the reign of Queen Mary, remembering his elder brother who had not been so lucky. He recalled with horror the acrid stench of his burning flesh and the filthy Catholic onlookers who had enjoyed his pain. Determined to shorten the anguish of watching his brother burn at the stake, Walsingham had incited the throng into action.

Walsingham began flaming the embers with his makeshift flag attached between two poles, flapping at the flames. The riot of people all around began to do the same, waving their broomsticks at the base of the fire, engulfing the pyre with wind. His brother Richard had asked him to make it so.

"Do not let me burn slowly," he had pleaded.
"Then you must go. Leave England's shores at once,"
he had begged, "for there is no one to fan your flames
here, after I'm gone. Do this for our parents, please."

During Queen Mary's reign Walsingham had strayed away from his Protestant attire, the simpler, darker, drabber clothing, often worn by other like-minded Protestant nobles. Instead, he wore in his pocket a rosary, and he made sure a cross swung from any piece of clothing especially around his neck. He made a habit of blending in, of appearing as if he had always been in a room. He practised leaving clues to his whereabouts throughout the corridors in which he roamed. He conversed with men and convinced them he was privy to their discussions. He noted what men wore and for how many days at a time. He took copious notes on everything and anyone of importance. He noted who was trusted with vital information and could recall every rendezvous location he had used.

Walsingham had been in Paris again during the Huguenot slaughter of 1572 and had witnessed the murder of their Protestant leader Gaspard II de Coligny. He had been unable to save his friend, whose throat and torso bore the skillful penetration of knives used to kill swiftly. His foreknowledge of the Medici plot had not been without pain, for he had chosen to allow it to take place and watched as it snared thousands of other Protestant believers. That subsequent slaughter of innocents tormented him daily.

He recalled a woman whose countenance he could not forget, a woman much like the one he now thought was on her way back to the walls of Westminster Palace. Surely he thought, this is not the same woman as last time. He shook his head and stood trying to recall the scene he witnessed in Paris. That woman had died. He knew it. He had seen her there, on the ground not far from others whose bodies had been slit open, eyes gashed out, crosses burned into their skins. Her hair was blonde, much in the style of the traveller. It was short, curly as if it had been cut off in a hurry, just as the traveller's was.

"Why?" He remembered asking why. When he had looked back, the smoke had concealed most of her body from view, but her hand had still been visibly holding that of a small child's. The two of them had looked out of place.

When he returned later that evening to collect the names of the slaughtered, her body and that of the child was gone.

She lives again, he had thought momentarily and then dismissed the idea as foolishness. No one could have survived such a slaughter. Somebody else has retrieved her. Maybe she floats in the Seine, and many more would be thrown in as well, he thought. There will be many unclaimed, and, after all, a Protestant cannot be buried in a Catholic gravesite.

Catherine de Medici's Catholic piety even permitted the sacrifice of her own children to obtain control of her empire. She was a master of manipulation. Walsingham had seen through this veil of Catholic piety. Power was what drove Catherine de Medici. He had witnessed the destruction of true faith within the Catholic Church. This was one more reason to despise this religion, he thought. But he was very grateful, however, when his post as emissary to Paris was over.

Walsingham had witnessed Catherine's Catholic hold over her people's minds. More importantly, though, Walsingham had learned the power of deception and vowed that he would never be caught by anyone, nor would the outcome of anything be attributed to him. Unlike Catherine he knew how to be invisible. As a Huguenot conspirator, no ties would ever be associated to him. Walsingham would be remembered in history but never caught. And unlike his minions and monarch, he would lay down the rules of deception and capture of individuals, and if that traitorous traveller were to come upon his shores, then this time she would pay the price of her indiscretions.

Walsingham was reminded now of Owen's troubles with the current queen. Owen had remained a staunch Catholic despite Walsingham's dire warnings. He loved this man for the loyalty he had shown him in the past, for it was Owen who had helped him escape England. It was Owen who had written to him, even visited him in Paris at the end of Queen Mary's reign.

Owen had remained a friend and been rewarded as Walsingham's spy for a very long time. Owen's skills were now exceedingly good. His tutelage of Owen had paid off. It was like they were brothers again, secreting away and recording the goings-on of nobility, the classless and the dangerous intruders who frequented London's streets.

Walsingham had convinced Owen to take a Protestant wife, one easily manipulated, in order to gain favour with the queen. Edith had

43

come from a minor noble Protestant family and was placed within close proximity of Her Majesty Queen Elizabeth's inner circle. This gained Owen access to Elizabeth's castles and the many private residences she stayed within.

Owen had become a valuable asset in the protection of Her Majesty, the Queen of England, Wales and Ireland and indirectly Scotland. Little James, he imagined, would some day become the king of Scotland. The likelihood of Elizabeth ever marrying and producing an heir was diminishing with each passing month.

However, that did not stop her or Cecil from conjuring up numerous attempts at gaining a dowry for her hand in marriage. It was sufficient to keep her treasury in gold and coin.

After Henry VIII died, Walsingham had guided his son and heir, Edward, in the ways of the Protestant faith. During Edward's short reign, Walsingham gained favour with the young king and became the protector of the realm. Edward's Book of Common Prayer had been printed in the common tongue of its people. It had shocked and outraged Catholic believers.

Latin was the preferred variation of scriptural doctrine. The Pope of Rome was outraged at this flagrant misuse of doctrinal matters. The interpretation of scriptures was the domain of priests and cardinals, not for boy kings, unlearned men or the king's sisters, Mary and Elizabeth, nor for women in general.

Owen, Walsingham and Walsingham's brother had been involved in the translation of scriptural Latin language into that of contemporary English. The coinage gained by each man had allowed Owen to acquire property and Walsingham his silver, gold and jewels, easily transferable from county to county, even countries. His fortuitous choices had provided quick coinage for escape during Bloody Queen Mary's reign.

Owen and Walsingham had managed to conceal their intentions for writing these blasphemous documents under the guise of spying for the Catholic cause. It had saved Owen from the burnings, but Walsingham's brother's fate had been sealed with his own piety. Fervent, though, were Walsingham's beliefs. They did not, however, include sacrifice of self. Longevity has more power. Duplicity is an art form, one in which he lavishly enjoyed.

Walsingham removed himself from his hiding station, one of several he had recently installed within the walls of Westminster Palace.

"Good day to you dear Earl of Leicester," smirked Walsingham.

"Walsingham, refer to me as does the queen. Robert will do in your address to me."

"As you would wish, dearest Robert," said Walsingham.

Walsingham then bowed gracefully towards Robert showing off long legs encased inside his stockings, emphasizing his slim elongated embroidered shoes. His padded doublet and collar gleamed in their newness. It's stitching revealing interlaced strips of embroidered silk strap work.

"How go your endeavours on behalf of Drake?" said Walsingham.

Robert lifted his left eyebrow upwards. "Whatever could you be talking of now, sir?"

"Surely you do not wish to have Francis Drake venture once again into King Phillip's colonies in the South Seas?"

"Not at all. Why would I? Well, there is the constant gossiping... if that is what you are harping on about. However, there is always talk of such things with Drake. He boasts so, does he not?" said Robert smiling sweetly.

"AH, yes. He does that very well," replied Walsingham.

"I assume you have heard of his boastings within these halls of late," replied Robert with a smirk.

"Quite so. The man is a veritable monster with his mouth. He causes great concern amongst the merchantmen who travel the waters in trade," quipped Walsingham.

"Do not worry so, my dear Walsingham. Her Majesty would not allow such a voyage to be convened."

"So you were discussing his proposed voyage then, I take it?"

"Not at all, Walsingham, quite the opposite, in fact."

"Ah, then you perhaps were considering his other voyage to the South Seas, for venture and gain. He speaks so easily upon the subject of this as well. Surely you were discussing this, then?"

"I do not remember any such discussion, Walsingham, indeed not. We were engaged upon a game of cards and entertaining Her Majesty with idle gossip about her ladies-in-waiting, and an amusing tryst with one of the new gentlemen just recently to court. Perhaps, you have heard about that too within these halls?"

Robert bowed his head towards Walsingham and strode on, dismissing Walsingham in his haste to be rid of him. Interfering clod, thought Robert.

"I bid good day to you, sir. I have errands to attend for Her Majesty."

Walsingham lingered a little longer amongst the tapestries and oak chairs lining the hallway to Her Majesty's Privy Council chamber, contemplating what he had just heard. He was not easily fooled. He had known all along of this aforementioned meeting and would be amongst its proposed voyage's principal backers, albeit secretly. But who will he exchange monies with this time? That had not yet been decided.

The adventurers in Elizabeth's realm were not necessarily trustworthy for they were only her corsairs and merchantmen and therefore not always reliable. Sebastian Cabot, was a brilliant adventurer, however, he lacked the necessary vanity for success in such open, uncharted waters.

Frobisher, adventurous more so perhaps than Cabot, but not clever enough to succeed, and his fool's gold find was a personal disaster.

Drake, the rogue, is perhaps the cleverest corsair in Elizabeth's realm and is proving to become its most brilliant. Handsome some will say, but more importantly vain. The most manipulative tool I have found yet, thought Walsingham. Utterly stupid of men to let this vanity of theirs get in the way of foresight.

Drake will become my tool in the most promising way. He will be used to serve this kingdom's realm to defy and manipulate the Catholic King of Spain. If only he could now somehow get Mary Queen of Scots embroiled in the affairs at court as well. What a prize to add to my list of accomplishments. How he despised the idea of another Catholic monarch on the throne. He had seen to it that her son, James, had been removed from that Scottish Queen Mary's care. Her infant will one day replace Elizabeth on the throne, he thought. Elizabeth will never marry. Unlike her father, she will covet virginity. He smiled at the duplicity of this. Walsingham remembered sewing that seed in Her Majesty's mind many moon seasons ago.

Walsingham was not fooled by Robert Dudley's trifling talk. These plans of discovery and plunder in the name of queen and country will take place. I shall see to it myself. And King Phillip of Spain will be prevented from the knowledge of its existence, for now. Phillip's reign over distant southern shores will be short lived, he concluded, especially if he had anything to impart on the matter.

However, if Elizabeth lets that coxcomb Drake quit her shores before the Irish issue is settled, she may indeed lose more lands to the Catholics. England has need of Francis Drake's particular talents at present, he mused. Drake's skills as a mariner are best suited to defences at present, not plunder and land acquisition, he thought.

A lesson in humility would suit Drake's countenance at present. He boasts too much to be let lose again just yet. Let him learn the folly of his mouth before he plunders along these distant Catholic held shores once more. The Irish could do with a thrashing as well.

Walsingham understood clearly that he would have to play Drake carefully, one hand surreptitiously backing another voyage of Drake's to lands unknown, and yet keeping his other hand active in Her Majesty's interests in the Catholic Irish discord. Drake's vanity was the way to control and steer him in any direction in which Walsingham needed for Elizabeth, his country and for Protestants, he thought. I have need of that rogue, Drake, at present, patrolling the Irish seas. Then I will send him off panicking the Spanish along all of their supposed shores. Plunder is especially lovely once it is loosened from Spanish booties. There is more than one way to flail the skin of the Spanish king and his heretical machinations. And after Drake's mistreatment by the Spanish Viceroyalty at San Juan de Ulúa, I'm guaranteed vengeance. Walsingham smiled at this thought. He knew very well how to manipulate Drake and allowed himself a hearty laugh.

Professor of nightmares

Kathleen understood she needed to purge all thoughts of Elizabeth I, Francis Drake and Francis Walsingham if she was ever to stop these nightmares. This notion of having been part of their world was ridiculous.

She knew that the Songhees told stories of Drake having visited their shores long before Captain Cook or Vancouver. These possibilities kept penetrating her mind like a worm burrowing into rotting wood. And there was plenty of rotting logs lying along the shoreline in Cadboro Bay of late, she thought.

Recently her nightmares had taken on a unique twist. Not since her childhood had she had such vivid dreams. Was it possibly the loneliness she had been sensing creeping through her bones? She recalled her childhood. Was this what was driving her visions, her fears of the dark? Doors opening slowly in the night, ruffling, hissing noises and the pouncing of their cat Cicero inside the closet chasing mice. Was this what she was recalling?

I hate mice to this day, and I hate waking up in the middle of the night to noises," she blurted out.

It was the smells in her nightmares that were particularly familiar now, again, reminding her of her childhood. The hippies had smelt like that. But her days of growing up in Vancouver's hippysville, Kitsilano, were long over. The smells that Kathleen sensed often lately, incense, unwashed bodies, smoked herbs and sun baked outhouse, rattled their way up her spine. Tingling in their pungency towards her brain.

"I have to leave the bloody TV on now at night. Darkness haunts me. Silly and stupid, I know, but I'm desperate now. I'll do anything to avoid those nightmares. Childish as that may be nonetheless, a light block from the darkness, from Elizabethan unrest, it helps."

Kathleen recalled her latest troubling vision. Maddox, her son, I wasn't pulling him back away from…His hand had slipped from her grip. And I wasn't screaming obscenities at anyone. I wasn't.

"You touch one hair on his body, and I'll remove your left ball with my teeth, and stuff it so far up your arse, your nose will bleed, you BASTARD."

Well, that I'm capable of saying. Hopefully none of the kids heard that nonsense, she thought, even if I have had a habit of talking in my sleep since childhood.

Kathleen's thoughts drifted back to that of Drake and his notorious affairs at sea. He had captured many a man and slave into his service willingly, though debatable. Nuno da Silva and Carlos Rodrigo Ortes, however, were plausible. After all they had travelled with him from the Cape Verde Islands off the coast of Africa and became valuable tools in his plundering of the Caribbean and the western coast of the Americas.

Kathleen's thoughts now drifted to the voices she had heard in the garden. Not only was her bedroom haunted, so too was her sanctuary. "My garden," she exclaimed. "My bloody garden is now talking to me."

Damn, that voice had seemed real, though. It was a deep, resounding sound, reminding me -- no, telling me to come back. Back to where, she thought, shaking her head?

"It is time for your return. I have waited long enough!"

You have waited long enough? Bloody nonsense, she thought.

"Begin your journey back into the past once more or I will take your precious sons."

Kathleen had gone stony white at that threat, her face taut, the muscles in her back tingling and her hands constricting the handle of her spade. Breathing deeply, she had gained some measure of control. Looking over her shoulders, peering into the neighbour's yard and all the while hearing a feint sloshing of water as if something was slipping across the surface of the sea.

And then her anger returned at the sound of his voice. He wanted to take her children.

"Take my sons. Ridiculous!" She had spat out at the nothingness.

Kathleen recalled how she had been pulling up weeds when the voice had made its pronunciations. I should have just ignored that voice emanating from somewhere amongst the roses. She had stood up suddenly when it happened, and then there was the sensation of something tugging at her pant legs, but there was nothing touching her when she had swung out at it, to brush off its gripping, dragging force.

I did love my garden, digging, planting, sowing seeds until that voice spoke to me, she thought. Its deep resonance had made me start and look out for its source, its body. And what was that tentacle I saw after plunging my spade into the muddy pool of soil in the raised bed. Kathleen shook her head quickly, returning her gaze back down at the pool of muddy water. Nothing, just my imagination, she thought.

Kathleen avoided the garden now, as the voice had repeatedly tormented her sanctuary. It was demanding in ever-increasing threats of the importance of fealty, loyalty and allegiance.

"Allegiance to what? You? Bastard. I'm outa here."

"Carlos," she said aloud. "I'll have to contact him again. He was helpful last year when these bloody nightmares began."

Thank goodness for running, thought Kathleen. So easy to clear one's thoughts, to be rid of irritating, uneasy imaginings.

Elizabeth

London 1576

Elizabeth surveyed her council chamber and sighed. When would these men stop manipulating and start producing some wealth? Standing again, Elizabeth rose from her well-worn chair, stomped across the oak floors with their tattered rugs and withdrew from the privy chamber into the private sanctuary where she most liked to think. Throwing open the doors to her chambers, Elizabeth smiled sweetly and stared across the room towards the hearth. Every lady in waiting looked up expectantly, pleased with any attention that their sovereign would and could mete out.

"I have need of quiet, ladies. Please gather your sewing pieces and leave my chamber." Kat Astley stood, crossed the floor quickly and placed herself close by Elizabeth and waited patiently until the ladies-in-waiting left the chamber. "Do you have a migraine, Lizzy? Can I call upon the Welshman Cadfael to attend to your needs again?"

"No, Kat. I have a need to speak with my sister that is all."

"Shall I find her for you or…"

"I will find her myself. Thank you, Kat. Go now and rest. You must take some time to recover from your cold. You will do me no good if you cannot take better care of yourself."

Elizabeth took her governess' hand and gently squeezed it, breathing in the musk and rose scent of her dearest friend and admirer. Elizabeth will grant her former governess many quiet days in the near future. She will even attempt to prevent her from breathing in the sometimes foul odours of her half-sister and cousin, Catherine. Yes, the daughter of her mother's sister and her father King Henry shared many secrets. But there will come a time in the not too distant future, a sudden sadness within the governess' bosom, which will sorrow Elizabeth greatly.

Kat dropped her head in recognition of Elizabeth's tone and authority, gently gathered her skirts and quietly removed herself from the room.

Elizabeth surveyed the space, taking in the embroidered bedclothes and cushions.

Her ladies had done Elizabeth well, always making ever more luxurious cloths and fashioning them into rich outer garments and robes. She hoped they enjoyed what they did, as she had not enjoyed the sewing required of her by her sister and former monarch Mary Tudor, her now deceased sister, Queen Mary. "Bloody Mary, they called her," Elizabeth said aloud and softly. "I don't even miss her presence any more, not since she had me imprisoned in the Tower of London. Whatever will my people refer to me as?" she mused boldly and then quickly dismissed the thought.

Queen Mary's intimidation of young Elizabeth within the White Tower of London had eradicated any need to continue her own stitching. Mary's insistence on Catholic symbolism in Elizabeth's stitching in the end became futile and pointless. The vile taste of her half-sister's piety, the stench of Mary's fury in the burning of her heretics, still lingered in Elizabeth's nose and throat.

Her ladies would continue to enjoy their tasks. Elizabeth could not ever again idle her life away with insignificant chat and embroidery. In her kingdom, Elizabeth would rule, not men. Elizabeth would do the telling. Elizabeth, Queen of England, Wales and Ireland would dictate the matters at court, not her councillors or men-at-arms, she thought.

"Never again will I be controlled by the likes of royally blooded men."

Elizabeth moved along the corridor and secreted herself along the inner passageway to the stairs leading to the Tower's turrets. It is here that she had seconded her older sister and cousin. It was a pity that Catherine chose to spout so often of her importance as Her Majesty's kin. Elizabeth could not have her talk this way, as if she were heir to the throne.

She may, however, be of great use as a bewitcher. Her skills at prediction have so far yielded truth. But as her keeper, this had often caused Elizabeth harm. Catherine had a habit of offending with her poisonous tongue.

Cardinal Wolsey had Catherine declared a witch long before his own execution by their father Henry VIII. Elizabeth's past was continually haunting her present circumstances. She had replaced the portraits of former queens, consorts and traitors upon the walls of her palaces.

Her mother's headless body no longer haunted her thoughts. The dark eyes of Ann Boleyn pierced the soul of Elizabeth daily and fortified the strength emanating from her spine. Robert Dudley's father's head no longer rotted outside the walls of the Tower. And Jane Seymour's corpse now lay gently decaying in its marbled cask beside that of her formidable father's.

Katherine Howard's youthful portrait served as a reminder to her ladies-in-waiting of the duty due to Elizabeth and the need for discretions in the matters of fornication at court. Their images looked out at their Virgin Queen with less arrogance now. They stood as reminders to those in her court at the futility of vanity, deceit and personal pursuits.

But it was perhaps the portrait of Lady Jane Grey that strengthened and chilled the bones of Elizabeth the most. This dainty figure's portrait hung in many rooms of Elizabeth's palaces. Her intelligence and arguments of defence were written in letters and revealed her determination to disobey the orders of traitorous parents. Elizabeth kept them close at hand and reviewed their contents privately, often.

It was well known at court of the beatings that Jane Seymour endured for refusing to marry and carry the duties of royalty upon her shoulders. Only when she was coerced into believing the futility of her views did Jane give way. The use of her sisters as a weapon, that they too would be forced into marriage with an unwanted husband and kingdom, that she did relent. The slender young neck of Jane gracefully rose up the stairs of her execution scaffold and laid its head modestly, forgivingly, acceptingly down upon the axe man's block.

Thirteen defiant lonely days had been the length of her reign. Her ghost is still said to wander the halls of the infamous White Tower of London. How could her sister have believed that Jane would harm Mary Tudor in anyway? It was well known of her refusal to accept the crown.

But that was Mary, at the hands of her suitor and soon to be husband, King Phillip of Spain. How could Mary let that man into her bed, let alone her kingdom? Queen Mary Tudor hadn't ruled England, King Phillip of Spain had. She gagged at the disgust of it all.

Bloody Mary had begun her reign of terror with persecutions upon the most loyal of souls. Elizabeth's imprisonment in the White Tower of London with Robert Dudley had formed a bond between the two prisoners. Her release at the hands of King Phillip of Spain at the marriage of her sister Mary to Phillip had released her from the tower's confinement.

It was only afterwards that she suspected that his insistence of her release was based upon his assumptions that he would need another

English queen to wed upon Mary's death. For his elderly bride Mary was not well in mind or body. And perhaps the youthful figure and mind of her much younger sibling could be advantageous to Spain. Elizabeth spat the bile that rose into her mouth out.

Elizabeth's shoulders released their grip momentarily and lengthened her neck from its frame each time she passed by her sister Mary and Phillip's portrait. The revulsion of Phillip's presumptions and flirtations shuddered their way past lesser men and emerged triumphantly from the smirk of Elizabeth's grin and the fiery eyes of her own cagey endeavours.

Elizabeth mused on the thought that perhaps the sins of the Tudor lineage have wrought this deformity of soul that allows Catherine, her half-sister and cousin the dark power of prediction. In time, she may learn wisdom and begin to curb her unnatural utterances.

Her perch above the reaches of court, though, had so far been of great import. The view along the Thames has its advantages. Catherine had seen many comings and goings about Elizabeth's realm from atop the walkways and passages of the tower's turrets. The tower's traitor's gate could be seen, as too could London's only bridge. Merchantmen, ambassadors, assignations, burgers, freemen, townsmen, laymen all could be seen and sometimes heard from Catherine's placement above Westminster's pathways.

Catherine was kept hidden from court and used at the queen's pleasure. Only when it was necessary and advantageous was Catherine allowed to wander or mingle with the others at court. For she set an edge of friction and demonic countenance upon any resident with whom she was engaged if released for too long amongst the stone and mortar. Rumours had circulated that even the vermin and ghosts scatter and hide if left too long within her council.

However, at present her secrets, her knowledge, her dangerous thoughts, these Elizabeth had need of now. Catherine will predict the timing of Drake's voyage to the South Seas. And this time, she must explain her deranged ramblings about this traveller, who begins again her voyage with her sons. From her lips will ensue forth the truth of this tale of a traveller, who roams from one realm and into another at will and with no impediment? Preposterous! Not in my realm she won't.

Of what possible traveller could she speak of so highly when Walsingham knows nothing of it? Or does he know, and is he using it to attain power and knowledge to engage in dangerous liaisons and treaties. The thought of intrigue behind her back made her blood boil. However, she needed to greet her half-sister with caution. Information was what she needed most now.

Elizabeth wondered at the possibility of travel forwards and backwards in time. What would she change of her past and spent days? Would she change anything at all, her future or death? Will there be more pain, more loss of soul? Will her dignity be preserved in time? What will become of her realm, and who will threaten the security of her kingdom? Who will set the best fortune upon her reign and what truths will be ushered and from whose lips?

All these thoughts mingled inside her brain. But these thoughts were not jumbled. She had a clear idea of what lay before in the talk of this traveller come of late. Elizabeth wanted to stop these rumours from spreading. Myths were dangerous, and this one had to be eliminated quickly. Especially if there were to be substance to its meaning.

Elizabeth quickened her pace along the corridor that led to the narrow passageway to the spiral stone steps of her half-sister and cousin's chambers.

Carlos

June 2002

Professor Kathleen O'Malley picked up the phone at her desk at the University of Victoria and then placed it back down again. Her cell phone, she realized, couldn't be traced, at least not by the university. She needed to call Carlos, but not on campus. Kathleen felt a desperate need to see him. Carlos had an ability to negate her nightmares' ferocity, and she wanted desperately to understand them as he did. It had been a year since her last nightmares, but they had begun again, and this time Kathleen's children were ... She shook her head. This has got to stop. This was something Professor Kathleen O'Malley, the traveller, was not willing to put up with.

"Traveller, I'm not a traveller. Oh God, I need to get control of myself."

Carlos Rodrigo Ortes, time traveller, healer and pirate recognized the ring tone on his phone. Finally, he thought she is willing to make contact again as she must.

"Professor, it has been too long. I am glad you have called."

"Carlos, we -- no, I need to speak with you again. The nightmares."

"Yes, Kathleen, it is time for us to speak. We have much to talk about."

59

"How would you know that?"

"I always know."

"I'm going to ignore that statement for now. When can we meet? I have a break from classes for a few hours now, but I'd like to go for a run first, clear my thoughts then meet if that works for you?"

"All right. Go for your run then meet me in Cadboro Bay afterwards, at our usual place."

Kathleen closed the cell phone and reached for the gym bag she kept behind her desk.

"I'm going to run these thoughts out of my head."

As she ran, Kathleen made a mental note of her thoughts. Keep a diary of these dreams; note the time, date, weather, news items, moons and tides. There has to be a logical, methodical, scientific explanation involved. I will root out this evil from my mind. Questions to ask Carlos.

One, why are they happening again?

Two, what methods does he propose to deal with them?

Three, create a spreadsheet of tools to use when nightmares occur.

"That's logical. I can deal with that."

Simple really, Kathleen thought. Rid my mind of beasts like the Kraken. That's a myth. Then eliminate the triggers that cause nightmares. Then…then what she thought?

Waffle, gag myself and stop teaching Elizabethan history. Well, that's not going to happen.

Kathleen looked out across Cadboro Bay. "Humph, the beast lay sleeping nestled in the sand, me thinks. Oh, how the boys love climbing all over it."

Cadborosaurus lay amongst the sand in dutiful slumber, its repose more innocent than sinister, its big teeth somehow inviting, nothing like the mouth of that beast she had seen last night.

Shit…refocus, breathe, you're almost there. I can sense him, yet I cannot see him. Why and how does he do that?

Kathleen slowed her pace from a fast run to a trot and finally to walking. She breathed deeply, smelling the salt of the sea on her tongue. Water, I need water and lots of it.

Kathleen saw Carlos looking at her and stopped. He waved his hand and beckoned her to come over. He has been running as well. Hmm, I didn't know he ran.

There is a lot you don't know about me, he thought and smiled. Soon you will know more.

Kathleen walked towards Carlos and hesitatingly smiled back. She sat down at the table outside of the coffee shop.

"I didn't know you ran."

"There is a lot you will find out about me someday but not now. You came here seeking my help again."

"I said I needed to talk."

"About nightmares, you said." He smiled.

"Ya, I know. It's starting again. Only this time my children are involved, and I'm not interested in having nightmares about my children."

"Tell me about them, then, your nightmares. Let us sort them out again."

"Listen Carlos, I need to pay you for your services. You cannot just help me for free. I have insurance that will help pay for our sessions."

"No need. My services to you are free."

"Why?"

"Because we have history to discuss. We have history together, remember."

"No, I'm not going there. We don't have history together."

"You will remember," said Carlos.

61

"Carlos, let's just put that disagreement aside, for now. I need your help, and I know you can help me."

"Yes, I can, but you must believe in our past together."

"I cannot. I will not. Let us forget that nightmare for now. There is a new one which needs to be eliminated from my daily thoughts."

Carlos leaned across the table and picked up Kathleen's hand in his. He caressed her fingers without looking into her eyes.

"You will remember. You have to. Otherwise, I will not be able to help you fully. And things may go terribly wrong," he said and stared into her eyes.

"Carlos, stop that."

"Stop what," he said gently.

"Carlos, I asked for your help, and I remember you saying you would help me again if and when those nightmares returned. That is our past."

He let Kathleen's hand slip from his fingers. He nodded and sat back in his chair.

"I did offer you help, and I will help you. But first, you must acknowledge that we know each other from before, from a time that was important to both of us, from a time when you helped me."

"Carlos, I have a memory of a nightmare only, which you helped to eliminate from my thoughts. I remember that nightmare seeming very real, but it was not. And now I need you to help me again, please. I don't mind paying you for this."

"Kathleen, I do not need your money. And you have at least acknowledged, to a certain degree, that we have a past."

Carlos put up his hand in protest.

"It is enough for me for now that you have remembered that particular nightmare, as you call it. So what is it that you see now?"

Kathleen hesitated. She did not want to reveal everything she had seen in her dreams to Carlos yet. She needed to sort them out first for herself, but the bits involving her children were particularly disturbing. She swallowed and took a deep breath after closing her eyes. Kathleen's sons, Maddox, Woody and Kitt were jumping off the side of an Elizabethan boat into the Thames River in London. She shook her head. That's not what she wanted to share yet with Carlos.

Kathleen took another deep breath and opened her eyes. Carlos sat back in his chair with his hands in his hair, his face pale and confused.

"Carlos, what is it? You are not well? We can do this another time. This is not important if you need help." Kathleen began to rise.

"Sit, I am well. I did not realize this change had occurred in you. That is all. It is very serious. We must talk. Tell me more of your dreams."

Carlos did not tell Kathleen that he had seen that same vision just now. It disturbed him to think that Sir Francis Drake was now employing these tactics on her to get what he wanted. Children, Drake had promised, were never to be part of this.

Kathleen hadn't told Carlos anything yet, however, his demeanour had changed so rapidly she hesitated before beginning.

"I'm not sure if this is the right time to talk, perhaps another day. Maybe I've got silly ideas in my head. Let's forget what I was so disturbed by, for now. We can talk later."

"No, we must talk now. You called, and I want to listen. So begin. Tell me what you see."

"I dream not see, Carlos. I dream."

He nodded his response. "For now we will call these visions your dreams. Go on, tell me your dreams."

Kathleen closed her eyes again and heard that word repeat itself inside her head. Visions, visions. These were not visions. They couldn't be. They were nightmares. I have nightmares she concluded, only nightmares.

"I see myself in Elizabethan England, imprisoned in the Tower of London with a woman I call Edith. And then suddenly I am free again only I can't tell whether that freedom is before or after my imprisonment. And I'm always running from someone. Their faces are obscure, shadowy and blurred, but I am searching for something that I don't want to be looking for. My heart aches. My mind won't stop seeing things. It's the same nightmare over and over again. Each time it occurs, though, I see more ugliness, more wretched people begging me. Sometimes they are even throwing things at me." Kathleen opened her eyes again. She wanted to see that pale face begin to look normal. Only then would she be able to believe what he said in response to these nightmares.

Carlos nodded his head his face no longer had its former complexion. Such a rapid change, thought Kathleen. He needs to see a doctor too.

Carlos leaned across the table. "I need no doctor to help me and neither do you."

Kathleen's mouth dropped open. She shook her head. "You can't be listening to my thoughts."

"I can hear your thoughts when you are in danger. You must believe in that, for only then will I be able to help you when you need me most."

"I am not in danger, Carlos. I'm in Victoria, not London England in the Elizabethan era."

"This too is true for now," replied Carlos.

Agreements Made and Broken

Carlos was furious. Drake had changed the rules to suit his means, and he didn't like it. Children were never to be part of his plans. He had promised that. However, now after seeing Kathleen's visions, he knew that change was happening, changes not agreed to. And he meant to stop it.

Summoning Drake was not always easy. He could be frequently complacent, and right now was not the time to be thus. Their history together was set. He could not change that. It was because of Drake that he lived on in another realm and would continue to live after another lifetime's worth of living memories. It was an opportunity he had agreed to, to extend his existence beyond man's normal lifespan.

Helping Drake in return accomplish that which had been denied him in history was an easy bargain to agree to, for the privilege of longevity and a chance to gain more time on earth as a living being. He had never doubted it before, its appeal. In fact he had thoroughly embraced as much of living in this century as he could.

The agreements were many, more than he had understood. First of all, Drake had wanted his journals and maps retrieved from

Elizabethan England, a feat not without peril in its grasping. Carlos had yet to find out where Elizabeth had absconded with them.

The trouble was what was he to do with them once he got a hold of them? It was not like he could just deliver them to a library or museum. They needed to be discovered amongst other missing documents or even hidden inside of something insignificant and rarely asked for at a museum or archive.

And then how was he to disgorge their contents without eliciting suspicion at its authenticity? It was an impossible task, no doubt, to which he had found no remedy.

The other troubling agreements were difficult and sometimes perilous. Returning to certain scenes in his past life had not been without consequences. Repeatedly dying at the hands of the inquisition, until he had found several individuals who could master the art of transference, was and had been wretched. His body and mind had had to be cleansed after every occurrence.

Transference was in itself another problem to grasp a hold of. Its sensation had been alarming, even disturbing at times. And then teaching others to transfer had not been without peril as well. There were, of course, the reluctant ones. And having to put them through numerous recurring death scenes had reduced his numbers of willing participants.

Kathleen had managed to transfer successfully, but unfortunately, her willingness to believe in its advantages was troublesome. She was a strong-willed woman, more intelligent than most of the men he had attempted to transfer willingly.

Often when transferring, he had come into contact with the Shaman whose portal he and Drake used. Shaman was not a pleasant man at first until he had agreed to help in the closure of its portal.

However, the pact that was made between them continued to be limiting. He would have very little time to achieve all of Drake's goals within that time frame that they had agreed to. And the tool he had engaged in closing that portal consisted of engaging the traveller, the woman whom Drake had used to save him from imminent death at the hands of Drake's own men. This was the very memory, which the traveller, Kathleen, remembered as a nightmare only, stubbornly refusing to believe or acknowledge how real it had been.

The traveller, with the help of Emily Carr, an eminent writer and painter of her time, was perhaps the best adversary he had. She believed in Kathleen's ability to be able to close Drake's portal. Emily had recognized her as the one to be able to accomplish this task. Kathleen, the travelling professor, had a knack of always doing the right thing, regardless of others protests. And the fact that her travels, in her time world happened to coincide with the places Drake had been to, further convinced Emily that she had chosen the right person to do their bidding. Emily believed that with Carlos' help they could depend on great things from this professor of lore and history.

Shaman, on the other hand, thought Carlos was not as convinced, especially as Kathleen had been used finally to bring forth my emergence into modern times. He was furious about this. It meant that Drake had succeeded in manipulating the spirit world to his advantage once more, an advantage that the shaman was determined to eliminate quickly. The Songhees spirit world was becoming increasingly agitated by the abuse of this white man in their domain.

Carlos took to the pathway leading down to the shore. He had waited until sunset when the water's surface carried the moon's glow across its breadth. He slipped off his shorts and shirt, wading into the sea. However, he was careful not to engage in discourse with the

Kraken. This was not his time to go back. It would be the traveller's soon enough, and he wanted to extract from Drake a promise not to engage that woman's children in this venture.

Carlos swam out beyond the cliffs and slipped beneath the surface of the sea. He dove deep beneath the waves, calling out to Drake as he went. Drake's replies were weak, which meant he was either ignoring him or temporarily back on land for his daily hour's reconnaissance into Elizabeth's London.

After several more attempts at requesting Drake's presence immediately, Carlos confirmed his suspicions. He was being deliberately ignored. Never had Drake kept him waiting this long. What game was he up to now? Impatience was never one of Drake's faults when he was alive. Why now?

Yes, it had taken Drake almost four hundred years to learn how to manipulate this spirit world of the Songhees nation. However, he had accomplished it. He was making progress. What was the hurry, anyway?

Had Drake discovered his alliance with the shaman and Emily? Carlos decided he needed to be more careful in his approach with these two in the future. They would need to meet him on land next time for their hour's worth of foraging. Convincing them of the need to do this would be problematic. Neither of them wished to be on dry land ever again, preferring instead the comforts of the spirit world and their people. Family, was as always, more important than acquisitions.

Transference

Cadboro Bay
June 2002

Her children had been taken. She was sure of it. But once again after checking on their whereabouts, she was satisfied that they were still at home sleeping. These nightmares have got to stop, thought Kathleen.

"Once you retrieve my journals, they probably will. I'll have no need of you by then. You can go back to your work, your children and your former existence."

Kathleen chose not to listen to that. After all she knew there was nobody here in her room. She slept alone these days. In fact she preferred it that way. No one could then see or hear those voices that kept ringing, calling out at her, speaking to her. She had enough worries at present raising three boys on her own, without snide comments on her level of sanity at present.

Once the kids were off to school, she would head down to the beach for another run before teaching her day's first history class at the university.

Carlos could feel the pull of the Kraken before he realized what it meant. He had ignored it purposely. He was angry with Drake and his abuse of power over the lives of his travellers, in particular his hints of taking Kathleen's children into Elizabethan London.

But then it occurred to him, what if that pull was not meant for him? Would she go again, and if so, would it be willingly? Drake had a knack of taking those he felt most useful, even if they had no wish to transfer in time. Dropping what he was working on Carlos left his condo in haste and ran outside, leaving his door open. The beach was only a block away.

Kathleen sighted the beach as she rounded the pub. And now for a sprint across the sand, she thought. She looked at the Cadborosaurus as she ran past it. It was nestled as usual in the sand, harmless cement beast, blinking its lashes out at her.

Ah, there's some splashing in the water forty feet from shore, she thought. The sea was looking promising, nothing but a few rippling soft waves coming ashore. A seal popped its head up and disappeared down again. "Humph," she said aloud, continuing on with her run. "I wonder if you have found some choice meal."

Reaching the end of the beach, Kathleen turned back around and sprinted across it towards the cement beast. Endearingly she looked towards it as she passed it. "My children have played on that beast. What lovely imaginings children have." And she laughed out loud. "I can't help smiling at you, my mysterious Cadborosaurus and your lovely myth of a lone beast prowling the waters off the bay." Again she laughed out loud.

Another louder splash brought her head around towards the sea. There amongst the flotsam floating on the sea's surface a man's head had emerged, his black hair plastered to his face, his arm breaking the surface of the water, grasping at the air. He bobbled there, momentarily before slipping back under the water.

"Shit, he's drowning." Kathleen felt a burning tingling sensation run along her spine. Haunting past dreams flashed before her eyes. She shook her head. She had to find him. She had to save him. He was going to drown, and she could feel that. Now this was real, not those bloody nightmares.

Kathleen turned her head at the sound of her name. She waved at Carlos, pointing towards the sea. Good, she thought, someone else has seen him. I'll have help now.

Throwing off her light jacket, Kathleen ran into the cold Pacific waters. He wasn't that far from shore, and so she called out to him as his head surfaced once more.

"Over here. Can you see me? I'm coming. Hold on. I'll be there soon."

He slipped beneath the surface momentarily before his head came up again, and she could see him gasping and spluttering. His face appeared distorted, his lips swollen and blood appeared to be coming out of his nostrils and mouth.

The water had been cold when she had entered it. By now she could feel her feet had left the security of the sandy bottom. She was calling out to him but was uncertain if he could hear her. His thrashing was getting more agitated and desperate. Back down he went.

She pulled at the water before her, ignoring the cries from the beach, where Carlos was calling out to her. She kept gliding over the waves as quickly as she could, bobbing through them as the sea kept pushing her forwards. A wave crashed over her head, and she surfaced knocking herself into the side of the man.

He stared into her eyes, his pupils dilated. He seemed to be kicking at something beneath him. He was frightened by something below the surface, his panicked cry every time his body was pushed by the waves confused her.

What was it that was causing him such distress? she wondered. Kathleen, realized that she would have to push him away from herself and then dive beneath him, coming up behind him, so as to grab the back of his neck, enabling her to hold his head above the surface. This way he could be convinced he was not about to die. He drove his arm out towards her, and she pushed him away. His startled cry, "ayudar, ayudar" startled Kathleen and made her confused.

He speaks Spanish, she thought, but that didn't matter right now. He was going to drown the both of them if she didn't do something quickly.

She plunged herself below the surface and could feel his thrashing movements beside her. He twisted, turned and bobbed beside her. She would only have a few moments to grab the back of his head before she surfaced again. Kathleen reached out to grab the back of his head as he slipped back beneath the sea, something almost pulling him down, she thought.

That's when it took hold of her, wrapping its tentacles around her waist, and dragged her down, deep into the sea. Her muscles tightened. Is this what he had felt below him. My God, she thought.

She felt more tentacles working their way up her body. Her nostrils filled with the salt of the sea. Her muscles cramped. She looked up towards the surface, as her body was flipped sideways and pulled further downward. The man above her rose up and down again. His form fading farther away as each new tentacle wound its way around her.

She grasped at the beast's long thick tentacles and desperately tried to pull them off. It gripped at her harder, swirling its body around her. The enormity of its size loomed in front of her, as it held her just slightly out of reach of its gaping innards. She felt the light pack she was wearing beneath her discarded jacket, as it was crushed and twisted up against her back. Her water bottle dug deep into her waist and then popped out beside her, shooting towards the surface as if possessed.

Kathleen felt the steel of her pen, as it dug into her shoulder blade and the pressure of her latest notebook. Something she had always ran with just in case she needed to write things down. She thought then only, of the lovely pinkness of its soft leather, creamy unlined sheets. "Vellum" she tried to say out loud. Nothing, however, but salt filled her mouth. She spat, but nothing entered or came out.

I should be dead by now. Why am I not dead, she thought. Her mouth became dry, pasty, and her nostrils filled with the smell of smoke. A hand reached out towards her. A woman slowly made her way towards Kathleen from out of the beast's mouth. A shaman then followed the woman out. Kathleen shook her head and closed her eyes.

Is this what it feels like to drown? She tilted her head up towards the surface of the sea. One last glimpse of the sun's rays before I leave this world, she thought. But what she saw confused her even more. She could clearly see herself and the man she had entered the water to save above herself. She was kicking hard, one hand grasping the back of his head and long black hair, the other arm pulling backwards through the water towards land, her feet furiously kicking towards the safety of solid ground.

I was just running, wasn't I? This doesn't make sense. How can I be down here and up there at the same time?

Kathleen felt the tentacles grip the side of her head and force it down. She stared directly into the eyes of the man before her. He smiled. His long dark hair flowed freely around his head as the swell of the water moved them through the force of the seas currents. A tall woman, slightly plump, hair knotted up on top of her head smiled at Kathleen too. They were mouthing something at her. She couldn't understand them and shook her head in confusion.

The woman frowned and turned towards the shaman. He nodded. The shaman looked back towards the beast holding fast to Kathleen. He brought his hands up to his mouth and blew bubbles towards the Kraken.

The Kraken opened its gapping mouth even wider, sucked in the sea around them, drawing the three of them inside its enormous cavity.

Kathleen felt her lungs explode with pain as she was drawn into its mouth. She felt every stinging slithery noodle-like teeth as she passed through into its innards. She floated above the two figures, pushing herself away from them. Pain seared through her fingertips. She gripped her hand and tried to right herself as if she was swimming, feet downwards, head presumably above the water floating, looking out at the masses of other swimmers and the loveliness of the shoreline. Kathleen shook her head once more. She was not above water. But how could she be inside a beast's mouth, she thought?

Kathleen drifted down towards the two below, righting herself as the sea pushed them around from the outside.

"Who are you?" she yelled at them.

The woman raised an eyebrow.

"Your memory is short," the woman snapped back at her.

"I am Emily Carr. This man you know as the Shaman of the Songhees Nation."

Kathleen turned and cocked her head sideways, folding her arms across her chest.

"No, you are mistaken. I'm drowning. Why aren't you?"

They both laughed and smiled back at her.

"This isn't a joke, you know," she yelled at them.

The shaman moved forward and grasped hold of Kathleen's hand and dragged her towards himself.

"No, this is no joke. You must begin your journey back. You must bring back his heirs this time, or you will lose your own to him forever."

The shaman released her, but what seemed to Kathleen more gently than he had grabbed at her before. The shaman, his face now was watching Kathleen, her face contorting, grasping at memories.

Kathleen tried hard to recognize the two before her. Nothing but a black emptiness filled her heart after the mention of her own children. A deep aching curdled in her stomach. She felt cold and lost. Now more than ever, she desperately wanted to reach the safety of her own home. Where were her children, thought Kathleen? She wanted to feel their soft young skin, to smell them after a bubble bath, to drop them off at their school and whisper gently once more into their ears.

"It's school, you know. You're to have absolutely no fun whilst your there. OK?"

She could hear their reply now, their giggling and their ha-has. She watched them run off smiling, waving back at her, running towards their friends.

"At least she recalls her heirs," said Emily now turning towards the shaman. "She will recall more. I can assure you of that."

"We will see. White man has not been our friend, as you well know."

Kathleen looked between the two colluding mirages.

"My heirs?"

"My children?" she yelled at them.

"Yes," they replied in unison.

"Who has my children?"

"Drake," they both replied.

Shaman raised his paddle and his eyebrows simultaneously. "DRAKE," he spat back at her.

"DRAKE, DRAKE, Drake...who?"

"Klee Wyck, she is not the one. Only you thought she was." He turned to signal to the Kraken.

Emily, grabbed hold of Shaman's paddle. "Oh, she's the one. She'll just have to suffer some more before she realizes what's going on. I'll see to it that she makes her way back there again. Listen just a while longer. You'll see."

Kathleen rolled the name Klee Wyck around in her head. That's the Native name for that writer and painter from the late 1800s, but she's dead. She died in 1941 or 42. This is impossible! Emily Carr is dead.

"1943 to be exact," replied Emily. "Brain cells are on. That's my girl. Now who do you remember as Drake?"

Kathleen wondered how this woman could read her thoughts so well. She reached behind her head and felt the stickiness of something at her neck, wiping her hand across her neck and bringing it around to look at, she saw the oozing mess of congealed blood in her hand. She gagged and spat out even more blood and watched as it swirled around the three of them. Images of an executioner's block loomed in between herself and Emily and the shaman. She saw her children jumping once more from the side of a ship she recognized as the Golden Hinde in London, and they then disappeared from view just as quickly. Men on horseback galloped through her, brushing her aside and further distancing her from the two smiling individuals trapped with her in this whirling, gyrating mass of fleshy pulsating muscle.

An axe swung down between the shaman and Emily Carr further pushing Kathleen away from them. Shaman shook his body and backed further away as the water around them turned red. He had recognized something else, thought Kathleen. His face contorted, his mouth had opened as if to scream a warning.

Kathleen looked back over her shoulders. A crowd of people stood gathered around her on the ground. She saw herself kneeling before a block, her children reaching up towards her with her journal clasped in her son Maddox's outstretched hand as a young man pushed the children closer towards her.

"DRAKE, YOU BASTARD," she roared out at him. "Jesus. Shit. No, I'm not going back there again." Kathleen shuddered with the realization of that memory.

She stared across the slowly disappearing forms of Emily and the shaman.

"SIR. I WOULDN'T CALL YOU A SIR, YOU BLOODY PIRATE."

Kathleen struggled to get lose from the Kraken's hold and cried out at the fading figures of Emily and Shaman, but their forms were fading fast towards the light of sun.

The Kraken tightened its grip pulling Kathleen further inside its cavernous mouth, forcing her deeper inside its gullet.

"Wait," she cried out towards their fading images, "Why me? Why me? she cried desperately.

"Because you can," echoed around inside her head. It repeated itself over and over again. Slowly fading away, she could just hear them.

"Because you can. Seek out the one you know as Edith," she heard softly before the return of the phrase, "Because you can. Only you have been able to survive in their world so far. Remember to seek out Edith," whispered the voice of Emily fading now into nothingness. Dark cloudy swirlling smoke surrounded her, pain seared across Kathleen's body.

She struggled in vain to release herself from the grip of the Kraken's tentacles. She felt herself being sucked through its stomach, its intestinal juices digesting her face and hands before her.

Her bones ached with each crushing blow from the tentacles ends. She imagined being pinned inside of a washing machine, whirling around the Kraken's tightly formed insides of the interior, as she tumbled over and over again in the darkness, things pushed at every part of her body.

She swirled back and forth, up and down. One moment she was sideways rolling and rolling, head, body and hands held tightly by the beast. Then she was travelling upwards. Back down she went again then back to rolling. Her lungs felt tight, her mouth sticky. She could smell them. Suddenly she smelt their hair. "Maddox, Woody, Kitt," she screamed out. She heard them laughing with someone, an unfamiliar voice. Her body shook violently. She felt suddenly cold, helpless, constricted but alive nonetheless.

When was this going to end? Where are my children? she thought. What has he done to them? What BASTARD takes a woman's children from her and uses them as hostages, she thought? Despicable!

No, this can't be happening. I'm drowning. This is what it feels like when you're dying. Your memories return, and we as people relive those things. She stopped, realization dawning with her uplifted brows. Her children weren't dead. She wasn't drowning. She hadn't had real memories, and these were her nightmares playing themselves out inside her head again. Any moment now she would wake up, covered in sweat, shaking and looking for her perfectly sleeping children, nicely tucked up in their beds.

Kathleen saw daylight above her again. Ah, I am waking, she thought. Murky waters swirled around her. The movement was quick and fast pulling at her like the tide withdrawing across the sand. Her body shuddered once more, and the pain ceased its hold of her bones. She tried to breath but only took in dirty cold water. Reaching skyward with both hands she kicked her feet furiously. The surface she thought. I have not drowned after all. But where is that man I went into the water for, and who the hell is Edith, sprung into her head?

Kathleen's head popped out of the Thames between the pillars next to the shore. A rickety dock lay next to stone stairs leading up to the safety of land. She didn't understand. Where the hell was she? She swam towards the stairway where a woman was racing down them towards her. The woman stopped, clasped her hand to her mouth and cried out.

"No, no, not you again," cried out Edith. "He will kill me this time if you come back. Go away. Please, go away. You cannot come here again."

Kathleen pulled herself up out of the water and onto the stone stairway leading upwards from the river.

"I must find them," Kathleen shouted out at the woman running away now from her.

"Edith," she stammered. "Please, help me find them. He has my children."

Kathleen's mind raced. How did I know this woman's name? she thought. She looked up at the woman she had called Edith fleeing back up the stairs in fright.

"Wait. Stop," Kathleen cried out again. "Please, help me."

Kathleen turned her head back towards the water. She looked down towards the lone bridge, spanning the river.

"LONDON, the THAMES," she shouted out loud. "This can't be."

Turning back to the almost disappearing form of Edith, Kathleen exclaimed, "Shit, what year is this? This can't be right?"

There'll be time to worry about that later, she thought. Right now I have to catch up to the only person I seem to have a name for. That woman knows me. Why?

Kathleen bolted up the stairs towards the only person she thought could help her now.

"Edith," she cried out desperately. "Edith, who's on the throne?"

Edith was struggling to run along the shore in the gown that she wore. And it was not long before Kathleen was able to come up alongside her.

Kathleen grasped hold of Edith's hand and pulled her back towards her. Edith's face was stony white.

"Who's on the throne? Is it Bloody Mary?"

Edith paled even further and shook her head. She tried to pull her hand away from Kathleen. But by now Kathleen held fast to both of Edith's hands. She gripped Edith's wrists and shook her entire body firmly.

"Please, I am confused. I do not want to be here. And for some reason I don't know you don't want me here either."

Edith tugged at her hands, eyes wide with fear, tears running down her cheeks, gasping at the air around them, spluttering nonsense. She looked away from Kathleen, whimpering softly.

"Thank God it's not Bloody Mary on the throne." She turned her head away from Edith, momentarily, glancing quickly at the Thames River. Its fast flowing waters indicated the tide was moving out to sea. She could feel Edith pulling back from her, attempting to get away. Kathleen squeezed tighter, sharply pulling the struggling woman back to her. Pillars holding docks lay high above the water level. One lone bridge clustered with housing spilling over its sides crept across its breadth. On the far side of the bank she could see shipyards and a church. The Tower of London lay opposite the shipyards at the other end of the bridge, and the same side of the river upon which they were as well. The Towers encompassing walls loomed around it. Slowly Kathleen turned her head back towards Edith.

"Who, then?" she said. Who has claim to the throne, Edward or Elizabeth?"

Kathleen saw the terror, flick across the dilated pupils of Edith's eyes as she mentioned Elizabeth's name

Edith stared into the eyes of Kathleen, this interloper, this woman, as the traveller who had brought much pain and misery to her the last time she had left these shores. She had anticipated further bruising every day she had denied her husband the knowledge of this woman's whereabouts. Owen had been cruel in his beatings; she still bore the scars of his knife and hot poker. Her own father would never have dared hurt her mother. She had wanted to be married to a Protestant like her father. Why were Catholics so cruel, she wondered, or was it only her husband who inflicted his torture on women?

"Elizabeth," stuttered Edith. "Why have you come back?"

"I told you I don't want to be here. I actually don't want to believe I'm here. This is some monstrous cruel joke. It's a bad dream. I'm going to wake up anytime now and be back home." However, Kathleen knew this was not going to be the case. She needed to get out of here and fast. And if that bastard has taken my children... but she forgot all of that instantly as Edith tried desperately to pull her hands free.

"Edith, please, I have to find them. I have to find my children. Drake has taken them. Help me get them, and I'll leave you alone. Help me, please."

Edith stood there in disbelief. The last time the traveller had come, Owen, her husband had almost killed her with the beatings.

Edith shook her head, her eyes wide, desperate, tongue sticking to the top of her mouth, teeth clenched together.

"Edith, please, my children are in danger."

"He will kill me if I speak of your return. Please be gone from here. I cannot help you. He is angry with you. You have made him look a fool. And he takes his anger out on me when he has no one else to beat."

"I don't know what you're talking about Edith, but I can help you, if you help me. And who is it that hurts you so?"

Edith shook her head again. "You must go find your own way this time, please."

Kathleen looked into Edith's eyes. Her dilated pupils, her wide-eyed anxiety and her opened mouth said it all. Edith knew fear at the hands of somebody.

"Who hurts you, Edith? Who does this fear come from?"

"O-Owen," she stammered, "my husband." And she looked away, tears forming in her puffy eyelids. She turned her shamed reddening face away from the woman who still held her hands, squeezing them so that the blood throbbed to the tips of her fingers.

Kathleen released one of Edith's hands, as if realizing the pain she was causing in the frightened woman's face and hands.

"I will not let him harm you, Edith," she whispered. "But you must help me find my children. You know about my children, don't you?"

Edith shook her head and turned away. She would not look into Kathleen's eyes at the mention of her children. Kathleen understood the fear in those bloodshot eyes, but she also had seen the flicker of joy that had momentarily swept across those terrified eyes.

"I will leave you in peace when my children are back with me. I need to find them and bring them home. I will do anything to protect them. I'll even make a pact with the devil if I have to gain their freedom. And I will keep seeking you out until I find them. Do you understand that?"

Edith stood there avoiding Kathleen's gaze. She shook her head in defiance. Her pale face confirmed everything Kathleen needed to know. Edith was as much a prisoner as her own children and she were.

"Drake will not cross me and win. I will find them, Edith, and I will bring them home with me. You can come with me, far away from this place. You will never have to be beaten again by your husband."

Edith momentarily gazed back at Kathleen. Then the fear resurfaced across her face, muscles contorting, teeth clenched and eyes bulging along her pale puffy face.

"Ask the queen's cousin and sister, they are one and the same, where your children lay at night." Edith's lips had quivered at the mention of Catherine, and her voice had softened to barely a whisper.

"Catherine Carey is the one whom you should speak with, not me, but be wary of her. She is the daughter of Mary Boleyn and King Henry VIII. Catherine wields much power but is dismissed by those who would have her executed and is sometimes referred to as the witch who resides in these turreted tower walls at every corner of the castle." Edith looked up towards the castle walls and the turrets, her body shuddering at the thought of being seen.

"Catherine floats between these turrets conducting her witchcraft. She will only take you, traveller, to them if you are willing to disclose something new she can report on to the queen. But be wary, as the walls have eyes, and they tell all."

Edith pointed to the base of the closest turret with her one free hand. A large oak door loomed at its base in the distance.

Kathleen nodded her head in acceptance.

" I will find you, though, when I am in need, and I am sure I will need you again."

Edith's eyes widened in fear, but she did not shake her head in response. She instead pointed towards the other end of the castle, towards the gardens and gate near them.

"Is that where you reside? Is that your home, somewhere beyond that gate?"

The two women stared at each other seeking out some kind of knowledge from the other. Both needed some reassurance, but none came for either.

Edith twisted her remaining wrist free, and Kathleen willingly let her go. She had to show Edith some trust after all. But had Edith given her enough information, or was this just a trap? She needed to let Edith know that she could trust her, even if she did not trust me, she thought. It was a start.

"Go now, traveller. Be gone from here. It is not safe to be seen next to you in your clothes. Men's clothes are to be worm by men. You would be wise to find women's clothes to put on your body." And she backed away from Kathleen. Then she turned and fled running past the hedge away from Kathleen, glancing back only the once and disappearing inside the garden.

Kathleen watched Edith as she skirted around the hedges leading to the doorway at the other end of the castle.

Kathleen now looked from the disappearing form of Edith towards the oaken doors at the base of the turret and wondered what on earth she was going to do next. She contemplated heading back towards the Thames. She noticed that she was dry! How could this be? Every bit of her was dry. No sopping mess invaded her bones, hair or clothing. She looked up only at the sound of men roaring and cursing. She heard that name that Edith had called her.

"Traveller! Catch the traveller."

Kathleen froze. I've been betrayed. She will pay for this. But at the sound of further cries of "the traveller," she realized this was no time to wonder why her clothing remained dry or why Edith had betrayed her. She ran instead towards the castles turrets and the safety of the doorway at its bottom.

"Open" she whispered. "Please open."

What she hadn't realized, though, was that Catherine had seen and heard everything that had just transpired between the two women.

Catherine reached down and retrieved the silky smooth journal left behind by the traveller.

"She has returned," Catherine now laughed out loud. "I have you now, traveller. I have you now."

Appearances

"Catherine," blurted out Elizabeth. "Begin at once to explain your ramblings, and pray tell me what is of such importance that you have need of my urgent presence?" demanded Elizabeth.

Catherine's lips quivered then split apart revealing blackened teeth. Clapping her calloused hands together, she rubbed them repeatedly and broke into a generous smile.

"Young Elizabeth, come quickly. I have found the portal which can yield the information you seek."

"Portal? What portal? Why do you always speak in such riddles, woman? Explain yourself. What do you mean by this foreign word?"

Elizabeth watched as her older sister and cousin, now self-proclaimed crony, stepped quickly over to the desk and removed a leather-bound diary from the depths of a drawer. She thrust the book, bound in rose-coloured leather, into Elizabeth's hands. Warily Elizabeth smoothed back the folds of soft leather with her fingertips. She tugged at the lacings which tied its coverings together. Unexpectedly it smelt fresh, unsoiled by the drippings of fat left upon unkempt fingers. Its colour soft and enchantingly pleasing soothed the burning eyes of its beholder. Catherine flipped open its pinkness and revealed a most puzzling writing velum, smooth, shiny, thin, light yet crisp and cold to the touch. The peculiar foreign script of its author revealed rudimentary, ugly, plain thick cobalt blue penmanship. Although readable it lacked beauty and grace in its strokes of ink, thought Elizabeth.

Could this vellum which lay in Elizabeth's fingers reveal and predict the future as had Catherine? Does it hold the security of her kingdom's secrets amongst its soft pinkness? Is this the tool needed to find and begin travel into and out of an era? wondered Elizabeth. Had my father used it in his pursuit of his need for a male heir? Was this the tool he had used, and if so why did Catherine now possess it, she thought?

"See here, look at the page now." Catherine pointed a gnarled and trembling finger at the opened page. The vellum was whiter than any Elizabeth had ever beheld. Suddenly before their eyes, words began appearing upon the page. Elizabeth gasped and took a step backwards. At that moment, the words temporarily stopped appearing on the page.

"My dear sister, you must watch the vellum. It will appear again. Look and whilst you wait, more words will appear. The traveller is amongst us again."

"What are these words that appear so unnaturally upon this page?" Elizabeth snapped. Her head lifted quickly away from the offending diary. She paced impatiently before her sister and sought out the eyes of her delusional sibling with a knowing careful incisive stare.

"From whom have you taken this?"

"It begins again. Look!" cried Catherine.

"What begins again... what is this book? How have you possession of such a thing? What black magic do you throw out at me?"

"It is the traveller's. She is amongst us again," Catherine repeated.

Elizabeth breathed quickly and pinched her thigh beneath the folds of her immense gown, gritting her teeth with fury as she struggled to remain calm.

"What is this sorcery that you lay before my eyes, witch!" she demanded.

"It is not I, dear sister, who should bear the brunt of your anger. Heed not your temper with me but at the woman who writes these words."

Elizabeth breathed deep and slowly, regaining her self-control quickly.

"What woman? Speak plainly with me now, or your head shall be impaled upon those turrets you reside in at present."

The slippers of nobility and race tapped the stone pavers upon which she stood with her left foot and coolly, confidently a tight smile breached the exterior boundaries of royal lips. Penetrating black eyes stared icily from within fine red lashes.

"Cousin, sister, I lay before you the answer to your realm's troubles, if only you would listen. It is not I with whom you should be aggrieved, but the disappearances again of that woman and her sons."

Elizabeth arched her red brows and cocked her head to one side.

"What woman and her sons? Come now, speak plain, or you will not live to regret your defiance!" Elizabeth regained her breathing pattern and turned her mother's black eyes upon the soul before her, penetrating the older woman's stare. Elizabeth wondered what amount of common blood coursed within the bones of the sister before her. She knew exactly who this traveller was, but she was not about to let her unfortunate sister, that pleasure of knowledge. Nor was it something for Robbie to know of just yet.

"It is the traveller and her sons. They have come again. We must find them and secure them to the Tower. They have information that will lead to the protection of your realm."

"How Catherine? What could this traveller have that affects my realm?"

Catherine snatched the diary from Elizabeth's hands and flipped the vellum back to another page. Having found her weapon, she thrust the offending book back into Elizabeth's hands. Here amongst its whiteness, ordered neatly by date, lay page after page of the decrees of Elizabeth's realm, and her letters of state, copied in a most inferior hand. And most distressing of all, Elizabeth's letters, her most private musings to her dearly beloved Robert Dudley, copied out before her.

Reeling backwards, Elizabeth cried out, grasped her slim hand to her forehead and threw the leather journal, letting it slide across the stone floor in the direction of the doorway. Elizabeth heard it slip down a few stairs. She would pick it up on her way out of her sister's chambers. Only then would she begin to understand its writings, she thought.

"For now your head will remain upon its slim neck. Any utterances about this diary to anyone and I will remove your head and limbs myself. Go back to your potions and poisons. I will have need of you further if what you say proves true. And remember, the longer you insist on raving about predictions and time travellers in my court, you will remain ensconced in this turret. You may be my sister and cousin, but that does not prohibit me from removing your head from its royal, bastardly shoulders."

"As you wish Your Highness. As you wish. I only have your realm's interests at heart," murmured Catherine sanctimoniously.

"Hmm, we will see about that, Catherine. We will see."

Elizabeth closed her sister's door and picked up the journal. She clutched at the strange object, pressing it close to her, crushing the delicate lace of her gown against her chest. The rope of pearls that she caressed and twirled during times of worry and stress now dug into her ribs and pinched the back of her neck. How could the words she had written to Robbie appear upon these pages? What sorcery has been played out here? And how is it that Catherine has got her hands upon it? She swayed slightly from the shock and the overwhelming implications of her most personal writings copied without her knowledge. Elizabeth lost her footing and slipped on the stone spiral stairs leading down from the turrets above her rooms. She grazed her head, dropping the journal as she reached out for a handhold, catching herself from slipping any further.

Kat having patiently listened to the goings-on of her queen and Catherine leapt out from her listening post below on the stairs, which led up to Catherine's rooms.

"Your Majesty. What is wrong? You are pale. Are you wounded! Let me call the guards." Kat had momentarily dug her nails into the crevices of stone to support herself and that of Elizabeth. She winced briefly from the weight of her slight queen. Kat's health and age would not permit her to give support to any woman, beast or child for more than a few moments.

"No one has done anything, Kat. I merely slipped upon these cursed stairs."

"You should not be going about the castle's turrets alone, Your Highness. There are spies about this realm with poisoned arrows… you did not go about the walkways outside, did you?"

Elizabeth smiled at her dearest governess and sighed at the magnitude of adoration and worries that emanated from devoted limbs. She recalled the sensation of being watched at close range which had precipitated the fall and slip upon the stone stairways landing. Whoever is behind these tapestries, she thought, did not radiate fear or intimidation within her bones. It was the knowing of hiding which bristled her being. Who dared to lurk and spy upon their monarch so brazenly? Is this spy a rash or sound-minded individual? For this would reveal much about the intruder.

"No, Kat, I did not. I merely wished to converse with that damned sister of mine. She has given me a foreign scripted journal to decipher. Your assistance would be most welcome, however, in retrieving this book – I dropped it when I slipped, and it must be somewhere upon the stairs above," whispered Elizabeth gently.

Kat's eyes glossed over with worry at Elizabeth's words.

"Elizabeth, let me help you back down to your rooms. I will seek out this object shortly.

"Kat, listen to me, I felt a presence here amongst us, and just before you appeared, the journal slipped from my hands, almost as if it was taken… It is a most glorious colour, so you will not mistake it from these damp grey stone walls. It is a book bound in rose-coloured leather, so soft to the touch, and weighing mere ounces. It cannot have gone far," whispered Elizabeth.

"You're Highness. There is nothing here. Please come away from here immediately."

Elizabeth breathed gently, quietly and gazed kindly upon her old governess. Gathering Kat's face between her hands Elizabeth tenderly stroked the moistened cheeks and wiped away the tears, which had ran down Kat's face.

"Kat, if this journal is not upon these stairs, then it must be in the rooms of that witch of a sister of mine above us. Let us go and retrieve it. Come we will go together and find out what sorcery or trickery she has played upon me this time."

Loud banging could be heard below outside. Looking out through one of the stone crossbow openings, Elizabeth glimpsed a commotion in the courtyard. The guardsmen and Robert Dudley were desperately trying to enter the castle's lower turret door. Some of the men carried drawn swords and knives. In their haste to ascend the stone stairs in pursuit of their quarry Robert had neglected to remove the barrier, which prevented their entrance. This passage had been used many times by Robert and Elizabeth, but the catch and lock at the bottom door needed pushing on at just the right place before it would swing open outward. The weight of his men behind him had prevented its easily accessible door from opening. The placement of a key was normally needed at night as well. The lubricated hinges of the door were kept greased and cleaned by Walsingham himself. Very few men knew of its importance in escape for Elizabeth, but the three who did used it often.

·"Whatever could Robbie be doing down below with the guardsmen, Kat?"

"Did you not hear them earlier, my lady? They have been downstairs for some time. I heard them myself, that is why I came to find you. Someone has breached your private entrances. Come, we must depart immediately. There is surely evil about. Your person is in much danger."

"We will do no such thing, Kat. Ascend these stairs with me at once, for I will not be fooled any longer by that deceiving sister of mine."

Grabbing Kat's outstretched hand Elizabeth lurched forward dragging her governess quickly behind her. The echoes of their every step rang down the ancient stairs to the ears of the waiting men below. The pounding of the door from below reverberated in the small space, making Elizabeth and Kat's ears ring with each blow. The tapestries lining the landing to Catherine's chamber billowed slightly as the door below finally opened. Elizabeth banged on her sister's oaken door, only to discover it was unlocked. The door creaked open with the determined impact of her fist to reveal Catherine laying face upwards and moaning in agony, the source of which neither Elizabeth nor Kat could fathom. They ran quickly towards Catherine.

A sudden coolness entered the chamber from behind them. Elizabeth turned and looked intently at the opening from which they had just entered. The sudden coolness reminded her of the presence of a person behind the tapestries. There was no fear associated with this presence, but its enveloping blanket stirred and alerted Elizabeth to change. Change had been forced upon her before now. The accepting of which she knew would be the challenge. This moment of realization had passed quickly for Elizabeth. She glanced sideways. Catherine's eyes opened wide and gazed upwards at the stone ceiling.

"Elizabeth, sister, she has come and gone again. She has taken what is yours. You should not have gone and left me as you did. Now you will have to wait again before she comes, for I do not think she will be back for some time now."

Elizabeth doubted her sister's remarks, for she still felt this presence within the stones walls. It waited patiently, secretly and furtively. She would rise up to its challenge and greet its bold demeanour and survey and control its next appearance. Elizabeth recalled her memory of King Phillip's visit to her in the Tower of London's White Stone prison. She had known before he arrived that he would order her release and had been guided and comforted by this similar feeling and premonition before. One more premonition was about to surface and she would wait quietly and patiently for its arrival.

It had brushed a warm rush of contentedness, power and control over her. It washed away all her doubt and fear. This was a trustable feeling. It had served its purpose in exposing itself only once before King Phillip's arrival. But she would purposely not recall that memory. Virginity of this England's queen would never again be doubted or challenged.

"Be quiet, woman. Do not speak of this again," snapped Elizabeth.

Catherine let her gaze fall on her sister, kneeling beside her. Gently she placed her right hand inside the slender hand of her much younger sibling. The trembling had subsided, and her breathing evened.

Whispering with what Elizabeth recalled as her sister's old voice, the one in which reason and logic had resided, she began to retell all that had occurred in the preceding hours.

"Elizabeth, dearest sister, please, do not look so scornfully upon me now, for I have seen her. She was amongst us. The traveller has come again. You must embrace her when she comes amongst us next. She carries knowledge of your kingdom in that journal. She must be thwarted in her descent homewards." Catherine sighed, expelling her foul breath and revealing blackened teeth.

The clamouring of armed men could be heard ascending the spiral stone stairs, and their banging and scraping of scabbards along the way awakened Elizabeth and the others to their situation. If they were not careful, those pointed blades would redden the very backs of their gowns before anyone realized whom they had pierced.

"Raise yourself up now, Catherine.

Be quick about it. Rise, rise, rise, now," shouted Elizabeth.

The women got to their feet quickly, withdrew to the window nearest the door and composed themselves for the onslaught of men-at-arms. Linking arms, Elizabeth threw back her shoulders and straightened her back, prompting the others to do the same. In this regal and courtly posture, she reached for their hands, gripping tightly upon their fingers. Composure and stature is an important asset to any royal personage, and Elizabeth exuded these qualities in every aspect of her manner.

"SMILE, ladies, and do not show your fears. It does you no good. These men-at-arms are merely attending to our safety."

"Smile? How can you ask us to smile?" cried Kat.

"Smile as my dear sister has stated. Do it and you will come to no harm," snapped Catherine.

Catherine's sudden harsh voiced rang with a knowing tone. She had noticed the change, which had gripped the shoulders of her younger sister. She had begun to believe finally, she hoped.

Elizabeth drew her head upwards and clenched her teeth once together. Experience had taught her how to prepare for the unexpected. Becoming a royal seldom allowed the weak to reign for long. Forced confidence, taut jowls, piercing stares and cunning curt remarks were the trademarks of her father and mother's bloodlines. Elizabeth's power at mastering the art of persuasion had begun at an early age. She had adored her father, and she could persuade him to grant her many favours despite the temporary withdrawal of royal status thrust upon her by her mother's apparent adultery and her father's pursuit of a male heir.

"Be amused, ladies, and welcome these good defenders of my realm with pleasure and thankfulness, for they are doing a splendid job, do you not think?" laughed Elizabeth amusedly.

Kat slipped down and inch or two, leaning against the wall for support, before Elizabeth could haul her back upwards to a courtly, upright position.

"Everything will be fine now, Kat. We will discuss this further in quieter settings and with that potion of Cadfael's to loosen my dear sister's tongue. We shall have a game of it with my sister being our victim until she confesses everything which she hides."

Elizabeth could see a faint smile appear on both her comrades' faces. Each amused by the other's belief in the truth being revealed. She could feel it as well for they loosened their grips slightly upon her hands. They straightened and shifted their feet into that of a lady's stance at court. One foot turned out with ease into the ever-familiar position. Right heel to the opposite foot's inside sole and both feet pointing exquisitely fine leather soles outwards. The dance with the men could now play out, their courtly demeanour hiding any fears that were so recently present.

"YOUR HIGHNESS, YOUR HIGHNESS, WE COME. HOLD ON, WE ARE NEARLY THERE!!" shouted Robbie from below. The echoes of his words played and danced upon the chamber's walls.

"YOU SHALL COME TO NO HARM, FOR WE ARE HERE TO DEFEND YOU AGAINST THE TRAITOR WHO HAS COME AMONGST US!" cried out Robbie.

"Oh, how he does amuse me sometimes. What valour! Would you not agree, ladies?"

"He has many qualities, which are of use and very amusing, would you not say?" sneered Catherine.

"Quiet, Catherine," snapped Kat. "Her Majesty has no need of such talk. She is pure and unheeded by men's desires of the flesh."

Elizabeth let out a very long loud sigh. Startled, both women turned and stared at Elizabeth.

"Your Majesty!" cried Catherine, with an amused grin. "Surely you have curbed your desires for that rogue, who so quickly ascends these stairs?"

"As have you?" quipped Elizabeth.

"They are here," whispered Kat, "make ready."

Three heads turned in unison, readying themselves for the onslaught of knives, swords and men.

Thirteen men clamoured up the stone stairway and burst through the doorway, one by one. Robert Dudley led his men each driving their swords forward as they climbed the stairs and lurched forward through the open doorway. They began tumbling over each other when Robbie skidded to a halt halfway across the narrow turret entrance and enclosure. These rooms had formerly been decorated in an enchanting style by Henry VIII as his frequent paramour's retreat. It was easily accessible from the royal bedchamber below.

Robert had not yet spied his quarry or distinguished Elizabeth from the three female figures before him. Beyond this entrance lay other rooms and corridors. Falling over one another at this sudden stop, men began trying to avoid the very pointed ends of each other's weapons. In the melee, Robert was knocked to the ground, as were all of his men. Shirts, leggings, fingers and even part of an ear lay bloodied, torn and dishevelled in the heap. Elizabeth gasped in relief as Robbie picked up the tip of an ear and handed it to a young man in red livery that Elizabeth familiarly recognized as Edwin, who was wincing and bleeding profusely. Edwin had been imprisoned with Robert and stood by as his most trusted servant. The three former prisoners had shared many walks together amongst the stone of the White Tower.

"Lose anything else, Edwin?" stammered Robbie."

"No, just my bloody ear, you damned fools. Get up, you bastards," yelled Edwin.

Grumblings began in earnest amongst the men. Then as they began to realize that Her Majesty the Queen stood waiting, stamping her foot in agitation, an uncomfortable silence descended on the room.

"What is it you seek in my sister's quarters, Master Dudley?" said Elizabeth with a warm smile.

Master Dudley bowed as low as he could whilst on his hands and knees and began to extricate himself from his men.

"The loss of part of your ear, Master Edwin, is most unfortunate. My sister here is good at stitching. She will see to your wound once I have found out what it is that you all claim to have been chasing."

Gripping the torn and bleeding hole in his ear Edwin bowed quickly and looked fondly at Elizabeth. "Begging your pardon, Your Majesty, but my ear will be stitched by the willing wife at home. She will be quite pleased that this is all that I have lost in the pursuit of that traitor."

"What traitor do you speak of, Edwin?"

"It is the one who begins the speech of foreign tongues and asks questions regarding your realm. She attempts to hide her womanly form inside men's clothing. A woman has no need to hide and secret herself from her kind."

"Ah, that one. You have no need to worry so, my dear man. It is a trifling matter but not one that endangers my kingdom at present."

"Your Majesty, have you seen her?" exclaimed Robbie.

"Yes, why yes I have. She is of no consequence for now," declared Elizabeth staring directly into Robbie's amazed, rounded almond coloured eyes.

All eyes turned now and looked between Robbie and Elizabeth. Was she covering up for another mistake of his, or had she really seen this woman? Elizabeth stooped over her friend and offered her hand.

"Please, Master Dudley, do tell. What has brought you into my tower in such haste? Did you see her too?"

"Aye, we did," piped up John from the back of the pile.

"Is that so, John. What was she wearing?"

"Aye, it ... she was ... I don't know, come to think of it, Your Majesty."

"Well, I do. Look amongst you now, and have a good look at your-selves, for if she is here, and you have chased her all the way up those stairs, then she must be amongst you."

They searched each other then for some form of recognition. John's small hands, Gresham's freckles, Elwin's big nose, John Cabot Junior's blue eyes, Edward's thick forearms, Master William's black hair, his brother Mathew's vibrant red... Edwin's ear would now become one of those recognitions, thought Elizabeth.

She looked up at the sound of the light flap of fabric from the landing's tapestries. Soft footsteps pattered down and then up the stairs. Elizabeth felt the warmth and tingling of the presence, which was about to emerge. A moment of silence amongst the melee allowed Robbie to recognize the sound as well. Gently squeezing his hand in earnest, she pressed her finger to his lips to silence him.

Elizabeth turned towards the open doorway and greeted the woman before her, strangely dressed in muted linen leggings and a tightly woven woollen tunic, similar perhaps in design to that of her men-at-arms, except for the distinctive womanly shape of her breasts. Stooping quickly, the small blonde woman removed her shoulder garment, crouched down and retrieved an object from the floor, only just visible now that the doorway was fully open. A slim rose journal could be seen in her hand, which she quickly covered with the cloak, wedging it beneath her armpit, concealing it completely under her shoulder wrap. Elizabeth realized she had glimpsed again, though only for a moment, the distinctive journal her sister and cousin, Catherine, had so much of late talked about and she, Elizabeth, had so recently held within her grasp.

"Is all as it should be, Your Majesty? whispered the traveller, Kathleen. "Shall I go below and fix the doorways shut?" asked the woman standing now at the top of the stairs.

"As you wish," said Elizabeth gently. And with a quick nod of her head the woman descended downwards clutching the journal.

The woman had disappeared back down the stone spiral stairs, as slyly as a fox and before Elizabeth's words had finished passing through her lips.

"It is the traveller, Kathleen," whispered Catherine.

Robbie and Elizabeth's eyes met at Catherine's mention of the traveller's name. Both glanced at Catherine quickly and then locked eyes momentarily. Elizabeth smiled sternly then knowingly she gripped Dudley's hand compelling him to silence.

"Catherine." Elizabeth jerked her head in the direction of the woman who had just disappeared. Motioning again with successive jerks of her head towards the stairs, silently willing the vacant looking Catherine to follow the interloper down the stairs. To Kat, she held out her arm preventing any movement forward. The men continued on with their searching of each other's identities, oblivious to the goings-on around them. They had witnessed the agility and speed with which this interloper had emerged and disappeared before.

Henry pinched Edgar to obtain his distinctive yelp. Harry pulled up Francis' shirt to see his purple skin markings. Albert slapped Henry for laughing, a disturbing habit of his when fraught or caught off guard. Albert smelt foul -- eating raw garlic does that, and everyone knew that but Albert, who still maintained it kept the spirits at bay. Harry farted. He did this when things confused him, a sure way to distinguish him from an imposter.

"Have you or your men seen her before now, Master Robert?" Elizabeth asked and helped him to his feet. He stood up too closely beside her and gently responded to her push. Elizabeth moved quickly away from Robert to ensure the men would not recognize the familiarity with which the two former prisoners would later converse.

"Yes, we have."

"Which of these men amongst us has seen her before now?"

"A few of them have."

"Whom, Robbie? Be more specific."

Glancing over his men, Elizabeth watched as Robbie's eyes squinted. His jaw line tightened and clenched browning teeth. She could almost see how he was recalling those moments of conversation about the foreign imposter.

"Edward," he blurted out. "Albert, John and Henry," he continued.

"Anyone else," demanded Elizabeth quietly.

"Maybe Edgar, yes, I believe Edgar has seen her as well," whispered Robbie.

"Silence your men on their talk of her, on pain of death."

"Why?" he retorted.

All eyes had now focused in on Robbie and Elizabeth, deeply engaged in their hushed conversation. The men began whispering amongst themselves.

Elizabeth straightened herself suddenly and stepped one pace away from Robbie.

Robert Dudley bowed towards her just as quickly. Elizabeth turned towards her men-at-arms.

"You may practise this exercise again, my men-at-arms. However, next time I expect your weapons will be found in something else besides your own flesh. Perhaps standing on your feet instead of falling about the foyer of my sister's private chambers would suit your purposes better, would they not?" snapped Elizabeth in a ringing voice.

The twelve men-at-arms began muttering again in disbelief. Their awkwardness at not bowing before their sovereign evident upon the brows of fellow men. The righting of bodies into prone respectful subjects began. The disengaging of weapons, buttocks, knees, arms and elbows from one another had ceased in their eagerness to stand up and bow before their queen.

Elizabeth waited until all the men had gathered and replaced their weapons inside scabbards. Edwin clutched his bloodied ear part. Smiling now and revealing her browning teeth, she addressed them with kinder eyes. She dropped her head slightly, indicating further silence and dismissal.

"You may leave, and thank you for securing the tower so quickly from harm, even if it was done rather badly." She laughed.

"Kat, see to it that Cadfael is called immediately to attend to these men and their wounds."

Elizabeth stared her men out the foyer, silencing Robbie in the process with a curt nod of her head towards the door.

Kathleen was as confused by the people she had just met. The conversations she had witnessed in regards to her journal puzzled her immensely. Kathleen had not yet realized the importance of objects brought from one realm to another. The complications of travel into another world would be learned at a later date. At the moment all of her energies were required to focus on the retrieval of her sons so she could get the hell out of this place.

History would not be changed or altered lightly. It is therefore governed by the laws of the past, present and the future yet to come. To alter the course of history is to harm the future and the inhabitants who reside within its eras.

Within the journals pages, historical events could be revealed, but if placed in the wrong hands, well, then what would become of the world as we know it. Kathleen had yet to grasp that she held within her journal the power to alter and change history, as it is known. Oh dear, what a troublesome prospect to behold.

Francis Drake had known about the power of objects and their ability to change history. He had learned this power at a great cost to his soul. His promises not kept to the Cimaroons, Natives from the shores of Nova Albion and the captives he acquired throughout his illustrious career had forced upon him the fate of the spirits. Upon his death at sea, he had not ascended to God's world, nor had he descended to that of the devil. His punishment came in the form of servitude to the spirits of the Native people whom he had befriended and left behind on the shores of the Pacific Northwest. They would possess his soul until he fulfilled his promises and returned their Native people and the belongings he had taken as trophies for exhibition.

In death he had learned how to manipulate the souls of others. He could transport individuals across time. His aim, though, had wandered and time had twisted his humanity to vanity and personal gain. Vanity replaced his need to ascend to heaven. Recognition had not come for the discovery of the iced locked waterway of the Northern Arctic passage. The truly rightful mapping of the Pacific North West coast of the Americas had evaporated with his death in the Caribbean. It would take him centuries to learn the powers of persuasion, which would enable him to transport people from one realm and into another, but he had finally mastered it.

Now he could present to the world of academics of the twenty-first century, that indeed he had discovered more than any other explorer before or after him. And his rightful place in history would be recorded fully, his greatness, his glory restored. People would remember Drake for whence he had been. They would understand how he had endured the silences imposed by Her Majesty Queen Elizabeth. He would enjoy the fruits of recognition in death that he had been denied in life.

His feral heirs would live again upon distant shores, which bore theirs and his DNA. What he had not learned quickly, though, was how to keep these travellers alive successively. At each attempt, the lives of most of these travellers would be imperilled. This was a most annoying perplexing problem until of late. This one traveller, Kathleen, had successfully been brought onto Elizabethan shores and been returned unharmed.

She had been returned again after her unsuccessful attempt at retrieving his journals from Whitehall's palace. In her refusal to do his bidding, he had mistakenly convinced his close cartographer, a Spanish man, into his confidence. Instead of Carlos remaining here with him, she had taken Carlos, a keen and masterful cartographer, back with her into her realm. Drake would have liked to have consorted with him more. However, he would get Carlos back somehow. But the time right now was not to think about that. Instead it was time for Kathleen, the historian, to fulfill her vows. Having sworn her to these vows at the tip of his blade, he thought he could now make her do his bidding. This traveller, Kathleen, had proved most unwilling to do as she was commanded. He had had to finally take her precious children as a bargaining tool to convince her of her folly at resistance to his plans. However, now he thought perhaps she would bargain for more if he played his hand right. These children would one day become men, and if they too could travel from realm to realm, then... he smiled at the thought of it. The traveller might not be needed after all. Men were so much more willing to lose their lives for riches, he thought.

Secrets

Catherine moved quickly down the stairs and out the corridor from Elizabeth's rooms past the fools waiting for an audience with the queen.

"They are so preoccupied by the exit of one person, and the anticipation of another's turn at gaining favour with the queen, these fools had not recognized the intruder as one of falsity," blurted Catherine. "But then fools are too easily and far too frequently born at court. I have gained favour with Elizabeth again with these tidings from this comer of words and wisdom, upon whose pages delicious secrets appear. I have want of that journal for myself. It has such power within its pages. I shall know of who to curry favour to, whom to avoid and more importantly, those words, they reveal what is hidden in this kingdom. Walsingham will be pleased. He is a man of much importance, and I must stay alert where he is concerned."

Now this traveller, thought Catherine, how shall I gain her trust? What must I say to dissuade her passage from this realm? Her children... I must speak of her children. They must be captured. This will stop any woman from leaving. She will have to deal with me once I have her children, she thought.

The sound of Catherine's hurried footsteps carried along the long stone corridor. Kathleen slowed her pace, straining to listen to the footsteps behind her more closely. Were there many or just one man following her? What had Elizabeth said to them inside the turret? Had the queen really just let her go? Was this a trap after all? Doing her best to make no sound as she continued to move along the passage, Kathleen heard the lightness of the step following her. It is a woman, thought Kathleen. She could hear the swish of voluminous gowns. How they must weigh her down, she thought, suddenly grateful for her own choice of attire.

Kathleen could not yet return to the comforts of her world. Avoiding capture and the exposure of her world would endanger the lives of her children and others. She understood the pursuit of them would lead her further into danger. Drake had lured her into this place before, and she had escaped. It was coming back to her now, slowly. She recognized these walls, the places she had just been to, the conversations she had overheard, but how she had left still eluded her. What still lay ahead she could not fathom, but what she did now realize was that the footsteps following her were getting closer.

She could hear the woman's breath was steady, quick and not laborious. She will have strength, this one, thought Kathleen. What weapons will she be hiding within the folds of her gown? She must take heed. This would be Elizabeth's doing, and therefore she must be prepared. Kathleen's mind raced. Where could she hide amongst the stone. The corridor was dark, long and full of hangings and paintings. There were no furnishings to slip behind.

If I can just get to the other end before she reveals herself to me... For she knew the woman sent after her wanted something. But what -- what does this woman and Queen Elizabeth want?

Turning a sharp corner, Catherine paused as she espied the traveller named Kathleen hurrying down the corridor. The familiar paintings of her father and mother hung from the walls. Elizabeth's mother's picture had hung inside these walls of late. There it was, beside her own mother's familiar face. How different the two sisters looked and yet how similar.

Mary Boleyn's blonde hair contrasted with that dark brown black of her sister, Ann's. Their high arched brows both rose regally upon high foreheads. Their almond shaped eyes differed only in the colour emanating from the canvas above. Ann's dark iris and Mary's amber globes glistened momentarily as they stared down at Catherine. Thin parted lips shone rosily as did their painted cheeks. Mary's nose was petite and rounded as was Catherine's. Ann's bore the familiar long thin nose of her daughter Elizabeth. The thin small hands of the four women matched that of their grandmother's, Elizabeth of York, the quiet, reserved mother of Henry VIII. Ann's oval shaped face differed from that of her older sister Mary's and its softer, fuller, rounder one. Catherine's bosom matched that of her mother's. Ann's reflected the thinner, flatter form of her daughter, Queen Elizabeth. The bones of nobility, Boleyn and York heritage, emanated from the portraits, which hung majestically above Catherine.

There had been murmurs and gossiping when Elizabeth had revealed the presence of her mother's image in this hallway. Elizabeth's parentage was of utmost importance to the young queen when she ascended to the throne. Only now, though, did she have the confidence to place that offending face upon these walls. No one dared to make snide comments about Ann Boleyn any more.

"Wait!" Catherine cried out, trying to slow or stop the traveller's escape.

"Wait for I have news of your sons."

Kathleen felt the bile rise quickly in the back of her throat. Her heart started pounding, thudding inside her chest tearing from her lungs the very breath that she had just taken in. Gasping for air and steadying her nerves, she prepared to face this tormentor and regain some kind of control. Before she turned into the danger that now befell her disheartened soul, Kathleen checked her watch the digital face was blank.

Her thoughts raced. Had Drake's need of her sons slight bodies, immature natures and boyish adventuring spirits compelled them to believe in the power of the everlasting life. Had he instilled into the minds of all the boys whom he employed upon his ships this belief system? If he could indeed manipulate this gift of travel, could she benefit from its knowledge as well? Kathleen dismissed this thought immediately. That was a fool's thinking, and she was no fool. Drake has used this power of travel as a tool.

It's his tool, she thought, a tool for those who understand how to use it wisely. It must have its detriments, though? Maddox, Woody and Kitt would be alone somewhere right now. They were mere boys to Drake, easily hidden within Tudor buildings. Kathleen would have no power over Drake just yet. She knew she would have other issues to deal with first.

Entrusting the likes of Elizabeth's servants and corsairs would become her most challenging endeavours. Kathleen would learn to swallow the bile which rose within her regarding Drake's capture of her children. She would in time find his vanity useful in the pursuit of her goals. She would even contemplate changing history as it has been recorded in order to barter for the lives of her children. She as of yet, though, did not know whom she would be bartering with.

Kathleen realized that she would have to face Catherine. Bracing her shoulders and straightening her back, she slowed then stopped from her brisk walk. Clenching her free arm's hand she dug her nails deeply into the palm, wincing under her breath at the pain, trying to distract her racing thoughts and beating heart. Inhaling slowly, she cocked her head to the left and nipped the journal closer to her body with a quick motion from her elbow. She glanced over her right shoulder to reveal herself to Catherine's grinning face. She calculated the distance to the gardens and recognized the futility of escape. She would have to face the woman whose voice was calling out to her. She stooped and collected as much dust and dirt from the floors around her. It was a considerable sum. She squeezed her hand tight and held its contents, her only weapon of distraction. She turned and hoped she would not have to pitch it into the eyes that now bore into her own.

The older woman was fast approaching Kathleen now, her skirts rustling as she held them above her slender ankles, revealing pointed shoes. Her fashionable court slippers were embroidered the colour of precious jewels. Her lacy kirtle looked torn, but upon closer scrutiny was merely gathered peculiarly to one side. Her hose were shimmery, faun coloured and loose about her calves. This peek into intimate Tudor finery disappeared as quickly as it had appeared when Catherine dropped her gathered gown and flung her arms wide.

"What say we take a walk about the courtyard outside, and you tell me how it is that you slip in and out of this world and our realm without ever revealing whom you are," said Catherine, offering her arm to Kathleen and smiling eagerly.

"I do not know of what you speak, my lady," said Kathleen as she bowed as low as she thought necessary, never letting her eyes leave those of her adversary.

"Come now, surely you and I can be of use to one another? We are not enemies, are we?"

Kathleen examined the woman's black eyes. Was there truth in those eyes or merely deception? Did this woman really have knowledge of her sons, or was she just willing to say anything to get her attention? Does she need me more than I need her? And with whom does she converse with besides Elizabeth? Kathleen weighed the situation carefully before responding.

"We are not enemies, my good lady. I too have need of some air, but let us not gather outside in the courtyard below. The southern walkway between the castle's turrets that leads to your chambers has certain advantages, does it not?" The arched brows of Catherine revealed the surprise Kathleen had hoped to provoke. Would this disclosure of the walkway's presence enable her to have the advantage, or would it merely put her in even more danger, she thought?

"If you so wish. If this is better for your present condition, then yes, I will walk with you there," said Catherine. Kathleen was puzzled by this momentary diversion.

"Your clothes, dear lady, look to your clothes. They attempt manliness, but it is too obvious a disguise, at least for the likes of me. I too have dressed as a man when in need of particular things. But your breasts are too large for it not to be noticed up close. You must pad your tunic more to suggest a stauncher belly. You must hide your womanly figure better than this."

As Catherine took Kathleen's arm, Kathleen could feel the other woman's long fingers poking into her waist, brushing her hand across her forearm, searching for and then lingering over the journal's corner. Once again their eyes locked, piercing each other's thoughts with questions, wonderings and ideas. The coldness in their eyes radiated back mutual distrust, the envy and the fear of one another.

If she were to gain anything from this encounter with Catherine, it would have to be trust. Catherine could become a valuable tool in her pursuit for justice with Drake, but first, she must learn to listen to the things which were spoken. For her children to survive in Elizabeth's realm, Kathleen would need to learn the power of deciphering post haste.

Kathleen turned slightly away from Catherine and gazed directly into her eyes. Catherine relaxed her tight grip upon Kathleen's hand and noticed the moistened eyes of her foe.

"I do believe you are right, my dear Lady Catherine. I shall have to hear all of what you have to say on this. I too am in need of escape from time to time. You must be very clever to mask your beauty from the eyes of men."

Kathleen would need to watch over Catherine very carefully. She had witnessed first-hand the conversations between Catherine and Walsingham through the peephole in Kat's room. She had found many a spy hole cleverly located within this castle's walls. The clarity of conversations she had heard delighted and frightened her.

Someone had designed these spy holes perhaps for aggressive means. They were certainly conceived for a specific intent. These weren't mere convenient places to reside in unnoticed? They were suggestive of covert actions, improper, furtive or indecent coves of refuge. She had realized their advantage quickly and was thankful so far as to the frequency of their locations. As a child Kathleen had hidden from her brother's ire on many occasions. She was used to desperately needing quick refuge. Her thoughts were suddenly averted with Catherine's next jibe.

"Your children are well cared for. They are big for their age. Your cooks must have great talent to entice children to eat so well. How much do you pay them?"

"My cook must eat what the children eat. It is an incentive that at present works." She thought of her plump mum back home and suddenly longed for her fat inducing diet. It's familiarity brought back pangs of fear into her breast. Her heartbeat raced.

"This is a clever persuasion, indeed. I will take heed and follow your good example, kind lady."

"Where is it that Francis Drake resides at present when he is not conversing with Cecil and Robert Dudley? Does he take the air along the greenway at St. James Palace, or does he stay within Richmond Castle?" Kathleen asked in an offhand manner.

"We can talk of these things once you have changed clothes and spoken to Her Majesty," said Catherine.

"To which Queen Elizabeth do you refer to, my good lady, for there are several past and present Queen Elizabeths of this England?" She enjoyed the look of horror and confusion that flashed upon Catherine's face. The sudden whiteness of Catherine's lips and cheeks revealed her weakness. Information was the tool she would use, she thought, on this cunning little vixen and then thought differently about it. She felt guilty momentarily at the woman's panicked look.

Kathleen took in the look of Catherine's widened eyes. She had hit pay dirt. The fear of not knowing whose monarchy she would live through manifested in the sudden clenched jawline of her adversary. Catherine's step slowed and faltered. She stumbled and swayed slightly against Kathleen.

Gently, lightly, Kathleen reached out for Catherine's hand. She took it in hers and squeezed the fingers that had recently probed her body seeking out the journal. She moved Catherine away from her side and gently guided her around to face her.

"Do not be alarmed, good lady. It is the future I speak of, not the present or the past. There will be another Elizabeth, who will reign far longer than your dearest Elizabeth. An Elizabeth whose people also seek her out for consolation," whispered Kathleen. She realized too late that she had spoken for too long on the subject of Elizabeth and mistook the quietness of Catherine as fear. Deception of character was a skill, which Kathleen had not yet learned. It was, however, a necessary skill for survival in Tudor England.

Footsteps could be heard beyond them in the corridor. Kathleen's departure must be attained quickly. The advent of encountering more individuals was alarming her. A foreshadowing of frequent hiding again pumped the blood within her veins and thumped her heart into action.

"Where is Drake?" whispered Kathleen.

"Pacing in the gardens within the maze," said Catherine. "He likes it there," she added.

"Thank you, dear Lady Catherine. Now we must go before Walsingham is upon us." Kathleen unlocked her fingers from Catherine's and grinned at the bemused woman who stood before her. She leaned in closer to Catherine and whispered.

"We will meet again, my lady, and soon, I think. You must inform Her Majesty that there will be another Queen Elizabeth. Queen Elizabeth II. That history will record her as the first Queen Elizabeth, Gloriana, and her reign will come to be known as Elizabethan, a Golden Age. And tell her that the reign of the second Queen Elizabeth has of yet not ended."

"You must also tell her that my journal will not help anyone. Now go and reveal to Elizabeth all that I have imparted, for she will want to know of what I have said." Turning quickly from Catherine, she slipped away deftly, quietly.

Catherine's thoughts raced. She contemplated following her adversary, but the news of what she had just heard held her in place as the traveller fled. Catherine, looked about and realized that her captive had indeed escaped, but she knew where to look for her. There were not too many places to hide in the queen's gardens at present. Her thoughts wandered. The traveller had revealed the coming of another Queen Elizabeth, and that Her Majesty's reign would be recorded as "Glorious and Elizabethan."

"I must impart this news to her at once," she whispered. Catherine turned back towards the corridor from which she had come.

"I must evade Walsingham," she said aloud, "for I do not want to reveal this knowledge to him. I must be the first to reveal it to Her Majesty. She must be warned about this traveller's assumption of ownership of the journal." For now, though, she thought the traveller would keep her head upon her shoulders.

Kathleen knew she would have to speak with Elizabeth I to explain to her everything that she had just revealed to Catherine. If she did not, what would become of her if she were captured? If she had to, she thought, but if she hid herself well, she might not need to speak with Elizabeth again at all. First, though, she would seek out and speak with Drake.

"I do not believe that my children are here now. But why does everyone keep referring to them as if they have seen them. Catherine spoke only of their presence as if to catch my attention and hold onto me, but why? What does she want? What can I give her?" she whispered softly to herself.

"Keep moving. Get out of this castle!" she said aloud to herself.

Walsingham will be fast upon my heels too as well. The spiral stone stairwell leading to the kitchens and servants quarters would be her best option now. She would hide behind the Tudor tapestry lining the lower end of the stairwell with all its decomposing parts and lingering odours. Within the stench of festering spent semen spillage, urine crystals and dank, grimy sweat droplets of its former and coming secretors, she would hide until it was safe to emerge. This rank passage has its benefits. She had heard the kitchen servants talk of its ghostly haunts. Not even dogs dared venture into its chamber. She would cover her nose from the stench and the sting of its filth in her eyes and maintain her grip upon that blasted journal. However am I to get my children out of this mess, she thought.

Arrogance, Pomp and Circumstance

June 1576

Kathleen recognized Drake immediately when she entered the gardens. A man of average height strutting away, amongst the yews and hedgerows, who looked determined and yet was distracted by his thoughts. His countenance appeared kind. A groomed beard, slightly pointed, matched his elfish ears and clipped moustache. Long, amber, embroidered stockings were held in place by leather bindings cinched beneath knees capped by fluted upper leggings of similar amber tones. His waist was encased within the confines of leather and silk ribbons drawn down to a point extending beyond a slim build, hovering over his codpiece.

Does he dress this way every day, or is he hoping to impress the backers of his forthcoming voyages? Everything about him is neatly tucked, crimped, folded and layered, she thought. How can he wear all that in this the heat? Is this an indication of his determination regarding this all-encompassing journey which controls his thoughts? Is this strutting of vanity affected by these stones or by the tranquility that invades these gardens, or is his purpose here merely contemplative and thought-provoking? she wondered.

Drake watched for her. He knew she would be here. He expected it. This scene had been repeated before. And she would continue to come into these gardens until she understood there was no other way around it. This traveller would have to obey his rule this time. However, time was running out. His momentary possession of the living Drake would wear off soon enough. His soul would only inhabit the living body for less than an hour, and this woman had kept him waiting far too long. He did not have much time left. Soon the real Drake would emerge from out of this mirage of twinned souls.

Kathleen was angry. Does he care at all about the lives he plays with in this pursuit of his goal? She wondered about telling him everything or nothing or just some of the trials that lay ahead, or would she merely let him know that he would make this epic voyage. The coming and going of which will be before him, within these fourteen months. Or is it seventeen, she would need to know what year she resided in at present first. She stepped quietly from her hidden vantage point, stealthily coming into step with the man.

"Good day to you, Francis," said Kathleen. She had been determined to unnerve and rattle this rogue, who had kidnapped her children.

But she had not yet learned the lesson of the vanity in men and would learn very quickly to decipher its providence.

Drake delighted in the intrusion, which showed itself before him. He had known she was there all along. He had an innate ability to detect change when it fashioned itself before him. The winds of time and travel were ensconced inherently in his bones. He was not easily startled. Covert actions rarely escaped his notice. He was a man with eyes that interpreted the movements of men well, a skill he had learned at sea.

His cousin the adventurer, Hawkins, lacked these discernment skills. Drake could foresee disaster before it befell him and his men. Drake had survived the betrayal of the Spanish at San Juan de Ulúa better than had his cousin. All his men had survived without even a scratch. The broken bones and the torn skins of Hawkins' men were evidence enough of the superiority of cousinly skill.

"This is unusual attire for a lady of court, is it not? Do you come before me as friend or foe, or do you have word for me from her Highness?" said Francis.

"I have no word for you from Elizabeth, nor do I wish to harm you unless---"

"Unless what? Come now, you cannot have any grievance with me. I have offered you no insult. Speak freely woman, for there are more pressing things of which we can address beyond that hedge."

"I have no wish to press or address issues with you beyond that hedge. But you have information which I would be grateful to receive, Sir Francis." She realized her mistake in address. Her face reddened.

Drake cocked his left eyebrow and strode languidly around her. He openly surveyed her ample breasts and rounded curves with a lingering long look. He stepped closer and shifted the leather strapping which held fast his scabbard and sword.

"I am yet to be made 'sir,' lady, but someday perhaps. Now run along and aggrieve me no further, for you are of little use to me at present, unless you wish to relieve my present tension."

Kathleen stepped back. She closed her mouth and bore fiery eyes up at the smug face standing before her. Her blue eyes rapidly changed to green. This was a trait which normally only her mother noticed. But Drake had been watching, and he too could see the forthcoming lashing from Kathleen's insubordinate tongue. Heated throughout, her normally flushed cheeks darkened to crimson. Desperately she tried to control the trembling within her limbs. Here was a man with whom she would teach a lesson. He would never understand the rage of panicked motherhood.

"I would not screw you for anything, you filthy bastard," she said. She inhaled the stench of this century within her nose. She would never, ever sleep with a man so full of himself.

"You may be finely attired, but your over perfumed reek permeates a clear distinction between your century and mine," she snapped back at him.

"If you have no interest in servicing my needs, then why do you seek me out in this lonely garden?"

"I have news of your future. It concerns your pursuit of travel near and far, travel for which you seek permission from Her Majesty. But first, you must begin by telling me all you know of the three small boys, those who came upon you with smiles and wonder deep in their bones. Do you recall their mischief and foolish tales of things, which surely could not come to pass? They spoke of voyages, beyond these shores, of times afar and ancient sailors' ways, of sailing ships, of men and boys, of golden bars, of cannons shot, of feral faces, of bows and arrows with markings, of the people of the Southern Seas. Entertaining tidbits to be sure. Do these tales also invade your talk of late?"

Kathleen sought after the sense of knowledge that lay within those glinting orbs and vainly arched brows. Does he know of anything, or has this forced impossible venture been an enormous mistake? Do I push for more or demand an answer? Can I goad him into action, withholding the bits of history pertaining to him? Would flattering his ego work? she wondered.

She had not expected the suddenness of his movements forward nor the speed with which he had grasped her hands. His one stride had encased their proximity swiftly. His taut face exposed the creases beneath weathered eyes. His beard neatly trimmed, bristled against her forehead. His pungent smell emanated his recent application of abundant lilac waters. Acidic breath and spittle washed over her face. Kathleen gasped at the strength within the hands that clamped down on her wrists and drew her near. The slamming of his chest against her side was fast and the quickness of those feet which kicked out hers, startled her. Kathleen relinquished air and inhaled sharply as her buttocks hit the dirt.

"Be quiet, woman," he hissed. "There are ears and eyes about this place, many of who wish you ill. Do not trouble me with your petty needs, or I will turn you in as booty for myself. The queen is in need of entertainment, and you will do nicely. I have need of your predictions first, before you impart your knowledge to her Highness. Your heirs are fine for now, but I will make no promises for their safety if they enter my realm for their own purposes. There will only be protection for those who mind their manners and do the bidding of better men."

"Of better men? Hah. They are but boys, you stinking, filthy man." Kathleen spat the words out at Drake.

"Silence, there are men nearby." Drake had heard the approaching men. Boots crunched upon the pathways beyond the stone building. The whiney of horses had alerted him first to the approach of others.

"Be still and quiet your tongue," snapped Drake.

Kathleen lowered her shoulders to the ground and stared at the figure above her. Drake placed his boot across her thigh and pressed gently down. The two conspirators locked eyes for a brief moment before Kathleen recognized the voices approaching. With a quick dart from his eyes Kathleen acknowledged her cue to roll quickly down the verge and hide beneath the ferns and brush below. Safely hidden, she noted the point of his boot and thinness of his sole that had been upon her skin. The smelling of dirt was far superior to that stench of ale, perfume and sweat, she thought.

"Have you seen anyone of new and foreign dress about the maze and gardens, Drake?" called Robert Dudley.

Drake looked at Robert and paused momentarily.

"There is no one of any consequence here, my good men. Pray who is it you seek?"

"A woman has come wearing men's clothing. She must be found. She carries beneath her cloak a journal, bound in a peculiar kind of leather. I believe she may be the spy amongst us. I wish to speak with her. If you see her, engage her in conversations, which will divert the causes and concerns from across the channel. You know of what I speak. Guide her into my rooms, and I will be sure to speak on your behalf to Her Majesty. There may be more than coinage that comes your way if we can locate this woman."

"Certainly, my good man," acknowledged Drake with a slight nod. "Good day to you and your men."

Kathleen lay still, drinking in the earthen smells of snapped fronds, weeds and brush. Her side was sore and aching. Fatigue was etched in every wrinkle, and her hair felt like straw. At least this was an opportunity to lie still in safety and collect her thoughts, even plan her next course of action. Kathleen's mind raced at the thought of where her children could be. She wondered if they had eaten anything in this realm and whether it would harm their bellies. She needed to find them quickly. If they stayed here too long, she did not know what would befall them or herself.

She snapped out her thoughts. My journal, she thought. They cannot get my journal. She knew deep within her bones she could not leave this place without it or her children. She needed to find them and get them out of this place. Please God, keep them safe, she thought.

She listened to the chink and chafes of cloth, of knives the tingling, the crunch of boots upon the soil. Kathleen strained her ears to pick up the sounds. Voices carried further away. They were retreating, she thought. She could smell the fresh dirt on her clothes and face. It felt warm, dry, safe and familiar. Looking across from where she hid, she watched as Drake surveyed her prone state with a smile and that arched brow of his. What is in this for him? What does he want from me? She would have to get out of here and leave without conversing with Elizabeth. This was the one thing she had always wanted to do, to speak with a sovereign, in particular the Elizabethan one. She was so close to being able to do this and yet in so much danger if she did.

She needed to find Edith. She would help her. Edith had been kind and concerned for her children when they had spoken before. Kathleen's bowels cramped, and she briefly considered trying to relieve herself but quickly realized that famished and aching as she was, the only thing that would remove itself from her body would be vomit. Her throat ached, and her tongue felt too big for her mouth. This thirst would have to be quenched and soon, but how and what with? She was not about to drink the water. She didn't drink much booze, and gin wasn't an option. Ale it will have to be. Ale. It is the only safe thing to drink in this realm, she thought.

The food here looked questionable. It reeked of unfamiliar things. She had seen what went into the gruel pot in the kitchens. Bits of everything, slop from the kitchens butchering, rotten pieces of vegetable, lots of spices, she suspected, to cover up the stench of what had been thrown in. Was everyone expected to eat this food except the nobility? Her heart dropped at the thought of her children. My god, what have the children drank and eaten?

Drake surveyed the woman lying on the ground before him, nestled inside the shrubbery. She blended in well, he thought. He had heard

Walsingham speak of the one who comes and goes within realms. He grinned, and all at my doing.

This woman would be good for more than just the breeding of strong sons and brats. Strange as she looked, she spoke in rhythms not familiar and yet sounds that were familiar. Her children were amusing, quick, agile and alert. Her children will make for good companionship aboard my ships, he thought. Strong and inquisitive, they will learn fast, and can already tie many knots. But their size could be troublesome, for they're hefty lads, almost as big as some of the ship's men. They will be costly to feed.

"Stop your squirming about woman and quickly get up and out of here. There is a passageway in the next hedgerow across this path. Fetch up that journal and follow me, and I will take you out of here."

Kathleen hesitated momentarily.

Everyone seems to be aware of my journal. It has a power to mystify and alarm those who have read it. There are parts of it that could be read by these people. Other parts are hidden. Why, she thought?

She began to understand the importance of keeping it secret.

Too much information, even the wrong interpretation of that foresight could be dangerous. What if it was used to predict the future in a way that altered history? She did not relish the idea of leaving the journal behind. What if she could not find it in time to leave this world behind? At least here, no one will be expecting it. It would be safe and surely the risk of leaving it here hidden amongst the shrubs would be better than the risk of being caught with it. Rolling over onto one side she carefully lodged the pink journal beneath the fallen leaves of three seasons past. Covered with leaves and brush and smeared with dirt, it was as close to invisible as possible, she hoped.

She would go and confront this arrogant man and stop him from using her children. She stood carefully and brushed herself off.

She did not yet realize that she would have no power in the future over how skillfully Drake would convince her children to voyage beyond their own familiar shores. His abilities at persuasion were only just emerging to her. In death he had come to master the art of persuasion and used it to fulfill his desire for everlasting glory. His ability to move through time repeatedly had been useful. However, its limitations were still confounding to him.

He could not yet remove his documents into the future without them disintegrating before his own eyes. But he believed she could, and he would make her bring them forward in time. It would ensure the validity of his travels around the world. His determination to be recorded as the greatest adventurer could destroy the lives of many, but he wasn't worried about that at present. He had lost certain scruples in death. His need to remain within the spirit world of the feral people to obtain his objectives was clear. Sacrifices would just have to be made.

History would be recorded and adjusted to include within its pages the truth about the greatness of his personage. He was at liberty to do what he wanted with those who travelled backwards and forwards in time to do his bidding, or so he believed. The problem, though, was that he couldn't control them fully. It took him 423 years to master a degree of some control. Some were wilfully difficult to control. Others were very easy, indeed. This traveller, on the other hand, was becoming difficult to reason with. Perhaps John Stowe, the historian of London, would be able to help out in this manner, though, he mused.

Stowe and Drake had equal amounts of vanity amongst themselves. Drake had approached Stowe after a successful short voyage forward in time. The two men had embarked on a plan to eliminate those who got in their way and to record the truth of history as it should be. Stowe had a particular grudge against another man in London, the playwright William Shakespeare. Drake agreed. This mere actor and man of writing had twisted the recording of history and replaced the truth with lies about England's kingdoms once too often.

Shakespeare's blasphemous writings must be eliminated. They needed to be taken out of London's history. The man had no shame. The fact that his work survived that of John Stowe's was ridiculous. John's work was brilliant. It recorded everything in the daily lives of good Englishmen and the accomplishments of England during the glorious Tudor reigns. His work was superior to that of any playwright.

And so therefore Shakespeare should be eliminated from recorded history.

In conclusion the two men had colluded to eliminate any of Shakespeare's writing and hide all of Drake's work, secreting it away from the hands of Elizabeth's men and councillors so that Drake could bring his documents forward in time at another date in time. They would bring both their work beyond the time of the great fire, beyond those dark days of Cromwellian rule, beyond the destruction of London's bombings and into the light of the new age of reason.

There were of course several impediments to be worked out. Remembering what era one was in when travelling forward had proved somewhat difficult. Each time he revisited an era, his memory improved. However, it was difficult to stay focused for lengths of time. His biggest worry within the spirit world of the Natives was that it would take him a millennium to retrieve all of his documents. He had no interest in having it take this long to prove his voyage of discovery along the Northwest coast of the Americas. Time was of the essence. Bringing forth others into the milieu was much more promising and productive.

Walsingham surveyed the scene below him with an amused grin. How foolish these people were. He had seen everything that had taken place between Drake and this foreign traveller woman. Her juvenile attempts at concealment were fruitless. He watched the interesting game of hide and seek they played out below him. He was a keen observer of people and could decipher their body language well. Everyone had weaknesses that betrayed them. There are distinctive lying patterns in people's movements. One's individual habits, slight voice changes, little movements with hands, a removed awkward stance, the quick dash of the eyes upwards or too the left before relocating the subjects eyes to his own, these were some of the subtle cues he looked for instinctively.

For Walsingham it was all about recognizing these little impediments in speech, or faltering rhythms and tones, noting the style of address to one another. Sometimes he just needed to watch the placement of feet and hands, all of these were his little telltale signs of lies and deceit. It made distinguishing the truth from fiction a most enjoyable endeavour and a very advantageous skill to possess.

Kathleen watched as Drake raked his eyes across her body. He did it with the practised ease of someone used to evaluating inferiors for whatever advantage they could offer him.

He is a filthy bastard. How can he even think of me as being remotely interested in his lust? He is sadly mistaken, she thought. These people are foul. She was going to have to hide herself in some other kind of way. Seeking out Edith now was ever more paramount.

Drake looked from side to side and stepped forward then hesitated before changing course. She was confused. He was not heading through that second hedgerow after all.

"Wait, where are you going now?"

"Quiet woman. We have to get out of the gardens. Go at once before me into that stone shed. We will commence our talk in there."

"I will do no such thing." Kathleen looked about, spotted the gate at the end of the herbaceous borders and took off at a sprint.

"You will not get in there. That gate is always kept locked. It is for Her Majesty the Queen. Only invited guests are permitted entrance. She is the only one with the key. She keeps it on her person day and night."

Kathleen grabbed the handle and pulled at the lock.

"Damn it all anyway" she muttered. Turning towards the oncoming Drake, Kathleen pulled out a small Swiss army knife from her pocket and began attempting to prize the knife open. It remained stuck, and every line where once a tool was concealed began to blur and fade. She didn't understand what was happening. Why couldn't she use this? Was it because he approaches? Was he not to see this? Was he not to see tools from the future?

Drake removed his own blade from the leather sheath dangling at his side. It was bejewelled and shiny and sharp. She watched as he swung the blade widely, slicing off the heads of foliage, deadheading with one swift stroke. He advanced and placed the point of the blade beneath her chin.

"You will do as I bid, woman. Now get thee into that shed. I wish you no harm, merely to conceal you from Walsingham and Cecil. You have knowledge I want."

As he lowered the blade from beneath her chin, Kathleen stared into those brown eyes trying to decide whether this was a ruse.

"Why can you not ask me now? What is it that you want to know? Why not, out here?" Kathleen demanded, planting her feet defiantly.

"Walsingham sees everything, and he will report our little meeting to the queen. I have no wish to anger our good queen. You have something about your person that I want. Walsingham wants it as well. Your journal, where is it?"

"I do not have a journal. I carry no such thing," said Kathleen.

"You lie. I have seen it amongst your things."

126

The whiney of horses brought Kathleen to silence. She had heard the commotion before Drake had finished his words. Both looked intently at each other. She noted how he quietly slid the blade back into its sheath. The soft leather silenced the ting of steel. His hands now free, he grabbed hold of Kathleen' shirt and pulled her towards the shed, roughly squeezing her forearm to forcefully direct her movements. With his other hand, he put a finger to his lips and walked backwards to the stone entrance and gently leaned on the door. Kathleen noted that the door did not squeak, but moved silently, easily. This would make a great escape. Doors this heavy did not generally move with such ease. Someone else must make use of this doorway, but for what, she thought?

Drake kept his hand on her arm as the group of men passed by. Their voices could be heard discussing what Kathleen was wearing

"A woman wearing men's clothing, you say, Master Dudley?"

"Yes," he replied, "and rather inferior ones at that."

"Can you really see her bosom? I would like to see that," snickered John.

Their voices were fading now as they passed the stone wall, which enclosed Drake and Kathleen.

As they listened to the footsteps and voices fading, Drake relaxed his grip on her arm. She could just make out his clothing and face. She could not tell just what kind of barn or shed they were in yet, but the smells of sawdust, rust, hay and dung were present. Horse dung? She wondered whether whoever made regular use of this place also concealed their horses in here as well as whatever else they used this secretive place for.

"Do not speak," he whispered. "Wait until the horses pass completely."

They stood in silence, Kathleen glaring at Drake, goading him with her defiance, as she twisted her arm. She tugged and pulled at her sleeve, pinched his hand, anything to distract him from his listening intent. The steady rhythm of the horse's hooves moved past them. She did not want to remain in his grasp. She didn't like being held against her will. The voices of men walking their steeds past the shed momentarily distracted her. She stood silently now, not knowing which of these men, those outside or the one inside, posed the bigger threat. They stopped.

Murmurs and scratching sounds echoed around inside the building. Just go, she thought, go away. She needed to get out of here. She hated enclosed spaces. She recalled having hid in garbage cans as a little girl to avoid being held in a corner with her hands and feet behind her. She had preferred the stench of garbage and large bins than the confines of the corner, on her knees, whilst mum's choice of babysitter trapped her between the walls corner and the back of her chair. Her knees ached with the memory of the punishment of two hours confined by a bully. She could feel Drake's breath on her face. He was closer, much closer.

"They will pass", he whispered. "Young Master John has to pass the waters." His grin confirmed his thoughts.

She could hear it now, the distinct piddling of urine against the wall. The tension in her shoulders relaxed. How like men, she thought.

Kathleen had always harboured the desire to be able to do that. Her bladder echoed the need of a good piss right now. She giggled at the thought of how a woman standing up to pee might startle and alarm her confiner.

She had laughed at the babysitter when she meted out punishment. Time and age had taught her how to get even without getting caught. She was adept at letting her abuser guess that she was the cause of their grief, but left little evidence to outright confirm her as the culprit.

Moving a sprinkler could have wondrous effects on the wooden floors of the babysitter's second floor apartment. It wasn't truly two floors above the ground as the first floor apartment was only halfway visible having only a snippet of windows for light.

She sensed Drake's mood change. He dropped her arm and brought his hand up to her mouth and pinched her lips with his fingers.

Determined not to allow this cocky man to assert his authority over her, she bit down on his finger and did not let go. He tasted dusty, leathery. She could hear him gritting his teeth, cursing her softly. She released his finger and spat out his dirt from her mouth. They stared at each other again.

"I see you have courage, woman, as do your young brats. It is interesting what our heirs inherit, is it not?" he whispered.

"What do you want from me," she responded fiercely.

"I want to know how you got here, and who sent you into our realm?" said Drake.

"What? exclaimed Kathleen, the profoundness of his statement furled in her brow and tightly pinched lips.

"Who sent me?

"You, you bastard. You sent me. That's who. You took my children. I want them back."

Drake realized his mistake, his soul was leaving the current body of the contemporary Drake, and he only had moments left with the traveller before the real Drake emerged.

"I did not take your children. But you can have them back soon. However, first you must give me that journal Walsingham wants."

Drake could feel himself leaving the body he inhabited and the real one emerging, sombre, enraged at being inside this stable with a woman much inferior to him. His thoughts tumbled between the two souls locked temporarily within this body.

"I do not have a journal, but I do have knowledge of your impending journey to the South Seas."

Kathleen stared at his taut face. His face changed then. A glint appeared in his eyes. The lines on his face deepened, his nose rose into the air, and his chin pointed itself magnificently forward, as if on cue.

"What?" he hissed.

She could see his focus change dramatically from that of her to that of a voyage. She imagined any voyage could do that to him. Familiarity grew within his countenance. He stood erect, his eyes glossed over at the work which would be needed. She goaded him on.

"Your voyage to the South Seas will be forthcoming, but you must bide your time. The time has come when Elizabeth will have need of you here for the next fourteen to seventeen months. The Irish issue has not yet been solved. You are needed here for now. You must prove your worth to her. You must reveal to her your skills at home and your abilities at convincing men to follow you. Your Majesty has need of your skills to squash this rampant Catholic desire festering on English soil. The Irish are not yet quenched in their thirst for Catholic blood on this realm's throne. You are needed here to assist in this endeavour for the queen. You must do her bidding willingly, or else she will not let you venture again farther than your own shores."

"How do you know of these things? You are but a woman and a stranger to this court? Who have you overheard?"

Kathleen could feel the length of his sheathed blade on her thigh now, as he pulled her in close and spat his words out. Still determined not to let him intimidate her, Kathleen kept her expression composed as Drake visibly seethed. Her eyes stung now from the stench and rot within this temporary prison. With watery eyes, she stood her ground and told him exactly what he wanted to hear.

"Elizabeth will send you on your journey," she said. "You will lose many men in conflict and one boy overboard. You will capture a Portuguese pilot by the name of Nuno da Silva off the Cape Verde Islands and release him back to the Spanish. With the help of Nuno, your captured pilot, you will locate the northwest coast of Nova Albion and declare it for Her Majesty. Walsingham must not know of what I speak. It is up to you to convince them of the importance of this voyage. Only upon your return from this voyage will your revenge of San Juan de Ulúa be complete."

Kathleen watched shock, realization, and satisfaction form in succession on the face before her. His smile told her she had his attention now.

"I have told you what you needed to hear, NOW give me back my children, or I will not be able to complete all that you have brought me here for. All that I have just revealed will not come to fruition if you impede my way."

With one eyebrow cocked, smiling at her Drake replied, "Children, how interesting. I have your children, do I? Well, then on one condition," he said. "I want those boys on that voyage, for they will know the way."

"Never! You can never have them again. It is not written in the journal. You cannot change yours and England's history yet. The time has not come for history to change its course. Your journey must begin without them." Without my children, she thought.

"Change history? No, I create history," he smirked.

"You will have to find other ways to redeem the sins you commit along your way. And you will commit them in the name of your God. But not with my children, you won't."

"Yes, I probably will commit some sin." He smiled back at her.

She left him then standing there, satisfied, bewildered and amused. He had puffed out his chest like a peacock. All that remained to be seen was the shimmer of blue and green feathers fluffing and strutting their selves about the shed. His piercing brown eyes shone, and his limbs quivered with anticipation. She left him there, prancing, preening himself and slipped away out of the darkness.

Walsingham waited patiently on the walkway between the turrets. Only when he saw the traveller emerge from the shed did he move. He watched as she travelled quickly across the gardens towards the servants' entrance and the kitchens below. He noted she had not retrieved her journal.

He waited again for the signs of her adversary to emerge from the shed. Drake too ignored the journal as he headed for the castle's other doorway. Walsingham noted the proud man's gait, his strut, the determination of his chin pointed in the direction of the courtier's entrance. This was a man with knowledge. He noted how Drake's clothing was still firmly tucked about his waist. No courtship or lustful embrace had taken place. He noted the poise of Drake's movement, the utter disregard for all around him, except the entranceway to Elizabeth's court.

The transferring of information was Walsingham's job, not this traveller's, he thought.

"I shall take your journal, traveller. I know you have need of it to return to your realm. For I know all about Drake's abilities at present. His soul does not fully possess this realm just yet."

A shaman's foretelling

Return to the earth
What you have taken
Or be taken by the earth
And remain within the belly
Of the Kraken

John Stowe's Study 1604

"Why"

"Why what, little John?" replied Stowe, as he squinted his eyes and peered over the top of the drawings he had been showing to all who gathered in his study. John anticipated what question was coming but held his tongue. He liked it when his flock asked questions. Better they listen to my stories than that playwright's.

"Why? Why is she coming back? Why do you need her?

"I need her to do…something that has been left undone for far too long. Very soon she will appear again in our realm."

Silence invaded the room. Edith's eyes opened wide. She shook and trembled. Several men took hold of Edith and steadied her quivering body. John looked over his flock of interested listeners and smiled. His drawings of the traveller, the Kraken and the beasts of the lands of

Nova Albion had frightened and delighted his flock. He could see the looks of fear in the dilated pupils before him. He watched as fingers rubbed together and reached out for something to hold on to. Bug-eyed anticipation rippled across the room. He knew they wanted more.

Cicero, an enormous cat stretched out his front legs extending his claws and dug into the pillow he lay on. He yawned, looked over at Master Stowe, bowed his head lowly and laid his head upon his front legs as if listening and softly lowered his lids. Slits of his narrowed eyes shimmered. His fur shook slightly, and his ears twitched quickly.

John put back the drawings into his chair's pouch.

"The traveller is needed little John because...she made a vow to Good Queen Bess and to Sir Francis Drake. Now it is time for her to fulfill that vow." John continued to look into little John's eyes.

"A long time ago when Francis Drake and Queen Bess lived, there came to our lands a woman, a traveller from another world. She had supposedly lost her children."

John sat back in his chair.

"What good mother loses her children, I ask you."

"Some of them willingly lose themselves, Master John," whispered Edith. "I have seen them do this."

"Yes, some children wander where they should not," said John raising his eyebrows a degree or two.

"However, like most young mothers, this traveller wanted them back." He snapped back his reply. "Now, the place she came from has many spirits. And these spirits agreed to help her for a price. The traveller bargained with these spirits in order to gain her children's freedom. What she promised to do for these spirits was to capture the souls of their dead and missing children and bring them back to life. The spirit people could not go on this journey with the traveller, but promised to keep watch on her soul for as long as she fulfilled her bargain."

"These spirit people," began John, "inhabited the world of in-between."

"Do you know what I mean by this, little John, Lizzy? John looked directly at Edith?"

Edith and the two youngest children shook their heads.

Master Stowe smiled. His eyes lingered over the three boys who had recently come into his home as orphans. Maddox, Woody and Kitt were all grinning. The boys sudden appearance into John's household had come with a fair number of questioning by his servants, especially the women who assumed they would have to care for them as well as their own. However, John had managed to stifle any further worries by engaging Edith into service as their guardian and keeper. So far Woody, Maddox and Kitt had played their part and had even managed to befriend nearly all the inhabitants of his household and outer courtyards. Initially there had been some moaning of sorts about these urchins, who had invaded his household; however, the newness of their arrival was still creating gossip, a fact not lost on John. John was well aware of the dangers of hiding heretics. So as long as they continued to parlay, he would protect them from the evils of the courts, where they were bound to end up.

The newcomers' dialect was becoming the most troubling aspect for the adults. Not so, for the other children. The new arrivals had taught them much, like climbing trees and making forts within the forest. They had been shown how to throw overhand, farther and more accurately. Maddox, Woody and Kitt had devised a game with sticks, in which they pushed hardened dung across the yard whilst running. And a most curious contraption through which to shoot that dung had been erected and then dismantled by the adults when it was deemed too dangerous and impious when it was played on a Sunday.

Woody, Maddox and Kitt's clothing was deemed to be of a superior cloth than that of the local children. However, it had been decided that these children must have had hard times come upon them, so the consensus was to allow them to adapt to rural London life and remain safe for now amongst Master Stowe's household. Master Stowe had assured his staff that his servants' children would not suffer under the influence of these foreign children. The orphan's clothes were to remain upon their backs unless nosey parkers or people asking too many questions lingered.

"The world of in-between is that place in which Sir Francis Drake and the traveller reside forever or until their bargaining has been resolved."

"IT IS THE PLACE BETWEEN HEAVEN AND HELL… BETWEEN THE LIVING…AND THE DEAD."

Every neck swallowed the saliva sucked from its shallow opening. Tongues clenched the roofs of mouths, teeth closed tightly. Little fingers tightened around littler fingers. Adults made the sign of the cross upon their brows and chests.

"It is that place where spirits live and roam about. These are not ghosts or demons. They are travellers, and they possess the bodies of human form to fulfill their requisite vows. It is a place of no sleep, little food and longing thirst. They must remain in the world of in-between until all that has been promised is complete."

"How do they get there?" squeaked Edith.

"Ah," sighed Master Stowe. "They have been sucked into the mouth of the Kraken of Nova Albion. It is a large beast far into the North Sea. Farther west than the setting sun in the lands of the Northern Seas." John waved his hands in the direction of west.

"It is the place also of the these Natives and their spirits, where chieftains rule and shamans lurk within darkened forests."

Master Stowe leaned over his desk and whispered.

"The Kraken is the most feared creature of the seas. Each sea has its own Kraken. English sailors are familiar with these beasts, which inhabit our seas. These are great monsters with a tangle of long sucking arms, which draw in their victims. They wrap their arms about ships, dragging all on board deep beneath the foaming sea's waves to be forever lost, sent screaming into the depths, many fathoms deep."

Stowe sat back in his chair, glanced down at his fingers and began to remove the dirt which had lodged itself underneath his nails. How he hated dirty fingernails, and he sighed looking up again and leaned forward once more.

"Very little remains afterwards. Bits of broken masts and ship float aimlessly lost upon the deep blue darkness. Never does a body surface. The Kraken sees to it that every tasty bit of man is ripped apart, shredded and eaten whilst the blood of man drips from its teeth."

Stowe sat back slowly in his chair lifting his shoulders to his ears in a circular motion. He breathed deeply and exhaled slowly.

"The Kraken of Nova Albion not only eats its victim from the seas but also from its lands. It hunts its prey, seeking out the lonely walker of the woods. It climbs up creeks, over large boulders bigger than this house and drags them back under the leafy green water's rolling abyss from which it comes. No one is safe from the Kraken."

Edith wobbled momentarily. Stowe knowingly glared at her to keep quiet, raising his eyebrows as he stared directly into her pupils.

"The Kraken must compete for its prey with the Sasquatch of the forests and that of the Cadborosaurus, which roams the islands and estuaries of Nova Albion. The Sasquatch is a large hairy creature, one and a half fathoms tall. He is a wild hairy-like man of the woods with big paws and feet. He carries fire in his hands and burns the forests where men try to sleep. He speaks only to the shaman of spirit clans. These spirit people admire him, so I am told. These spirit people see him through the mists that lay down their smoky cover upon the rivers and streams, which lead to their vast lakes and roaring rivers."

"The Cadborosaurus is a large saltwater eel-like creature. It measures six fathoms long. Its rounded head encases two large golden eyes and a long snout with gnashing teeth. Its body slips below the surface, flicking its tail out of the water before pushing its head up through the waves and laying it atop the crest. It is as black as night and can best be seen at dawn slithering its way across the sand banks which line the shore of Cadboro Bay in Nova Albion."

"Spirit bears roam the inlets. These white bears inhabit the thick green forests, pushing over bracken and shrubs. They lie down amongst the seaweed and float across streams. Their thick white fur glistening as it shakes off the cold clear waters. They roam. They catch salmon with their paws and rip its flesh open, sucking out the entrails with their snouts."

Stowe sat back in his chair and lifted his goblet to his lips. His throat was dry and his mouth parched. He took a long pull of ale from his tankard. He wiped the spillage across the back of his hand.

James looked across at Master Stowe with an open mouth and wide eyes.

"James," he said quietly, "how do you think the Kraken puts these travellers into...between?"

James shook his head. "Not know, sir."

"Well, James, it grabs hold of the feet or arms of these travellers with its long slippery tentacles, opens its mouth and sucks them into its belly swallowing them whole. He then spits them into the depths of the sea, where they enter the realm of...in-between. They roll and roll around beneath the waves, never able to catch their breath. They emerge into our world, gasping, spluttering, arms all flailing about."

He stood then and flung his arms about making circling movements where he stood. He grasped his throat and coughed, spluttered, gagged and flopped down upon his chair laying his trembling arms and head upon his desk. His hands twitched, his boot kicked the desk.

"NOOOOO," cried the souls within his study.

Stowe lifted his head slowly off of his desk. This was the part he enjoyed most, watching and searching for the eyes that believed.

"Master Drake, with his great drum beats out a special rhythm across the seas when he wants to move his travellers across time and into our realm. This drumming lets the beast know when it is time to capture and not eat. It is said that this beat captures the rhythms of the waves, stills the waters beneath the Kraken and allows the traveller into...between."

"It has taken Sir Francis Drake over four hundred years to master this beat. He captures his traveller in the year of our Lord 2002, two years past the second millennium of Christ's birth."

More crosses were crossed upon the brows of men and women. Mary shook her head and counted her fingers over and over.

"Another Queen of England reigns supreme upon these lands. Queen Elizabeth II in the traveller's realm is now in the forty-eighth year of her reign."

"Another Queen Elizabeth," cried James.

"Yes, James. She is married to the Duke of Edinburgh. His name is Phillip. He bears no resemblance to the former King Phillip the II of Spain. He is taller, thinner and a Protestant."

Stowe looked over towards Cicero the cat and wondered how much more he should tell them before he sent them on their way. He needed them to believe all of this was a story. He placed his fingers beneath his chin and rested his head upon his knuckles.

"Drake was a Master of the Seas, was he not?" asked Stowe of his listeners.

Numerous heads nodded in assent.

"When Drake returned from his voyage around the world, he brought with him, maps and charts of the seven known seas. The charts and stories from the lands of Nova Albion were hidden from you and me. Those lands were given to King Phillip II of Spain by the Holy Roman Catholic pope, Gregory XIII. No English blood dared walk upon them until Drake. It was a dangerous journey, but also it was a journey of hope. This hope was for a safer passage through stormy seas unhindered from Catholic control."

"Good Queen Bess wanted to keep our shores safe from King Phillip's invasion, but we all know what happened, don't we?"

More nodding of heads of assent could be seen.

"This hostile king invaded anyway. He threatened our good queen and the very lives of England, did he not?"

More nodding and agreement ensued.

"Our queen stood the test of time. She sent out Sir Francis Drake to defend our shores, did she not?"

Nodding children and adults acknowledged Stowe.

"Drake beat his drum and struck out at King Phillip's ships with his fleet of fiery barks and scattered those evil men upon the rocks of the Northern Seas and into the mouths of the Kraken. Every screaming, terrified, succulent soul slithered down into its belly, never to be seen again."

"Still wary, the queen prevented Drake from publishing his accounts. So he took his tale to the Netherlands and published his new Map Of The World with them. There it sits far off in another man's land, under the control of another king."

"So shall I begin to tell you now the true stories of all of Drake's voyages?"

Master Stowe looked about his study meeting every eye that stared into his.

"Drake has come back to me. He has beaten his drum once more calling out to the Kraken. It has raised its large head from deep within the cold seas and opened its mouth wide. Drake threw himself into the mouth of the Kraken of Nova Albion, whereupon he was swallowed... and spit back out into...the world of in-between. It is from this world that he seeks counsel with me."

Stowe lent forward again, tapping the side of his nose.

"What do you think Drake did in this world of...between?"

Heads shook sideways, for they did not know yet.

"Well, he went back to the lands of Nova Albion, the world of the people he had earlier met in the land of Natives, of spirits, of shamans, Indian slaves, chieftains and their sons and daughters. His ships were laden with Phillip's gold and silver. And they laboured heavily along these shores carrying more than treasure with them. The hulls of his ships were covered in seaweed, mussels and the favoured slime of the Kraken. She would lick the oozing mess from the bottom of Drake's hulls, rolling his men across the waves. Drake knew he would have to lay anchor and scrape off all of these gifts from the sea. But where could he do this, and which of these feral people could he trust?"

"His men were worried and feared for their lives. The Natives of these Western Seas had at times been hostile, killing several of Drake's men. It was upon the shores of Nova Albion, though, where he met and befriended the Natives of that spirit land. They came out to his ships in long hollowed out trees. They sat two abreast with great oars pulling their little ships nearer to the hull of Drake's ship, the Golden Hinde. Their welcoming cries were calming and cheerful. These Natives brought with them gifts of food, of roots, berries and the white skins of their spirit bear. Their chieftain held out a great long pipe decorated with carvings, decorated with dyes of red, white, blue and yellow."

"For six weeks Drake and his men laboured on the shores of Nova Albion careening the hull of his bark. The Natives watched, brought food, skins of raccoons, pelts of beaver, sea lion meat and smoked red fish. In exchange, he taught them the songs of sailors, gave them pieces of iron, buttons, cloth and knives. When he left them finally, he was given one last gift...the daughter of the chieftain and two other companions for her."

"But, sir," cried Edith. "Women are not allowed to travel with men on ships."

"Oi, that's bad luck. 'taint right to have a woman on board ship."

Murmurs of assent and nodding heads looked around the room.

Stowe ignored this last call out from his flock. Drake had assured him long ago that women were indeed aboard many a ship.

"Do you know what else he brought home to England's shores from the land of Nova Albion?"

Shaking heads greeted him again. He sat back in his chair and closed his eyes before replying.

"The shaman's curse. In accepting the chieftain's daughter, Drake made a vow of allegiance to the shaman. This vow between men who do not understand each other fully was unfortunate for Drake. For now he resides within the land of...in-between. He was forbidden to enter heaven or descend into hell until he brought back to the shores of Nova Albion all the descendants of the daughter of the chieftain. And there he lies still, taken from our world, into the mouth of the

Kraken who has spit him into...between. He must fulfill this vow or forever be held in...between."

"Is it like death, sir? Is he cold to touch?"

"No, Edith, he is not cold to the touch, but he cannot taste, feel or be seen. His voice will echo deep inside your head. He will torment your brain until you listen to all he has to say. He will whip up the wind and slam your door closed. He knocks over things and puts other things in your way. He moves items across the room and whispers in your ear when you are alone. He inhabits the very presence of a room when he visits. He will only visit you when you want the stillness of a quiet place. It is when you are the most alone that he will find you. He will follow you down the street, into the alleyways and even into your bed."

Stowe looked over the tops of the heads of the children gathered around him, into the eyes of fathers, mothers and his servants. Open mouths greeted him. Edith appeared to be swaying again, and the men who stood by her grabbed hold of her and shook her.

"Now, Edith, this is but a tale. Go about your chores, girl, if you cannot put a stop to your swaying."

"Here, here," cried out the men holding her up.

Edith stood her ground. She wanted more.

"No, I will not fall down. I have charges to look after. I must remain with them."

"Very well, stay," said Stowe.

"Do you know who else can enter into...between?"

"The Kraken," called out Nicholas.

"No... the Kraken holds onto the world of...between. I mean, who else can go into...between and come out into our realm?"

Silence once again greeted him. Heads shook sideways. Little heads looked into the eyes of littler eyes. Adults shifted uncomfortably against each other. Some even backed a little ways off from Stowe.

"The traveller can. She was taken by Drake and the shaman into the mouth of the Kraken and spit out into our world. She sleeps amongst you at night, and walks the alleyways of London town searching... lost in our world, seeking her children that Drake has also taken into the mouth of the Kraken."

"Why?" said little John.

"She is the chosen one. She must find the heirs of the chieftain and return them to Nova Albion. If she does not, then her own children will perish. Edith, you must look after her children. These temporary orphans here before you are her children."

Seekers

June 1576

Walsingham removed himself from the walkway between the two towers. His view of the Thames from here had been most rewarding. He had espied many a person traversing the waters about London. His use of Catherine as a tool within Elizabeth's private circle of ladies had produced many a linkage to goings-on in the castles Elizabeth reigned over, but more importantly those that were closest to London.

Catherine had served as a faithful sister and cousin to her monarch. Her depiction of proud, cocky and occasionally deranged bastardly heir of Henry VIII was complete. Walsingham had paid her well to perform her antics. She had become known for her knowledge of others. He had seen to it that she knew too much about others. She was as sought out for her tittle-tattle as she was for her amusing, vain-like qualities. She could be relied upon to embarrass all those who needed embarrassing.

Often her price was cheap, as her need to be sought out was greater than that of her purse. Therefore she became easily accessible to those who needed her services. In their bid to gain access to Her Majesty, the elite of London were often in need of Catherine's advice and services for a price. Walsingham was aware of these clandestine actions and therefore saw to it that she was released from her rooms when affairs of court dictated his needs most.

Catherine was to be governed always, especially now as Her Majesty might be involved in the pursuit of this traveller. Walsingham needed Catherine for the moment to disengage from her pursuit of the traveller. Retrieving that journal was of more importance than the movements about the courtyard below or the kitchens in which Catherine might find his quarry.

He sent word for her using his pigeons, fat, useful, well-fed little birds for communicating with his spies. He sent two short notes off, one note each tucked into the leg bands of his pigeons.

Owen received his first.

The Traveller comes. Secure her. Reply.

Catherine's reply came back first. Walsingham's left eyebrow arched at the fine script of his queen. He had not meant for Her Majesty to read this.

Secure traveller to prison, Reply E

Owen's on the other hand was more promising.

Kitchens secure, reply.

Walsingham had wanted to interrogate this interloper before Her Majesty became involved. He did not know yet what powers the traveller possessed, and he intended on finding this out before Elizabeth. It was for the queen's own safety that she should not question the traveller yet. He reasoned he would tell her. Walsingham needed more time to investigate this idea of a traveller. He sent one more pigeon to Owen.

Owen could see most occurrences from his perch. The far end of the stables could be seen through the window. He had witnessed the interchange between Drake and the traveller, who Walsingham now wanted Owen to secure.

Owen recognized the blonde traveller immediately. He recognized her shape as she wandered down the passageway. Owen could see most occurrences from this vantage point. The hallway leading to the kitchens ran behind his back. He could hear most conversations easily, having placed listening holes beneath pictures and tapestries. He had placed mirrors of brass above many entranceways. Their reflecting qualities could easily be discerned.

Owen immediately understood the urgency of Walsingham's message. This woman posing as a man would cause discord and fear amongst the queen's cooks and bakers. The traveller's attire was alarming and her hose improperly tied.

She possessed a familiarity of his place, which irked and maddened him. She knew far too much about his home and his watch. Impertinent, conniving little wrench. He would personally see to her demise once Walsingham had secured everything he wanted from this filthy bitch.

Everything about this travelling woman was sinful. Owen wanted to wallop her for her inferiority and foolish attempts of masquerading as a man but especially for escaping from his grasp before. Owen entwined his fingers, pushing his palms outward, cracking his knuckles. "She won't evade me this time," he sneered.

The traveller had entered his and Edith's rooms. He watched in the brass reflection as she removed the oddly shaped vest and shoulder wrap. His pulse raged at the offence of this. Her features were unique enough but were of better use for the purposes of men in taverns. She could arouse the interests of men in more fulfilling ways. He watched as she covered her body beneath Edith's gown, struggling and straining at its pulls and ties.

"Who does she think she is, wandering about my private chambers and using the things I have bought for that pathetic wife I'm attached to?" He spat out the bile, which was building in his throat and sneered.

He clenched his fists into a ball and then released them, cracking his knuckles, one of the telltale signs of his anger. He then removed his thin blade from its sheath and ran the edges along his belt. A fine cut appeared along its length, joining a series of others. His memory recalled the others who had succumbed to his ministrations via the blade's useful persuasive qualities. Bloodletting had its advantages, and inflicting terror was so very satisfying. He smiled at the blades sharpness and replaced it inside its sheath.

"You will find my blade a most persuasive tool in loosening your tongue," he spat out, as a grin stretched across his face in triumph.

Had his sympathetic wife found another lost soul to mother? He would find out soon enough, he thought. Edith would tell him everything. She always did. She knew better than to lie to his face. The back of his hand saw to that.

Owen had seen to it that Edith was chosen to be the one to taste the food the queen ate. However, he had not been prepared for the unfortunate likelihood of others being attracted to Edith. She had fast become a favourite of his chosen cookery staff. Getting rid of his wife was no longer possible via poisoning.

Worst of all, though, was Edith's penchant for children, and it angered him immensely. Edith had made allowances for women with children and saw to it that the maids and servants were well fed, especially their children. This endeared Edith to all who came into her pathetic little circle, concluded Owen. It would make getting rid of her more difficult but not impossible. The eventuality of her demise was already settled in his thoughts. This inconvenience of providing for a wife would end soon enough. And Walsingham's inability to see the lack of his need for a Protestant wife was becoming irritating.

Owen continually chastised Edith, tormenting her.

"You have the curse of a barren woman. You will never have children of your own. It is God's will that you are so barren," he would taunt.

In truth, though, he could not afford to have his wife locked away in confinement during pregnancy. Nor to have her attentions displaced elsewhere. A childless woman was more easily controlled. Her needs for nesting and reproduction could be used as bargaining tool to do the bidding for more important things. But once he was free of this encumbrance, her life would cease its hold over him. He smiled then, and his eyes glinted with the satisfaction it would bring him.

"Useless wench," he spat out. "Useless, except for fornication. There are plenty of whores," he hissed, to satisfy his needs.

"What need do I need to have for a wife?"

Owen recognized the flutter of wings approaching and looked expectantly for his next missive. He received a second pigeon from Walsingham. His eyes narrowed. He sneered. "Pathetic," he snapped.

Rose Journal, hedgerow, buried, secure, reply, urgent.

Owen ignored the message for now. He had other business to attend to. Securing this traveller to the cells would be next on his agenda; then, the journal would be located. After all it was just another bloody book. He despised books and all their falsities. Having to make despicable translations of the Latin Bible into readable English text for commoners to read had been one of Walsingham's more despicable requests, especially as it had almost cost them their lives at the beginning of the reign of Bloody Queen Mary.

"Another stupid woman, and I had to endure her litany of reforms, despite her Catholic intentions. The marrying of a Spaniard who claimed England for his own was unforgiveable. Stupid, silly woman." Owen shook his head in revulsion.

He had instructed Edith to keep the brass plates above the doorways as shiny as possible, just in case Her Majesty Elizabeth came below in need of food. It was necessary for Her Majesty's safety he had hissed at her. It was Elizabeth's habit to eat very little when in the company of men. She feigned at eating, as she was fearful of becoming corpulent and fleshy like her father.

Henry VIII had been a man of appetites, fitful moods and at the end of his reign, violently thrashed out at anyone close by. Owen harked back to the beating he had endured as a boy because of that, Catholic turned Protestant king's transgressions. Henry's attempts at fornication were legendary. Owen's mother's rejections towards Henry resulted in her disgraceful banishment from court.

Owen's punishment had been to remain in a blasphemous prison, until Walsingham relieved him from its clutches. His own father had left him in there to rot, never bothering to secure his release. He smiled at the memory of his father's demise. It had been easily enough done. Instinctively his hand reached out for the blade. Useful little tool he grinned. He never bothered to find his mother, selfish woman that she was.

Not that he missed her that much. He simply resented her even more. Women in his mind were to obey the orders given them. Owen's mother should never have refused His Majesty's desires upon her flesh. Now they had to scrimp and work hard for their keep. If his mother had been more cooperative with Henry VIII, even producing a bastard for his grace, then he, Owen, would now be a titled landowner.

"Foolish, selfish, woman," he said, disgusted with his mother's disobedience.

Queen Elizabeth was everything her father was not. Despite her Protestant rearing, she had proved unwilling to persecute Catholics with relish. Beheadings and public drawing and quartering had subsided, although they had not been abolished either. Her penchant for bloodletting was not as virulent as her half-sister's and Henry VIII's had been. Even the burning at the stake had subsided considerably, although he smiled recalling he did enjoy watching the chosen few who did succumb to its flames. Owen recalled how much it amused him to watch Walsingham's brother die at the hands of Bloody Queen Mary's orders. Walsingham had engaged the crowd into such a fury and outrage at his own brother's burning. Owen had admired his Lord's ambition at fanning the flames higher and higher. Owen only wished the screams of agony had lasted longer. It was a particularly well-attended and spectacular burning.

However, now those events were not frequent enough to ease his leanings towards violence. Queen Mary was dead, and her half-sister now reigned. His need for slaughtering now came at the tip of his own blade. Quite a satisfactory elation, and he felt the need of another quenching running through his veins. This traveller would do nicely, he thought. Playing first with his victim's fears and then their bodies.

Walsingham had enlisted him in the control of Queen Elizabeth's kitchens. Many came begging for food or work. Many came to gain entrance and elicit gossip about his queen. Even more came to claim acquaintance with her. He would control who entered this castle and any other residences she might venture into. He smiled at the power it bestowed on him.

Spies are everywhere, he thought. What does this one, this traveller, want this time?

Having abandoned his perch, Owen now sought out his wife. He kept watch of the traveller through the brass plates. He would not let this quarry vanish. Edith was feeding a small girl when he found her.

He had not understood this need in women to have children. It disgusted him. Children were not a responsibility he wanted. But needs could be turned into gains if properly controlled, he mused.

"I see you are feeding our hungry again. This is God's will, I take it."

"Yes, husband it is. What else would God have me do for Him?"

"He would have you obey your husband more often, would he not?"

Edith tensed and averting her eyes from the child, she looked at her husband's face. She knew by his rigid stance that suffering would accompany that look unless…

"Yes, husband. God would. What is it that you need of me?"

"Good. We have an understanding. Come. I will need you to see to the stores. Someone has been pilfering again."

Edith released the child's hand and fearfully surveyed the room with furrowed brows. He noticed her back straightening and the biting of her lower lip at the implied accusation. She did not like it when he accused her, and he knew it. She clenched her fists and stood up. Her dilated pupils and colourless face showed the first signs of alarm. Her breath was shallow, quick and produced the first trembling in her torso of remembered beatings. He enjoyed the silence and palpable fear he had forged. Her shuffling feet or darting glances brought a sudden attention to order. This was the product of his power and the tools of his manipulations. Order was restored with the swiftness of his tongue.

"COME."

She followed him then out the doorway and into the hall. They walked past the other kitchens into another hall and towards their rooms. He rounded suddenly and grasped her arms.

"Be silent with what I am about to impart. You are to find that woman who you have given leave to wear your clothes. She is to be entertained and held by you. Take her to the storerooms. Engage upon her your need to have children. She will listen to you."

Edith stared into the intent eyes of her husband, his spittle splattered across her face. Tears formed in the corners of her lower lid. Her arm hurt from the tightness of his grip. He smelt of beer and sweat. Her bowels and stomach churned, bile rose into her nose, but she kept it there, unable to release its sting. She recalled how vomit had further angered her husband, her disgraceful behaviours inflaming his brutality. He despised weakness, he had told her. She willed herself to train her bodily urges. Losing another tooth to his violence again was too much, too soon.

"Do not tell her where her children are held. I will kill them if you do," he spat out.

Edith trembled at the thought of losing those lovely plump boys she had found.

"Now make haste. She is in our rooms changing into your clothes. I did not buy clothes for you for foreign spies to wear."

He pushed her then enough to make her falter, but not enough to make her fall.

He knew she would not look back at him. He had trained her enough not to do so with the back of his hand. She would recover her tears quickly, wiping any traces away with the swiftness of an obeying woman. She would do as told. He sneered at her back and then grinned at his command of his wife.

"I will give you one of her children to keep if you do as I instruct," he hissed.

She rejoiced at the mention of him gifting one of those children to her. He had briefly given her a glimmer of hope. One of those children she thought, but which one. The little blond one like his mother or one of those impish redheaded ones? Their blue eyes shone now in her memory of them.

Edith hurried along the corridor to their rooms.

Treachery or Allegiance

June 1576

Owen quietly slipped outside and motioned for a new boy emptying kitchen slop from a pail to come over. Children had their uses, and the newer ones freshly arrived, agile, quick, clever and hungry could be sent into places men would not go. Children understood it was not their place to ask questions.

"Find Master Walsingham, young boy. You know of whom I speak. Tell him the newly acquired lambs have fled."

He pushed the boy along,

"Be quick about it."

It took Owen little time to locate the rose journal once the boy had gone. It was delicate, smudged and bore no resemblance to the script with which he was familiar. It smelt of her. She had slipped past him and into his wife's clothes, reeking.

Owen wrote another quick note and attached it to the pigeon's leg.

Lady with Thyme and Sage arrived. Rose secured.

Owen felt he had accomplished all that was needed now in this pursuit of the traveller. Was this his opportunity to eliminate Edith?

A smile breached his lips. He would follow the women. There was no escape now.

Kathleen had witnessed some of the interplay between the man and Edith. She had seen their movements in the reflection of the brass-like mirrors.

Kathleen's tensed jaw line and boring eyes met those of Edith's enlarged red moistened ones. They stood and stared at each other, neither one looking away.

"Good day to you, lady. I was hoping to find you in your room again," whispered Kathleen.

"Why do you wear my clothes?" said Edith.

"When we last met, you told me not to wear men's clothing. I was hoping you would approve of my change in attire. I need help from a friend. I can pay. I have money." She held out her hand and produced a gold sovereign.

Edith's eyes opened. She liked touching coins. Owen did not entrust money to women. She looked from the coin to the woman before her. Back and forth her eyes travelled. She recalled how he had said women were not capable of such matters.

"How is it that you are allowed to have a gold sovereign?" Edith whispered.

"Many women keep the family's purse, my lady. You need only know how to manage, count and record it wisely," said Kathleen.

Edith shifted her feet uncomfortably. Kathleen could see the discomfort that this statement had produced. Edith breathed deeply regaining her strength to speak out against another adversary. This woman whose children she might keep if she behaved as Owen had asked. Shamefaced, she challenged this interloper whose presence had caused Edith's latest bruises.

"I have this knowledge, but I do not view the control of my family's monies as the rights of God-fearing women. How is it that your husband has allowed this sinfulness to be endured?"

Kathleen carefully placed the coin back in her wrist pouch. She noted the other woman watching her as she did this.

"Who gave this man the right to take such liberties of money away from you?" imparted Kathleen softly. "I have need of coin as much as any man, especially since I travel to inhospitable places as these walls," she said looking around the drab little room and its tiny cot of a bed.

"Why are you here again? What is it that you want this time?" trembled Edith.

"I have come for my children, as well you know. We spoke of them before. I must find them and remove them from the danger which waits. You know of what I speak."

"You must come with me. It is not safe here," said Edith.

"NO, not yet. I saw him hurt you. Why do you let him do that?"

Edith's defiant, embarrassed chin rose quickly. "He is my husband. I must do his bidding."

Kathleen changed the subject, in part due to alarm and in part to elicit knowledge.

"I think you are the one who is in danger, not I."

"He will kill Maddox and Woody, if you do not come with me. You must come away with me now!" whispered Edith. We will go to the storerooms. You must secret there with me."

Kathleen leapt forward and grabbed Edith's arm. She pinned Edith against the wardrobe. Edith winced and went white. Kathleen grabbed the woman before she could faint and settled her into a chair.

The two women's breasts pumped their fury and fear outwards towards one another. Kathleen attempted to gain control of her now silently tearful captive, shaking her into looking at her.

"Where are my children? Where are they? What have you done with them? They are mine. No one can have my children. I will kill anyone who harms them." Kathleen looked into the eyes of her captive and understood the fear she saw radiating from every pore and orifice this woman possessed. Her breathing was shallow, her lips white and trembling, her hands small and scarred. She had been beaten recently. She could see the bruising forming on Edith's neck and wrists.

Her fury rose. Kathleen gulped in air and steadied her own breath while she watched Edith gain control of herself.

Edith had not yet fully understood why these children had come into her life, but she liked them, wanted them and needed them. She had vowed to look after them in the only way she knew how, from a distance and through the friendships she had acquired by being the wife of a respected man.

She knew Owen had these children. He had grabbed them soon after she had found them wandering in the gardens, picking cherries. He seemed to know they were coming. She did not understand why they were here or their vaguely familiar broken English in which they spoke. But their smiles and happiness were reward enough.

Edith didn't know where they might be. There was talk of a man, an important man, one who made a living upon the seas. She had been fearful for them then. Many a child was apprenticed, but not all were treated well. The life of a seaman and that of the children they hired was an evil one. Her mother had told her that. There were sea witches and serpents that snatched the likes of hungry children into their depths. The rolling seas would swallow them up and eat them. Their tummies would swell from the hunger at sea. Men sometimes came back, most of them cried out in their sleep from the terrors they had fought. Her mother and aunt had spoken of it often. The sea was no place for the little ones, even the plump, happy ones she had found.

They were big children, but they were without sin. This she could feel. They were without guilt when she had asked them where they were going, why they had eaten the queen's cherries. They had asked what queen and where they were?

They had giggled and laughed when Edith had told them about Queen Elizabeth. Maddox had told her of another Queen Elizabeth, but she did not have the red hair of Edith's queen. Their queen had four big children. They had told Edith she was pretty, that she looked like a mummy. She had held hands with Woody and Maddox by then, as she walked them into the queen's herb garden and then into the orangery.

But then Owen had found her, and they had to be taken away from her. He had told Edith not to speak about them to anyone. But unfortunately, she had, and now this traveller before her wanted them back. Edith couldn't give them back, not yet anyway. She longed to see such happy robust children too… touch them again. She could not lose them to anyone. Neither would she let the serpents and the sea eat them.

"You cannot have your children back yet… he won't let you have them," Edith whispered. "He will feed them to the serpents if you do not go away from here."

Quietly, Kathleen took Edith's face into her hands and gently rubbed away the tears now streaming down her face. She looked into the eyes of a beaten misguided, untutored woman.

"Where is Kitt?" she asked tentatively. "Where is my third son, the other redhead? What has he done with him?"

Edith's eyes opened wide as did her mouth. "There is another one? You have three sons? How? Why do you have so many and I have none? This is not fair. I am a virtuous wife." Edith's eyes moistened with the grief of a sinful, barren woman.

"It is the curse of bad wives to be so barren. I do not understand. You are a bad wife, and yet you have children. Why does God punish me so? What have I done to provoke his ire?" she cried out. "Please God, forgive me. I will do better. I will obey my husband." She closed her eyes and made the sign of the cross upon her breast.

"You haven't done anything wrong, Edith. You're not bad. Evil men have tricked you into doing things that are not God's will. These men have told you lies, blasphemous lies. God will see to it that they're punished, not you. You must help me find my children and safely return them to their home. I will help you find a better man, one who does not beat you or tell you lies."

Edith looked into the eyes of her foe and slowly, sweetly smiled. She would not let this sinful woman take her newly found children away. Owen had said he would give her one of them. He had never offered her anything before. She would have both of them, not one. She would protect both of them. She rose from her seat and motioned the traveller to follow.

"We must go to the storerooms, where things other than food are sometimes kept. There is a place inside which holds keys, keys to open the doors through which your children went. To get the keys we must go below, where the spiders hide and the rats ferment. There is much darkness there, upon the stairs to which we descend. Come quietly, for I do not want the maids and servants to gaze upon your face."

Edith turned into her rooms, picked up the taper by her bed and deposited it into her apron. She looked back at her quarry and placed her fingers to her own lips. She motioned for her to follow.

Kathleen realized then it would be another four hundred years before women of her generation would come to know and appreciate their freedoms. What if she helped this one before her time and life were over? If Drake could manage to bring people back in time, perhaps she could bring them forward. She could rescue this woman and her own children. Together they could all be saved, but first she must regain Edith's trust. Her children's lives depended upon it. Kathleen would find her children, and when she did, she would forbid Maddox, Woody and Kitt from ever talking to strangers again.

She would find them and enter into the portal with all of her children, including Kitt. Had he not come? Did he not wander into this realm, or was he still too young yet for the likes of these evil men and this horrid filthy place? I have no choice but to use this poor woman, Kathleen thought. I have to!

Kathleen noticed Edith look up into the brass plates at either end of the hallway once again. She wondered who had put these mirror-like hangings upon the wall. There was no one at present reflected but herself and Edith. She remembered seeing shadows move across these plates as she had entered the building. Who else besides Edith uses these mirrors? It would be prudent to recognize and use this well placed tool. Being careful and unwatched was going to be more difficult if I am to find my children, she thought.

Kathleen kept her eyes moving at all times. They walked the hallways, around corners, through door after door. She noted that everywhere they went these magnificently polished brass plates hung. They hung above doorways, at ends of halls, above tables. Her spine tingled and nearly froze as she noted the passage of shadows flick across one plate after the other.

They were being followed, she thought. Edith brought them deeper and deeper inside the castle walls. Every hair on her body now took note, stood up and sharpened to a point. Her edge of reason propelled her fingers to seek out her knife now locked within her hose and body purse. She must lose the dress of a woman, for it is far too cumbersome for escape, she thought.

Edith slowed her pace and stopped at a doorway. She lifted a latch, removed the tallow from her apron and strode inside. She motioned Kathleen to come inside. The room was dark, damp and musty.

Kathleen hesitated momentarily until she saw the shadow flick again. She bolted inside the darkened room.

"Close the door quickly," said Edith.

Kathleen closed the door partially, allowing for a sliver of light from the hall to penetrate. She fumbled with her dress. She would remove it now, she thought. Better to lose this body attire now while she could.

The door clicked closed, the sound of the latch clasping its metal hook rang out and echoed around the now darkened room.

"Owen, Owen, let me out," cried out Edith. "I am locked inside with this sinful one."

The sound of metal scraping on metal pierced the room, its low dull grinding thud made its answer. Edith began to weep.

Kathleen breathed slowly now trying to gain her composure. She was not sure how to deal with her emotions. She was angry, afraid and betrayed. "Think, woman, think," she repeated to herself.

"What is in this room, Edith? Why does it have a lock?"

"I… I cannot say. I am forbidden, and he will harm us both if you ask me too many questions. He does not like questions. He does not like women who wear men's clothing or borrow my dress. He is quite angry with me. I should not have told you about your dress.

"He won't harm you. I won't let him."

"You are nothing. He is a man. I am a married woman. I must obey my husband."

"Well, I wouldn't."

"I will not listen to this talk. The devil has called, and you appeared. It was my sin to listen to you. Now I must pay. I will have to pay for your sins and mine."

162

"You don't have to pay for any sins. You haven't done anything wrong. You are as kind as your husband is cruel. He has tricked you. He is the one who taught you about these sins, isn't he?"

The darkness which divided these women also united them. They were both captives now, and Kathleen intended to unite them further.

"Edith, we are both trapped down here, but we can get out of here. We can both escape. You can come with me to my world, but you must help me. We can help each other."

"How can you help me? You are only a woman, and what do you know that can help me?"

Kathleen fumbled within her hose and sought out the lighter she had brought along with her. She remembered the knife, which would not show its blades when she had wanted to proffer it before Drake. She had wanted to let him know she had meant business, but it had melted into one solid piece. The things that were not of this realm. She hesitated. Perhaps these things were not to be seen. That doesn't mean they cannot be used? It would be wise to be careful in the use of this lighter. Maybe if I held it in such a way that Edith could not view it, I could use it. Maybe if Edith saw how I could produce fire, she would begin to believe and trust me.

"Edith, I'm going to show you something from my world. It will produce a flame, which will light your tallow. It's something which you cannot see. So I'll enclose it in my hand. Remove the tallow from your apron, and I'll light it."

"You are the devil. Only the devil can produce flames. Do not light this thing of which you speak. It will harm us. It will harm me."

"It will do no such thing. I do not want to harm you. I want to help you. Edith, let me help you."

Kathleen removed her lighter from inside her body purse and dropped her gown back down. The rustling of her skirts produced a whimper from the now trembling Edith. She held her lighter within the palm of her left hand and used her right hand to mask the shape and form of her lighter from Edith. She lit the flame and stared into the eyes of her astonished comrade.

Edith's eyes looked from the flame, which came out of Kathleen's hands to the eyes of her enemy.

"The devil has come to visit me. I am to die now. Have I been so terrible a wife? Is this the curse, which befalls a barren wife? Forgive me God for my sins." And she made the sign of the cross quickly across her bosom and forehead.

Kathleen stepped back from Edith and sighed. This was a woman sorely treated and misled. This will take a lot of work if I am ever able to make amends and befriend Edith this trembling woman before me now. I will have to teach her to trust me!

"The devil has need of light, so produce your tallow and let us begin our journey," said Kathleen sharply.

Edith obeyed, trembled but obeyed. Edith looked into her apron and retrieved the tallow. Kathleen came nearer to Edith and lowered her hands to the edge of the wick.

"Close your eyes, Edith." She obeyed again.

Kathleen lit the tallow and put out her lighter. Then she removed the tallow from Edith's trembling hands

"We must work together now, Edith. We must get out of here."

Kathleen watched the Edith move away and into the corner farthest from her. The empty barrels that lay on either side of them seemed as vacant and empty as that of the eyes of her adversary, as they faded into the darkness and away from the tallow. Edith swooshed through the hay, as she walked backwards towards the stone wall, kicking up dust, which hung momentarily before drifting back downwards. The smells of decay, limestone and clay heaved themselves into their nostrils. Kathleen sneezed and coughed and coughed. Edith stood there silently watching the coughing and watched as the traveller regained her breath.

"How is it that the devil can give you beautiful children?" whispered Edith.

"I am not the devil, nor do I have the devil's children," replied Kathleen.

The two women locked eyes and stared at each other, maintaining their distance. Edith stood transfixed, motionless and incapable of understanding. Kathleen realized she would have to make the first move. She regarded Edith's gown, her demeanour and her fear. Looking away from Edith, Kathleen searched with the tallow for a place to sit down. She looked around the room, at the floor, the walls and the barrels. She needed to make a space for the two of them to converse, in a less adversarial manner.

"I tell my children that sometimes if you look closely at the things that frighten you, the things that you don't understand, that they turn out, after all, not to be so scary."

Edith shook her head back and forth, covered her mouth with her hand and whimpered in the corner

"Let's set up a table of sorts and some chairs."

Edith stood immovable, her eyes following every move which Kathleen made. Kathleen thrust the tallow at Edith.

"Hold the light high, so I can see more than the dirt on this floor."

Edith took hold of the tallow with trembling hands and followed Kathleen around the room with her eyes. She watched as Kathleen righted barrels, found crates to use as chairs and pushed aside the hay, which was strewn about the room. Kathleen sat down upon a crate and indicated for Edith to settle on one herself. She patted the crate with her palm and motioned Edith to come near.

She waited....

And waited...

And waited...and still Edith stood against the stone of the wall. Kathleen noted that her shoulders had relaxed somewhat. She no longer seemed glued to the wall.

She waited....

And waited...

And waited... Edith looked at the table, the seat she was to sit upon and at the table again and then shifted her feet.

"Why have your children come to torment me with their loveliness?" whispered Edith. "It is not fair that I, a good wife, am so barren and you the product of sin can have so many."

"I am not the product of sin, Edith. I have children for a reason. I wanted them, and they want me. I was meant to be a mother. I was chosen to be a mother. I am a good mother. You will be a good mother. Your instincts, your attention to the needs of others, these are the qualities of a good mother too. Your patience is a virtue well-suited to motherhood. I can help you even if you are not able to bare your husband's children, but you have to talk to me."

"How do you know that I cannot have children?" whispered Edith.

"I don't, but you believe that you can't. Who told you that you're barren? Did Owen? I believe you can bear children, Edith. You can certainly look after them, as you have been looking after mine, haven't you?"

Edith moved closer to Kathleen now...almost to the barrel's edge.

"Who told you that you cannot have children, Edith? Was it your husband?"

"Yes."

"I think he is lying to you for his own sake, to control you, to have you do as he wishes. Does he stay in your bed at night, or does he slip out and go elsewhere for his lovemaking?"

Kathleen watched a flushed, embarrassed Edith as her eyes swelled with tears, and her breathing quickened.

"Give the tallow to me," said Kathleen. I will secure it to our little table. Come sit with me.

Edith sat before Kathleen like a broken doll. Her head hung low over the barrel table, and she wrung her hands repeatedly. Kathleen leaned forward and gently took hold of Edith's hands. She caressed the weeping woman's hands and fingers until there was silence.

"I'm your friend. I wish you no harm. I'm here to find and retrieve my children. They must come away with me. You must understand. They don't belong here. I believe it is the seaman Drake who brings them here for his own purposes. In time he will be remembered by the Spanish as El Draco, the dragon. He wants to use my children for his gains. He will take them if I -- we do not stop him."

Edith looked up into Kathleen's eyes.

"Francis Drake presses them to go on a voyage with him," said Edith. "He says they are strong, healthy, quick limbed and smart."

"Who helps Drake besides yourself Edith?"

"My husband, Owen. He says that Francis wants them. He says that I am to keep them well fed, that if I do as he wishes I can ha…"

Kathleen looked into the eyes of her adversary. This woman has been promised my children if she behaves and does what Owen wishes. The Bastard. How dare he control my children's safety this way?

"What has he promised you, Edith?"

"Nothing," blurted out Edith.

Kathleen stared at Edith and rose out of her seat.

"You will surely burn in hell, Edith, for you have just sinned. You have lied to me. I was going to help you, but now you've sinned. I don't think I can help you now," spat out Kathleen.

Kathleen moved away from Edith and tripped on a ring in the floor by her feet.

"You cannot escape that way. It goes nowhere," cried out Edith.

"I think it does go somewhere. And you will come with me, won't you? To watch where I go, to see whom I seek, won't you?"

Kathleen leaned over and traced the edges of the boards. With her fingers she outlined the latches on the floor.

"Where does this lead, Edith. What lies below us?"

"It is nothing. Nothing at all. You cannot escape. There is nothing below for you."

"I think there is," said Kathleen. From her kneeling position she pulled up on the ring and glimpsed the stone stairwell below. A glimmer of light, she thought, pungent, cold air entered her lungs. These well-worn, stone stairs were going to be their escape," she thought. "The Thames must be just below us now. It has a landing for unloading and disembarkation, doesn't it?"

"Excellent. We will leave from here. Do you not smell the water below that awaits us, Edith? Have you never seen it from here? Or do you still lie to me to cover up for your husband?"

Kathleen listened for Edith's reply, but it did not come. She is fearful of my plan of escape. That or she knows of something below, which I do not. There is no choice. We must escape, she thought.

"Let's talk about the children as we leave. I believe you hold their interests near and dear to your heart. You want them as safe as I do away from danger, do you not?"

Kathleen broke off the tallow now glued with wax to the table and motioned Edith into the depths below.

Edith hesitated momentarily and then began the descent into the darkness. The two women slipped quietly down the stairs. Kathleen let go of Edith's shoulder and took her hand into hers.

"Let's follow the salt in the air." The faintest draft was now pushing its way past their noses and up into their former prison.

"Why do you let him bully you? He doesn't deserve your loyalty," said Kathleen.

"He is my husband, and I am to obey him," came Edith's curt reply.

Kathleen looked at Edith now and felt sorry for the woman who descended before her. Does she think Owen will kill her? Is this why she does as he wishes? How many other lies has he told her? What will he do to her now that she has escaped and followed me? She contemplated leaving Edith behind. It might save her from further harm, even death perhaps. But Kathleen needed Edith desperately. Edith knew where Maddox and Woody were hidden.

Kathleen seized Edith's arm and squeezed. "Who has my children, and where are they?"

Whoever it is that wanted her children would not take care to save them from any Elizabethan dangers. She tried to recall when the plague settled into London. Had it arrived yet? Were they in the midst of its pungent decay?

Kathleen shook Edith with a force that startled her.

"Tell me now, woman, before they come to harm."

"I told you your children are with Master Drake. He wants them. You must get them from him. I do not know where they are."

"Drake, that bastard," said Kathleen.

"He is a man of importance. He comes here before the queen and asks her many things. Sometimes he is very mad and swears about the things of which he cannot have. Owen has forbidden me to talk to him. Turning away from the traveller, Edith motioned with her hand.

"It is this way. You can leave this way. But after that you must leave me alone."

"I think not, Edith, for we have escaped the clutches of your vile husband. He would not like that, especially if I left on my own. He will beat you again. I have seen the bruises on your arms and neck. It is Owen, isn't it, your disgusting husband, who inflicts these marks on you? You must come with me. He will think you have command of me then, and you will not come to any harm."

Kathleen quickly followed Edith down the hallway of stone and breathed in the smells of spices, which wafted past them. There was movement ahead of them. She could hear the crunch and scrape of crates being moved about. The slop of the Thames lapped at the sides of stone. Edith slowed to embrace the arched entranceway with a sigh.

Voices echoed back to them from the waterway ahead.

"Edith, don't let these men impede our way. You must order them to take us away from here. Remember whose wife you are. Bark your orders clearly. Let them know who owes service to whom."

Edith stopped and turned to face her foe. She looked into the confident eyes of the sinner. Determination greeted her. The strong arm of Kathleen turned her away and propelled her forward. They stopped at the end of the long dark corridor. The traveller moved closer still and whispered into Edith's ear.

"Breathe now…slowly…long deep breaths control your voice. Do not let it tremble with fear. You have nothing to fear from these men or from me," whispered Kathleen soothingly.

Kathleen watched as Edith gained control of her breathing, gathered the strength she needed with the movements within her shoulder blades. She gathered up her skirts with clenched hands and moved forward. Kathleen blew out the tallow, placed her fingers over the wick and quieted the flames and smoke. She placed the warm tallow up her sleeve and gathered her skirt as had Edith and slowly moved forward to catch up with her.

With swiftness Edith flicked her hand and arm towards the boat and shoreline, motioning the men to move aside and find a rower. Kathleen noted how quickly the men gathered nearby leapt into action. She saw too the nod of heads in Kathleen's direction and the motion of men picking up ropes. Were these for the boat? Uneasiness surrounded her entrance. The men were wary, suspicious, thought Kathleen. They look so dartingly at me?

"We have need to go ashore for Her Majesty. We must cross over the Thames, bring us closest to Tower Bridge, to the nearest pier closest to it and be quick about it. We have need of obtaining items for Her Majesty," barked Edith.

"I hope Her ladyship is in good health as is the queen, my lady," said one of the men.

"Her Majesty, is indeed, in good health. I shall inform our queen of your good wishes upon my return. You have no need of worry. We merely wish to acquire trinkets and vellum, as Her Majesty likes to write so often and has need of the finest vellum and quills. You are familiar with the shops which I frequent. If my husband so wishes to find me, you may fetch me from one of these. He does so like to worry, does he not?" Edith glared at the men.

More than one eyebrow shot its way into the heavens. Edith chose not to respond to the lie she had just told. She knew these men well. They would report back to Owen, and Owen would know where to find her then. Edith stepped over the rail, which held fast to the long ferryboat. The traveller followed Edith and climbed into the boat. The two women sat down and waited for the oarsmen to disengage their ties and place oars into rings. The waters were smooth at present, although fast, and the boat slipped quickly out into the Thames.

Not much was said between the two women who sat quietly beside one another. Instead they watched the men intently. Kathleen had noticed the arched brows of the men, and was wary of the ambiguity of Edith's statement about Owen's worry for Edith. These men were not fooled by Edith. Fools could not live long in a place such as this. They know something is amiss, thought Kathleen. Edith has left them a trail to follow. Deception works best when the betrayed are unaware of the deception, thought Kathleen, and she leaned in towards Edith and whispered.

"All I want is to retrieve my children and go back to where I came from. You can come with me if you want. I have need of a good nanny."

Edith shook her head sideways. "No, no do not lie to me again," she stuttered.

"How many children do you have, my lady," asked Edith. Both aware that their conversation might be overheard

"Why have you been blessed with so many?"

"I have three boys, Edith. I have been with child seven times. I have lost four."

Edith's eyes saddened with this new knowledge from the traveller. She too had lost her children and survived. Edith recalled only losing the one. She almost retched at the memory of the loss. Owen had beaten her so badly at the mention of her pregnancy. The next day the babe had left her body. She had never since been able to conceive.

Kathleen turned her gaze now to the shoreline. It was different than she remembered it to be, not what she had expected. There were no familiar buildings except the Tower of London. Although Traitors Gate was no longer blocked up, its gates were pulled tightly across, but the stone stairs leading into its prisons were still clearly to be seen.

The South Bank was empty, its buildings gone. Pasture and sheep roamed where buildings should have been. Westminster Castle in the far distance behind them resembled nothing like what she knew.

The Jewel Tower stood there in the back somewhere, but Big Ben was missing. She longed for the familiar, the phallic pickle with all of its thrusting prominence.

London Bridge was nowhere to be seen. The smell of fish and chips, cod or haddock deep-fried umm, she thought and licked her lips. She could almost taste the bangers and mash, mum's bubble and squeak. She was hungry. A good ploughman's lunch would go down well with some British beer, she thought, until she remembered where she was.

Edith and Kathleen remained seated long after the boat bumped them into the wharf and was tied up.

"Your Ladyship, we have docked. Is this not where you wished to be?" stated the rower.

"What? Oh, yes. Excuse me, I was thinking of where I must go to first," she stuttered, embarrassed by the questioning.

"As you wish, my lady. When is it that you wish to return? Shall we stay?"

"Look for our return on the south shore. We will wait for you there on that pier further down towards the queen's palace."

With a nod at the men Kathleen and Edith moved away from their boat and ascended the stone stairs to the shops above leading them to Tower Bridge. The hustle and movement of men and women and the call of children swallowed up the women as they moved out of sight.

The two oarsmen did not leave the pier. They tied up the boat, and Henry slipped quietly up the stairs to follow them. Henry had orders to never let Edith out of his sight. The other oarsman remained within the boat and kept watch out at the wharf from which they had embarked. He too was a faithful servant of Owen and shuddered as he recalled the beatings, which accompanied that loyalty. He would wait there until daybreak if he had too, until he was summoned, if need be, by only one man, Owen.

The Problem of the Traveller

Walsingham and Owen discussed the problem at hand. How does one interrogate this interloper, the traveller, now without the queen's permission?

"Owen, it is important that we secure her immediately. Then we shall interrogate this interloper who invades our courts. She has knowledge which I need," spat out Walsingham in frustration.

"The traveller is trapped within these walls. I have her and my wife, Edith, locked away in the stores room."

"Good. Who lies within the castle's prison at present?" said Walsingham.

"There are many which reside below, Your Lordship. We have but one and twenty at present."

"We must feign an escape by her, then, and remove her to Richmond. She will elicit much, I think, with the devices at hand there, do you not agree?"

"I do, however, there is also the problem of my wife. I believe she has sympathetic tendencies to all and any who are capable of baring child. Foolish woman."

Owen gripped his hands together and wrung them energetically.

"She should be strangled into silence," he said. "She is weak and mindless. She thinks only of children."

Walsingham stared at the problem before him. Owen had become most problematic lately. He was becoming too independent and violent. Rumours of his handy work were becoming too well known and discussed.

Owen would need to be given infinitively more jobs decided Walsingham. He must watch for the signs of treason. He had seen it grow inside others besides Owen, far too often. He winced at the thought of eliminating his longest friend and dismissed the idea as quickly as he had thought about it.

"How would you silence your wife, Owen?"

Walsingham watched as the startled and delighted face before him transformed. The muscles on his left chin pinched themselves into a half grin, his eyes opened wider and his left brow arched skyward.

"Perhaps she should be put to the rack as well as this interloping traveller," quipped Owen.

"What other terrors could you enlist to silence our captives?"

Owen moved away from Walsingham then and paced about the room.

"There is the problem with the kitchen staff. Edith has many friends within. They will protect her. She must not be removed forcefully. I think an accident must occur. The staff must witness this accident," he stated.

Walsingham considered the problem of Edith and Owen. Edith had been useful, but was the time such that she needed to be silenced? Permanently? How much would this affect the servants? She had made so many friends. Could they use the grief of Edith's faithful servants as a ruse to elicit hatred towards their captive, though? He needed to think more on this problem. The traveller had proved herself a valuable asset in the past, and he knew that. This bothered him immensely. Was this tool of information on his monarch worth protecting. It was an intriguing problem to solve. I do so like these little puzzles, he thought.

"How useful do you believe this traveller to be Owen?"

"Ah," Owen smirked. "She is aptly endowed and could be put to use in the brothels. She might be useful for gathering information from our foreign visitors," he grinned. "And I would be willing to convert her into that service for your needs, if necessary."

Walsingham pondered the very thought of such a move. Dignitaries were always in need of fornication, and exotic woman were highly sought after. The whiteness and straightness of her teeth would be alluring enough. Her short blonde hair was not, but those blue eyes were always a particular fascination for men. He pondered this possibility.

"I have a problem before me, Owen. This traveller carries information within her mind which must not be lost. She may be useful as you suggest, however, there is still the problem of Elizabeth. Elizabeth knows of her existence. She will want to interrogate her personally. We must secure her first and decide the fate which will fall upon her later."

She might just be as valuable as Catherine has suggested, he thought. Did she really possess these powers of prediction? How much knowledge did reside in that ignoble head? he wondered.

"There is much to be done with her yet! However, first I must decipher this inferior hand and script," he whispered.

What implications will lie ahead of us? And how much decipherable knowledge can be gleaned from this journal's vellum? What precautions can I implement to impede the traveller's purpose and keep Elizabeth from the evil that lurks inside those foreign bones?

Walsingham paced the room, and from time to time he let his eyes wander over the limbs and ligaments of his friend. Owen's stature was big, but not clumsy, and he understood the power of attraction he elicited from inside London's brothels. Perhaps, thought Walsingham, Owen spends too much time fornicating. I will have to send him on another voyage and soon. The problem of Queen Mary of the Scots and the Irish Catholic uprisings will need addressing soon as well.

Walsingham could see he was going to have to keep Owen from attracting too much attention again. Perhaps luring him out of London along with Francis Drake was what the pair of them needed. Both men had become too astute at procuring their needs! It was time to take control. He needed both men to do exactly as he wanted them to do! They needed to earn their desires, not just take them.

It did not take Walsingham long to decode the traveller's script. What it had revealed to him, though, was the importance of securing this woman. She had obtained more information than most. This was a problem, which needed to be addressed now.

He noted her handwriting was inferior to his; however, she had procured classified information, and he needed to know how. Who else had seen this journal, and where did she glean her knowledge.

"Let us go now into the stores room and retrieve our guest," stated Walsingham.

The two men left Walsingham's rooms. They travelled quickly downstairs and through entranceways and corridors. Owen unlocked the latch and entered the empty storeroom.

"Edith has betrayed me," spat out Owen.

"I think not. She will take heed to listen to your wishes, my friend. Perhaps they are engaged below with the oarsmen."

The two men descended further into the castles depths, and the sounds of the Thames slapping itself against the stone abutments greeted them. Walsingham led the way and slipped quietly onto the stone pier. Owen spotted his men immediately. Wesley was ensconced within his sloop, which must have carried the women to nearby Tower

Bridge, he thought. He noted Henry was not with him. He must have followed, as instructed when irregularities surfaced.

The other men were busy attending chores. This was the queen's private pier, but it was also Owen's to enjoy and engage in activities necessary for the protection of Her Majesty's realm.

This was a pier used for private engagements, and its usefulness and proximity to Tower Bridge was indeed necessary. Prisoners, thought Owen, were never taken down here. Nor would he let it start to be used for escape.

"Owen, we must find your wife and the traveller quickly. There is much at stake. Go quickly now, he whispered, take your men, secure her to the tunnels below Bermondsey's church. It is more secure for releasing illicit information from that traveller's tongue."

Walsingham's jaw tightened. He clenched his teeth, grinding them. The traveller had escaped. Twice now she had eluded his grip. She was more slippery than an eel, he thought. Elizabeth must not know of this lucky escape. He looked sideways at Owen's brooding face. Secure! "Humph." She was not. Foolish of Owen to put her here, letting this interloper evade his capture so easily!

"Humph. Your third attempt at escape will not be so fortunate, me lady. Nobody escapes from the Tower!"

Escape

June 1576

Walsingham sent word to the queen via a servant to inform Her Majesty of the traveller's escape. His writing was that of a man of confidence. She will not get far, he thought. He had men who were even now fast on her trail, by land and river. Owen will flush her out first. And then he will release their captive only once they had purged the traveller of all her information. Elizabeth has no need to know about this yet. Walsingham's men had signalled of her whereabouts. The traveller will be back and secured before nightfall he assured himself.

The traveller's impertinence was annoying. She would explain everything written in this journal. He flipped its vellum open and looked at the milky white pages. He noted the inferior script. Its simplicity was intriguing. Did it have some secretive messages hidden within?

He had informers everywhere, and yet she had appeared without warning. He did not like that. No one had seen her come. No one had found any trace of her presence. That was probably good. Easier to dispose of any bodies that way.

If, as Owen had suggested, they use her in the brothels, she could be pressed to elicit information for him. He dismissed the idea immediately. She would not lie easily with any man. He recalled how Drake had emerged from the shed fully clothed, not unkempt. No, she was too independent. He needed to confine the traveller in a place far from London's eyes. She would disrupt everything.

Hampton Court or Greenwich, he pondered?

Which palace has more implements to extract information? Where could he hide the body? And why did she have to take that wife of Owen with her? "Damnation, she will have to die too. I didn't want to do that."

Edith had been good for Owen. She hid him well enough from his Catholic tendencies. He flipped the journal shut. It was the only way to keep Owen safe from prying Protestant informants. He needs a Protestant woman at his side. One who will not speak the tongues of a Catholic heretic!

Owen has been useful of late, but he has also been a worry, thought Walsingham. He is far too promiscuous. There have been more than a few ladies of the brothels to dispose of. His insatiable lust will be the end of him if he does not take care. There is a time and a place for these things.

"We will need to speak of this again," he said aloud.

Needs

Sticks and Stones can break your Bones
But Words Can Never Hurt You
Or Can They?

Francis Drake strode quickly towards the privy chamber. He knew he would have only a few moments with the queen. It was imperative to impress upon Elizabeth the need for England to stymie King Phillip of Spain. Drake's need to thwart the Spanish was equally pressing upon other mariners nerves as well. Drake's lip curled upward at the thought of his betrayal by the Spanish skirmish at San Juan de Ulúa. His escape had been perilous.

"The bloody traitors," he spat out. He had lost several good men during an exchange of prisoners to secure their free entry into the port at San Juan, for their ship's urgent repair.

However, the Spanish had reneged and set upon the English, killing many. Only Hawkins and Drake had managed to loosen their ships and escape. Later after the attack, he had been accused of abandoning his fellow seaman by Hawkins, his cousin.

"It was because of me that Hawkins got away from them at all! Lying bloody Spanish bastards."

"So much blood lost," he sneered. "I will not be made to look a fool again," he snapped, and spat on the ground once more.

Elizabeth was formidable. How was he to garner her trust? Surely after all he had gained for her purse she would now consent to let him go abroad and pilfer in the interest of England once more. He had brought Elizabeth six cargo ships laden with gold, pearls and emeralds. And he had secured sugar! He had brought Elizabeth many secrets from the Spanish held islands in the Caribbean. The queen owed him for this, and he would remind her of that.

That traveller had indicated that I would sail soon but when? When will I be off of this England? I need to set sail, for it is in my blood. My veins pulse fastest when the sea roils. I have need of the salt, of the sea air in my beard and the sweat of my toil in my palms. Does Elizabeth not understand this desire within the bones of her seamen?

Drake looked over his attire. He was wearing one of his best doublets. His hose were of the finest silk. He looked down and admired his legs flexing his calves. He adjusted any slight twist in the fabric that would impede Her Majesty's viewing. The turn of his ankle and his strong muscular calves always caused a stir amongst the ladies at court. His confidence waned slightly when he remembered he had not brought with him his ornate codpiece.

The queen always looked at men's codpieces. This was one of the many rumours gossiped about her. He loved the power it stirred in him when she looked at it. Drake was glad that his monarch was not a man. A king would have demanded its possession. Queen Elizabeth's momentary glance at her male subjects' codpiece had indeed caused many an eyebrow to raise skyward. What thoughts were really brewing inside that majestic noble head? he wondered.

Elizabeth was strict, demanding and driven, much like her father, but her needs were different. She worried more about her people. She wanted to be seen and liked by them. She was kinder than her siblings and father had been, shrewder even and more learned. She could be talked to, addressed as someone who could make decisions and reason probabilities, unlike her father, Henry.

Drake decided he would appeal to the queen's mind. Her need to be liked was immense. He would remind Elizabeth of how beautiful she looked today. A simple comment on her dress would suffice, he mused. Next he would ask what she was reading. Elizabeth was a thoughtful, well-read monarch for a woman.

Then of course there would be the talk about her shoes and her choice of colours today and how marvellous they looked on her. Elizabeth was fond of seeing colour at court.

"Colour is joy at its elemental best and sorely needed to brighten the dreary days of winter," he recalled she had said.

Drake fingered the emerald in his purse, the gift he would present to her upon her giving permission for him to set sail again. Drake considered himself a generous man. He extended his hand as if the glittering emerald shone in his hand. He'd recently had it cut into a large rectangular shape.

"I will not give this to her unless she procures for me my privateer's licence once more." And he brought his hand back down to his side.

He stopped and looked again at his ankles. He turned and lifted his left calf upwards.

"Yes," he said. "I do have a lovely calf muscle. She will like that."

His thoughts wandered back to the conversation he had with the traveller.

"That wench didn't even mention my hose. How rude. She will have to be reminded of her duties to compliment."

Drake fixed his gaze now on the doorway ahead that lead into Elizabeth's privy chambers. On either side of the door stood two finely dressed sergeants. Their pikes rose headily above them as they stood looking unblinkingly ahead. Marching forward and striding briskly Drake's nose rose upwards almost sniffing the points of the pikes.

Drake's hand was reaching out to grasp hold of the brass handle on Elizabeth's door. The sergeants leaned quickly forward, crossed their pikes barring his way.

"Sir, what business have you with the queen?"

Drake pulled back his hand and stood glaring at the two guardsmen. He looked at their uniforms and smiled.

"You have done well to be on your guard, sentinels, but you must stand aside now. I have business with the queen, which does not merit your knowledge. Send word to her that Francis Drake approaches and wishes to converse with her about the realm. Be quick about it, for it is urgent."

"We have orders, sir, not to let anyone near the queen."

"Says who?"

"Walsingham, sir. He wishes to have the queen kept safe. There is a foreigner about, someone who has got loose. We are ordered to bar everyone from entry to Her Majesty's chambers."

"There is no foreigner about. This is folly, and she is harmless. I have spoken to her. She will obey. I have her word."

Both sergeants looked at each other then. Both heads turned towards him, and their eyes opened wide. They reached upwards with their pikes and brought them down hard on the ground with a thud, raised them again and thud. They crossed their pikes again and repeated that motion three more times.

Thud, thud, clang,

Thud, thud, clang,

Thud, thud, clang.

The sentinels did not uncross their pikes, but held them there in place, above the ground.

Drake stood stalk still. He knew the call of trouble when he heard it. This was a complication not planned for. Straightening even taller, Drake raised his head and nose higher. The simplest thing to do now was insist there was official business of the utmost importance to discuss.

It was not long before men could be heard running along the corridors. Drake waited patiently examining his nails. He was glad that he had washed and cleaned his nails. He knew how much Walsingham hated dirty fingers and hands. Walsingham was sure to arrive shortly as well, he thought. Walsingham always seemed to appear within minutes of any palace skirmish. He had not envied the man's position. His need to control almost every aspect of court life had at times been frustratingly annoying, but Drake understood its need and place.

Drake too had complete control and mastery of his ships. It was essential and orderly. The seas, he recalled, could be fickle. The littlest of issues upon the decks could turn into the most monstrous ones within seconds.

Drake had been furious over the loss of the nimblest of boys on one of his voyages to the Spanish New World. The boy was lost overboard, just off the Cape Verde Islands. The lad had been caught up in untidy ropes left improperly secured. It was a tragic loss, but one that had not gone unpunished. He had seen to it that the inebriated souls who caused this loss of life had been tied to the mast and whipped thoroughly.

Drake thought of the new children. The plump, well-fed little urchins would make good seamen one day. They will grow up under his tutelage, and he would pick their quick minds for all they could yield. They had shown great strength of stomach as well, for the winds and tides of the Thames had not bothered them at all. It was easy to tell that they had been upon the seas before. Their efforts of climbing his ropes to the crow's-nest as a test had impressed all his men.

They had even swum in the river with ease. Most of his men could not swim, but these boys played in the salt chuck like they were fish. They dove off the decks and retrieved items thrown overboard, climbed up the ladders and gleefully smiled. They had played a game of it. Drake's men were placing bets on them in the end. These children had even gained coin from his men with their antics.

These urchins understood quickly how to decipher each of his men's different dialects. They spoke well and could even read, although their enunciation was appalling. They could play at cards, bet with his men and tolerate the ale to a degree. Drake stood there at the queen's chamber doors, lost in his thoughts about those most entertaining children.

However, the comments by the men had been somewhat of a curious nature, something that was not easily tolerated onboard ship. It led to too much discord. Even if they were correct this time as to the dress and fine clothing these children were wearing, the children's shoes were of the oddest fabric, having black straps, which bound their feet to them. A most extraordinary sight as there appeared to be no undoing of this strapping around their bare ankles and feet. Try as his men could, there was no getting off of these most interesting shoes.

When the children explained about their black straps, their voices dissipated, unnervingly, as if they could no longer speak. Once the subject of the shoes was diverted from my men's thoughts, these children's voices returned.

Drake pondered on the absurdity of it all because he knew he had felt something when the children had silently spoken.

"And yet their breath was evident upon my hand. I could feel its warmth and force emanate from within little lungs," he said aloud.

Startled by this speech the men holding their pikes glanced quickly at each other and brought down their pikes with a...Thud, Ud.

Drake stood straighter, unimpressed by the latest thudding. Lifting his head upwards and directing his chin outward he met their gaze with a knowing smile. He understood just then what this was all about. Walsingham had put these sentinels into play here.

Drake dropped his shoulders slightly and brought his hands up from his sides holding the right hand out in admiration for its elegance and then lowering it slightly to tap a tune on it with his left hand, humming as he did so.

Walsingham men's boots echoed clearly now on the stone stairs leading upwards to the queen's chambers. Other boots and voices could be heard scampering towards the Privy Council rooms where these livered men now stood barring Drake's way.

"What have you heard of the traveller?" he asked.

"Nothing of a traveller, sir, just one of them foreign spies running about the palace grounds," said the shortest man.

"I've heard that it is a witch that roams about."

"Really," quipped Drake

"And she scratches her nails along the stones."

"Nonsense."

"Makin them bleed the reddest blood ever to be seen."

"And that if yus touch it."

"Be quiet, you fool," snapped Drake.

"Your soul taint never getting ta hevin," shuddered the muscular one.

Drake grinned. "You fools. Witches tear men's eyes out first," he sighed. "That's what makes the walls bleed."

Drake enjoyed the utter look of horror on the faces before him. He wanted them to spread the news of her arrival. The more he goaded these men into believing her capable of harming them, the safer she would be, he concluded. She would not want to be seen when these men and others recoiled in fear at her presence. She would then have to seek out an audience again with him. She would soon need Francis Drake for protection, he mused. He could gain from her the information that he needed. Information that would persuade Her Majesty to let him forage, plunder and wreak havoc upon Spain and the Pacific Ocean.

"Ultimately," he said aloud, without realizing it, "I could ruin that Spanish King Phillip's Catholic reign of terror upon us."

The men now looked at Drake and crossed their pikes extending their arms out towards him.

Walsingham had heard the thud of the pikes' flat end hitting the floor. It was a sign, a call for help. The queen's privy chambers had been breached. He would have to put aside for the moment this disturbing element of the traveller's breach.

He gathered his cloak around him and hurried off towards the thudding. What now have these morons let past? He would have them flogged if her chambers were disturbed and his papers, which resided on the queen's desk at present were removed, altered or marred. His quick sharp clicking heels clomped past oiled paintings. Dust swirled in the shafts of light streaking through windows that were left behind by his billowing cloak.

This sudden alert of the queen's chambers being entered was alarming. Who else had heard the call, he thought? He would need to quiet the panic, which this call had stirred. The queen would not be amused by this intrusion or its restriction on her person. Her Majesty hated these incursions.

He had wanted to restrict the queen's knowledge of the traveller's escape. The queen had seen her, he was sure of it. He could feel it deep within his bones. Had they spoken to each other yet? he wondered. They must have. The queen's curious nature into the matters of court life and the affairs of state had bothered him more in the beginning of her reign. He had understood her need to preserve dignity, strength and leadership. Her father, Henry VIII had also possessed fine skill at governing his lands. Elizabeth had grown on him, though. Somehow she had a way of finding out everything and demanding more control of state secrets than he thought necessary.

Walsingham had put in place a series of spy networks. Bargaining with coinage had proved many times more useful than the rack. He could elicit more loyalty for the crown's protection simply by making sure that the bellies of little ones were well fed.

His spying urchins were welcomed with food from the kitchens and lodgings in the barns. Edith, he thought, had been good at making sure all children within her reach would not go hungry. Knowledge of their activities at night and during religious events throughout London had been concealed from her. Walsingham had decided that any child who told Edith too much was never again seen at the kitchen's doors. They understood, these littlest of spies, how to answer Edith's questions with skill.

He had taught them the art of spying. Listening carefully behind furnishings, tapestries and draperies was just one way of relaying important information. Acting out well-rehearsed skirmishes allowed his teams of urchins to pickpocket, distract and steer their quarry into various directions. This allowed for the switching and snatching of vital items of importance from unsuspecting foreigners. They had perfected the art of pretend sleep and stupidity. Their lithe little bodies could get into the tiniest of spaces. Walsingham used multiple hand codes and signals to detect and decipher the parlaying of London's notorious foreign spies. Relaying information quickly and precisely had its rewards.

Walsingham could find anyone, anywhere, including the far reaches of Yorkshire, Devon, Wales and parts of Ireland. He sneered. Bile rose up into his throat. The Catholic unrest in Ireland was brewing once more. This would need to be addressed and quickly. This was a job for Drake. Any talk of a privateer's licence will become directly linked to Drake squelching this Irish discord across the channel.

Scotland needed controlling as well, he mused. However, England's holding hostage Mary Stuart had done much to quell the unrest up north. Scotland had such an unruly crop of men inhabiting its shores.

Walsingham spat on the floor in disgust. He would make sure little King James VI of Scotland would grow up a Protestant. One day that Scottish king will rule England but not yet. Not yet, he smirked and grinned.

The Celtic Catholic Scots had been pushed aside in favour of the Protestant Kirk. Queen Mary dethroned, her reign ended. The imprisonment of Mary by Elizabeth and Walsingham was convenient for the Scots. Queen Mary's fate, unfortunately, had not yet been decided. Her newly anointed toddling son would reign over Scotland in due course. His upbringing in the meantime was being supervised with the strictest Protestant English ideals, he thought.

If this Queen of England does not marry, then James the sixth of Scotland, the last of the Tudor line will succeed England's throne. Such a shame to have Scottish blood reign over English lands. Still Henry VIII's grandnephew will have Tudor blood at the very least.

There are the Grey girls, of course, but women, another woman on the English throne. "Ungodly. Utterly intolerable," spat out Walsingham.

He thought about how he could manipulate the populace into fearing the traveller he now sought. She could be harmed if he was not careful. Her usefulness had not yet been decided. The rack would come in handy if she proved unaccommodating. Coinage would provide nothing from the likes of her.

He would send out his urchins to locate the traveller. This will require food and tainted ale! Then she will be brought back to Hampton Court, away from the prying eyes of Cecil, Elizabeth, Catherine and the court. The kitchens at Hampton Court will be this traveller's final destination, if she does not elicit valuable information, he concluded.

"She can work for me if she tells all. Otherwise, she will be put to an end. I will have no enemies in my encampment," he spat out.

I will pay well for her capture. He smiled, his sideways grin revealing browning teeth.

I will find out what you know and destroy all those who attempt to get in my way.

The Irish trouble was brewing once again. The lands of the dark-haired Catholic Celts with their Norman blue eyes always needed an English thrashing. The pope has had too much influence over these people. Walsingham had met many a Catholic during his absence from England during Queen Mary Tudor's reign over England with that pious overbearing King Phillip of Spain.

A Catholic Spanish king had walked the streets of his London spitting his bile upon English earth. His codpiece had never matched the grandeur of Henry's, though, he thought. He had fathered as many bastards as Henry VIII, perhaps even more. Phillip's child would never have remained alive had it been born from the bloody womb of its mother, Queen Mary Tudor. Walsingham had seen to it that Mary had drunk plenty of the spiked coffee, which induces vomiting at the onset of pregnancy.

"That foolish woman had believed her womb capable of bearing children, humph." He smiled at his own ingenuity.

His knowledge of the preventing herbs for such an occurrence was vast. Mary had been given a daily dose the moment she declared her interest in Phillip.

He slowed to a walk as he approach Elizabeth's rooms. As Walsingham rounded the corner, which led up to the doors he espied one of his urchins and signalled for him to retreat. A quick flick of his right forefinger at the temple and the trail of his finger circling his ear and tapping his cheek indicated circle back and wait. The one he had instructed to follow him was just barely audible to his ears. Nonetheless, he could hear the urchin's retreat. He made a mental note to himself to lighten the sound of the urchin's footstep with even softer leather on the souls of his shoes.

Turning the corner, Walsingham saw Drake standing before the raised pikes of the guards. Drake's head was cocked absurdly high, his nose leading the way towards the doors.

"Drake, Drake, Drake. Whatever is it this time?" quipped Walsingham.

Drake turned his nose only slightly to the side and sneered ever so quickly before breaking out into a full, toothy grin.

"Master Walsingham, how pleasant it is to see you again so soon. Could you tell me what it is that impedes my access to the queen at present? Surely there is no impediment upon my nature that requires such harshness from the queen?

"There is indeed no impediment, Drake, to your person. I have merely put in place measures to ensure the queen's safety from the Irish problems which have so lately caused the realm concern."

He stood there observing Drake raise his eyebrows and watched him as the point of his beard and chin dropped 45 degrees. He smiled at the complexity of thought, which furrowed between the seaman's brains and brows. Drake cusped his chin and pulled on the hairs protruding from his chin. He stared deeply into Walsingham eyes. The two men stood analyzing each other for the briefest of moments, long enough to glean the other's intent.

Master Walsingham surmised Drake had no intention of letting him past these doors. He had used the Irish uprising once too often for Drake to believe.

"The Irish, you say. How is it that the Irish can cause so much havoc of late? Surely they are of little consequence to our shores. The troubles late last year were put down. The Catholics have all but been driven out of Dublin, have they not," said Drake?

Walsingham observed the silkiness of his speech and the lilting lightness with which he had spoken. He so enjoyed watching the transformation of speech, and the switching on and off of charm to induce loosened tongues. His observational powers were astute. Not many a man got past his powers of detection and deception. He enjoyed this art of games he had mastered. He too could induce spilling tongues to reveal man's most inner thoughts.

Walsingham read now the desires of adventure frothing like waves off the sea. Here stood before him a man lost when not roiling amongst the Kraken monsters, which lurked below its surface. Drake could feel the power of the wave's movement beneath his feet, the lifting of loosened boards creaking and turning with the strain of its ropes, ties and sails. It was in this man's blood, his swagger and hand jesters were like that of a sail billowing, his chest moving in time, in and out like some great big breath sweeping across the bow of his ship. Walsingham knew just how to engage Drake to do as he wished.

Drake observed the shrewdness of Walsingham brows and his sudden silence with keen interest. He understood he was being observed, judged and manipulated. He would need to be more careful. Walsingham knows too much about my desires, but he does not know all of them. He grinned. I know where I will be going next. Ireland will need to be squelched before Walsingham lets me attack King Phillip's cargo of gold again. He will want to have all of his shores and England's lands quieted before ever he, Drake, garners and promotes another voyage of discovery. That is what that traveller was alluding to. He grinned again.

"How is it that the foreign traveller knows so much about my impending journey to Ireland to still its defences?" quipped Drake.

Walsingham pursed his lips and hid his annoyance at being read so quickly. He had not thought Drake to be so quick to observe.

After all he had only just completed that thought.

"Hmmm," he replied.

"So, you have gathered information from the traveller too, I see!" replied Walsingham. "Yes, you will be needed soon to squelch the Irish discord."

Drake ignored the last comment. "Where is the queen at present. I have information for her about her realm. I wish to speak with Her Majesty in private."

"I will see to it that she hears of your wish, dearest Drake, but at present, she is engaged on another matter. You will have to wait. Surely, though, matters of her realm fall into my care? I see to it that all goes as she plans. What could possibly be of such import for you to cause these men here to be alarmed? You did set off the alarm, did you not?"

"I did no such thing, Master Walsingham, as you well know. You have set this elaborate barrier up for your own purposes. A rather well-known and talked about one," he said dipping his head down.

Walsingham tipped his head forward in acknowledgement and raised his left eyebrow mischievously. Walsingham's grin, confirmed the temporarily barring of the doors entry for now.

"You spoke of a foreign traveller," said Walsingham. "Of whom do you speak, Drake? Perhaps instead of talking to ghosts in the gardens, you should go back to the sea from whence this apparition surely came." Walsingham noted from the twitch of Drake's lips and the pertness with which they came together.

Drake swallowed hard and glared at the man before him. How had he known about my encounter with the traveller? Who had reported this transgression of royal import? He would need to be more careful where he commences speeches with the traveller, he thought. Her children would need to be scurried out of the city with much haste. He did not want Walsingham to interfere with their whereabouts. They were his to be used as he saw fit. These spry, quick-witted little urchins would not become one of the many of Walsingham's little army of spies.

The two men stared at each other as the guards looked on in bewilderment. Walsingham heard the clomping of Her Majesty's shoes before anyone else. It was too late, he thought. This man would have words for the queen.

Damn it all, he thought.

Pursued

Pray
Soul Seekers
You're 'N God's Way
Irreverent to Things Divine
Sacred Vows, Obedience to Queen
Rash, N Smouldering, Conceit
Driven, Maniacal Reasoning
History, Chasing
Quarry

London 1576

Edith's eyes darted to and fro as she climbed the stairs from the wharf. Her attention was preoccupied with the noises issuing forth from the emerging street before her. She hesitated for too long at the top of the last of the great stinking stairs. Her hesitation caught the attention of Kathleen who grabbed at her wrist.

"What is it Edith? Why do you pause so long? Are we in any danger?"

"No more than usual. I think we are followed. Do not look back," she mumbled.

Kathleen heard then the patter of a boot as it skidded to a halt on the stairs below them. Her pulse quickened. She wanted to look back. Silently she surmised that to do so would give up the fact that she understood they were being followed.

She nudged Edith on with a little swing of her hand but held tight to the sweaty palm of her friend. She imagined Edith to be a friend. She hoped that they could be. She wanted to protect Edith from the great wrongs that had been committed against her.

"Surely not," she said aloud.

"Surely not what?" asked Edith quietly. "What is it that you see?"

Kathleen shushed her friend and gripped her hand gently squeezing it repeatedly.

"No, I do not think we are in danger."

She hesitated then, just long enough to recognize the man standing across from them on the street.

She had seen this man before on the cover of a book she had read recently. He looked gentlemanly enough, but what was his name, and why did she remember that face to be so kindly, she thought.

"Look before you, across the street," said the traveller. "See the man in the long coat, holding the writing vellum, the one with the long pointy beard? Do you recognize him?"

Edith's eyes darted over to where the man in his coat was looking back at them. He smiled, nodded his head and began to cross over to them.

"I do not recognize him. He is no one I know of. Who is he?" Edith said?

"I can't remember, but I do recognize that face. It is a friendly face, is it not?

"Yes, he has kindly eyes and softness to his features of someone who is gentle, not inclined to the bad humour of this city, I think."

"A man of the country would you not say," whispered Edith?

"We must address him as if we are expecting him, so as to not alarm our follower. Perhaps this man will be of use to us in our escape of them."

Kathleen moved quickly up the last stair and strode out in front of Edith. She held fast to Edith's hand, looked the thin man who approached in the eyes and smiled warmly at him.

"We have met before, have we not?" She extended her hand now to shake that of his.

His eyes looked beyond them now to where a form had emerged behind the women. He bent his head then in recognition of the two ladies.

"Lower your hand, my lady," he whispered.

"That is not proper for a woman to do, as you well know. This is not your century. These things you do will alert others to how different you really are."

"Bow now," he barked.

Both women dropped their heads in recognition of someone with whom they were supposed to be acquainted. Kathleen brought her head up slowly, turning it just enough to glimpse the brown boots of the man who had followed them. She guessed he was at least three metres behind them. Those boots, she had seen them before. They were two-toned leather boots with fine stitching. But where, she thought, where had she seen him?

"I am Master Stowe at your service, my ladies. If you would follow me, I believe we have some matters to discuss, do we not?"

Kathleen began to stutter her reply, "Oh, my...surely you have not yet written your biography of London?"

"Ladies, if you please, follow me," he snapped at them. "We must make haste." He stared hard and long at Kathleen. "Your mouth will get us all in trouble if you do not shut it. Now, be quiet woman. You have duties to perform and a few lives to save, do you not?" he hissed.

Edith furtively glanced over her shoulder then and shuddered involuntarily. "He is gone. We are safe," she nervously laughed. Her companions locked eyes momentarily.

"Edith, we're not safe. We must not tarry. We must go now with this good man."

As they followed Stowe through the streets, Kathleen surveyed her surroundings and looked for the familiar markings of the London she knew. But they were not to be seen. No giant London Gherkin stood on the North Bank shores, no Tate museum. The White Tower was visible farther down shore on the opposite side to them, though. No impending buildings stood in the way on the South Bank shore. The Millennium Bridge was gone. The eye and its great round wheel nowhere to be seen. She wondered if the Clink was further down from them. She could not remember when it had appeared in London. Was it the nineteenth century or the seventeenth? she wondered.

"Is the Globe Theatre before us soon?" she asked.

"It has not yet come," he whispered.

"These things are before us, and yet you have seen them, have you not, Mistress O'Malley?" he stated with an arched brow.

"Yes, I have, but…"

"As have I." He stared at her.

"Y- You have…?" stammered Kathleen.

"Of course. How else would I have known to be here in your hour of need, and it is a great need, is it not, my lady?" he replied.

"Why? What is before us? You know something. My children, do you know where they are?"

"Of course I do. There are duties, however, that you two must do before any more of this talk of children. Do you understand of what I speak of?"

"No, I do not. I'm just here to get my children. Where are my children," she spat out at him?

"Then you shall suffer the same fate as Master Drake, I fear. For he too is ensnared, like you, in the pits of the spirit world. He has come and gone again. As will you, if you do not heed what I say."

Edith paled as though in shock. Her fearful eyes were wild with the ungodly talk that had been spoken before her.

"Edith, look lively. Do not bend your will to harm. That is but a moment in time, long into the future. The troubles, times and travellers of your present day do many wicked and wild things, but you will come to no harm as long as you do as you are told."

He had spoken his words softly, and they echoed inside Kathleen's head. How lilting his voice had suddenly become when he had spoken to Edith. His person appeared transcendent. She reached out then and took hold of his sleeve just to be sure. She tugged again and looked hard into the eyes that bore into her own. They were deep, dark black eyes. *You are real enough, she thought.*

She tossed her blonde head up and asked, "John Stowe, is it, the biographer of London?"

This time he inclined his great pointy beard towards them. "It is I, yes."

"Then what is it that you'd have me do to secure my children from harm? What year is it?" Kathleen blurted out angrily.

He shook his head then in exasperation. "Why do you forget these things?

"Tell me. Tell me now!" She spoke out loudly.

"It is 1576," he snapped.

Kathleen looked around at the fields that lay ahead. Sheep roamed in great numbers amongst the crags, stone and grass before them. The street was winding now ahead into the fields. She looked back behind her and could not see anyone following them. She noted, though, how her mind doubted that thought. They had walked a great space from the dock, stairs and wherrymen. The stench from the river had subsided somewhat, but still lingered in wafts in the breeze that floated up to them. The little landing they had emerged from and its inhabitants was a very little distance from them but not forgotten. Rows of houses clung to the edges of the shoreline, a hodgepodge of shambled thatched roofs totteringly close to falling into the river. Why had they come here? Was this some kind of fate that she could not avoid? Ahead in the distance a church spire loomed. She remembered the bear-baiting rings and wondered if they were active. Would anyone else recognize her, she thought.

"You said we have met before?"

"I did, and we have and will again perhaps..." he replied with an arched brow and grin.

Kathleen turned her head towards him and stopped in the road. She looked at him and shook her head.

"Okay. No more riddles." Her furrowed brows and crossed arms indicating she would go no further. "What do I need to do to regain my children from this vile place?" she said.

John Stowe stopped his movements and closed his eyes. He spoke without opening them.

"You have a duty to perform, as you well know. Our queen will not let Master Drake sail. He has caused quite a stir across the channel of late. Her Majesty wishes to keep him chained to her side. I mean, to her shores," he blushed as if in love.

Kathleen looked at the man before her. I will keep his secret crush of his queen quiet for now. However, it could be put to use somehow. It may even help me escape from here, she thought.

"What has this all got to do with me, with my boys, my sons? What have they done to deserve this?" She threw her hands into the air in exasperation?

"You have been chosen, as have your children, to compel our queen to release Master Drake into the seas. He is destined to discover your shores. You have no choice. Either you will do this or your children and eventually you will die. Probably, he smirked, a most horrible death. They burn witches you know. If you do not heed your tongue and questions, you will be easily marked as a witch, as will your children," he snapped.

"NOoooo," squealed Edith. "He has promised them to me. He said they would be mine if I obeyed him. I will obey him. You will see. They are mine."

Both Kathleen and John looked at the frightened woman. She had become agitated again and wrung her hands profusely in front of her. A worried, alarmed look of desperation filled the hollow of her eyes.

"They cannot burn children. They would not," she murmured over and over again. "They would not. Please say it is not so," she pleaded with him.

Kathleen looked at the troubled woman before her. She knew now that Edith could be turned to her side. She would not let harm come to the boys, even if she did want them for herself.

Kathleen turned to the man before her.

"Why have you come, and how did you know where to find us?"

"We have spoken before and will again if you don't do as you are told. I have a duty to my good friend to carry out as you well know."

"What friend," she snapped back at him?

"Francis Drake, good lady," he snapped back at her. "Now move along now, quickly, down that road more quietly. We have perilous business to attend. You are needed in high places, as is this pathetic wretch. No thanks for your interference. You could have left her out of this. Inflicting your values on our world misdirects our mission and causes more problems than is necessary."

Kathleen stood there, stunned by what he had just said.

"Yet you demand my assistance? What is this duty?"

Stowe ignored her and pushed Edith aside.

"Quiet your tongue woman. You are in a man's world now. Know your place," he said in frustration. He rolled his eyes skyward.

"We are being watched from the river," whispered Stowe. He lifted his shoulders upwards as if shrugging and scanned the shoreline. He watched the men, maneuvering closer towards them, pretending to be looking for passengers to go back towards London town, calling out, "Ferry for a farthing to tuther side."

"They will follow us in their wherry until we reach Tower Bridge."

"It is there that I mean to help your cause and your escape from Walsingham and Drake. For they will both be after you now, as is our queen," he chided more softly.

"Now, come, we must get you to safety. From there we will plan how to approach the queen and plead Francis Drake's case. Keep your journal concealed beneath that gown. You will need it to place before Her Majesty."

He turned abruptly away and began his march towards the village huts, which lay ahead of them, the steep looming spire of the church beckoning them on.

Kathleen wondered how she was going to retrieve the journal now hidden in the foliage. She recalled the delicacy of the way the queen's petite hands had rubbed the long string of pearls that hung at her side.

Another meeting with Elizabeth, she shuddered, belying the immense strength of the black eyes of Ann Boleyn boring into her own blue ones, the halo of fiery red hair inherited from her father, Henry VIII. Kathleen shuddered again in recognition of the trouble yet to come. How will I save us? she wondered.

They trudged on, mindful of a boat on the river having gone ahead of them a ways and then returning to pass them again. She wished she could see inside the boat to be sure that the boots she had seen earlier were aboard. What if they are not and he is following us still. That would indicate two followers. She made to turn around for a better look, but John pushed her shoulder.

"Move on. He is behind us, as he should be. Do not be worried he will not harm you. I have his promise."

Edith spoke then for the first time in a long while.

"Did you pay him, then, a goodly sum to keep us safe?"

"He will not harm you child. Now hush."

Kathleen had pondered on his words. What had John meant by needing to plead Drake's cause to the queen? Why was she to be put before the queen? Why would she give up her journal to anyone? It was her only means of knowing who was who and distinguishing factual events from legend. Thank God it's well hidden, or is it? John had mentioned her use of it and the queen's need of it. What could they possibly need my journal for?

"My God, the journal! What if they find it?" she spoke softly.

"We have to go back. My journal, it is in the queen's gardens at Westminster."

John spun around and faced her.

"WHAT? You foolish woman! How are you going to convince the council to send Drake without that journal?"

204

His look was incredulous. He stopped walking and turned his head back towards Westminster. He had raised his hands to his head and rubbed his cheeks and brows with them.

"That journal is your only way out of here. How could you leave it back there," he snapped?

Kathleen looked at the back of his head and long hair. She could smell rotting flesh and the salt mixed with tidal sludge wafting its way towards them. Momentarily distracted by the smell of putrid offal and blood emanating up from the ground, she felt dizzy, and an overwhelming urge to vomit racked her guts. She would not give in to this urge. She would fight it. She would not vomit. She hated vomiting.

She recalled her moments of uncontrolled sputum, puke and mucus gurgling up her throat in the isolation ward of the Bone Marrow clinic in Vancouver. Five weeks in hospital without access to her lovelies had kept her focused and determined to come home and see them, but even peeing had made her vomit. The stench of chemicals had stung her urethra. Her feces were even more vile, the slurry of curry like mush dribbling out in spurts burning its way into the bowl beneath her. Thank God she had the beaker to puke into at the same time. If she could stop puking and gain weight and show that she could eat, they would let her go home soon. It was what had kept her going, her lovelies, her children. She must control her urge to vomit again and maintain her focus. What is it that they all want from me anyway?

"Why are you here? What is it that you and everyone else around here wants from me? Where are my children?" she spat out at him. And then promptly farted and puked at his feet.

He backed off slightly, unnerved and disgusted by her base display. He looked at her then very sternly and fixed his gaze upon her face, diverting his eyes from her ample bosoms escaping from the bodice of Edith's dress. "You have been chosen to do God's work. You must convince Her Majesty to let Master Drake go on his journey."

"Why? Why me? Why should I do anything for you people?"

"If you do not help, history will be wrongly recorded again. Master Drake has not been accorded his rightful claims to the shores of whence you come. You must take back to your shores the evidence required by your learned men, the proof of his claims to the discovery of your lands."

"What? You bastards!" she spat out at him. "You kidnap my children for this?"

Kathleen shook her head in disbelief. She was furious, and her face was white with the shock as she realized her children were now pawns in this whole affair.

Ignoring her outburst, Stowe continued along the path with Edith in tow away from the stench of her vomit.

A chill wended its way down Kathleen's spine. She felt sick again. Tears formed in the corners of her eyes, and her breathing staggered its way into her chest, thumping in and then gasping as if grabbing at a vanishing air supply. Her body ached with the pain of sorrow and then numbed into nothingness, as if her limbs did not exist. She plodded on not knowing how or where he was leading them. She prayed that he would give her some kind of clue as to where they might be. She would enlist the help of Edith, she thought. She had no other choice.

Stowe stopped and turned, determined to get the traveller back on track.

"I do not understand your reluctance to do what has been decided for you to do. You do want your children back, do you not?" he looked at her then more softly, his eyes gentler less creased, a lack of fierceness about him.

Kathleen stared back into his face and silently studied the man before her. Could she trust him? Could she coax him to reveal some source, some trace of their whereabouts?

He studied her countenance, her searching eyes and woman's form. She was not a big woman, but she was stronger looking, more muscular and taller than the women of London. That alone might distinguish her too much. She will need to be covered more, or that frame of hers will attract too much attention as it probably already has. Her blue eyes were clear and unbroken by redness and pus. She was healthy, he thought. Those Celtic looks would bring in a few lusty men at the brothels. Her short reddish blonde curls might provoke the devil to come out in her, though. On second thought perhaps the brothels were not the place to hide her. He would take her somewhere else.

"If you do not do as Master Drake has enlisted me to help you do, he will surely take your children with him on any voyage that he so wishes. They will not necessarily survive such voyages, as I am sure you are aware. I am merely his aide in this, as he is in mine. I must write my biographies of London, and in doing so he will help me rid this young playwright William from history in return. It is of mutual benefit that I now help him in his quest. Now stop your blustering and pretense and get on with God's calling. Get it done and soon."

His face was flushed with the exertion of ranting at Kathleen, but she was still confused. No God would 'call' people back in time. There must be some other way of explanation. She tried to recall the moments in her garden, the walks under the oak trees in Ross Bay. The lovely September fall leaves which had mingled amongst the deciduous foliage floating to the earth. Her mind wandered back to the sight where… no, it was merely a temporary vision of coloured light forming itself into shapes like humans as she strode past the graves in the cemetery. Ross Bay had and was still the most peaceful graveyard she had ever been in, its statuettes meandering pathways and abundant foliage had always intrigued -- no, beckoned her in, down the paths to the water's edge and the deep-sea smells.

The smell of the salt brought her thoughts back to the present. She looked at the confused, terrified face of Edith. She knew then that whatever this journey was about, she could not leave without this woman, a woman who had cared for her children and spoke of them fondly. A soft caring woman, owned and controlled by the evilness of these men and perhaps the women surrounding her.

Kathleen looked kindly at her charge and took her hand in hers.

"Edith," she spoke calmly now, "do not look so alarmed by what this man has said. I will take care of you. I promise to get you out of this mess we are in."

John Stowe looked at both women and spat on the ground. He motioned them on with his clenched fist.

"We have no time for these sentimentalities. We must set foot lively along this road and get thee hastily out of here. You have much to do here in this realm and then get back to whence you came. You have no authority here, and your presence must be kept secreted. You have been wrong to involve Owen's wife in this mess. She will pay dearly for it, and there will be nothing you can do about it."

He took hold of the traveller's right forearm and gripped it fiercely.

"You are in a man's world here, woman, and you must tread more carefully. I have but a few options to keep you safe. This woman here beside you, I cannot vouch for. I have no instructions to keep her safe. Now get along this road ahead of me and keep a steady pace. Avert your eyes from behind and beside there in the river. You have attracted enough attention for one century."

He separated their hands and pushed the two women along ahead of him, grumbling as he did so. "Normally you women should be behind me. This is a great insult that I have to herd you along in front of me like this."

"Who is that other man following us?" Edith asked Kathleen her voice trembling and slightly pitched.

"Hush!" interjected Stowe. "He has been chosen by Drake to accompany that Irish woman beside you. It is of no interest to you, dear lady. He has this same uncanny ability of travel, which possesses their souls. You should stay well clear of the two of them in the future, Mistress Edith."

Kathleen could not recall how she had managed to arrive into this realm. Her mind had only registered that he, Drake, had taken her children. Why had her children been pressed into this realm as well?

"Why me? Why was I chosen for this mysterious task? I don't understand," she hissed at him softly. She could see Edith's whitened face and trembling form as she moved slightly ahead of Kathleen.

"Why indeed are you so simple? Because you have been here before," he schooled. "You have the power to move into our realm like no other. You have travelled on our shores, my shores, during your own century. It is this alone that allows you and that man behind us to travel to and fro. The two of you have visited as many shores as Francis Drake has. This is important. And it has been told to you many times. You are a brainless, vomiting woman. Get this knowledge into your head and whence there, keep it."

Kathleen still did not know what she was expected to do. All she wanted was to get her children and leave here. The stench of sixteenth century London was revolting. She had seen far too many corpses floating in the river Thames. It reminded her of the sea of slaughter visible in Rhodesia during one of its many fractious governments. How the greed of man had been revealed on television, she thought, brought out and displayed the worst of her era and society.

Would there never be an end to such injustices in this world? Her head was swimming with thoughts. How was this all tied together, and what was she to do? Why me? What do I possess which would make me valuable to these people? What do they all want from me?

She stumbled along beside Edith, with Stowe following. The weight of the dress she had borrowed from Edith, the hem now saturated with river goo seemed to weigh her down. She felt like she was drowning, suffocating. Her breathing had slowed with her thoughts. She could feel the leggings she wore beneath Edith's dress twisting with the friction from the folds of her heavy gown.

She thought of Queen Elizabeth then. Her veins raced at the thought. The whole incident of the journal retrieval had seemed almost dreamlike. It was as if her body had been trying to catch up with these current times, the one she was now stuck in. The fog which had encased her soul was familiar yet different. She remembered how it felt like to acclimatize in Cusco, Peru. The heaviness in her chest had lifted after two days. Her mind had recovered its fog later that second day. These sensations had been similar to what she was experiencing now. She had been bold with Elizabeth, too bold. Why had she acted like that? And why did Elizabeth let me go?

Who could she trust? Did the man following ever so quietly, stealthily, like some cougar in the forest of home have a mission to complete as well? Why is he able to transport in time as well as Stowe had indicated? Was this man John Stowe telling the truth? She feared not.

She must focus on the positive, take nothing for granted and listen carefully to all that was said to her. She must look out for signs of trouble and find some kind of ally quickly. Above all she must not vomit any more of the bile that was building and trekking its way up into the regions of her throat. She would need to show some fortitude and strength in front of these people.

She viewed the village, which enclosed them on the South Bank of the Thames. Everything looked so different. She tried to recognize her vacation memories of London with what stood on its shore during the evil times in which she now found herself. Was the Clink here yet? Was he leading her to that prison? No, he had said that he must hide them. But why?

Who was he hiding them from or for? And where the hell are my children? I've got to find my children.

Orders

Westminster Palace
June 1576

"WALSINGHAM," yelled the queen. "Where is she?"

"Your Majesty," replied Walsingham. "Whomever are you referring to?"

Drake studied Walsingham with amusement. He would enjoy this encounter with the queen after all.

Elizabeth rounded the corner, her heart racing. She could feel her chest heaving against the stiff bodice of her dress. It was warm today, and her body glowed from the effort of carrying the weight of her gown. She slowed her pace as she approached the men, who stood before her chambers.

Walsingham had turned towards the billowing folds of cloth bearing down on him. Elizabeth was furious, her fingers gripping the beads hanging from her neck. Her dark eyes shone, and her red brows furrowed and creased above them.

She stormed over to the men and stood before Walsingham and Drake. With a slight recognition of motion towards the guards she released her beads and waved the pikes out of her way.

"You know perfectly well whom I am referring to," she blurted. "Come, we must talk, both of you".

The guards opened the great oaken doors leading into the queen's chambers bowing as they did so.

Elizabeth led the way into her study and stomped across the floor, flinging herself down into her chair. She placed her hands upon the table and pointed her finger at Drake.

"Not a word out of you yet, or I will never, ever let you leave my shores again. Both of you must sit and be quiet. I must think. Turn around and do not look my way."

The men turned quietly away from Elizabeth's gaze.

Elizabeth pondered what she was to do with Drake. What did this man need from her now?

"Ah."

Not realizing she had spoken aloud. Her mind raced, she would use this opportunity of Drake's arrival to pursue the traveller. She would use him to locate and inform the court about the traveller's presence in her court. She wanted that journal found before others did so. If that traveller has knowledge of her letters from Robbie…she couldn't bare anyone else knowing what he had said in private to her.

"I have a task for you, Drake. There is a woman amongst us who lingers in my court without my approval. She must be found and brought to me immediately. She is a spy whom Walsingham needs help finding. Go and bring her to me quickly," she snapped.

"She is no spy, Your Majesty, but she does hold information which would be of import to you," blurted Drake.

"Then go and get her. Bring her back to me at once. Do all that is necessary to accomplish this task." Elizabeth leaned over her desk and glared at Drake.

"It is imperative that you bring her to me," she whispered. "I will not issue you a privateer's licence without that woman found. Now go. Do as I bid. Impress upon your monarch your powers of deduction."

Drake bowed towards Her Majesty and turned towards the door. He thought about what she had said and frowned. "Damn," he said aloud.

"I beg your pardon?" quipped Elizabeth.

"Your Majesty…"

"Go, Drake, be gone. Bring me that woman." And with a wave of her hand she dismissed him and sat back in her chair. Her lids revealed the fatigue she felt within her heart. She would not let Walsingham know how she felt about her Robbie.

"Walsingham. We have much to discuss."

Elizabeth looked about her room scanning its entranceways for movement. She needed to be sure the traveller was not at present amongst them. She had felt disadvantaged inside her sister's rooms above. The traveller had appeared and disappeared too easily, she thought. Her gut instinct had been to let her go. Better to know and befriend one's enemy than not. But was she the enemy, or was she really this traveller in time that Catherine had spoken of? What knowledge did she have to impart. Why had she been able to duplicate her letters so easily? Who else had read that journal?

Elizabeth turned her attention now to Walsingham.

"I would like you to use your contacts to find that woman, as well. She needs to be interrogated by me and me alone. Do you understand this request and what I am implying?"

Walsingham smiled sweetly at his queen. He knew exactly what she was referring to.

"Of course I do, my dear Elizabeth. I have your best interests in mind as well. She will be brought back to you shortly. I have men out already seeking her whereabouts. It will not be long, of that I am sure."

He inclined his head towards Elizabeth and smiled gently at her again. He smelt the fire and felt the warmth of the coal's embers as they drifted across the table between them. He had a longing to pick up the poker and ram it into the back of the traveller's head. How dare she escape him? She will pay for this. It will be I, not you dearest queen who interrogates her first, he thought. After all he was the one responsible for this realm's safety and that of the queen's.

Elizabeth looked deeply into Walsingham's eyes. The countenance of his face shifted from reverence and obedience. His eyes glazed over she noted as his thoughts raced. His left shoulder dropped whenever he was plotting the demise of his quarry. She too could read his mannerisms. He would not take care of this woman, the traveller. She would have to do all that she could to save her from the likes of Walsingham's men. That journal's information was for her to glean over. And the traveller in time could be used for Elizabeth's gains. She relaxed her fingers and smoothed down her gown breathing in deeply to calm her hearts thumping.

"Do you believe this tale of the traveller?" she enquired softly of him.

"That she is a spy? Of course. What else could she be?"

"My sister has begun rumours of her being a witch, one who travels in between worlds, far different and distant from ours. One in which time has no boundaries. What say you of this, my spy master?"

"If indeed she so does belong unto this world of witches and souls, then perhaps we should put about that she is of a harmful nature to all who seek her? Let the public be warned of her impediments, and then let us see how far she travels thus?"

Elizabeth warmed to the idea suggested by Walsingham. "They will treat her like the plague. She will have nowhere to hide. Is this what you propose to do, sir?" she said.

"Something like that," he said, "but perhaps we should do more as well. We do not want her injured or captured by foreigners. We should also offer a reward for her capture. Make her finding a worthwhile endeavour."

Elizabeth smiled at Walsingham.

"Yes, see to it," she said.

"I want her found and all her personal implements brought to me for perusal. Nothing is to be left behind. She has a most unusual journal with her. I want it brought to me and no one else. Do not open it without me present. I want to be the first to read its pages."

She looked deeply into his eyes and exchanged deeply rooted locked eye contact with him.

Elizabeth heard the movement outside her hallway entrance from where they had so recently come. Walsingham heard it too.

"You must leave me now, I think! We have visitors. Deal with them quickly!" she whispered softly.

Elizabeth smiled at her spy maker and nodded an approval of the discussions that had just taken place. She indicated with her head that he was to leave via the spiral stone stairs leading to and from her sister's rooms. She mimicked writing with her left hand over the desk indicating correspondences and then clenched her hand as if holding something. She released her hand upward indicating her need to have Walsingham inform her of his progress via the pigeon couriers. She had enjoyed this quick and easy form of communication. It had pleased her immensely when Walsingham had shown her how he had used this method as one of his tools of speed in intelligence gathering. The trick of course was knowing when and where to send the correspondence and which particular bird to use.

Pursuer

Robert Dudley removed himself from behind the freshly beaten tapestry. He only wanted information to confirm his worries regarding Elizabeth's safety. The conversation between Her Majesty and Walsingham made it apparent that she needed him again. He had been right in assuming that woman, the traveller, was trouble and foreign to these parts. Foreigners, he thought. Trouble in large sacks full.

"I shall bundle you up inside the granary sacks and toss your mouldy jute into the Thames ebbing tide."

He briskly ascended the spiral stairs behind Walsingham. Robert had intentionally waited until he had heard the pace of his receding steps fade and the soft click of the locks latch engage. Walsingham would be up on the stone walkway surveying the river. He always went there and waited and watched and plotted his assignations. Anyone evading London soon lost themselves on Bermondsey's shores. He knew now in which direction he would find the traveller, thought Robbie. He was not going to cross over the river via the bridge. The slowness of movement across its divide irked him at the best of times. He would find a ferryman and flow down the river with its tide. He

217

would ascend the banks past the bridge across from the tower and make his way up into Bermondsey from the west. Horses were faster than one's feet, and he knew just who to engage in finding someone on the other side of the bridge's shores.

Robert hitched his belt tighter about his waist and secured his dagger within its sheath. He wanted to be sure that this interloper would be sufficiently concerned for her safety. He would abscond with his victim and bring her to the Clink's prison. Once there he could instruct the Bishop of Winchester to hold his charge for Her Majesty. And if the Clink were not secure enough, then he would ensconce her into the Tower. Elizabeth was sure to reward him in kindnesses. He did not want her money. He wanted her attentions and her hand in marriage.

Robert now considered the prospect before him. He would need to pay the required sums to keep this prisoner well fed and nurtured. She was far too important to Elizabeth, he thought, to be lost or mortally wounded.

"Elizabeth will want the traveller in fair condition if she is to elicit information from her," he said aloud.

He wondered if Owen had been summoned by Walsingham in order to secure this traveller. Knowing, Walsingham's trickery, he well imagined Owen's pursuit of the traveller had already been ordered. Robert had managed to descend the stairs leading to the street after confirming Walsingham's whereabouts. Robert quietly opened the exit door and looked out tentatively towards the river. He had no need of being watched himself. There were a few children about and a washerwoman but no hulking Owen or his manservants or Walsingham's urchins. Clearly, the pursuit of the traveller had begun. Perhaps he had waited and listened and followed for too long. Would he be too late? he wondered.

Robert smiled at the boy looking his way and nodded in recognition of one of Edith's charges. He was a slight lithe little thing with keen eyes and stringy hair. A recent acquirement of Edith's he presumed. She was adept at finding the scruffiest of children and turning them into valuable little workhorses. He enjoyed the transformation from lice infested, reeking, ragged urchin into blossoming tradesman. The woman's barrenness and her constant talk of it had rankled his patience more than once, but her transformations were becoming legendary.

He waited patiently in the yard, delaying his departure. There was something about the boy's eyes, which had given a need to remain momentarily. What was it he had recognized in his gaze, he thought? Was this boy more than an urchin? Was his purposeful stare intent on recognition? Blast and bugger it, he thought. Was this yard of urchin gathering more than it seemed? "Edith is not capable of such advanced training. She is a woman, a mother in waiting, practising her skills. That is all." He dismissed his thought quickly.

"Utter rubbish. I waste more time even now."

Robert looked up from his tarrying and glanced quickly in the boy's direction.

"No," he said a loud. The little boy was busying himself with the chickens. He recalled how he had enjoyed chasing them himself as a young lad. Staying near to the kitchens had more than once provided him with a tasty treat from the cook's oven. Warm bread and bits of cheese, torn crusts dipped into the lard crock melted into his brain, and his stomach grumbled for food. It had been a long day with little sustenance, but he dared not stop for a taste of pie or a bit of bread.

The boy ran around and through the chickens scattering them about. He wove in and out chasing them farther from the gardens in the direction of the east gate.

"Damn it, I wanted to go that way," he murmured. "It is the quickest way to the street. I shall have to exit another way via the Jewel Tower and the queen's garden's dock. It was shorter than Westminster's and farther from his quarry, but it would have to do. I shall make haste and move down river with a two oarsmen wherry."

Robert dropped the rag he had been polishing his boots with and moved quickly in the opposite direction. He did not bother to look behind him or notice the appearance of two other urchins emerge from the herbaceous gardens. They proceeded to watch and quietly stumble on after him.

The sentry easily chatted him up and opened the gate slowly, eyeing the boys who were following. They exchanged grins, Robert to the sentry and the sentry to the urchins. The sentry knew the game at play and delayed Robert as long as was necessary for the boys to slip past Robert's back unnoticed. He knew the kind of soft-soled leather boots Walsingham had provided for his entourage of wandering warriors.

The sentry had admired the attention to detail which Walsingham had enlisted and trained his little brood of bandits. For he too had risen within its ranks and been trained in the arts of deception. His belly he recalled had been filled with loyalty over the years, and his gratitude to Walsingham for his placement in Her Majesties' household was immense. He had not gone for wanting for some time now. Even when Her Majesty's purse had been without coinage for his work, he had remained loyal. His belly, he recalled, had always been full.

"The cook's makin' meat pies today, sir. I recon they be mighty hot sbout now," he chatted away jovially. "Ida says she bakes the best pies in London. What say you, sir."

Robert stopped and smiled pleasantly, leaned forward giving the sentry a warm cup on the shoulder with his right hand. His thoughts had returned to his bellyache again.

"She does, indeed, good man. My belly could use one of her pies, but I must not tarry. The queen wishes for an urgent matter to be attended to. I must fetch some little thing for her pleasure! You must keep watch for a new boy about the yards. He has scattered the chickens about, and the cook will not like this interruption to her flock. See to it that he does not do it again if he comes your way." Robert grinned back at the sentry.

The sentry raised an eyebrow and nodded his head. He would need to speak to the boy, but it would not be to correct his play, he thought. It would be to know precisely who the boy's quarry was. Later on, he would glean who Walsingham's latest recruit was.

"I hear there is a foreigner, a spy amongst us Your Lordship. Have you seen her?" quipped the sentry.

Robert turned around from his exit to the street and looked intently at the sentry. His mouth had dropped open and his eyes had expanded their roundness.

"Whatever do you speak of, good man? A spy is in Her Majesty's chambers? I think not? Surely you jest and tease at a man's heart?"

"No, good sir. I only mean to make comment on your recent foray into Her Majesty's chambers and the privy stair which leads up to her chambers. You were most agitated, sir, and your men wore worried faces. They were moving at an ever so quick pace, and you were leading them into some kind of scuffle. I was quite beside myself with worry, sir."

"Ah that...I was putting my men-at-arms through their paces. My men need to be on constant guard for the protection of the queen. It is my duty to see that they are well trained and ready at a moment's notice to defend her honour."

"Well, then, and did you succeed? All is good with your men-at-arms? Sir, I had heard rumours of a witch amongst us. Catherine, the queen's… Ah… whhh…sis…good lady had mentioned such a monster of a thing. I dared not believe it into being."

"Nonsense, dear man, nothing of the sort lies within these good walls. It daren't' enter, for I will fix it to its grave if ever such a being were to emerge within your yard's keep."

Smiling sweetly at the sentry Robert rose up to his full height and straightened his shoulders thrusting his chest out in his most strutting like of poses. He enjoyed this state of being and the breath that issued forth from his prominent nose. His height was above the average, and he took full advantage of its viewing by others.

The sentry surveyed Robert and watched as the strutting fool passed through his gate, and he smirked. The lure of this most prominent of men gave great pleasure to his sentinel bones. He resisted the urge to slam the gate with force. He too had learned how to pretend and hide one's feelings beneath his skin. There would be time enough later to gloat about his actions to Walsingham and Owen at the 'Owl and Hawk,' a little haven, it was, within London's walls for the nocturnal, subspecies of spies.

The witch was afoot, and her whereabouts was eminently needed. He the gatekeeper had new knowledge to impart. The traveller was lose and the seekers had been seconded on their next hunt. It was always interesting to him to see who was seeking whom and for what intent. It made his pulse race. He loved the chase and until just now had not realized how much he had missed it.

Robert moved quickly across the street and entered the gates of the queen's dock enclosures. He would make good time if he could locate a two-oarsman wherry. He must make haste.

Robert cherished the conversations with his queen. She would be very much in his hand if he could in fact secure for her the very thing she most wanted now. Robert grinned at this thought. It gave him great pleasure to be in the company of Her Majesty. He had grown tired of making love to an image and using the company of lesser women for his manly needs. If only he could make the queen pregnant with his child. Surely then she would marry him.

This traveller was a most perplexing problem, and he was alertly interested in her. She was buxom with fair teeth. This was a most promising prospect to encounter, although the shortness of her hair, well, that was beyond reason. A shapely woman must also possess a fine mane of long hair. Short and curly? No, this must be a mistake. Perhaps she is merely a boy of some years past ten with the curly locks of a Roman or Norman father. He dismissed the notion of a boy when his thoughts returned to the buxom problem.

"Well, perhaps one could look past this lack of womanly hair if, indeed, she possessed enough cleavage and displayed a willingness to be vigorously fondled," he said aloud.

Robert's brisk walk had slowed down considerably. He felt a warmth flow through his veins. A stirring of desire pulsated, and he felt the need for friction and rubbing.

"Oh, enough. This does no good. I must find her and soon."

Roberts's thoughts now strayed to what to do with the woman when found. How was he to restrain himself? How was he to report to Her Majesty with this woman in toe? He must show no desire for her in front of the queen.

"Unless of course," he said a loud. "I could get her banished. She could be played with at my will in an established premise."

He stroked his chest and pulled at his moustache and beard. He would show her the countenance of his walk and his shapely legs. A most irresistible sight for the ladies at court he recalled.

"How they all like me to prance about and ruffle the ends of their skirts with my boot."

He quickened his pace and made off for the pier at the queen's dock.

Deceptions

Walsingham strode quickly from Elizabeth's rooms. His movements were silent and quick. He had enjoyed observing the movements of cats in his youth and noted how quickly, quietly and stealthily they had foraged for food. He mimicked now the lightness of their steps up to the turrets walkway. He focused on elongating his movements in swift, soft landings on his feet. Gently pushing away from the stone, lifting his feet high, being careful not to drag or catch clothing along the stone perimeter of the stairs walls. He could smell the cleanness of the air as he rose ever so quietly and quickly upwards. The dankness of the bottom stairs exhaled with each upward movement as he ascended step after step upwards.

He knew that the movement detected outside Elizabeth's rooms had not been of his making. His urchins had been trained well in the arts of deception and hiding. They would not dare be caught making such a foolish mistake. So who, then, had been listening to his private conversation with Elizabeth? Drake perhaps. He was slippery and clever enough. But if it was not Drake, then who was it? He would find out soon enough. He always did.

Walsingham's thoughts now drifted to the probability of finding the traveller. She had been followed from Westminster Pier to the South Bank upon Bermondsey's shores and towards the bear-baiting regions. His men had reported the presence of another and the wife of Owen, Edith.

"Another," he said aloud. How had this third person evaded him? The South Bank was mainly fields and farmlands all the way to Greenwich except for the areas around Tower Bridge. Tower Bridge road ran south leading to the southwest and Plymouth. They would need transportation soon if this was to be their destination. Drake's encampment was down in Plymouth. Perhaps Drake had not been listening. But who then? I could have sworn on the pope's grave that it had been Francis Drake hiding. He was sure that he had smelt his perfume and could well imagine that pompous face clamouring for more action, but no, impossible, for there cannot be the same individual in two different places at the same time.

Walsingham quickly moved in the direction of his urchins

I must be informed of whom these women converse with and why. Had they made contact with others? he wondered. What was the real purpose of this traveller's presence? Is the traveller on some kind of mission? What is this mission, and with whom does she collude?

He recalled now the elements, which had been described to him. The traveller had worn a dress similar in length to that of Edith's. Her hair had been short reddish blonde and curly. She was reported to be strong, buxom and having straight white teeth. Her shoes were of leather, but they bore no fashionable heel, as was the custom for women. The presence of another was noted but not seen as of yet. She had been talking to someone. She had appeared agitated and annoyed. They had been walking in the direction of the bear-baiting rings. The traveller and her companions would certainly be within the region of Tower Bridge's south bank district of Bermondsey's shore by now.

It was a notorious place at best. Theatre companies were formulating on its banks as a way of escaping the confines and rules of London proper. It was a dangerous place with many of its citizens careful and observant. They were generally wary of newcomers, and yet the place was full of these very individuals. A person could easily be lost and or recognized if they stood out in their dress and mannerisms.

This alone, he thought, would be to his advantage in finding the traveller. It will not take his men long to capture her. He wondered whether she was stupid enough to attract attention and get herself and Edith ruffed up. He needed her, but not necessarily unharmed. Just alive would do. This traveller will be scared and easily frightened along Bermondsey's shores. It's insignificant little village and boat building yards held many moles. It would not take long to locate this irritation. Bermondsey's alleys were sweeter smelling most times of the year than London proper, or its only bridge, but its rancid bear, bull and theatre excrement could boil the blood and burn out the hairs in one's nostrils.

He would need to send men over Tower Bridge from its northern shores towards the South Bank to secure this most festering wound. Walsingham smiled. He would see to it that she was squeezed sufficiently enough to emit copious pustules of rotting lies and gangrenous facts. This woman knows far too much already about his London, where to hide and who to contact, he thought, but eliciting information from vermin was as natural to him as breathing. Besides, he wouldn't have to witness this torture. That was why he had Owen.

Catherine

Catherine stood before her half-sister and cousin Queen Elizabeth and watched as she paced back and forth across the flooring. Elizabeth had clasped her hands behind her back, her long pearl beads slid softly against her bodice as she moved about the stone rooms of Catherine's chambers in Westminster's turret. Her slippers padded softly along the boarding. Her pace was quick and quiet. Elizabeth's furrowed brows indicated deep thought. Catherine would not interrupt. The tongue of her monarch could be sharp when interrupted from her thoughts. She watched as the familiar lines and patterns of Elizabeth's face wrinkled their way over her face as she twisted and digested the news Catherine had just brought her. Catherine would wait patiently for as long as she could.

Catherine enjoyed these quiet moments between them. It stirred in her an acute bonding between the two sisters whenever she brought snippets of news as she had just done. The advent of another Queen Elizabeth, Elizabeth II, was succulent information indeed. She wondered if her hair would be similar to that of the first Queen Elizabeth. When would the first Elizabeth bare children to produce such an heir?

Whom would she sire them with? The excitement of it all was almost too much for Catherine. She itched to speak out but dared not. She would remain quiet. That way she would be privy to the confidence she now sought. Elizabeth married? How delicious. Catherine had forgotten for the moment that strange woman who dressed so improperly but her monarch had not.

Elizabeth could not comprehend. What other queen could Catherine possibly be referring too? She had no desire to marry and give up her throne to a man. She would not let some man weaken her resolve to govern over England, Wales and Ireland. She would need to suss out this foolish notion and stop it in its tracts. She needed men on the continent to think of her as some available ally, someone to possess. They understood too little. An ally was for her to toy with, not the other way round. She would keep her shores safe with false marriage proposals. She could never marry. A child was out of the question. It would only get in the way, as lovely as they were. But a bastard child to inherit my throne…never, she thought?

Elizabeth paced the rooms. She recalled her sister Queen Mary's brush with child. How her ignorance had led her to falsely believe she was even with child. King Phillip had not been in the country long enough to have fathered the child. His contempt for his new bride showed clearly in his manner towards the beaming queen. Phillip had not much liked his wife. His attentions had been more directed at herself Elizabeth. She had toyed with this man too. She knew it was the reason why she had lived and escaped from the tower. Phillip had insisted Mary release her from her imprisonment. Elizabeth shuddered with the memory of the place.

Elizabeth's imprisonment had been many months long. Her quarters lively enough, which had afforded her many long walks along the wall's enclosure. She had enjoyed the company of Robbie there.

They had both been imprisoned together. They had comforted one another on many an occasion. She had had to assure Phillip that she had no inclination to marry Robbie. She had agreed that it was up to Queen Mary her sister and Phillip, her monarchs, to decide who she would marry.

They had advised her to think on her values and Christian thoughts, and they mentioned how the evilness of papist beliefs would condemn her to death. Phillip did not want to order her execution, she recalled. He had been after her as some kind of prize. His lust was evident in his dark black eyes and his strutting manner around her. He did not hide his desires from his wife. He had no need to. Queen Mary was ignorant and disbelieving of all before her.

Elizabeth turned towards Catherine and smiled.

"She will have to tell us all of what she speaks, this traveller. You have done well, Catherine. Do you know where she is now?"

Catherine did not know. Her sudden stiffness betrayed her ignorance to her cousin. She shook her head but remained content. It did not matter to Catherine so much now where this traveller was. She cared little for her anyway. But catching her would be fun, a lovely game of hide and seek. Catherine had plenty of informers about the palace and along the Thames shops. She knew where everyone was hidden. Walsingham had seen to it that she knew where people were ensconced.

Elizabeth eyed her older sibling. Her impertinence of late was evident. Was she working for others, thought Elizabeth? Perhaps Walsingham would need to be instructed to keep further watch on Catherine.

Elizabeth moved over towards her sister. She leaned in and whispered, her black eyes shining brightly.

"You are not to speak to anyone of this news, Catherine. We will proceed with caution." Elizabeth looked coldly into Catherine's eyes and stared. She did not blink. Her lips had barely parted as she had spoken her words.

"It must not get out. The Privy Council must not hear of it. I will not have my men talking of further marriage arrangements just yet. I have not decided yet which alliance should be attained on the continent. This news will wreak havoc with King Phillip of Spain if he hears of it."

Elizabeth flicked her hand indicating Catherine to move out of her way. She strode quickly towards the grey stone staircase leading down into her private rooms. At the doorway by the entrance, she turned back. Elizabeth raised her left brow pointedly.

"Do not leave your rooms. I will fetch for you when I have decided how I will retrieve this traveller back into my palace. She will not escape from my grasp once caught. That was your fault!"

Catherine did not pale from her monarch's biting words. She was used to the insults and taunts Elizabeth would sling out at her. Walsingham had taught her how not to react to Elizabeth. He had taught her how to digest and retain information. Letting one's quarry talk too much was a gift of surprising delights. She enjoyed watching people squirm and talk incessantly. Their misfortune would be beneficial to her. Elizabeth had no idea how informed she was about her activities. Letting Elizabeth believe she had the upper hand in manners was paramount to remaining in her graces, however, ungratefully she was looked upon in the eyes of her monarch.

Catherine would only wait momentarily, and then she would seek out her quarry.

Cecil

Cecil's Study
Westminster Palace, June 1576

William Cecil known also as Lord Burghley got up from his desk. He reflected on the past few hours' events.

"There is a troubling matter which will have to be dealt with soon, but how." He rubbed his chin with his thumb over and over again.

Cecil's thoughts ran over the events which had led him into this quandary. The traveller, as she had been referred to, was gaining more information about his sovereign than he liked. Or was it that the people who had contact with her were exaggerating her capabilities?

The rumours circulating about the traveller were spreading and multiplying in their manner. It was not the mere lies of her apparent presence everywhere which concerned him so much, but the witchcraft and sorcery that were being bandied about. This could be useful in her interrogation, but it would present problems of state if she were not to be tried for them.

"If she is possessing of the knowledge that has been spread, perhaps it would be advantageous to keep her locked up and divulged of the secrets she has acquired. But this journal it must be found, and its source must be kept secret."

·Walsingham is not the only one who has contacts on our streets, he thought.

"I'm aware of your foraging excursions to the docklands seeking our traveller. I too will know when she has been recaptured." Cecil put down his quill. Now was not the time to be writing missives on the subject of foreign spies. Now was the time to think and find solutions to this problem and erase this inconvenience from the minds of London's inhabitants.

Cecil stood up, shook his head and then dropped it back down upon his clasped fingers now snug against his chest. His brow furled, creased and un-creased, with each pacing step like a bobbing bird upon the wave.

"Such a to-do. Such a to-do," he murmured.

"What is the best for England and Her Majesty? That is what is important. That is what I will do." And with that, he lowered his hands and brought up his chin.

"I must make a list of possibilities and their outcomes."

Cecil sat down upon his cushioned seat and wrapped his cloak across his leggings. A chill had risen within his bones, and he shrugged his shoulders together and shook his head and arms about until the circulation stimulated his thoughts enough that he could sit. He began:

Is she an enemy or an ally?
What knowledge does she possess?
What religion does she profess to believe, and
are we to believe all that she speaks of it?
Does she possess the convictions of the pope?
Does she mean to undermine the queen
with messages from his Holiness?
Whom does she report to?

Into the Mouth of the Kraken

Does her knowledge infringe on
our sovereigns abilities?
Will she be useful in our advancement
against the Spanish and the Portuguese?
What knowledge does she possess of the queen?
What characteristics of our queen is she aware of?
Will she use this to her advantage,
or will the queen be offended?
Will I have to remedy the queen's conscience to keep
this traveller alive or render her to the gallows?
Who are her contacts? This might be to our advantage
if the sources of these contacts can be trusted.
Could she be hidden for her own
protection from the people?
She must be made to either disappear or
be seen as a witch, spy, an ally, traveller,
court fool or even a magician.
What will be the outcome of her lies?
Will this traveller bring us into war with Spain?
Or will she avert us from disaster upon the seas?
Does she ally with the French, the
Dutch, the Spanish or the pope?
Is she of French, English, Scottish,
Irish or of Dutch stock?
Is there Spanish or Portuguese blood within her veins?
Where does she come from?
Is this land of the traveller known to our realm?
Why does she come? Is it to seek knowledge
of our tradesman and merchants?

Whom does she travel with, and why
does he not keep her in check?
What is it that she seeks, and can it be kept from her?
What superior qualities does she possess,
if any? Are they worth availing of?

This will surface under interrogations, thought Cecil. The traveller must be made to swear allegiance to the sovereign and make promises to the protection of this realm. She must abide by the rules of the council and Her Majesty if she is to remain in this kingdom uninvited.

This traveller possesses the elusiveness of a spy and the ease of a whore. Her mannerisms are charming, and she easily slips past men-at-arms. She has allowed the queen to see her and leave without fear of reprisal. She has a magical quality that relaxes and irks once she has left.

Her tongue is that of familiar but distant. Is it advanced in its progress or retarded in its growth? She lacks fear in her countenance and determination in her looks. She neither lingers about to be seen or noticed, nor does she hurry in her retreat. Instead, she elicits curiosity and admiration. She is a force to be reckoned with and reconciled too. Far too much power to be held by a woman of such low rank, he thought.

Cecil put his quill down and closed his eyes. This was a matter to be dealt with immediately.

"I must write another note highlighting these objectives and problems for the queen. This traveller may or may not be trouble for this realm, but she must be found out, and her outcome must be reported to stem this tide of rumours from its current course of disorder."

He breathed in the smell of the wax from his candle and lit another one from its flame and placed it closer to his writing table. Its light helped him view more clearly what he had written down in haste. He glanced over the document and quickly reread what he had written. He knew that something was missing but couldn't quite come to terms with addressing it in public.

A spirit lose amongst the populace would be a frightening occurrence. He had had images of his late wife wandering in his house for years now. He spoke to her softly when they were alone. He missed her company greatly, but he could not divulge this to anyone, especially the queen.

But his acute sense of the underworld and of the world where sprits arose from, lingered at the tips of his fingers, and he was itching to put pen to paper the niggling thoughts that invaded his being at present. But he could not release them onto the world. This was a world to which such sensitivities did cost lives.

If he could be but a few moments alone in her company, then he could be assured of her allegiance to the queen. Spirits rose and disappeared all the time. Some possessed enormous powers over others, and then some just merely wanted to be seen again and rub past their former places of residence, lingering, hovering, and prowling around what once was theirs.

It did no good to chase them, but leave them be, thought Cecil. Perhaps that was all this traveller really was. Someone from the past, trying to regain some former life, even if it were only momentarily?

Somehow, though, this presence was much stronger. Its spirit was growing stronger, and its time amongst us needed to be stymied before...the rumours became too much to squash and control.

Cecil rose again from his chair and took the vellum and his thoughts out of his chambers. Elizabeth must be informed of this presence and soon.

Sin

Bermondsey's Shores June 1576

The six priests hovered around the hearth's fire and rubbed their hands vigorously. They had gathered in secret. Their purpose was to discuss the troubling aspect of a foreigner in their midst. Being Catholic was only somewhat tolerated of late, and a restlessness had invaded their bones. The sighting of this traveller had brought fear amongst the parishioners. And calming the nerves of an already compromised flock was straining their dwindling reserves.

Although the Protestant queen's tolerance was known to be just, so also was her resolve to change her opinions. Elizabeth's temperament was not to be relied upon, as she could be fickle, hard to please and was seldom trusted by devout Catholics. It was always best to remain vigilant, quiet and unseen.

The restlessness abroad and across the sea to Ireland was disruptive and milked little favour with the queen's ministers. The only promising note was the constancy of her secretary, William Cecil, but he was a known Protestant, and the winds of change in favour of Protestant convictions was disturbing, rubbing off the veil of complacency and tolerance.

"There is talk of a spirit amongst us, who floats within our realm and makes reference to being present upon our shores in the far distant future. This is the devil's work! Witchcraft! Blasphemy must be exorcized. While some fearful peasants cling to the church, such utter nonsense threatens to scatter our flock and cannot be tolerated. We must put a stop to such talk. Let us preach the importance of the one true faith and restore these mindless parishioners. The consequences of heretical thought will be banishment from heaven."

"Here, here," were the murmurs of assent.

"You must bring your parishioners back into the arms of God, the true God. For there is only one God. He has no pretense. You know who your discounters are. Bring them into confessional. Make them repent their sins. These lies and blasphemous tales are the road to a fall from grace. Gather in your flock and arm them with the Lord's fury for their error in judgments. Forgive them for straying and elicit from them the source of this most unrighteous soul."

"Are you suggesting we gather evidence to prosecute this dissident problem?"

"Why, yes. We must remove this blemish of its sin. We shall exorcize this devil. Blasphemy must be met by the hardness of stone upon its back. Seek out and destroy the problem at hand. We must gather strength from this incursion into our faithful flock. Bring forth the rock of knowledge and stone the problem at hand."

"This is a forbidden practice at present." The priests nodded in unison.

"Then we must pursue this in the privacy of our parish. The flock must be protected from the evil which lurks. We shall take it to the crypts, beneath the earth's crusts and bury this problem with the other dissenters."

"Do you propose to leave this problem underneath the church's structure. Surely you suggest only temporarily holding it in the vaults below?"

"Here, here, surely not in the crypts…"

" I concur."

"Surely we cannot sanctify this soul within church walls."

"It must be met with death somewhere other than within the grace of our church."

"Perhaps it could be left outside of the city's walls where no connection to the church could be seen."

"Surely a burial would not be necessary for such a heretic's soul."

"Here, here," quipped the priests in unison.

"The act of the stoning must be carried out below ground closer to the fires of hell, from whence it has surely come from. But the body must be left clear of church grounds. Let it rot in the fields beyond Bermondsey's outer city walls."

A further murmur of assent and nodding of heads sealed this latest agreement amongst them.

"Now go, pray for a quick retrieval of this heretical soul's sin. We are bound by our faith to eliminate this filth before it infects our flock."

Chosen Ones

Elizabeth's Privy Chamber
1576

Elizabeth had received Cecil's letter. She opened it again and quickly closed it when she heard the rustle of skirts behind her. This was indeed alarming. She had not wanted her secretary to be involved with such matters. She looked up to see her lovely smiling governess fussily tidying her desk.

"What is it that worries you so, Lizzy?" asked Kat Astley.

"It is nothing, dear Kat. I have issues to deal with regarding the traveller whom you met briefly earlier in my sister's chambers. She is beginning to make herself known in too many quarters of my realm."

Elizabeth sighed and picked up her quill. She would need to write a quick response back to Cecil. She would order him not to engage in any activities that would indicate his knowledge of the traveller's whereabouts.

Elizabeth indicated with a nod for Kat to sit down. She put the quill down again and looked into the eyes of her governess. She extended her hand and touched the softness of the older woman's skin. Gently she caressed the delicate warmth.

"I have need of your services. I wish to write a note to my dearest Cecil. But I fear that there are eyes and ears about that will misconstrue my intentions. Therefore I would like to send you on a task. Please ask Sir William Cecil if he would attend upon me presently in my privy chambers. I wish for him to bring his papers as I have a writ, which must be signed in his presence. It concerns the traveller but do not tell him such. Only that I wish for his presence immediately."

"No, wait. Sit a while longer. I shall write out a short note. Give it to no one except him alone."

Elizabeth penned a quick note and sealed her missive with wax and the ring she wore on her finger.

Kat reached over the desk and retrieved the note. She placed it in the bosom of her dress. She winked at Her Majesty, curtsied and turned to leave the room.

"Kat," hissed Elizabeth.

Her governess turned quickly in alarm and quickly returned to Elizabeth's side. She leaned in close. Familiar with the wiles of her charge's moods. "Yes, Lizzy, how may I help you further?"

Elizabeth nodded her head. "Yes. When he has read this and put it back down, retrieve it from him and either throw it upon his burning fire or return it to your bosom."

The two women gazed knowingly. This was a common occurrence with Cecil when Elizabeth wished to keep him from harm and accusations. This he understood. She hoped that it would end the matter of further discussion upon the topic. But to write a writ with him she must. The wording would be crucial in order for him to be without blame for the outcome of this traveller. Elizabeth wanted that traveller found along with her journal. This confounding bloody journal with all its disturbing words and notations would have its consequences if discovered by dissenting villains. Walsingham would need to be consulted further as well, Elizabeth thought, and quickly.

"Quietly, softly, impart this note and news unto him my dear. I am dependent on your good services once again."

Kat nodded her head and went about the business at hand. She gathered up her skirts and headed out of the privy chambers. She knew which exits and hallways to find. Cecil would be in his study busying himself with the affairs of state. He liked to work alone, but was generally watched whenever he communicated with Her Majesty. Elizabeth placed a great value on his worth. She rarely made state decisions without first consulting him. His intelligence was formidable, but his tact was not.

Kat had always admired Cecil. He was a married man, who did not wonder. At times she had wished that he might, but she could never compromise Elizabeth's trust for the want of a good man. Her need to protect Elizabeth was greater than any other need she possessed. She had understood the trust between them. Elizabeth's need for control over men and her realm had equalled Kat's desire to maintain that image and remain faithful to Elizabeth.

I too will not be ruled by a man, thought Kat.

Elizabeth viewed her governess retreat with a knowingness of her intent. She would follow her instructions to the letter. Elizabeth's thoughts now wondered back to Cecil.

He was brilliant and the only man whom she could trust completely. There were many writs upon her hand that were mirror images of ones Cecil had in fact laid out before her. Their thought processes had become predictable, each considerate and respectful of the other's, each viewing the pros and cons of any decisions they made with equal verve and intensity.

Some days Elizabeth wondered if any progress would be made in her court. She relied heavily on Cecil in public matters of state but not subtle negotiations nor populous interventions. That was a job best suited to her spymaster, Walsingham. Rarely did she involve Walsingham in the boring anecdotal matters at court. His intrigues of late were of no interest to her.

Walsingham's insistence of Mary Queen of Scots plans to overthrow her kingdom was boring at best. However, Walsingham had prevented Mary from pleading her innocence in person and had kept Mary safely ensconced from public view. His knowledge of the circumstances of the courtly life and the mood of her people were things Elizabeth had entrusted to Walsingham alone. His intuition had served both of them well, so far.

"Walsingham…yes, I must engage upon his services," she whispered to herself. "When matters of the mind and my safety are concerned, then you are my man."

This realm as Elizabeth knew and understood it, was best left to her control. She alone would judge when it was necessary to engage in war and rage upon the Catholics who challenged her sovereignty. Elizabeth knew better than to enrage a man of King Phillip's personality into an act of war against her, a foolish endeavour that only kings would indulge their vain senses.

Elizabeth rose from her desk and headed for the rooms in which her ladies-in-waiting would be. She sought out the company of her ladies and spent a few moments listening to their comparisons of the silks, which had just arrived. She had to admire the cloth. It was of superior quality. Its silkiness was a pleasure to have next to her skin and to rub with the tips of her fingers.

The women would, of course, not be making the gowns they held, only adorning them with precious stones and embroidering of the current fashions. The attention to detail and the trimness of the fit were of consequence to her seamstresses.

Elizabeth had many ideas on the subject of her holiness and how she was to be viewed in the eyes of her realm. Her wardrobe, she reflected, had but one sole purpose. To make all who beheld her believe in the sanctity of her holiness. God's one true representative. It was her divine right to lead this doctrinal standard for her kingdom.

The pope, Gregory XIII had excommunicated Elizabeth from the Catholic Church and state. Gregory had mobilized a Catholic world dedicated in its obedience to him. In Gregory's opinion no king and certainly not this bastard queen, would be equal to him in status. There was only one anointed representative on earth who spoke for God, and his name was Pope Gregory.

He had issued decree after decree to Elizabeth informing her in biblical terms that Elizabeth was no head of church and therefore also of its state. All Catholics upon England and Ireland's shores were to obey his edicts not hers. The inappropriateness of Elizabeth's holy stated claim, he had informed Elizabeth was blasphemy. Elizabeth had been excommunicated from his Holy Roman Church just as her father Henry had been before her. Elizabeth smiled at the inappropriateness of his remarks.

Elizabeth's convictions of her right to be the head of England's church and lands did not need the authority of a backward, corrupt religion. Her supremeness was God-given. Elizabeth needed no man to impart orders upon her realm. Therefore her royal-state-of-being dictated her gowns to be ever so more prominently fashioned. As the head of the Protestant faith she needed to equal or better her Catholic counterparts. No pope would adorn as fine a cloth as she.

To establish one's superiority, one no doubt had to display one's wealth, even when it was not so apparently seen by her of late. The populous would never know. It was the poor who needed to see greatness, and she could give that to them.

She also saw to the needs of her yeoman. They too would need fine clothes to adorn their backs and legs. It was the symbol of wealth and power, which was so much more important in the eyes of the public. It impressed upon them that she knew what she was doing and could do it well.

Elizabeth enjoyed her encounters with the faithful Englishmen and women of her realm. She wished to be seen amongst them caring for their needs, even when she could not. Her ladies-in-waiting adored the attentions of the flocks that followed them around or made great bowing curtsies.

She had tried to address the needs of the poor by imploring the nobles of her city and counties to engage them in honest work and give them good wages. She had asked them to provide for the needy when they needed it most, but that was as far as she had dictated. Balancing the respect of her nobles and the needs of the poor was at times irritating and complex. Loyalty was more important than dealing with the backstabbing precipitated by taxation of her wealthier citizens. Let the poor of her cities pay the bulk of the taxes and imply that equal portions of taxation had indeed been retrieved from the rich.

The uneducated need not know the truth of the matter. So it did them no good in the knowing and caused infinite more trouble than it was worth in sorting out.

When the time presented itself, Elizabeth nodded at her ladies-in-waiting, the need for a private encounter with her sister Catherine. She excused herself from the ladies and ascended the cold hard spiral staircase leading up to her rooms.

Elizabeth sat upon the chair she most liked in her sister's rooms. She waited until she heard the quick brusque swish of Catherine's skirts before averting her eyes to the window's ledge. She realized all too soon the cold bite of the evening's summer winds would soon be bearing down upon her again.

Elizabeth thought now of the need to hold on to the warmth of the new eve's last rays from the comfort of her castle and estate at Hampton. Hunting and dancing were far more enjoyable than the confines of Westminster at present. And it would do her citizens good to see her out and about the town in Richmond. It would do Elizabeth's mind infinitely more good, to be enjoying herself rather than worrying about the presence of a spy or this traveller amongst her citizenry.

Catherine curtsied more abruptly than she should have. Elizabeth raised an eyebrow in displeasure at the feebleness of its intent.

"Catherine, do not forget the need to keep your habits plain and simple. A good curtsey towards me will never do you any harm. But this lack of deference will someday lead to your head being placed upon the spikes outside of London's gates."

Catherine reddened and curtsied gracefully again, nodding her head in Her Majesty's direction.

"It is just that we have much to discuss. This woman who roams about your realm, she knows a great deal about matters which are not of her concern."

"So you found her? Where is she?"

"She has escaped my presence, but she is spreading rumours of the kind that must be stopped. She claims to know of another Queen Elizabeth upon English soil, one who does not hold the same powers at court as you do presently. Surely you see the need now to capture and eliminate her? She is a danger to your person, Your Majesty." Catherine swept Elizabeth an even deeper bow.

"That is nonsense, Catherine. There is no other Queen Elizabeth of England at present other than myself. And there will only be one Queen Elizabeth in my realm, not two as you so state."

Elizabeth stared hard at the eyes, which drew in and wrinkled their brows back at her. Catherine had been impertinent to suggest that this other queen held no power over her court. However, this was a troubling aspect to consider. The chaos, which would ensue if these rumours were to be bandied about, would be enough to plant the seed of fear amongst the populace and stir divisional loyalties amongst her nobles. Elizabeth waved her hand at Catherine indicating she wanted her to sit.

"Be quiet about this silly notion of another Queen Elizabeth. I have other things for you to concern yourself with at present."

Catherine looked up and grinned. She would not drop this subject so easily. She would store it for future use. Catherine too had needs to meet out.

"Yes, Your Majesty. What is it that you wish of me?"

Elizabeth lifted her hand to the back of her head and rubbed the itching spot. She enjoyed the contact of skin on scalp and moved her head around pushing it into the extended finger, which probed this most uncomfortable spot beneath her wig. She longed for the relief of her lavender oil and then dismissed the urge and quit her finger.

She did not trust Catherine entirely and would see to it that she would remain guarded and watched by Walsingham for some time. She approved how he used her. She too had used Catherine's charms and exploits for her own purposes. Catherine, she recalled, had requested once to take part in the playhouses outside of the city's walls. It was forbidden for woman to engage and act upon the stage. Only foreign women chose this reckless career choice. Catherine was a fool who longed for excitements. Fortunately, there were plenty of excursions

Elizabeth and Walsingham could send her out on. It was Walsingham who had suggested she be used for gathering secrets from the men who presided at Elizabeth's court.

Elizabeth swung around towards her half-sister and cousin.

"I have need of finding Master Robert. I wish to know where he is at present. I have a job for him to do that needs your help as well. Go and find him…if you can!! And bring him back here with you this time. Do not leave his side. However much you enjoy his company, it is also my wish that you not tarry." Elizabeth's black eyes bore down into that of Catherine's.

Catherine's eyes twinkled in anticipation of this opportunity to meet with Master Robert Dudley alone. She had always enjoyed the company of this finely dressed man. And the similarity of the sisters increased his interest in her, she was sure of it.

What was it that Elizabeth wanted of him? Perhaps this did not matter so much as that she was at last to be in the company of such a man, on the orders of the queen no less. Walsingham need not know of this most promising adventure. That traveller and her references to another Queen Elizabeth could wait.

"I will be in my writing chamber. See to it that he is brought there. Be quick about it. Now go!" Elizabeth rose before Catherine had time to react to this latest command from her sister.

She watched as Elizabeth strode off down the stairs. She followed softly, quickly, hesitating only when she felt she could be seen or heard. Walsingham had taught her well, Catherine thought. Elizabeth never knows how closely I trail her, she concluded.

"I know exactly where he is at present," mumbled Catherine to herself. She had been instructed to inform Walsingham every time Robert Dudley got too intimate with Elizabeth. Walsingham needed Elizabeth to keep her virginity intact for the advancement of this realm, he had said. Only then could he induce the likes of a Dutch or German prince onto the shores of England.

Catherine smiled at the thought of Elizabeth under the spell of a German prince, but Catherine also understood the need for that prince to be well educated and well spoken. He would have to know much about the languages that are spoken at this court. Elizabeth's ease with speaking Latin, German, French and Italian had amazed most of the foreign dignitaries, who came to avail themselves at her feet. Catherine enjoyed the simpering sweetness of their sickly tongues. She understood all too well the intent of their presence.

Catherine could glean much information for Walsingham about the intention of these persistent warriors. And she loved to hide behind them, coming upon them quietly and blowing her warm breath produced the startle of fear Catherine so much liked to see in them. She could smell their sweat and almost taste the salt emitting from their skins. Catherine recalled how much she liked to lick the salt off a man's neck and enjoyed a goodly nip and hold of a tongue now and again.

Catherine hurried down the stairwell leading out into the small garden. She knew where Robert Dudley liked to preen himself in preparation for his visits to Elizabeth, her queen. Robbie also enjoyed entertaining certain ladies at court. And Catherine enjoyed watching him keep himself physically strong and lean. Often he could be found practising his archery and instructing his men-at-arms. Robert liked to challenge them to games of strength and endurance. He made sure that the queen's privy windows were nearby. Visibility of his skills and his mannerisms towards his men were attributes to be desired by all but especially by women.

The peacock, as Catherine had nicknamed him, was willing and able to strut himself with regularity. She closed her eyes temporarily and recalled the fleshy smell of men sweating. And there were several of Robbie's men whom she particularly liked to taste, but today she was interested in the sucking of saltiness from Robbie's earlobe and the flicking of that earlobe around her tongue. She had long yearned for the chance to be alone with him. And now that Elizabeth had ordered her to find him and bring him back, she intended to do just that. If it meant delaying him en route…well, her little peacock could rut away and Elizabeth need never know. Catherine skipped and ran across the stone enclosure towards the sentry's post. She could see him smiling at her.

"Hmm, I know how to please you and get my way," she murmured quietly. Men are such fools and so easily distracted she mused.

"Ah, but what delights they hold beneath their hose." She liked to see anticipation glow upon cheeks when she pressed against loins and the catch of their speech when she reached deep inside a man's groin. A little squeeze was easy to do and produced such luscious desires from clenched teeth and wetting lips.

Her own moistening anticipation for Robbie's lust and searching hands stirred her onwards. She would leave no doubt about her intentions when she met him. And any alleyway would do, she thought. He cannot refuse me when I am so availing of knowledge for him, especially from Elizabeth.

London's Bridge

June 1576

Tower Bridge was teeming with the lives of her resident merchants, as shopkeepers plied their wares outside of their cramped shops. The streets were less visibly slippery with London's filth from here. Chamber pots could be easily emptied over its edges into the swirlling Thames. The Thames, however, had its own filth to seep into the bones of its only bridge. Corpses periodically jammed underneath its ramparts at either end of the bridge. The dampness of mould was a frequent destroyer of timber supports. This city within a city hung out over the edges of stone, hovering above the ebbing stench of the Thames.

Tower Bridge's twenty curved, Gothic-like arches stretched three hundred yards across the Thames. Its stone surface extended forty darkened paces in width across. Rats rarely saw the light of day within the squashed houses that hovered above its stone surface, the breadth of which extended ten paces beyond the cold stones of its edges. Wooden supports required frequent repairs. Chamber pots were generally emptied at low tide. It helped to keep the slurry of human waste farthest from the bridge's inhabitants. The tide washed the rest upstream. Spiral stairs winding four floors ever upwards garnered its populace exceptional views on days of less corrupted air.

Walsingham's urchins had run across Tower Bridge's breadth onto Bermondsey's shores. They had skipped and laughed all the way across the bridge. Their instructions included keeping quiet until they had reached the church next to the bear-baiting pens. Walsingham had insisted on creating a diversion for the women he pursued. Churches were known sanctuaries, even Catholic ones. And he had surmised that the chased would seek refuge wherever they could.

Bermondsey only had one church. The urchin's goal was to draw attention to themselves, and thus distract the hated Catholic priests Walsingham so measurably wanted dispatched. To be a Catholic was not deemed a sin as of yet, although it brimmed on the rim of heresy, and therefore if openly practised, could subjugate its adherent's to the rack, a device developed by Catholics to torture supplicants into confession for their sins. An ironic twist returned upon the original perpetrators of extinguishing wickedness and sin.

Of course there was also other means of torture, burning alive at the stake, for one's wickedness against the church's doctrine, continued to be a crowd pleaser. It was a slow painful death so unlike the boring alternative, the chopping off of one's head with an axe. However, no mercy was shown to any of these sinful victims. The stake involved tying an unfortunate individual to a central stake or post, placed prominently within a favoured site. Piles of straw and twigs were bundled around the hapless soul encased within its kindling. The wetter the debris, the longer the victim lasted. In God's mind to burn one's soul alive, prepared it for a clean emergence into God's holy hands once more. Smoked and roasted to death was always a crowd pleaser.

The Thames tide revealed all of London's transgressions. The little wherries, which crossed her breadth, bumped their way onto worn docks. It was always best for travellers to cross at the ebb tide, but it was easier on the unaccustomed eyes and nose to pass at high tide, thereby lessening the burning vapours, which accompanied rotting drowned flesh and sewage. Low tide revealed more, however, than the stench of decay into one's nostrils. Children scampered across barnacled rubbish. They sloshed their way through oozing mud recovering sodden clothing or boots. They dug deep into the festering bodies recovering hoped for wealth encased within the pouches of its victims. If a dead seal or fish looked recently expired, it could be brought ashore and sold or eaten.

Once inside the church, gathering around the robed men, Walsingham's urchins pulled at sleeves and the sacred cloth of God. They cursed the traveller, taunting the anointed men of the papist faith.

"She comes to eat us, Your Grace. She is a witch. Please protect us from her."

The priest, Reginald, grabbed hold of the first urchin he could and shook him into silence. He slapped him hard across the face.

Malcolm winced, and squeezed his cheek to quell the burn of the sting. He glared back at this black robed enemy. It was worth the penny he thought.

"Be still, foolish boy. There are no witches inside this church. For if there were, we would know. It is our job. What makes you say such blasphemous tellings?"

David and Elway hesitated before backing away from the priests. They did not want to be slapped as well. They knew they could not leave. Not until Malcolm was free of the priest's grasp. The boys exchanged glances and Elway rubbed the stones which lay tucked inside his pouch. He fingered them long enough for Malcolm to see and smiled.

"We have seen her," said David. "She is with the woman who married Master Owen."

The priests, Albert, Edward, Reginald and Francis looked around the nave and quickly scanned the pews before them.

"Master Owen sent us to warn you, Your Grace," Elway lied. He quickly dropped his head in a bow. "The witch comes to take his wife Edith away with her. The witch must be found and retained, Your Grace."

"What costume does she wear, child? Tell us now," snapped Francis.

"We do not know," said Malcolm quickly. "But she comes with the Protestant Edith who married your Catholic friend Owen."

"We know of whom you speak. But why, say you, would she walk this way with a witch?"

"She does not know it, Your Grace, for she is under the witch's spell."

"Who told you she was a witch?"

"Owen did, Your Grace. He told us to tell you to make ready. You must protect the church from her. She carries amulets with snake's blood in them. She pours them over the souls of her victims to cleanse them of godly thought."

Reginald released Malcolm from his grip and sneered at the other boys within his church. He walked over to his font and dipped his fingers into its cleansing waters. He wanted to wash the stench of these urchins from his hands. He shook with delight at the thought of exercising his rights to rid his church of a witch.

"Tell Owen," he said, "that I wish to speak with him. I will convey more news of his wife when and if she comes our way."

His lips curled upward. He sneered at each of Walsingham's urchins. He would decide if this woman was a witch. Owen's Catholic loyalties could be relied on, he thought, but Walsingham's Protestant devotions, however, were not to be trusted.

Francis lifted his head up to God and mouthed a silent thank you to God for the news he had just received. "Your work, my Lord, will have its revenge," he whispered softly.

"Be gone from this holy place. Do not tell anyone of what you speak. Do not tell the flock of God what you have seen and heard. For God will roast your souls in hell if you do."

Francis stomped towards the boys with his arms outstretched at his sides. The urchin boys ran outside, around the side of church and climbed up the stones to its stained glass windows until they could peep through to see what the priests were doing. After seeing each priest lay down on the floor between the aisles in a prone position, the boys jumped back down and ran to hide within the churchyard's stone monuments. Malcolm climbed a nearby tree and perched himself within its branches. As instructed they would wait to report on the musky black robed Catholic warriors.

Terminating The Unnecessary

Elizabeth's Chambers
June 1576

Elizabeth reviewed the note penned by Cecil. "Questions. Questions. Always questions with you, dear Cecil. How you do complicate the issues so."

Elizabeth paced the room, rubbing her pearls for comfort. She could smell the fires of this irksome traveller's heresy. The traveller would burn in the fires of hell, her citizens would see to it. And if not they, then surely her church wardens would. She sighed. A witch is a dangerous person to be. I shall find it hard not to let them have her.

"But I cannot…"

Elizabeth held up the letter to the light emitting from the window closest to her hearth. She read Cecil's words over and over again. She shook her head and stood silently listening for footsteps. No, none, she thought.

"What knowledge does she possess of this realm?"

"Why had I let her go?"

"How is it that she escapes capture so easily? How does this traveller impart trust and quiet to one's nerves with such ease? Indeed perhaps Cecil is right. She must be interrogated. And the interrogation of the traveller must be kept quiet. Her removal from London must be seen too at once. I will see to the traveller being removed to Hampton Court, forthwith. I will see to her wants and mine and keep her safe for the present being," she muttered.

Elizabeth paced her rooms now that she had concluded her thoughts. Patience was not one of her virtues.

"Waiting. Waiting. Waiting. Why must I wait so for these fools? Where are you, Cecil? We have words to discuss," she snapped.

Elizabeth stomped about her rooms. She no longer wished to pace, and fury was rising with each step. Her breathing had quickened, her pulse throbbed at her finger's grasp upon the damned letter. She walked quickly over to the fire and fanned the flames sending sparks and smoke up the chimney's blackened flue.

"See, see the fires that will burn ye, you irksome woman? I know you can feel its heat. And I shall see to it that you do."

Elizabeth straightened up when she heard movements and voices. She placed her hands behind her back and fanned at the fire behind her. Her stomach gurgled, and she noted that it was time to eat. Hunger was ever-present in her pit. She did not like to gorge herself in front of her court or ladies-in-waiting. Her father's monstrous appetite had at times sickened her. She had hated the way people had implied he was grotesque, large beyond his years. They had not said as much, but their snippets and whisperings when he began to eat were apparent. Kat had informed her of this many times as had Catherine. Both were loyal to her, but with varying degrees of intensity, she had concluded. How does one keep one's stomach full with such infuriating distractions?

Elizabeth watched as the outer door to her chamber was opened. Quietly her two most trusted companions slipped in. Cecil was demure in his dark clothing. Kat in her lively way was radiant beside the man she secretly adored. Both looked at their queen with concern.

"I have brought you your secretary, Your Majesty. Shall I go and leave you to your discussions?"

"Yes...ah but first bring us some refreshments. I am tired and need some cakes. Please bring up some sweets and a pie, some cheese and the wine."

"Yes, Your Majesty. I am sorry that I am remiss in this as I know it is late already, and I should have...."

"No, no dear Kat. This is not of your doing. When you have seen to the food for me, bring along some stitching, sit beside us here by the fire." It will seem less formal then if anyone else enters," especially Walsingham, thought Elizabeth. She needed him too on this matter, but first she had to decide upon the fate of this creature and elicit enough information from Cecil as was necessary. And she would do all of that before Kat's return.

Elizabeth smiled at Kat and gently waved her off with a floating hand and dropped a slight nod to her elder companion.

Cecil watched as the two ladies graceful movements towards one another were carried out.

He had been brought up to notice these small courtesies and enjoyed seeing them played out with such fondness. His late wife had shown him such loving kindness. It was as natural to her as breathing, he thought. His wife had been a kindly woman in an unkindly world, but she was gone now, and so now he enjoyed viewing other's courtesies instead. It gave him hope of a better world to come, one whose success he hoped to help build.

Elizabeth turned to her secretary and indicated he should proceed closer to the fire. Cecil understood Elizabeth needed to discuss his note with urgency. He was to stoke the fire as usual when they met like this. The rustle and crack of the logs would cover their voices, but only temporarily. He would have to talk quickly to make his point heard.

This woman who travelled about this realm so easily must be stopped and put to...put to what, he wondered. She was troublesome, but she did have advantages that he thought could be useful in this realm.

"Elizabeth," he said. "She must be found and questioned. She has knowledge which might be gained for our... pardon Your Majesty, your realm."

"Sit Cecil, we must discuss this quickly."

Elizabeth looked over her shoulders for signs of movement behind the two tapestries that she knew had space to hide behind. The chambers doors were closed, and her stairwell door was closed and locked. She had seen to that earlier. She had covered the listening holes placed about the room. In fact she had plugged them with stale cheese and crumbs from her last snatch at food earlier in the day.

"You mentioned her contacts Cecil and her knowledge. How is it that she has these things, and why do you worry about them so?" she said.

"Dearest Elizabeth, it is the feeling she brings with her when she is present."

"Ah, yes...that...quieting...calmness...that descends in her presence. Is this some form of a trickster, do you think?"

"No, I too have felt it. She is like a box when opened, bringing relief and a hint of joy. And when it is closed and she is gone, it brings with it worry and complexities to the mind."

"I concur. She is like a favourite plaything, which has been snatched away suddenly. Longing for it is both irksome and sinfully pleasing. But find her we must, for if she is to fall into the wrong hands and is abused or misled, she could become troublesome, even dangerous if found."

Elizabeth and Cecil's eyes met. Each searched the other's dilated pupils and raised brows. The fire snapped them apart. Elizabeth breathed deeply, and Cecil recovered his thoughts whilst flaming the fires embers.

"This rose journal of hers…"

"Ah, so you too have seen it. It possesses much knowledge. It must be found, but it has been spied too by others."

"Ah," sighed Cecil. "You too have seen its pages, then, have you not?" Elizabeth nodded her head in agreement.

"Yes. I am shocked by what is written and in such an inferior script! I must get this document and glean more from what is upon its pages." Elizabeth shook her head and fluttered her eyelids. "I do not want fools hands on it. I did not mean you, my dear Cecil."

He nodded in understanding. He knew this monarch well enough. Elizabeth blurted out her thoughts most vigorously, without censuring.

He watched as Elizabeth abruptly stood and snappily waved her hands towards him. She turned and looked down at him, placing her slim hands upon her waist. "What knowledge does she impart that is so vital to this realm, Cecil?"

Cecil patted the hearth's chair and beckoned Elizabeth to sit back down. When she had settled back down, he leaned closer and lightly spoke.

"This we must find out, but my fear is…that whatever it is she knows…will be nothing compared to the stir of interest she will bring…and the unrest that will surely ensue because of her presence."

"Hmm. Yes, I must agree, but that she would or could have importance to my realm, surely not, dear Cecil." She watched as he bent down beside the fire and prodded the embers before placing kindling and logs upon its embers. He breathed in the trailing smoke and enjoyed the heat upon his face and hands.

"She has children with her, and she seeks them out. I have heard her asking for them from Master Drake. He seems to have knowledge of their presence and withholds it from her. It could be a tool for our gain as well."

Elizabeth got up quickly from her chair and paced the room. She placed her hands on her hips, again holding Cecil's letter pressed against her side.

"She has children with her...foolish woman? We must find them."

"Yes," he said, "she will be more willing to cooperate should we have them to hand, but you must show her kindness. I believe she does not want to harm you."

Elizabeth turned and looked down upon her kneeling subject. Cecil is right, Elizabeth thought.

"She does not want to harm me. How can you be so sure? Every true Catholic in Christendom wishes me cast out as the pope has dictated. How can you be so sure she is not of the Catholic persuasion, my dear Cecil?"

"No, she is not, of that I am sure, Your Highness," he bowed from his crouched position next to the fire.

"Ahhh...Cecil, clever as always." Elizabeth frowned. "How do you know this?" She demanded.

"As always Elizabeth, your kindly elder governess has informed me. She noted no cross worn about the traveller's person. No adornments. She is of the Protestant faith. A Catholic always wears some adornment. It is their way. However, Kat is worried. I have attempted to belay these fears of hers for your safety."

Cecil looked away from Elizabeth and into the fire. He needed to reflect and redirect his monarch. He needed to change the pace and fury of her heated angst.

"Kat is aging, is she not? Do not the aged worry so much more than the young?" smiled Cecil.

Elizabeth nodded in agreement and sat back down with a plump.

"So who else knows of her existence? Do you presume to know as much of this matter as well?" she snapped.

"There are others, and rumours do spread quickly, too quickly. Tongues are waggling already. We must meet this outbreak of gossip and squash its spread or ramp up it's telling."

"Why?"

"You know as well as I do that you must catch your prey by chasing it with fury, scare it into playing dead and then pluck its usefulness from it. If that means ending its life, then so be it. But if it proves worthy and useful, then you must protect it and make it swear allegiances to Your Majesty. It will want to play with you then. And it could be that this traveller has some advantages for us…Your Majesty's realm. She must know a great deal about it. I can feel it deep within my bones."

Elizabeth's eyes widened, and she arched her eyebrow.

"I watched her play out her act with Drake when he was molesting her in the privy gardens earlier today," replied Cecil.

"She showed great courage, and her mannerisms were that of a woman on a mission. She convinced him to let her go. He walked away from her. She has powers over men. You might find her skills useful in the controlling of some of your disaffected adversaries. Those who want something from you…may find her…or shall I say, this traveller may be made to find…make herself useful to us."

"You are beginning to sound more like my spy master than my secretary, Cecil." But her smile was evident upon her face. She had straightened in her chair, and her regal mind was at once off in its darkness, thinking, plotting and worrying.

Elizabeth had not wanted Cecil involved in this matter. She had wanted to protect him from the consequences of this traveller's presence in her realm, but it was now too late, and she sighed. Getting up again Elizabeth blew her frustrations out through her nose and humphed and stomped her way around the room. As her thoughts carried her onward her pacing slowed, and she began to replace her fury with action.

Although Cecil had become involved now, perhaps his talents for notation and wit could be used for the purposes of recording all who had come into contact with the traveller. His value would be twofold, she thought. Firstly, he could record the sightings, and secondly, he could then come up with sound reasoning for those sightings.

The more facts which were laid before Elizabeth, the more she felt she could control this situation to her advantage. Cecil was wise in the matters of state, but she did not want him meddling in the control of populous sentiments. That was Walsingham's position. "Something he does very well, indeed," she said aloud.

"Pardon, Your Highness," said Cecil.

She waved her hand at him distractedly and did not reply.

Cecil was her man of letters and Walsingham that of intrigues. Her men as she revered to them with Kat were agreed on many matters of state but with differing means of outcome. Cecil was her plodder, and Walsingham was her doer, a man of swift action and intent. Walsingham frustrated her intently sometimes with his actions and secrecy. She needed to keep him in close contact in order to be abreast of all his incursions. She would have to summon him next, thought Elizabeth. But first she must address these issues upon which Cecil had sent and put pen to paper.

"Cecil, we must get on with finding out what the traveller knows. We agree that she has knowledge, far beyond the average woman of this realm?"

He inclined his head in her direction and nodded.

"Good. In this case agreement is good. We must come up with reasoning for her greater than normal knowledge if it be questioned."

"Why, surely there can be no reason for a woman to know so much?" replied Cecil.

Elizabeth turned towards him and glared, raising her eyebrow again. She recalled how much she had hated as a child and young woman when men had been so condescending towards her. Only when it became apparent that she would be queen, had Elizabeth enjoyed any sort of freedom from this intolerance to her independent thoughts.

She stomped her foot at him.

"This woman does not come to harm me, but her actions inadvertently might. It is this that we must note and make a plan about. She is after something. It is that something that we must locate. This will reveal all. It may even be to our advantage to find useful purpose for her other than that which she pursues."

Cecil looked away from Elizabeth and bit his tongue to quell his aching heart from speaking of the dreads, which bore down upon his soul. The demons which could be made to come out of hiding in the people's minds by the presence of an unknown mysterious traveller were worrisome and curled the toes within his boots.

"Cecil, you may burn this letter upon which these words convey your deepest worries and fears for the safety of your queen and my realm. I thank you most humbly, but do not fear so. Record only those sightings and come up with a plausible reason for which she may be reckoned to. Together we will gather enough information to either gain such insights as are necessary to the protection of this realm or… enough distrust from the actions which result from this traveller's encounters to render her contrary to her value."

"Your Majesty, please…I am worried."

She would summon Walsingham next, she thought. Elizabeth moved closer to Cecil and gently squeezed his shoulder. They both heard the patter of Kat's footsteps coming with the aforementioned refreshments. Elizabeth smiled broadly.

"Still your heart, good sir. I do know how to terminate the unnecessary."

Escape And Capture

Bermondsey's Shore
June 1576

John Stowe moved slower now that the bear rings were close by. He had noticed too the pair of brown boots, which had followed them along their journey across from Westminster's pier. This must be the man Drake had sent to move this traveller along in her avowed quest, he thought.

"Edith, my child, you must get yourself back to your husband."

"She cannot go back there, Stowe. Owen will hurt her."

"That is not your concern, woman. You have duties to attend to for our mutual friend. Edith must be got from here and soon."

"You are not listening. I will not let her go back to that bruising husband of hers."

Kathleen took hold of Edith's arm and shoved Edith's wrist under Stowe's face.

"Look at what he does to her. He is a beast, not a man. He does not deserve her."

"That may be so, but she will die if she is found near you. Owen and Walsingham will see to that."

Kathleen opened her eyes widely. She looked over at Edith and back again at Stowe shaking his head back and forth.

"No, I will not let her die. She comes with me. I will see to her safety," replied Kathleen.

"You cannot. They are afoot. We are being chased as we speak. You have not even noticed the man who walks quickly beside and all around us. I must speak with him now. He is here to help you get on with the job at hand. Your quest I recall…

"I have no quest. I am here only to rescue my children from this damned awful place. So where are they?"

Stowe looked up and pulled a locket of red hair from his trousers. He proffered it under Kathleen's nose.

"Does it not smell sweet and familiar?"

Kathleen swallowed at the lump, which rose in her throat. She needed to counter this threat at her heart with calm. She took in a long slow breath of air to calm her trembling hands and wondered whether her voice would betray her thoughts.

"There are more than a few whose locks adorn that sinful colour," she spat back at him.

"Ah, but none so finely combed as this. Look how well it shines, dear lady. No street urchin would possess so fine a lock." He lifted his eyes to meet hers and smiled. "You have no choice. Release the woman you call Edith, and I will see to it that your children fare well."

Kathleen licked her dry lips and swallowed the bile, which had risen into her mouth. She hated the taste of vomit and its smell. She needed to control her disbelief and her feelings. Her fingers felt cold and her arms weakened. Get hold of yourself, woman, she heard echoing inside her head. What did it all mean? And then she remembered the anger that she felt once before when threatened by a rogue Rottweiler. How she had hated that dog? How angrily she had responded to it? She had not run away but stood her ground, yelling and swearing at the beast. And then she had chased it all the way back into its yard. Throwing rocks and anything else she could at it. She spat then and reached for the lock of hair.

"I do not run away from danger. And you are only a man." She grasped hold of his hand and dug her nails into his flesh. She released her hold of his hand when the lock was relinquished into hers.

"She stays with me. I will need her to help me. And I will help her. Do not get in my way."

Stowe smiled at the traveller, Kathleen, and dropped his hand back down to his side.

"Who is this person following us? I have seen him as well?" Kathleen recalled the familiarity of his boots. Where had she seen that particular two-toned colour of brown, she thought? It wasn't from this era, or was it?

She enjoyed the look of surprise on his face and understood that he had thought he had the upper hand in their situation. Perhaps they were becoming equals in the game they were playing. She hoped so at any rate? She watched as he looked back across his right shoulder towards the Thames.

"He searches too, lady. It is best if you let me speak to him. Your quest to save this wretched soul before you will be your children's undoing. But perhaps this is the logic of a woman. This sinful disobeying and these thoughtless actions will be your downfall. I have seen this in many women. I do not understand this lack of gratitude and help you and your kind reject from your superiors. You will be best served in your search for your children if you were to think on what you have been sent here to do."

Kathleen raised her head a little higher and glared at Stowe. She turned towards Edith. "Don't believe everything he says. I won't let

267

them harm you." She took hold of Edith's elbow and pulled her near, holding hands. Kathleen could feel the woman trembling. Edith's tear-stained cheeks revealed her fears. Kathleen pulled her close and took Edith's face in her hands.

"I won't let them harm you. I'll take you back with me. I'll find a solution to this problem. He's a man. His tools are to belittle, lie and cheat when he cannot get his own way. Don't be afraid of him or your bastard of a husband."

"You speak from some knowledge," replied the voice at her back.

The hair on Kathleen's back bristled its way up her spine. She had not anticipated this rear advance on her situation. The boots, she thought. He must be the boots that Stowe was referring to.

"I recognize your Spanish voice, sir, but I can assure you too that I am not afraid of either one of you."

She turned slowly towards the Spaniard now grinning at her. His face, even his countenance was familiar, but she could not quite figure it out. His curly dark locks were long, and he had a beard. Was that the difference? she thought. But where had she met him before now? All danger left her torso as their eyes met. They stared at each other longer than was necessary. She felt uncomfortable and confused. She backed away slowly as a name came to her. Carlos, she thought, as images of an axe sliced through her thoughts. He smiled back at her then, almost thankfully and nodded ever so slightly. She shook involuntarily and moved back away from him a cold shiver weaving its way back up her spine.

"Carlos, are you to be trusted then in this realm?"

"You will see," he said with his upturned grin. "We are not all as you make us out to be."

"Then show me the way to my children."

"I cannot do that as of yet. You have a mission to attend to first. It involves a vow, which needs to be addressed. Several vows, unfortunately, that you have made on behalf of your children's welfare. There will be more made, unfortunately, but these too in time will be forthcoming as well. These too I cannot help you with as yet either."

Kathleen and Edith backed away slowly from the men before them. Each woman was gripping the other's hand tightly.

"Vows, I make no vows to…"

"Uh, un," He raised his hand in protest. "Do not ask any more questions of me. I have your safety to consider at present." He raised his hand and pointed towards Edith. "Go. Take her with you whilst I commence my speech with Stowe."

Edith looked across her shoulder towards the Thames. Her head jerked back towards him as he addressed Edith personally.

"Edith, you must tend her, follow that one's lead." He pointed his hand at Kathleen. "Do not leave her side. She will help you… She will help you in many ways." He nodded.

"Now go, both of you. Get into that church and hide yourselves until we come for you. Do not speak to anyone." He waved his hands in the direction of the steeple rising behind the bear-baiting ring. It was a small church, with a little yard and fields around it. The stone walls surrounding its back enclosure were neither long nor large.

Kathleen looked closely at its farthest reaches. She searched for visible features, something that she could recall later, something that she could depend on to look the same in the dark of night. She grabbed hold of Edith's sleeve and propelled her towards the church at the back of the bear ring. She wanted to be clear of any possible interference with other men. She searched for the signs of children, for other women to sooth her heavy heart.

Kathleen recalled how when back at home...where is home, she thought? Where was she really?

"Forget these thoughts, echoed the voice within her head. Find them, bring them home, bring our heirs home."

Kathleen trembled suddenly and shook her head clear of the voice she thought she had just heard. She dismissed the voice. There was a mission just now, and that was to find her children and get out of this place. You can do anything, her father had once said. It pounded inside of her skull. You can, you can, you can do anything you put your mind to do, anything. Her muscles tightened and she squeezed her hands furiously.

"Stop it," blurted out Edith as she pulled her arm from beneath Kathleen's tightening grip.

"You're hurting me, just like him. You said you would help me." Edith's whitening face worried Kathleen.

"I am helping you, Edith. It will be all right. I'm sorry for all this trouble, but we'll get out of here. I can help you. Don't believe anything Stowe says; just listen to me. We must hide and quickly. Do as I instruct you to do and follow my lead in everything. Try not to be afraid. You must not be afraid. They win if you do that."

Edith was openly sobbing now. She was confused and shaking with fright. She lived in a world of meanness. Her life had been short, hard and long. Kathleen could see the defeat rising within her sagging shoulders and the despondent saddening face before her. She would have more than her enemies working against her with this woman now a part of this quest to find her children. How was she going to meet the needs of hiding two women whilst searching for her own flesh and blood?

"Edith," Kathleen said quietly. "Don't give up on your hope of having your own children. There will be another man to come into your bed. One who is gentle and kind. I can help you find another man. Count on it."

Edith raised her head slightly. A flicker of shine entered her eyes momentarily. A glimmer of hope rose from within her distraught heart.

"He will never let me go," Edith whispered.

"I'll find him and destroy him. He is a beast, a bully and he doesn't deserve you. I have friends, and so do you. Together we will make this happen."

The two women walked slowly on towards the back of the church. Kathleen looked for signs of trouble. She smelt rotting flesh and caught the wisp of a breeze upon her forehead. She breathed deeply and winced slightly as Edith leaned upon her side. She wrapped her left arm across Edith's shoulder and patted her.

"It will be okay. It'll be okay, Edith…"

Kathleen paused momentarily in her speech. She thought she had heard the patter of feet behind her. She glanced quickly across Edith's back. No one there, nevertheless Kathleen had sensed a presence nearby, regardless. There were others here who followed as well, she thought, but who?

"Now, let's not look suspicious. We must act like two women on our way to church. Hold your head up. Don't look about. Walk as if you know where you're going. Don't give anyone the opportunity to suspect anything else is going on."

Edith rose slightly at these words as if guided by some repetitive motion. The doing of walking along the streets of London was easy. It was a familiar activity to do of late. And Edith liked the temporary freedom it afforded her whenever it was made possible by the needs of Elizabeth her queen. They both looked up when they heard the sound of the iron forges banging as they rounded the end of the bear ring.

Smoke rose from the chimneys of the forge. Men were busily pounding out its steel. They seemed content in their doings. None looked their way. Edith spied the first urchin leaning against the wall of the little church enclosure. She had seen him before now in Westminster's yard. She smiled at him. He grinned back. Kathleen watched the familiarity pass between woman and child, the tenderness of someone who had reached out to another in need. However, though, Kathleen felt no kindness directed her way.

"Edith, he's been sent to follow us. I believe he'll help you, but he may not help me. We need him to help us both."

Edith turned towards Kathleen and searched her face.

"I do not understand this. It is all too much. I want to go back now."

"You will be able to go back, but not now. First we must find refuge in that church and await the arrival of the two men we just left."

And in the meantime, thought Kathleen, I'll have to decide whom to trust. The two women entered the church quietly.

They walked into its enclosure softly, Kathleen hesitating momentarily at the sight of the priests lying prostate on the stone flooring before them. They sidestepped them avoiding disturbing the black clothed forms lying on the floor. The first prone form was chanting his machinations.

Edith moved Kathleen into one of the pews next to his head and over towards the stone wall on their left. She pulled and tugged at her sleeve, the two women gliding quickly across the floor. Kathleen smelt the incense as it wafted past them, and felt a ruffling next to her long skirts. Straw and lavender had lain scattered about the floor, as if it was absorbing the decaying stench, which rose into their nostrils from below their feet.

A sudden chill descended into Kathleen's bones. Her gut lurched forward at the hint of movement from behind them. She felt threatened, unsafe and instantly wished she had not entered these hallowed walls. The smell of rotting flesh exacerbated the overwhelming, feeling, growing quickly within her breast. Her hair felt instantly prickly. A cold chill ran down her spine. She heard the weapon being drawn from its sheath and quickly shoved Edith sideways. A blade shot past them and clanged onto the stone wall, dropping to the floor in front of them.

"Edith, get down, now. There is evil afoot."

She pushed Edith behind the pillar and took hold of the knife at their feet turning around to face their attacker.

"How dare you attack me," she blurted out at the sneering face of the priest.

"How dare you enter my church, WITCH?" he snapped.

"You are no priest. You are a blasphemous lying bastard in the guise of a priest. And by the putrid decaying smell of this place, you are a murdering bastard as well!"

They locked eyes and glared back at each other. Kathleen noted his hands rubbing something beneath his long black habit. She glanced quickly across the room and noted three other robed attackers coming their way.

"You have friends, I see. How convenient for you. Do you always work together? Are you that afraid to work alone?"

Kathleen smiled at the priest. Her confidence grew with the anger brewing inside her head. She needed to get herself free of this mess. She backed up slowly towards Edith. The oak door they had entered the church through was now blocked from escape. She glanced quickly about, summarizing her escape routes, deeper within the church. The nearest escape appeared to be closest to the altar, at the far side of where she and Edith were now. She beckoned him closer with a cupping of her hand, waving her fingers towards herself.

"Come," she said. "Let us see what false priests are really made of."

He lunged at them. His anger fuelled with purpling rage on his face. His eyes bulged, and spittle spurted from his lips.

"How dare you enter the sanctity of my church, HERETICAL WITCH?" he screamed at her.

Kathleen slammed the heel of the blade into the side of his nose. She could feel his cartilage break and the gush of blood stream down her front. It disgusted her, the taste of his blood upon her lips. She spat it out and kicked his feet out from him. He slammed down onto the stone of his sanctuary like the broken corpses, which lie beneath them.

"Edith! Run! Head towards that doorway! Quickly," she shouted. "I will follow you."

She grabbed the stunned woman and pushed her over the prone priest moaning at their feet. She leapt over him, only to be grabbed by her foot and flung down onto the hard cold stone of the church's floor. She winced from the sudden lack of breath that met her. Fear and adrenalin shot through her veins and she kicked out at him, thrashing, hitting his hand and face. He groaned, and it gave her enough time to roll away from him and rise to her feet. The other priests were upon her before she took a step. They slammed her into the cold stone of the wall.

"WHAT IS GOING ON IN HERE," came the deeply accented voice from across the nave?

The startled priests let go of her. It was all she needed. She grabbed the two closest to her breast and banged their heads together. Brought her one foot up placing it on the smaller one's hip and pushed him towards the third stunned priest crowded around her. They stumbled into one another. Another chance opening to escape. Run now, she thought. She glanced quickly in the direction the booming voice had come from, but found nobody, no personage about. She did not care to know who had issued it. Edith had disappeared through the far door. She too needed to make her escape. She ran.

Kathleen ran through the opened door straight into the arms of Owen's men. Edith was struggling to get away. Owen slapped Edith into silence.

"Be quiet, you foolish woman." He nodded with his head towards the wherries along the shore, where his men stood, his destination clearly known to Edith. Terror gripped her eyes, and she pleadingly sought comfort from the men who dragged her backwards, Thames ward.

"No, no, not there," she squeaked, whimpering and crying softly.

Kathleen found herself raised and dangling against the rough stone of the outside wall. Two men held her aloft. A dagger was placed between her thighs, just six inches above her knees, its sharp edge pointed upwards. She spat at her captors.

"Leave Edith alone. She does you no harm. She is innocent in this matter. Do not let her blood be spilled. Your conscience will not forgive you. Your sins of hate will bar you from heaven, just as it does for those priests back in there with their false, ungodly ways."

Owen slapped her hard. She bit her tongue and could taste her blood swirlling, mixing with the saliva. She coughed up her bile, and spat everything into his eyes. He dropped his blade slightly, and she pushed herself away from the wall with her feet launching herself out at Owen as she did so. He stumbled backwards, as one of the men still holding her up against the wall fell forwards onto Owen. Kathleen grabbed the hilt of Owen's dagger, ramming it under his nose as he fell. She could feel the crunch of his nose as it broke. The warmth of his blood splattered her hand as she pulled it away. Her third captor held tightly to her and she dragged him halfway down the street towards Edith.

She turned towards him suddenly. He jerked his head backwards, away from her probing hand. It gave her enough time to climb up his protruding knee and slam her dangling foot into his crotch. He dropped down quickly, groaning, cursing.

"She is a bloody witch from hell," he spat out.

Owen had rolled over and onto his knees. He took the blade, which now lay beside him. Grasping it he threw it at her. Kathleen winced at the prospect of that blade slicing through her belly, and she dove sideways. She had thrown up her hand to defend her face, but not before she felt the slice as it flew by. It had nicked her arm. The warmth of blood trickled down her arm. It was a slow trickle. Nothing more than a graze she hoped as she turned and ran towards the ferrymen and Edith.

She heard the voice echoing beside her, familiar in its sound, but could not see him. Her spine tingled with the memory of the voice.

"You must keep faith. I will see to your rescue. But I cannot help you from this debacle you have now found yourself in. You are on your own. Go quickly. There are things you must do. Do not forget this."

"Go away. Just go away," she said to no one.

"Edith! Hurt them! Spit, slap, punch them! You must help me get us away from here!"

Edith did nothing but sobbed as the men dragged her towards the wherry. Kathleen swore under her breath.

"That Bastard. I'll kill him."

She could hear the stomp of hooves before she saw them. Dust swirlled around her as Robbie and his men arrived on horseback. They dismounted and took out their weapons.

"We will take this prisoner for you. Give her to us now."

"Says who?" snapped Owen from behind them.

Robbie smiled his boyish grin. Raised an eyebrow and smirked.

"Says...Her Majesty...the queen. I have orders to bring her back to the Tower. The queen wishes to converse with her subject, as is her right. This woman here," he said pointing his dagger at the traveller, "has information to impart. None of which interests you. Release her forthwith or be thrown into the Tower yourselves."

Owen sneered and glared at His Majesty's favoured friend. He nodded for his men to back off Kathleen.

"I will take my wife with me, then. Bring her to me now," he barked.

"I think not," said Robbie. "She too is of value at present to Her Majesty. She will be let go when we have released all that we can from her as well."

Kathleen took a temporary breath of relief. She struggled with calming herself. Robbie avoided all eye contact. He used hand gestures to round up his men to encircle the women.

"Walk on traveller," he hissed in her ear. Nodding to his men in the direction towards the crossing of Tower Bridge. They moved in unison towards the bridge and kept the women between the horses they had ridden in on. A man was placed in front and behind them. Their progress was slowed and cramped as it wove its way past the merchants, carts and the people who jeered at them. Rotting vegetation was thrown at the two women. As captives of the queen's men, it was assumed they were little more than common thieves due their comeuppance. More than a few bits hit the women, however, mostly though, their newly formed captors and rescuers got pelted.

"You have caused us a great deal of trouble these past few hours, but you will pay its price. Now move along more quickly. These horses hooves marching along beside you, show no mercy when they are provoked," smirked Robert.

The procession made slow progress across the darkened interior tunnels of London's bridge. Shopkeepers edged closer to the posse, which slinked its way across. Merchants whispered to their wives and comrades. More than one eyebrow was raised. Heads bobbed respectfully at Sir Robert Dudley as he lowered his head in recognition towards assorted businesses he frequented. Escorting his captives ever forward, he attended to common courtesy. He noted Walsingham's urchins wending their way ahead of his men. He smiled and took note to address Her Majesty on all that he had seen. These urchins of Walsingham's must be encouraged to ally their allegiance to him, he thought to himself. I too have been followed, and I have certainly been remiss in my seeing.

"Elizabeth will be pleased," he whispered softly to himself.

He stared at the back of the traveller's head and noted the shortness of her curly reddish blonde hair. Most uncommon, he thought to himself. Her dress clearly not closing at her bosom was nonetheless discreet as her undergarments poked through its gaps. He noted the oddness of her shoes. Leather to be sure, but not black, as a servant woman's should be. He had never seen such small brown ankle bound boots without binding's securing them to this woman's feet. Foreign women were a wonder to beholden, but perplexing in their ways of dress and manners. How easily would this one come to his bed, he thought.

John Stowe and Carlos stood closely inside the church, which so recently had held their charges. Each looked around hesitantly before whispering and nodding assent. Their task of directing this traveller to do for Drake his bidding was becoming more complex. Perhaps the dangled carrot of her children would induce this woman to remain on task and complete this most important job. Weaving through her wreckage was indeed annoying. Clearly her loyalties were jaded, mused John to his confidant.

John decided he would move the traveller's children away from London town and into another century immediately. Only once she has regained her belief in her ability to travel forwards and backwards in time would he release her back to whence she came.

However, thought Stowe, I will need another bargaining chip to keep her from reneging on past promises. I will make her commit to having Drake use her precious children in the future. Perhaps a ten years' reprieve in her timeframe would suffice. Stowe smiled at his own ingenuity. And I shall endeavour to use William Shakespeare in my plans as well. There is more than one way to skin two cats at the same time, he thought mischievously.

Walsingham's Inconvenience

June 1576

Walsingham did not like the turn of events laid out before him. The traveller had escaped his clutches. His ferryman and the dockhands had spotted her. Her recapture was of the utmost importance. And now Elizabeth was in the fray, demanding that he bring this upstart woman to her without blemish, bruising or blood spilled.

"How bloody inconvenient." He stamped his feet in protest, kicking out at the straw lain floors encasing the stench of his realm.

He paced back and forth about his rooms. He had need of answers from that traveller. Why was she here? What did she want? Whom did she know? So many questions to be answered, he thought. It was bad enough that he had to deal with the meddling Scots Queen Mary Stuart at present, but he would see to that queen's beheading soon enough. It was all in the timing. And a good little Catholic loves to confess so trustingly to her priest. Another Catholic queen in his realm. He spat a great wad of spittle tinged with blood. He had nipped his tongue again in fury.

"The problem with Catholics is their innate ability to lie and then be forgiven so readily by a priest for that sin," he spat out again in disgust. "Why commit the sin in the first place. Catholic sinners. I hate those who sin so filthily and with such deplorable disregard for the Lord. Blasphemous, stupid, wretched, soulless, idiots."

Walsingham stood still. He would use their despicable ways against them. He would plant in their priestly Catholic ears the seeds of dissent, and they will lead him to her, he thought. It will be their actions, which when discovered will bring about their abrupt sinning end. The blood they spill will manifest two completed tasks with very little effort on my part. No blame will be placed upon or near me. The glint within his eyes shone brightly now. He took a long breath and rose steadily to his appointed height.

These priests so corruptly attached to his man Owen would find a noose tightening around their corpulent necks. And if they happen to harm or are caught with his quarry, then they will certainly be caught. There is no escape from me.

He was about to tighten again another screw untidily loosened. Oh, how he loved this game of intrigue he parlayed about London town.

Bard, Beast and Belly

The Bard's emergence into play
Befalling of the fates
Promises, promises and
Voyages yet to be made
The beast's belly
And souls wait.

Stowe's study 1604

Stowe looked across his room. His flock of believers looked back at him.
He thumped the outside of his chair again, banging onto the drum
in its pouch. "Waump, waump, waump," the noise vibrated outward.
Stowe leaned over his desk towards them.

"Do you know who else can enter into the world of…in-between?"

"The Kraken," called out Nicholas.

"No… he sighed. The Kraken holds onto the world of…between. I
mean, who else can go into…between and come out into our realm?"

Silence once again greeted him. Heads shook sideways. Little heads
looked into the eyes of littler eyes. Adults shifted uncomfortably against
each other. Some even backed a little ways off from Stowe.

"The traveller can," he bellowed out at them. "She is taken by Drake into the mouth of the Kraken and spit out into our world."

Stowe pointed his finger at them, rocking it up and down at them.

"The traveller sleeps amongst you at night, and walks the alleyways of London town searching…lost in our world, seeking her children that Drake has also taken into the mouth of the Kraken."

"Why," said little John Stowe?

"She is the chosen one," he whispered now softly back at his youngest grandson. "She must find her children. If she does not, then they will perish. Edith, you must look after her children. These temporary orphans here before you are her children."

Edith looked down upon the children of the traveller. Maddox with his blonde hair was thin and tall, Woody and Kitt both redheaded smiled back up at her from the floor where they sat. The traveller's boys were the same age as some of Stowe's grandchildren, however, more robust, plump and strong.

Edith admired the strength of the traveller's small children at six, eight and ten. They had followed her around for a while now in their newly planted home, placed into her care by Stowe. They had teased and played with the other children on Stowe's estate. Edith could not always understand their talk and often wondered why they whispered so behind her back. But her chores and this new responsibility had kept her too busy to waste much time figuring out what they said to whom about her.

Edith had wondered at how simply she had been got from her husband Owen and his men. She remembered a disturbing memory of an acute danger. It pressed worryingly against her breast, taunting at her, ridiculing her safety here. Why did it feel so fleeting?

Distracted by her thoughts, she looked up startled to see all around her now looking at her. She could feel the heat rising into her breasts and face as the others present in Stowe's study followed her gaze back and forth between her charges and Stowe their master. Silence gripped Edith's cheeks, and she clenched her teeth down hard. Edith did not like this attention.

This sudden attention fostered an acute desire to run and hide. Usually these incidences of attention brought about beatings from Owen. Edith looked down at her hands in embarrassment. They were pale. She felt a chilling tingling running up her spine, and she went rigid with fear, frozen to some ungodly place. Was this place purgatory? Was this hell? She wondered how she had got here. No memory of this place existed in her thoughts. Why was she here? She looked up now towards the traveller's children. Recognition of these children brought a weak smile to her face.

"Now, now, Edith, and my friends gathered round. Do not look so alarmed. The traveller's children are not here to harm you. They are only here to play with momentarily. They need watching over for their own safety. We are all their guardians and must look out for the coming men who will follow and try to take them away." Stowe raised his eyebrows in defiance.

"And we will not let them take these good children, will we?"

An uncomfortable shifting of feet and movement away from Edith and the orphans began its slide. Stowe watched in silence. He knew he was going to have to divert the interests of these forthcoming men away from his household. The children of his surrounding household would forget quickly enough about these orphans and continue their pursuit of something interesting and new. He wondered how many would survive past ten. He cleared his mind of that fateful thought. So many children had been lost in this realm already. The adults, though, would quickly move away from and distance themselves in any way they could. These temporary orphans' imminent departure would soon be viewed as a blessing to be forgotten.

Stowe admired the ingenuity of his own plan. He counted on this for his plans to remove William Shakespeare from his glories was brewing. Shakespeare's disappearance from Stowe's world would finally come to fruition. I shall lay the foundation of that demise soon, he thought and in the process eliminate all his writings. He smiled at the formulation of the plans brewing inside his glorious brain.

"Ah, let us not forget our story," mused Stowe. "We must continue and find out where these young boys are from," pointing his finger at the children of the traveller once more. Stowe retrieved the drum from its chair.

Maddox recognized the signal that was meant from Stowe's words first. Maddox had seen the drum being pulled out of the pocket of Stowe's chair. It was familiar to him. He had seen it before in the museum at home. It was a Songhees drum, and he had been allowed to beat it once before on a class trip to the museum. They had been told to expect a sign of a time when they would need to be gone, and their exit from this realm into a more dangerous time was soon to begin.

"The traveller must begin her journey back into the belly of the Kraken in order to secure the release of these here," He pointed his finger towards the traveller's children. "Temporary orphans. And you must all guard her children here." He waved his hands in the direction of the traveller's children. He looked about his chamber and viewed the startled eyes that met his. Stowe grinned and laughed out loud.

He knew that the traveller was stuck in a time not near that of her children, but Stowe also knew that he would soon have to bring these children of the traveller's back to her. Maddox, Kitt, Woody and the traveller had a journey to embark on.

Stowe concluded that he would send the young William to escort them as well. Stowe considered for the moment, eliminating this emerging playwright even though Drake had indicated that this was not the appropriate time to do that...Stowe had so far managed with Drake's help to capture the little playwright before he would grow too big for himself and his company of players. Stowe was determined to thwart William before he even got started. Such an upstart, pompous young man and not a word of which he speaks or writes is truthful. It would be better, however, Drake had said to eliminate William in another way. Perhaps even replace Drake's own documents that were held in Whitehall Palace with that of William Shakespeare's. That way all of William's plays would be lost in the coming destruction and fire of London in 1666.

Stowe made the sign of the cross. He was thankful that he would not live long enough to see that onslaught of flames jettison skywards as they marched their destructive forces across London town.

"Ah ha, I have foiled you once again."

Relief met most of the faces Stowe glanced upon. He noted that several of his flock had not been convinced by his forced laugh, although his work here was coming to its conclusion. Amongst his flock were those who would begin their descent backwards in time and become part of the past, where if he could manage it, they will remain, unknown, lost, forsaken.

It was up to Stowe to choose who could be lost into the abyss of infamy and possibly pass through the belly of the Kraken. For he, John Stowe, had the power now, not Drake. Stowe shook his head, took a deep breath and wondered. Could I eliminate William despite all that Drake had suggested...or should patience prevail and should he follow his good friend's advice?

Stowe did not enjoy the prospect of losing another of his men to questionable circumstances. Perhaps dispatching William at this time was not the best solution, however delicious the prospect of it was. At stake was the voyage of Francis. It had to take place. Drake's documents needed to be retrieved from Whitehall Palace before they befell the fire of 1666.

But that voyage had yet to take place. First, though, he had to teach the traveller a lesson as agreed to by herself and Drake many distant moons ago. That woman simply had to believe in the probabilities and existence of transference. Thereby making it possible for her to retrieve Drake's lost documents from future destruction. Only then could she be sent back in history to retrieve them once and for all. But first of all she needed to converse with Drake's Queen Elizabeth to allow him a licence for privateering. Then he could begin his journey of circumference around the world. This time his journals would be duplicated. Stowe broke out of his trance and thoughts. He needed to convince his flock to distance themselves further from the traveller's children and Edith. Soon they would need to be used again to convince their most disobedient mother.

"You have forgotten, haven't you, the story?" he said quickly. The chieftain's daughter is awaiting capture too. She must be returned to the belly of...," he said and waved his hands about back and forth across his desk towards those who still listened.

"The Kraken," yelled the children.

"Yes." He nodded. "This princess must be got from her hiding place. She lives still and dwells within the walls of London town. Our traveller must find her and bring her back to her people. The land of the Spirit Keepers is a sacred place of immense beasts, which wander aimlessly across its lands. It is the land of the white spirit bear and grizzly bears taller than this room and of great winged birds that pluck out the eyes of foreigners stopping man from seeing his return home.

"Drake has slayed many of these beasts, but each time he slays them, more came back. They grow bigger each time they emerged from death, and each time they attempted to gorge upon his soul. Until at last upon Drake's death at sea, where they ate him whole and swallowed him down into the Kraken where he remains trapped upon their lands, until the traveller returns the chieftain's daughter and her heirs to them."

Stowe surveyed his rooms for the believers and the skeptics. He needed to know who he could trust with the task at hand.

"Did you know that another two Queen Elizabeths will come upon our shores," he said quietly. He waited for his words to foment.

"Another Queen Bess is to come?"

"Yes," he said quietly. "There will be two more Queen Bess. One will come to be beside her husband, the king. The other will rule as a man, like her predecessor and give this our England three possible future kings."

"This will be good, then," said a voice from the back. We will prosper under a Good Queen Bess" A murmur of assent rippled through the small group before him.

"You said two more Queen Bess' and one man Queen Bess. What do you mean by this talk of riddles," quipped the disbeliever emerging from his flock.

Stowe folded his hands beneath his chin and looked in the direction of William, the children's escort back in time, where he, Stowe, would see to the end of this young Shakespeare. He needed to have and make examples out of fools who mock history. Storytelling was done by educated men like himself, with clear minds whose duty it was to record the truth in history. Scholars like me, he thought, who tell the truth and do not meddle with facts.

"The next Queen Elizabeth to ascend our throne will not rule. She is not an heir to the throne, but she will be a queen nonetheless. She will, however, give birth to the next reigning Elizabeth. This third Elizabeth will be called Queen Elizabeth because she will be our second reigning Queen Elizabeth. This queen will inherit the throne, as did our late Good Queen Bess."

The shifting of feet began again.

"Is it not heresy to announce the coming of another queen? Are we not to be shamed because of this knowledge you impart, sir?" The young master writer, William, smiled. "How will King James like to hear of another queen reigning after him?"

Stowe looked into the eyes of his deserter with a knowing smile.

"We are storytelling here, my friend, not heretics making. You would be well advised to remember that. Storytellers are not heretics, as you well know. Scholars are better able to tell the truth of a man's reign than any playwright, wouldn't you agree? Speak to me afterwards and I will explain further the confusion of which I have caused you to believe."

William considered the advice given him by Master Stowe. He did not like this man. His actions were dangerous. He had only agreed to his ramblings of capturing this traveller when he had found out about her children being used as hostages of persuasion. Children were not to be used. He hated men who dabbled in self-aggrandizement for their own gain. He, Shakespeare, was well aware of the likes of this kind of man. And he understood too well that his part in this scheme was not yet finished. More would be required of him, but for now the safety of these children were paramount to his finding of their mother.

They needed to be reunited and quickly. Then that upstart Stowe and whomever, possibly Drake, he was colluding with could be stopped.

A shifting of more feet away from the distracter William had begun. Stowe noted William's keen eyes. He remembered the youth's ability to write had impressed. But where he had learned this complicated skill, he could not recall. But he would see to it that he never wrote another word. An upstart playwright would never again become more significant than the learned men of books like himself.

William stared back into Stowe's eyes. He understood and knew his place was elsewhere. He had been expecting a shift in this path. A calling had begun, a need to speak his mind more often, to impart the words of men and their foibles aloud upon the stage. His move away from the cottage life of Stowe would begin. London awaited, his need to walk its streets, converse with other poets had been foreseen. It was time, thought William. The voice he had listened to said so and had even encouraged his thoughts of late.

"Now, let us return to the lands of the beasts," roared Stowe. "There is much more gold to be found from their lands. And the late great, Sir Francis Drake will bring back to our shores the means to its discovery. More gold will be found on the shores where the black jaguars mouth appears. The beasts that guard this forgotten treasure are sharpening their teeth as I speak. They will not be merciful in their taking."

He had their attention again he noted. He enjoyed playing with them. He loved an audience. Writing history was necessary to feed and clothe his family and servants. But the need to tell stories was greater, and his willing victims ate up all he laid down before them.

"The traveller has made vows to our late Queen Bess. She has also made vows with Drake in regards to these children." He waved his hands again in the direction of the traveller's children.

Cicero stretched, extending his claws out and lightly touched the shoulder of Maddox. The young boy with his blond hair and blue eyes stared back knowingly. The two locked eyes momentarily. Maddox stroked the cat's head, and it closed its eyes. His mother was calling out to him. He could feel it. A longing ached inside his chest. He watched as the tear falling onto Cicero was washed away with one passing of the paw across his face. Cicero licked it clean and placed his paw beneath his chin and turned his head away from Maddox.

"I have told you about the belly of the Kraken and how it swallows and spits its chosen victims into the...world of between. But I have not told you of how it possess the souls it takes."

All eyes turned his way.

"There is a parting of souls that takes place. Those who challenge and like to fight will inhabit the fiercest of beasts. But becoming one of these beasts does not make you strong. For you are likely to meet other similar beasts from which to defend yourself from. Bears do not like to share their homes with others and will fight to the death to defend their den. Mother bears are especially fierce. They have been seen by Drake swiping the head clear off a man whilst he ran away in haste."

He looked across his flock of lost souls still willing to listen to all he said. Cicero the cat turned his head towards Stowe and gazed fixedly past his master's shoulder into the eyes of the large cat pictured in the tapestry hanging from the wall behind. Stowe noted Cicero's movements and turned towards the tapestry himself.

"See here before you these creatures from the forest. Look closely and recognize not one. For they are the animals that have been roaming upon the shores of Nova Albion. Look here. See this beast? He stands taller than the rest. Drake has seen a man climb these trees to escape this beast they call the grizzly. The beast itself cannot climb after him, but he shook the man out of the tree and ate his broken limbs one by one."

He paused for a moment to let them think about what he had said and then continued on. He pointed to the large light-coloured cat-like maneless lion. A lion had been seen many times in the baiting rings of London.

"The Kraken spit this beast out from its belly and set it free. Its body is longer and higher than my desk, and its tail is longer still. This mother beast, hides behind bushes perched above her victims in the forests. When it is ready, it will pounce upon you and toss you around like a mouse, dragging your bloody corpse across the path into the darkest part of the forest, and then it commences its feast of your flesh."

He turned back towards them, picked up his pen and pointed it in their direction.

"The Kraken will call upon its beasts when it needs them most. Only those who come to the shores of Nova Albion and do no harm to its beasts may pass safely into the world of…between. If a creature of the Kraken's control is harmed, it will take its revenge. You will lose your soul to it. The only way to be released from the Kraken's grip is by making a vow. The people of these lands believe in the powers of the Kraken and even worship it as a God."

"They shall burn at the stake for this sin," cried out Edith.

Stowe shifted in his chair, ignored Edith's exclamation and reached over to Cicero, stroking its thick black hair. He reached beneath its chin and gently scratched its throat until he heard the soft purring that Stowe so liked about cats.

"Drake has told me of the people of Nova Albion's rituals to the Kraken," he said not looking up from his petting of the cat Cicero.

"The people of Nova Albion place offerings of tobacco, fish, herbs and berries along the shore."

"Low tide is best, Drake had said. The coming tide lifts up these gifts and carries them into the mouth of the Kraken. The Nova Albion people believe the Kraken will protect their families from the ravages of other beasts if they gift and feed it. The people of Nova Albion believe their souls are taken away when they die and do not ascend to heaven but instead reside..." Reaching into his desk Stowe withdrew a large book.

"These animals here, I have drawn them for you. Here is the grizzly page, another page with salmon, another with a fox, a wolf, another of a large black and white whale. These are the gods of the people of Nova Albion. When their loved ones have passed away, the people of Nova Albion also believe they can talk to the spirits of their ancestors through the world of in-between.

"The brave ones walk into the forest for a week or more. If they emerge from the forest unshaken, then their soul possess the power to foresee the future and reside beside one of these chosen beasts. Those who fail the test the forest makes for them, remain lost, never to emerge again. Their souls echo out their warnings, bringing the changing seasons into place. Those who fail are lost inside winter's menace. Those who return can read the seasons and will help guide the forest's rites of spring, summer and the fall."

Stowe looked across his flock. One after the other looked back at him. He let them stretch their necks across at him. He could feel the heat of worry cross their brows.

"Now let me tell you more about the traveller. She too has come across the winds of summer and out of the belly of the beast. Her soul is being held by the Kraken until she returns that which Drake has taken from it. This traveller has made a pact with the Kraken to help it find and return the chieftain's daughter into the belly of the Kraken.

"The second vow this traveller has made is to Drake. She has promised to find evidence of his coming to Nova Albion's shores. This traveller, though, has forgotten the vows she made. She wishes only to protect her children from entering the belly of the Kraken. But a vow cannot be broken, as you all are aware. She therefore will continue to be tortured and played with by this beast and Drake who control all of her movements from now on."

Stowe looked away from his flock and picked at the drying skin from around his thumbnail. He bit it off after several pulls of its skin. It bled, and he sucked the blood back into his mouth and wiped his hand across his lips to remove the traces left behind on his lips. He spat the dead skin out onto the floor and looked back across at his flock.

"This traveller," he said, "has forgotten some of what was told to her. Most importantly that the entrance and exit into our realm has a forever changing bent. Its unpredictability has a way of causing unexpected grief. This traveller has yet to learn the power, which issues forth from the world of…in-between. And her escape plans from our realm will be challenged time and again. For she will continue to come into our realm for as long as Sir Francis Drake wishes for her to do so. He has many tasks for the traveller and her children to partake in willingly or not."

Edith smiled at Stowe. She didn't understand why just yet, but she reached down and placed her hands along the nape of her charge's necks. She felt the warmth of their pulse throbbing along the tips of her fingers. Their blood thus still flows, she thought. Her hand shook temporarily with the heat radiating out towards it. A vision of blood, a journal and her charges flashed across her memory. She shook these thoughts aside. No, she thought, I will not let anything harm her lovelies.

"Maquenna," he said, "take the boys outside now. This story will continue again, but for now I must get back to my writing." He looked over at the rest of the saddened eyes of his flock and smiled.

Edith replied, "Thank you for the story, sir. I will take the boys outside now. I will show them how to find the summer berries for drying and pounding into paste." Edith did not understand the reply she had just given Stowe, but it comforted her despite its oddity.

Memories and Prophesies

A Future for London is not easy to predict.
Merchants, Priests and Councillors are forever in the midst.
At journey's end a discovery awaits.
But who will see to its fruition? Perhaps the followers of Drake.
But will they be complying…and whose
realm shall be put to the stake?

June 1576

King Phillip had showered the young Elizabeth with monies and jewels from his conquests in order to gain her hand in marriage and retain his grip on English soil. She had favoured him for a while, toying with him, enjoying the resulting, albeit short, calm upon her shores, but she could not tolerate a Catholic monarch issuing orders upon England's lands. Her father had squandered away his monarchy in pursuit of an heir, and his wives had lost even more in his battles over lands and state. In the end Henry had resorted to robbing and dissolving all those who opposed his new faith, especially the rich Catholic monasteries.

Elizabeth, however, had continued her reign in her father and mother's new doctrinal beliefs. The Protestant faith would become her model, not that of the popish Catholic faith that now accused her of heresy. Elizabeth would show no mercy towards those who opposed her realm. Catholics would enjoy modest courtesy, but not open overt practising of their arts. The toleration of disdainful, problematic religions was a way of keeping the peace in her realm, but it had its limits, and she was not about to pander to their pressing issues.

Elizabeth looked up from her reading. State documents were necessary to the running of her realm. She had seen to the objections raised in her most recent arguments with Cecil and his insistence on addressing the issue of inheritance. Elizabeth had sworn to herself she would not be ruled by another. Her realm could not afford to be claimed by another foreign popish kingdom. If she were to choose any husband, it would be from reliable English stock. Cecil would have to put off another suitor in good time. For the moment, though, suitors were to be pursued only to the benefit of quieting European thoughts of invasion. Their useful offerings of money helped pay her way through her crown's meagerly funded coffers at present.

Mary had, as Elizabeth's predecessor, whittled away the country's wealth with her marriage to King Phillip of Spain. She had even lost the last stronghold on the continent to the French. No safe shores lay straight off England's coast to the east any more.

"That stupid woman," she spat out. "How could she have married herself off to that boastful, pig of a king. And of Spain, no less. Well, I suppose she inherited those tendencies from her mother, Catherine of Aragon. Stupid, stupid, woman, thanks to her I have enemies abroad."

The rustling of skirts in the foyer of her rooms indicated the imminent arrival of Robert Dudley into her midst. His charm was useful in keeping her ladies attentive and faithful to herself. They would not cross his sheets if they were to value their lives. He saw to it that they stayed pure as long as was possible. For once a lady was captured by the likes of the rogues who plied Elizabeth's corridors, and then their attention to her was forsaken or distracted. Part of this charming of her ladies kept them at the very most amused for longer periods of time.

Would he have news, she thought. Finding this invader amongst her staff was becoming a vexing problem. Her servants and lesser staff had begun to talk. She had surmised this was one of Walsingham's devices of capture. Who was this woman and how dare she copy her most private of writings? She would have to answer for this indiscretion.

However, Cecil and Walsingham had pointed out the usefulness of interrogation. Finding this traveller, as they called her, was annoying and jammed on her patience. She was used to quick results and had little time for the inabilities of inconsequential staff, but Robbie, Cecil and Walsingham had insisted this traveller possessed qualities that were different. She had a power for prediction, so they had said, which could benefit her realm.

That would imply that this woman was indeed intelligent. An intelligent woman would not reveal her sources easily, Elizabeth thought. A woman must always disguise her intelligence to further her causes. Never let your enemy know of what you are made of, she mused.

If they could not find this traveller, this meant that Elizabeth's own court lacked regard for her personage. Elizabeth would order the tightening up of her staff and be rid of these foreign influences who trounced in her court. This traveller would be made to obey Elizabeth's will and rule. Elizabeth would dictate her livelihood not the other way around.

Where exactly was this traveller from? That would have to be exposed. Her life's expectancy would balance on this knowledge. She was not opposed to Walsingham's idea of a quick beheading.

"To be done away with forthwith," he had said.

"What is the loss of another woman in this realm especially a foreign one?" he had said.

Elizabeth had shuddered at the complexities this man lacked. She was a woman herself, a royal woman nonetheless who had to act like a man in order to maintain some semblance of authority over her men. Thankfully owning a crown kept Walsingham in order.

Some days Elizabeth wondered about Walsingham's loyalties. His secrets, his pursuits, regardless of its origin, it too fascinated her. She had to admire his ability to find and relinquish individuals of their information.

Elizabeth knew Walsingham had a series of urchins at his beck and call. She had seen to it that they were well fed and shod. Edith had been useful in securing their allegiance. Cecil had managed to engage of few of them as well for her benefit.

Elizabeth made a quick sign of the cross across her breast and forehead in recognition of her fathers' insistence upon the manner of her education. From a very young age she had been able to speak with him in many languages. He had delighted in her cleverness. It had gained her more and more time in his presence. She valued this freedom it gave her over her house's governance. As Elizabeth had excelled in her learning, she had gained more access to Henry and time with her cherished brother Edward and his tutors. This had been one of the most joyful and rewarding times in her life.

Rarely did her father Henry banish her from his sight then. Her devotion to the new faith had garnered more respect in his eyes than had her sister Mary's devotions to Catholicism.

It had not bothered her when Mary, her sister and former queen had died. They had spent many good days in each other's company, but as Mary grew older, she had insisted on Elizabeth's conversion to the Catholic faith. The effect was to ram a void of distance between them. Mary's imprisonment of Elizabeth in the White Tower had further created a wedge in their relationship.

The Tower was a place for royal heretics to be held until execution at the will of the monarch. A chill ran down her spine as she recalled the familiarity of her own quarters inside the tower. The same quarters her dear mother Ann Boleyn had wandered in and lost her head to a French swordsman blade. A place in which, she now had insisted that the traveller be placed. A place reserved for the confinement of notorious royal blood on the way to the gallows or beheading. Perhaps this traveller deserved a less secure confinement, one in which more accidental harm could be meted out.

"NO...she must not be able to communicate with my subjects... she must be retained...in secrecy... and her movements controlled... observed for now," she said aloud.

Elizabeth looked up from her lapse in discretion and peered about her chamber for adverse signs of movement and sounds. Her heart beat with the memory of her own imprisonment inside the Towers cottages. How eloquently her mother had faced the swiftness of her death with grace. She had asked for and been granted the sharpest French sword possible. Elizabeth sat down and smiled at the folly of her Catholic adversary, King Phillip of Spain.

Elizabeth was most grateful for the previous transgressions of Mary husband's affections towards her. If it was not for these, she was sure that the axe would have dropped upon the whiteness of her neck. It had become apparent to him and his councillors that Mary would never give him an heir to his English throne, but Elizabeth could. She had been alerted to Phillip's designs on her by her gaolers. Even in her lowest most feared times, she had had friends and servants looking out for her person. It was a comfort she would not easily forget.

Elizabeth was favoured over Mary and Phillip by the people of England. Phillip, Elizabeth's saviour from confinement within the White Tower, has never thought that she would enlist the company of others and disregard his falsely flattering attentions upon her, albeit, though, with a cautious eye on being thrown back into the Tower.

Elizabeth recalled how Mary had been as mean and jealous as any wife would be. Phillip had regarded Elizabeth with lust more than once too openly in front of her.

Elizabeth had met her most coveted friend behind those walls of the tower. Robbie had been released as soon as she had gained her title to the throne. They had enjoyed each other's company as much as was possible under their gaolers' watchful eyes.

Elizabeth thought now, how little she would allow this traveller to roam about her former prison with its walls and oak panelled houses. Instead, this intruder and her accomplice, that wife of Owen's, would remain behind the stone enclosures of the White Towers exterior walls. They would not be allowed a fire to warm their bodies this night. A cold day or two awaited, and a need for sustenance would impart as much information as would do a racking at present. Let them suffer the ache of their bellies, she thought. It had done herself no harm as she recalled.

Robbie strolled through Elizabeth rooms and spent as much time as was necessary chatting up her ladies-in-waiting. He enjoyed his time with these women and was ever so thankful that they did not address their attentions towards him at present. He would introduce them as was necessary to the likes and attentions of Her Majesty's most loyal subjects. He was trying not to seem impatient, for his business with Elizabeth was urgent.

Owen had been remiss in his duties to Elizabeth's crown. Once again he had taken liberties, thought Robert. His flagrant assumptions had not gone unnoticed. Robert would see to it that Elizabeth was told every last detail of the traveller's treatment by Owen and his cohorts.

Edith had been calmed with a soothing tasteless potion. The traveller had seemed to be begrudgingly grateful for her escape from Owen's clutches. However, Robert did not trust her. She refused to address him properly or answer any of his questions.

"I cannot," she had said defiantly.

Most amusing, thought Robert, considering where she now resided. He abhorred the thought of using fiery tongs upon the likes of women. Scarring up those amble breasts would do no man any justice.

He looked about the rooms and caught the eye of Kat, who had been watching him closely. Kat always knew when he had information to impart. Robert would speak to her afterwards, once the ladies who had gathered around him had left. Kat was a wise sage, old bird, however much Elizabeth refused to believe it. She had informed him on many an occasion of indiscretions in the court and that troublesome half-sister of Elizabeth's.

Catherine was and continued to be a blight on his and Elizabeth's court, and he meant to be rid of her one day. She was, however, at times a useful theatrical diversion. But her incontrollable ways had infuriated him on more than one occasion. The wretched woman lacked consistency in her manner. Very unpredictable Robert mused. He hated unpredictability, and it rattled his nerves.

Elizabeth turned and smiled at Robbie as he entered her privy chamber. He looked confident and pleased with himself, she thought. Perhaps this problem of the traveller had been dealt a blow. She watched his body move carefully as he strode across the wooden floors of her private room. He enjoyed her lingering looks and she indulged him whenever she could. He was a man, after all, and needed copious amounts of attention, but with Robbie, it was never a chore. She loved his movements, his mannerisms and the familiarity of his stride in her private presence.

"She is secure. I have placed her within the Tower, but not in your former residence. I thought it unnecessary to grant her more comfortable surroundings."

Elizabeth smiled. He knew her feelings so well, she thought. She nodded in agreement.

Robert noted her change in face as he addressed her about the traveller. She sighed gently. He watched as her shoulders relaxed somewhat and settled back in her chair. She dropped her head in the direction of an available chair across from her writing desk.

"What has she said to you? Have you gleaned any knowledge from this troublesome interloper?"

"She speaks not. Only to say, she cannot."

Elizabeth's eyebrows shot upward, and her countenance stiffened.

"Well, she will change her ways. There are instruments of torture to induce her tongue to speech."

Robbie smiled at her and silently shook his head back and forth.

"Yes, there are, however, if what you say about this journal is true, surely then she must live then in order for us to find her turn coat."

Elizabeth nodded agreement.

"Do you think her mind impenetrable? Surely she will speak with a little inducement. We must find her weaknesses."

"Yes, that may work, but we must consider with whom she cavorts and where they reside."

"You think she has valuable information to impart?"

"I do…I do. She is clever and fights like a fox. I have never seen any woman escape the clutches of one of Walsingham's men before. She possesses mischievous arts and engages upon the use of the most curious means of escape.

"She escaped Walsingham, did she? How interesting."

"She also escaped Owen, Your Grace."

Elizabeth looked at Robbie and got up from her seat. She walked over to the window and stood there, her pearls clasped in her hand, her fingers rubbing the smoothness of her beads intently. Her thoughts wandered to the usefulness of such a lady in her realm. What else could she do? Elizabeth hesitated for a moment before turning her head around at Robbie. She rubbed the pearls again and again. Looking directly in Robbie's eyes, she said.

"She has skills in fighting, then?"

He nodded assent, lifting one eyebrow.

"Yes, she does. She does, indeed."

Elizabeth's leaned forward slightly, now clenching the beads clasped firmly in her hand.

"But she did not use them on you?"

"No, she did not."

"I see. Most interesting." Elizabeth moved over to her desk and leaned towards Robbie.

"What does she hope to gain from you?"

"Trust, I hope. She practically carried that wife of Owen's back with my men. She needs something from you, but I don't know what? I must find her out, catch her at her own game."

She nodded her head towards Robbie in agreement, but Elizabeth had already recalled Catherine's earlier statement of the traveller and her children. She smiled. She knew exactly what this woman wanted. She would have Walsingham find and secure her children somewhere safe from all who sought them. They must remain unharmed. She disliked so the torture of children.

Both heard the footsteps at the same time. Elizabeth sat down quickly. They looked closely into each other's eyes.

Elizabeth adjusted some papers and picked up her quill. She dipped its tip into ink and wrote a short note to Robbie. He watched her quickly write her missive. He knew her intent was to pursue this matter further. He reached across the desk quickly retrieving her note. He flapped it ever so quietly back and forth enabling the ink to dry faster.

Once dry, Robbie took hold of the torn parchment and tucked it into the leather pouch tied at his waist. He nodded and rose swiftly. He was bowing slightly when Walsingham strode into the room. He could feel the coldness of the other man's stare on his back. They had been civil to each other for years, but of late friction had arisen. Walsingham had made it clear that he would not support Robbie's desires for marriage with the queen. Of course Robbie had denied such aspirations at once.

"Master Walsingham," acknowledged Robbie with a nod and he strode straight for the entrance, neither expecting nor receiving a reply. Francis Walsingham smiled curtly and bowed before his queen.

Elizabeth noted the stiffness of the exchange with a raised quill to still Walsingham for a moment until Robbie left the room. This always seems to help ease the man's temperaments and engage him quickly in the purpose of his coming. She had learned well how to read her most loyal subjects. Occasionally setting them off against one another kept them in check and showed her who was willing to belittle the other. She would not stand for disloyalty amongst her most favoured subjects. And they understood this, as they should, she thought.

Walsingham bowed to Her Majesty and waited for her before being seated.

She raised her left hand and wafted it across the desk towards the seat recently vacated by Robbie. He nodded his reply without speaking. He too had issues which he did not wish Robbie to hear. He took his time to settle his waistcoat into place and crossed his legs slowly.

He did not look to see if Robbie had left. Instead he listened for the familiar pattern of soles clomping their way across the stone corridors. He noted Robbie's hesitation and mimicking tread.

He would have to speak to her carefully and muffle his requests. He placed his back directly in line with the unclosed door, clasped his hands across his lap and smiled at his monarch.

Elizabeth noted his pose and understood immediately the delicateness of the problem with which he had come. She leaned towards him slightly and raised her eyebrows. He understood this gesture, for it meant she wanted facts and quickly.

Softly he spoke, "Am I to understand that you have apprehended the traveller who roams amongst us?"

"Indeed she awaits interrogation as does the wife of your associate Owen."

"I would like to be present at that interrogation of these women. They are traitors…

"How so?"

"To your realm. They have confiscated items of secrecy and therefore need to be executed, Your Highness."

Elizabeth lowered her quill, looked across the room to the door and indicated with her head that Walsingham was to close the opened door. She watched him as he rose from the chair and strode quickly and quietly across the floor. She noted he made no sound as he crossed the floor. He seemed to know how to hold the door without it groaning whilst he closed it quietly. He glided back across the room and slithered back into his chair.

"What items of secrecy do you refer to, Lord Walsingham?"

Walsingham lent over the desk and gently removed the quill from Elizabeth's fingers.

"She has copied documents of your own hand, Your Majesty. She has seen your personal communications. As well she has engaged in copying articles of state secrets not yet made public to all of your councillors."

He stared hard into his monarch's black widening irises. She was not easily read, but occasionally could be. She sat back again with a long sigh. He waited for her usual stubborn indifferent reply.

"Have you gathered any proof that she has released this information?"

Walsingham put her quill back upon its rail, stroking its length with his index finger. He slowly leaned back into his chair.

"Why wait to find out. Dispatch her now and be done with the worry."

"And if she has valuable information from others to impart…what say you, then?"

His smirk and tilt of head showed more than intent to release such valuable information, if indeed it was valuable.

"Have you no mercy for the likes of women who might have only held that journal for another…what say you then, my dear man?"

"She may have done such a thing, but it is of no consequence to us. She will hold no great secrets, but it will show the likes of others not to meddle in state affairs. A standard and an example must be maintained for all those who sin against Your Majesty."

Elizabeth nodded in agreement. Walsingham, she thought, how he does like the intrigues. She knew he had a power of persuading others to do his bidding. Sometimes, though, she wondered if it was really all about securing her realm from harm. She rather thought Walsingham liked to stir the pot more than needed. He seemed to enjoy all these intrigues too much.

She raised her hand towards the empty glass upon her desk. Walsingham rose and crossed the floor towards the chamber, which held her ladies. He opened the oak door and indicated to Kat to bring forth Elizabeth's tray. They waited in silence as Kat appeared. She was relieved to see Elizabeth smiling.

"You are hungry. This is good to see. You have not eaten well of late, my dear."

Elizabeth rose and took the tray from Kat and smiled.

"Thank you, dear. I am famished. Could you see to it that the ladies are fed soon? They must be hungry as well." Kat backed away and nodded, before turning and walking back to the private chambers of Her Majesty's ladies-in-waiting. She closed the door, securing it from accidental opening. Both occupants could hear the drawing of drapes across the doorway ensuring privacy and silence from within their chamber.

Cheese, bread, cream, almonds, figs and pears adorned the tray. As well, two jugs of mead and wine with water had been made available. Elizabeth watched Walsingham pour out his own ale and her wine. They toasted and nodded towards each other. Their ritual of discussion over troublesome matters had begun.

Walsingham continued his persuasive notion that the traveller needed to be eliminated directly upon her interrogation, regardless of her output. She must be silenced. Elizabeth would not budge. She would be the one to decide fate's outcome. In time she hoped he would learn this, but as of yet he pursued his insistence on knowing what was best for the realm.

She would not let him take control. She was master of this realm, however much she enjoyed the process. Argument had its rewards. It invigorated her soul, and she pursued all possible outcomes. Her mind was forever clamouring for every available scrap of new information.

She longed for the days of learning, of reading and digesting complicated issues and language. These tidbits of oddities teased her senses.

This traveller had beaten a man at his own game, she thought. How had she done this? What arts had she used to evade Walsingham's men? This, she wanted to know herself. How is it that a woman can fight and evade capture by one man, and yet know when not to with another? This was a smart woman, and Elizabeth wanted to invade her mind before others did.

She sliced off a large piece of hard cheese and bit into it, chewing slowly. She enjoyed simple foods mostly, their taste often clean, clear and concise. The sharpness of cheese reminded her of simpler days as a girl without the complications of courtiers. Men were a troubling sort, always wanting something from her and her ladies. Men had tried on many an occasion to impress their personal needs upon her body, but she was unwilling to engage upon the delights of flesh. Childbearing was not to be. She would not bring forth into this world another motherless child. It was a pain she could not inflict.

Walsingham looked up from contemplating the softness of his hands. He had found a most interesting apothecary of late. One who had provided him useful, untraceable poisons. His potions had been unusual and easily blamed on others. Killing two adversaries through implication and suggestion was easily done. One would hang whilst the other suffered through a painful death. Planting evidence was easily mastered. Difficult Catholics often needed dispatching. It was much easier to control Her Majesties subjects via indirect means, he thought.

"We have all the evidence we need to eliminate these women," said Walsingham. "It is unfortunate that the companion, however, is the wife of one of your most loyal subjects. She must be dispatched as well."

"I do not agree at present, Your Lordship. I wish to interrogate these women myself."

Walsingham's amused grin said all that Elizabeth needed to know. She would not grant him direct access to these women just yet.

"Your Majesty, you would not want to witness these extraction events. They are most difficult on the eyes and belly."

Elizabeth leaned over her desk. "If I have to inflict the first blow upon their brows, I will do so myself. I am not afraid of violence. My stomach does not churn as does yours."

Walsingham feigned a wince at Her Majesty's reproach.

"Your Majesty, I only wished to spare you of this terrible event. There could be much blood. And vile blood has a contagion element to it, which would not be good for your person or this realm. You must let me help you in this endeavour to elicit information from this interloper of travel."

"How is it that she is known as a traveller and not by a Christian name?" demanded Elizabeth.

Walsingham placed his hands together and rested the sides of them on his lips and nose cupping his chin with his thumbs. He lifted them away slowly.

"She has roamed about the city swiftly and quietly. She wears beneath her borrowed gown the makings of a poor man's clothing. Her shoes are not laced and are of inferior leather with a tongue, which protrudes above her ankle at its base. These can only be the clothing of a traveller from foreign parts unknown." He displayed his hands outwards and shook his head from side to side.

"I do not recognize where she has come from, but I would like to deduce where this place resides. She has been seen talking to a spirit figure and taking instructions most unwillingly from him. This is an ominous, traitorous transgression. Her soul must be cleansed and purged of this evil. And your realm must be rid of such transgressions."

Elizabeth raised her eyebrows at the preposterousness of Walsingham's suggestions. There was no visible evil in her realm. Only the sins of man against man, she thought. True evil was tucked away, contained within sin. God would do justice to such doings. She had no need to interfere in the goings-on of God, but she would listen and quiet the noise, which would otherwise be noted and spread around by this master of intrigues, Walsingham.

"My dear Lord Walsingham, such indiscretions such as these will have an explanation. But between ourselves, we must deduce the nature of such folly on her part. As for Owen's wife, she is a mere servant and of no great influence on a trickster such as you speak about.

"Un…"

She raised her hand for silence. "When I have felt that there is no longer a need to have this traveller's neck upon my shores, I can assure you that every means possible will be used to dispatch her back from whence she came."

Walsingham nodded, but he was not satisfied.

Elizabeth noted that he was thinking of ways to convince her otherwise. His hands indicated their usual plotting position of late. He once more brought them up to his lips and nose placing his thumbs beneath his chin.

"I wish to interrogate this interloper myself," said Elizabeth. "I will determine with your advice as to the time spent inside the Tower. For now she remains its resident, as will Owen's wife. In a few day's' time, once some other intrigue breaches the curiosity of this court, I will have them moved. Perhaps we can move them with the help of Master Francis Drake. He has a way of keeping prisoners secure and the distribution of slaves below his decks from escaping. Removing her from London would be best, would it not?"

Walsingham nodded his slow response. "She must be dealt with quickly, Your Majesty, before these rumours about her spread further."

"Be assured Walsingham, I will see to it myself."

"Perhaps you could address the removal of these women with an order. I could then implement their transfer for you more swiftly."

"I will do so, but not yet. I want her to fret and be fearful for now. Placement in the Tower will be an inducement. Especially as they are to have no food or means of warmth for the next two nights."

Robbie could hear none of the conversation, which played out in Elizabeth's chamber. His anger rose at the prospect of Walsingham taking over from where he had left off. It was he who had secured this most interesting woman for Elizabeth. He was to be the one to help her decide the fate of these women. Perhaps it was time to enlist the help of Catherine again. She was good at spreading rumours and driving up the interest in other's affairs. He fumbled at his waistcoat and pulled out the note Elizabeth had written.

He read with interest what Elizabeth had written and smiled.

Find out who else knows her current whereabouts
and make note of who asks of her. Then report
back to me at once. We will decide between
us what is best for my realm. Do not be seen
or heard asking direct questions. E

Trapped and in Need

The Tower, June 1576

Professor Kathleen O'Malley stared down at the slumbering Edith and watched for the signs of breathing. She was hesitant at first to allow Edith the easily proffered drink, which Robbie had given. She had not drunk her own. She would not. Besides, there was little privacy and a distinct lack of a loo. She was not about to squat and aim above that filthy pot and have her gaoler watch. Robbie's men had been amused at her presence. They had peeked through the trap hole in their prison door far too often. What did they think she would do other than sit or sleep? Curiosity would get them a poke in the eyes soon if they did not quit.

She reached for Edith's neck to check for a pulse and tried to count her pulse. Her skin did not feel clammy or damp. How long would she sleep? Kathleen smelt the familiarity of her own skin and longed then for the wet, sweet smell of rumpled hair and clothing of her boys after playing, their overflowing gumboots, so full of the sea and weeds. Mud, scratches, blood, runny noses, torn and twisted clothing hanging out, all of it. She ached for all of it.

"What have they done with my boys," she mumbled softly leaning over Edith. "What have they done with them?"

Kathleen looked carefully across the body of Edith looking for signs of a purse or bag, which might contain useful items. She was looking for anything that could be used to inflict pain or help in the escape they so needed to make. Her chances were doubtful at best, but she had to try for her boys' sake. Edith would have to be coaxed into telling her what to expect next and where her boys might reside at present.

She pulled at Edith's waist and hoped she had found the makings for a weapon. Small bits of a powdery substance lay inside a hidden pouch. She removed the pouch carefully and tied it under her own dress, making sure that Robbie's men had not been watching.

She examined the contents slowly keeping her ears open and an eye on the latch at all times. A piece of twine, a small cross, a rock, some herbs in an amulet, coins, two keys… "An amulet…what does she ward off evil from?" she spoke softly? This woman is superstitious, she mused. Very pagan in origin, or is it something else? I'll have to watch for signs of ritual or anxiety at the discovery of the loss of this pouch.

For the second time that day, Kathleen found herself looking around for useful bits, which she could use against her captors, if necessary, or for escape. The room was empty other than straw bedding, an empty desk and chair. No logs were present for a fire. There was no water, nothing really except the coldness of stone and the constant lap of the Thames on the other side of her flagstone floor and the rock and mortar enclosure. Another door in their chamber led…she knew not where. But her own memory recalled walking up a spiral stone staircase as a teenager when visiting this ancient site with her parents in the late 1970s.

She shook her head clear of that thought. How could this be happening? She was a woman with her own children, lost in an inhospitable enclosure with a woman she did not quite trust, but she needed her to escape the bloody mess the two of them were in. She gathered dust and bits of mortar by scratching at the voids opened up by time and this prison's former inhabitants. Maybe she could throw these bits in one of her captor's eyes.

Slowly she gathered these crumbs and stowed them inside the pouch. Her nails were torn off from the relentless pursuit of mortar slag. Who else, she thought, had done the same? What were their crimes, heresy, traitor, or perhaps some mere poorly timed words? She shook her head. These thoughts would not help in her escape from here.

How many women had been here? Had the queen been one of its former guests, or had she been kept in the statelier buildings she had witnessed earlier on at their arrival? She had espied the black timbered structures from above, whilst being moved along, inside the great castles outer wall enclosure. At least, she thought, they had not arrived through Traitors Gate, but had been marched along the cobbled streets, past the crowds who clamoured around Robbie's men, dipping low to catch a glimpse of his female prisoners.

There had been whisperings, which she had caught snatches of. It had alarmed and reassured her that they were going somewhere other than the prison located in Bermondsey, the infamous Clink on the southern banks of the Thames. They had entered London proper now and were within its gates Kathleen thought, or were they? Did the White Tower and castle's keep belong inside or just outside of the city gates? Yes, she recalled. She was inside the gates, just below Aldgate and Whitechapel in the east end.

Perhaps there was a means of escape after all. There were fields beyond the keep. She had seen them from her position just inside the Tower's main entrance. Its high walls and walk had enabled a good view beyond. There were many fields in which to hide and perhaps along the Thames shores, maybe she could even find another wherry. She was pretty sure she could reach Greenwich. However, right now she needed a way to get out. She needed an escape route and time, precious time to locate her children.

What will they want from us? What can we give them to render a release for their freedom? She sucked on the ends of her bleeding fingers and bit down hard to stop the sting of her cuts.

Right now I need some outside help and fast. Memories flashed before her of Emily and the shaman. What was it that Emily had said about helping her, or had she just imagined all of this? Perhaps she would wake up soon. She usually did when her nightmares became too much to bear.

Two Little Birdies

Bermondsey's Church, June 1576

Owen gripped the handle of wood proffered before him, waiting for the sting, crunch and righting of his nose back into place. The priest Malcolm seized Owen's head between his hands whilst Albert pulled hard on the cartilage of his nose and brought it back into alignment. Owen swore he would get even with that woman over this indiscretion of hers. How dare she break his nose? Three noses had now been straightened. She had escaped his clutches and had been snatched by Her Majesty's favourite, Robbie, and had wreaked havoc upon his devoted servants of God.

"She will need to be dispatched quickly. Do not let her go again. For she will tear down this house of God and all that is in it. Blasphemous bitch!" he spat out.

Edward and Reginald with his proud long Norman nose nodded in agreement. Malcolm and Albert continued to wipe the blood off their hands onto their habits. Owen looked over at the open doorway before speaking again.

"We will need to find a way into the Tower's prison and dispatch that woman and my wife in your crypts below."

Albert with his bird-like thin appearance looked up.

"We're Catholic, Your Lord. We cannot go in there without risk of being slaughtered ourselves."

"Then you will disrobe yourselves from papal vestments and ingratiate yourselves into Her Majesty's faith."

"Owen," snapped Malcolm, "you need to work on your man inside. Walsingham's spies must be used, but by us this time." Malcolm's short stocky body stood firmly erect, and the bulge on his thick neck pulsed.

"No! We will enter that prison. Make sure we do not find our way blocked. And look to your back if we are. I will not be felled by a woman again," said Owen.

Edward shifted uncomfortably and shook his shoulders as if suddenly cold. His shuddering caught the eye of the others. They glared at him through cold narrowing eyes and clenched teeth. His weakness had been noted before. There was no room in their midst for a weakling who fretted and diverted their attentions from the use of force, even if he was a giant of a man. It would take the three of them or more to take the blond man down.

"Where will they have placed her? She did not go through Traitors Gate. That is significant, is it not?" said Edward defensively.

"How do you know this?" asked Malcolm.

"I watched them cross over the bridge whilst you lot were gathering your weapons. I followed their progress and that of Walsingham's urchins. I did not see the gates at the Thames bring forth any prisoners."

Owen raised his eyebrows in disbelief.

"You watched for that long without being observed yourself?"

He nodded. "I went down to the river and waited until I could see the crowds on the other side. I scanned the shoreline to see if any wherries approached Traitors Gate. They did not."

"Good. Then we can proceed." Perhaps he will be useful after all, thought Owen.

The five of them headed off towards the crypt below the altar. It was a place of special significance. They had exposed the bowels of men within its enclosure and strangled them with their own entrails. Owen preferred to watch and interrogate his prisoners using the hot tongs from a roasting fire. No one left this lair. That was never part of any bargain, however much he agreed to let them go. Freed prisoners could talk, and he needed no residual problems.

He would plan the demise of this most disgusting woman and his vile wife. He had no need of her now. As if he ever did, he thought. Perhaps this traveller has been useful after all. He smiled. Two little birdies killed with one stone.

Bargaining

—✕—

Spiritual Inclinations.
Double talk and unbreakable vows.
Inducements lead to lies, cheaters and snakes.

London's Tower walls June 1576

"Foolish woman. I told you to wait for me inside the church. Instead now, you are stuck inside the Tower's walls."

A winter's chill wound itself up Kathleen's spine... that voice. Drake, she thought. Riveted to the floor of her prison she slowly turned her head in the direction of sound. She peered long and hard at the prone figure of Edith quietly sleeping on the pallet. Kathleen felt a swift cold breeze pass by her left side, and she turned in its direction.

"Nothing..." This is too surreal, she thought.

She licked her lips, bit down hard on them and stood erect.

"You speak, but do not show yourself."

Kathleen looked around the small prison cell. No one was there. She placed her hands on either side of her head and squeezed her temples as tightly as she could stand and screamed. "AAAAHHH. You Bastard, how dare you talk to me like that? You're the one who got me into this mess in the first place. Show yourself."

The trap door on the thick oak door opened, and she stared into the face of her guard. His eyes were wide with curiosity. She ran over to the door and spat into his eyes.

"Witch." he swore and slammed the tiny door closed.

"You'll be paying for that witch…I'll see to it that Robert Dudley knows what you are."

Kathleen shook her head, censoring herself. "I shouldn't have done that." These men were her captors. She would have to behave and give them no more reasons to think illogically of her, she thought. There must be a way to be free. There just had to be. The safety of her children depended on it. Who else knew of their presence in this realm? she wondered. Think now Professor Kathleen O'Malley. What do you remember about this place? You've been here before now, just not in this century?

Kathleen looked over at Edith again and felt a pang of pity for the slumbering lady who had no power and few friends in this inhospitable city. She would save Edith, if at all possible. At the very least she would teach Edith how to defend herself from these conspiring men surrounding them.

I will need to find out just what Edith can do well and capitalize on this woman's strengths. She must be good at something.

The vibrations along the muscles at the base of her spine hummed like a finely plucked guitar string.

He comes again, she thought. This was is his signal, she recognized Drake's impending presence. Drake was about to communicate.

This is my opportunity to control you, Drake, not the other way around.

Kathleen smiled and waited. She would listen to Drake but not be dictated to. It was, however, unfortunate that she needed him now.

"Why do you not listen and do as you are told?" he snapped.

"It is not in my nature to do your bidding. I never said I would." She folded her arms across her chest and stood waiting. She did not notice Edith open her eyes staring at her back.

"You have been a problem for me ever since I brought you through the spirit world into Her Majesty's lands," he said.

"Perhaps. What of it?"

"You will do as I say, for you have no options left."

"We will see, for you are not the only one with distinctive powers, Sir Drake".

Edith strained to hear both sides of the conversation. Edith thought she could hear someone else speak as well, and yet there was no one else besides the two of them. Edith crumpled her eyebrows and squeezed the last drop of a tear from her eyes.

Kathleen sensed something moving around her neck. It moved away temporarily and then tightened itself again.

"Get away from me!" She was breathing but her mouth, nose and neck felt suddenly tight.

"The only way out of here now is by negotiation. You must ask for an audience with the queen. You must insist upon this. It is your only hope of escape, you obstinate woman."

"Why would the queen want to speak with me?"

"Elizabeth has sensed your presence and wishes to avert any unpleasantness with her subjects. They are a nervous, superstitious lot. Elizabeth has been led to believe in your powers of escape. This amuses Her Majesty, and you must avail yourself to her and engage in vows of secrecy. She likes secrets, our queen."

Kathleen turned and noticed Edith had moved. Edith is awake. She has heard me talking out loud? She must think I'm a witch. So too do those men barring the way out of here. Maybe I can use that to my advantage, she thought.

"Too dangerous," Kathleen whispered to herself.

Communicating and controlling with Drake required discretion. She walked softly towards the outer wall beside the Thames and spoke to him, goading Drake into a response.

"I have no secrets of escape."

"You have the advantage of time on your side," he said.

"What is that supposed to mean?"

"You are a long way from home, are you not?"

"Too far, no thanks to you."

She leaned against the stone wall and listened for the sound of the Thames as it slapped the outer surface of her enclosure. Its stench seeped through the rough slit of their glassless window. She could hear the cries of its wherrymen shouting their way across its shores. Men were everywhere, outside these walls, inside this castle and its keep, everywhere around her, and not one of them gentlemanly enough to be helpful at present. Chivalry has already begun its death toll, she thought and sighed.

She snapped her head around when the constriction on her throat loosened.

"It is my education which is my greatest asset, I believe."

"You are wrong, wench. Women like you are not educated."

"What's that supposed to mean, you fool? I'm a professor. I'm very educated."

"That's of no consequence to me. You are not an educated woman. There is no such thing nor ever will there be. There might be a few women who can read and write in a variety of languages, such as the queen. But you are not a woman of class, therefore you have no rank and no liberties in which to promote these ridiculous protestations."

Kathleen smiled and thought of the University of Victoria campus where she taught history.

"You are a delusional man, Drake, why else would you be here now? This notion of yours to change recorded history will not take place until there are primary source documents that are found, which verify your supposed journey up the Pacific coastline to southern Alaska. Therefore you will remain as the queen's best-known pirate who also managed to circumnavigate the globe. But that is all. However great that voyage might have been, there are no documents left to be had and pulled apart for all that its pages may glean to the known world."

"If you do not do my bidding, your head shall rot like all the other traitors upon the ramparts of Nonesuch House at the entrance to this city."

"Do your bidding? Think on, Master Drake. I am not amused or afraid of your delusional musings. I do no man's bidding."

Edith closed her eyes quickly when Kathleen turned around from her rooted spot and began pacing the room. She did not want to look into the eyes of the woman who had brought about the destruction of her life and chance of bearing children with Owen, her husband.

Owen would no longer want her and would think nothing of casting her out into the streets. The streets were no place for a lone woman. Mercy did not show itself on the streets of London. It didn't know how. Tears formed in the corners of Edith's eyes. Edith feared moving any part of her body. She did not want to respond to these blasphemous words in case it let that traveller know she, Edith, could hear every word the traveller and Drake were saying to one another. Edith did not want the traveller, her prison companion, to come near. She felt an uncontrolled shiver and prayed to God for deliverance from this hell she was now in.

Kathleen noted the trickle of a tear slowly running down Edith's cheek. This poor woman, what must she be thinking? Kathleen removed a scrap of cloth from the pouch, beneath her dress's skirts and bending over towards the prone figure of Edith softly dabbed at the smudged, puffy face whose eyes were squeezed tightly shut. She stroked the blonde hair of her companion and then laid her hand upon Edith's hand.

"Don't be afraid, Edith, I'll get us out of here. You'll be okay. I promise you."

Edith snatched her hand away and tucked it underneath her body. Edith rolled away from the eyes and hands of her tormentor.

"You are wrong, lady of foreign speech. Have you not forgot whose walls we are now entrenched in? This is our prison. We will never be released. You have caused the destruction of my life. Our gaolers will take it upon themselves now to torture us. They will call us witches. Witches are burned at the stake."

Kathleen took a long deep breath in and sighed.

"Not if I can help it."

Kathleen knew that what Edith had said could probably be true, but she was a twenty-first century woman! There had to be a way out of here. And she would need to motivate the frightened beast within Edith to help her take action against their guardians.

"We're not putting up with that!"

Edith rolled her head and body towards Kathleen. She leaned up on her elbow and searched the face which bore itself in front of her. A small glimmer of hope eased itself momentarily into her weary eyes.

"You will bear children, Edith."

"No, they will burn us at the stake. We are condemned before we speak."

Kathleen sighed and shook her head in Edith's direction.

"You're wrong. They want me to do something I've been unwilling to do. But if you help me, I'll reconsider, but I cannot tell you what it's all about. It would be better for all if I told no one."

Kathleen felt the now familiar chill run up her spine and knew her latest words to Edith had summoned Drake to hope. Kathleen, the traveller, wanted-- NO, she needed his help. And soon Drake would be the one doing her bidding. It would not be the other way around, she hoped.

"Edith, I know you can hear him speak to me. I've seen your movements in response to his voice. He is not the devil." At least not the one you're thinking of, she thought.

"I don't deny Master Drake being with us. He's our most precious adversary at present. Think of him as a gift, a way out of these stone walls which encase us both and prevent us from reaching our goals."

Edith looked into Kathleen's eyes, searching for some kind of recognition. This invasive woman who spoke only in riddles and nonsense and who brought havoc had an alarming and calming feeling upon her soul. This woman was indeed the witch who invaded souls. She would listen to its other voice, but she would not help it in its quest.

These things which had invaded her house could be rectified via the priests. Owen's priests, thought Edith. They would cleanse this witch, the traveller's soul. Edith vowed then to cleanse her own soul and confess all of her sins, only then would she be free of this witch. Edith would abide with this witch for now, this traveller, only until she could be freed of her clutches.

"Oh merciful Father, forgive me, for I have sinned. Lead me not into temptation. Deliver me from this evil which befalls me. I believe in your power and your glory forever more." She made the sign of the cross upon her brow and across her breast. "Amen" She bowed her head in prayer, her tears streaking down her cheek.

"He speaks. Listen to all he says," whispered Kathleen.

Edith nodded assent, wiping away the moisture from her face. She sat up slowly craning her neck upon her shoulder listening for the unspoken words.

"Okay, Drake, we know you're here. What do you want?"

"You know already of what I want. You must gather my documents from Whitehall and bring them forth."

"I can't do that yet."

"Of course you can."

"NO, I cannot, for you have yet to take your voyage across the seas."

"What? Do not talk riddles, woman, or I will leave you here to rot."

"You are mistaken. You have brought me back too soon. You have made a grave mistake. Your voyage of discovery has yet to be completed. You've brought me back too soon."

"You know of my voyages. I have succeeded where no other Englishman has been. I have accomplished a great deal for my queen. I am a wealthy man. You are a poor woman, who lives with her widowed mother and shows no duty to a man. You will do as I bid or your children will perish."

"That may very well be but not at this point in time."

"Do not speak such nonsense. You know what I want."

Kathleen smiled, for she knew then that he did not understand the exact date in time which he had sent her.

"This is the year 1576, Drake. You have not yet set out on your journey of discovery," Kathleen mused. "You wish for me to speak with our queen on your behalf. You wish for me to secure your voyage to the new lands. That I can do. But to retrieve your documents from a voyage which has of yet not taken place, that I cannot do."

"But you must, I have stated that you must."

"The voyage you wish me to retrieve your journals from has not yet taken place. Her Majesty hasn't even issued your leave, your vessels and your writ of privateer. These things have not yet happened, and they need to, for I can only do for you what has transpired. I cannot retrieve from your future yet."

Kathleen smiled, for she knew he now understood. Edith, however, looked alarmed and puzzled.

"You have brought yourself before the queen asking her for permission. She has yet to consent to your wishes, Drake. I can, however, help you with that. And we can come to an agreement about my sons."

"Humph… So, if this is so, I have erred momentarily. Still I have your sons, and you had better live up to your promises. There must be some way to retrieve my journals and maps? I speak from the other side, from the world of the raven and whale. I reside as you well know within the belly of the Kraken, and I can always bring you back."

"For now, though, you will remain in that place, Drake. However, do not forget too, my vow with the shaman, for there is also a way of removing you from controlling the world of in-between. And I will relieve you of this power some day. But for now you need to prepare yourself for a voyage to the green fertile lands of the Irish for your queen. Once you have satisfied Her Majesty Queen Elizabeth of your loyalties, then she will issue you that writ of privateer. Once you possess it, retake that voyage of discovery and place those items which you so desperately want within the belly of your current Kraken world. And bloody well don't lose them to her this time."

Edith's eyelids opened. Her enlarged pupils shone brightly, her mouth gaped open at the mention of the Kraken. Edith understood this beast of the seas. It had swallowed up her brother, her father and some of her cousins. This beast had spit out others, but had taken more than Edith's relatives with it. Edith had lost her home, her moorings and her way of life because of its ravenous appetite.

Kathleen looked sternly at Edith. Had she just heard Edith's thoughts now too? She brought her hand up to her own mouth and pinched her fingers closed across her lips. She shook her head in Edith's direction. Kathleen hoped Edith would not address Drake directly. This improbable scenario was complicated enough without another person communicating directly with Drake.

"What I can do for you, Drake, if you will release my sons is come to an understanding with Her Majesty about the importance of your voyage to the Pacific seas. And its urgency upon her realm and the implications and triumphs it will bring her."

"Implications! There are none."

The Armada will come. That is the implications of your voyage."

Edith felt the movement swirl its way across her back and around her belly. She shivered and brought her hand up to her mouth. Kathleen viewed the terrified widened eyes that met hers. She walked over to Edith and gently caressed the woman's back.

"Lie down, close your eyes, breathe deeply," she whispered. "He cannot harm us in here, but he can help us escape." She smiled down at Edith and gently closed her lids. "He cannot harm you. These are only words, a voice that penetrates and shows itself selfishly, a man who wants more than Her Majesty will permit."

"Am I to believe, that you prescribe that the queen will not grant my voyage? You have implied that I must remain within this beast for the rest of my days. Preposterous! You speak such tales. I will not believe such lies."

"I am speaking the truth, Drake. The year in which you have placed me is the summer of 1576. Your journey, if it is to be granted, will not take place until the fall of 1577. And you must make other voyages before to prove to Her Majesty your worthiness. Such an immense voyage has great risks. Can you convince her to let you go? I know I can."

"I will keep your children locked away if what you say is to be true. I will not release them. You must retrieve my journals and the maps. You will take back with you the trappings of my voyage. These things will be found. And you will find them."

"Only after you release my children."

"No."

Kathleen shook her head. This was becoming more complicated than she had anticipated. She raised her hands to her head and squeezed its sides again. She ran her hand across her forehead and down the back of her head.

"I don't think so. We must come to some arrangement, Drake. We must bargain with each other. It is the only way. Go away. You've made a mistake. I will help you, but you must help me as well. I cannot do anything you ask of me without first releasing Edith and myself from our prison walls. You must elicit our release."

"Humph. You shall make a promise of your sons. They will accompany me upon the seas. You will release them to my possession. It is the only bargain I shall make with you."

Kathleen shook her head. She would not give up her sons to this monster, who thinks to rule the seas. They are too young. They are but mere boys, she thought.

"No, they are not yours to take at your will."

"Then you shall rot where you lie. I will not help you escape the trap you have now found yourself in."

"And I shall not let it be known of your wishes. Your voyage it will not take place. You shall remain within your spirit world of shamans and Krakens, trapped by your vanity. Your world will cease to have the air which you seek to breathe again or walk upon the shores of the lands which you once discovered."

She paced about the rooms listening intently to sounds or sensations his mind might send forth. Nothing, she thought.

"Your world will cease to exist. You shall become but dust and echoes, withering away to nothing. Your infamy will vanish."

"Two can play this game, and you will lose your children in the bargain. I will send them on to speak with you."

Kathleen's throat tightened and became parched. A knot gripped her side below her breast and squeezed her gall bladder into spasms. She gripped the ache within her side and cursed at him.

"You Bastard." She realized her mistake too late. And tried to reclaim her composure.

"You will send my children into this prison?"

"No, I will send in men to teach you a lesson. I may even visit you myself when you are more inclined to listen. And you will listen, for I have your children. Do not forget what it is that I keep."

"I won't let you have access to my children. What men do as adults, though, I may not have a hold over." She would make sure her children never spoke to strangers ever again.

But Drake had heard all that he wanted. She had agreed to let him have them when they became men, a trifling ten years from now, and he would keep that bargain close to his interests. Oh, how foolish woman are, he thought.

Carlos and Stowe Debate

Bermondsey's shore, June 1576

Stowe recognized the coming voice echoing its frustrations from within the belly of the Kraken.

"He speaks, Carlos. What say we now, for we have lost them?"

The two men, one Spanish the other English stood shoulder to shoulder along the side of the church. They had witnessed the women's near death escape from the priests, the capture and release from Owen and his men. This had been a blessing but one which had also brought about another complexity. The women now needed to escape from the Tower.

"The priest, Reginald, has no like for women or Protestants," said Stowe in anger.

"He has no respect for Catholics either," sneered Carlos. "These are not good men. They do not abide by Roman rule."

Both men shook their heads and entered the doorway of the small church.

"We must not attract attention," Carlos continued. "Let us recover any object found to belong to the women, especially that of the traveller's. She cannot leave behind any evidence of her time spent amongst us."

They nodded agreement again.

"You are mistaken about Rome's rule, though. It is not yet reformed," said Stowe. "And many inquisitional interrogations are yet to be performed. Do not forget Carlos that you too are not of this realm. If you are to be caught by Owen's men or even Her Majesty's, you could suffer the same fate that awaits these women now. You would be seen as a traitor. Your corpse would hang from those iron hooks above the Thames."

Carlos, sighed softly and nodded his agreement.

"I will have to be careful and avoid the eyes of your Parliament, but I cannot leave her here. She has helped me in her world. I have evaded death because of her. She does not choose to remember this, but I do. And she has brought forth many others. We reside now within her community. She has even housed our children through the guise of them being international students."

The two men looked up at the approaching priest, Reginald. They stiffened at his movements towards them. His face, with a clearly swollen nose and bruised lips, looked more menacing now than it did before.

"She has done him a favour, I see. He suits that which sports upon his face," grinned Carlos.

"Ah, indeed, she has done him well," Stowe whispered back. "Hmm, Drake chose well, this one who travels."

"I do not recognize you as my parishioners. Where do come from?"

"We are merely come to pray, My Lord. It has been some days and weeks since our souls have been inside such a fine Catholic Church as this."

Reginald stopped and signalled for the men to follow him. He led them up to the altars first bench, beckoned them to sit and prayed for them, placing his hands upon their heads. It was not a long prayer. It was crisp, short and abrupt. He left them just as suddenly. They listened as his footsteps echoed past the altar and through the small doorway off to the right side of the church, its doors lay slightly open upon its massive hinge, but they could not hear the voices from within.

"Albert, use that slight body of yours to follow them. Edward, just follow them when they leave. Do not let them recognize that bulk of yours. Do not lose them," he sneered. "Report back all that they impart. Those two there near the altar, know things, too many things. I can feel it in my bones. That Spaniard may be a Catholic, but he converses with the Protestant enemy. He is not trustable."

"He could be one of King Phillip's men, sent to spy on Her Majesty, My Lord," said Malcolm curtly.

"You are easily fooled and misled, Malcolm. Do not put your trust in the enemy who cavorts with these blasphemous pigs. I will see to his drowning upon one of London's most prominent wharfs," laughed Reginald.

He spit out the bile and blood that had rolled between his teeth. He had saved it, working its way around his mouth. He had wanted to spit it at them and bloody the foulness of their breath. His disgust at foreign pretenders to his true faith angered and repulsed him.

"I will see to their ruin. Now go and do my bidding. We will disgorge the innards of Stowe's companion, later tonight. I have yet to decide if his corpse will emerge at low tide."

Reginald waved his bloodied tunic sleeve at them and sneered his browning teeth in the direction of the unwanted worshipers.

"Do not be seen by Her Majesty's favourite, for Robert will recognize you. I can feel it in your guts that you know of what I speak. Discard your robes and the authority they hold. Lose them. Glean what you can from the merchants upon the streets of London's only bridge. Let it be known that the traveller and Edith are witches."

The priests looked sideways at each other, confused.

"Who is this traveller?" They spoke in unison.

Reginald sneered again. He could not stand stupidity, and he was always amazed by what element of men could inhabit the robe of priest. His rank in the church had come quickly, but then he had not faltered from the true faith and the torture of its non-believing supplicants. Some of his brethren were not so inclined to faith. Pity, he thought. Reginald's implements of torture were well known, even sought after. But he had not given up their location nor would he. They were his, he thought. "All mine," he said softly to himself.

"The traveller is that women whom Edith has dragged out of Her Majesty's palace. Do not act such fools. Have you not forgotten how the queen's favourite spoke of her to Owen and his men? Pay attention. It will do you some good in my eyes and that of your church. Be gone all of you. NOW!"

Reginald turned his back upon his fellow priests. He stormed away from them and leaned over his desk. A few drops of blood smeared the vellum which lay across his desk. He did not bother to wipe it clean, for he wanted to remember that witch and what she had done to him.

"NOW," he repeated.

Both Carlos and Stowe looked up from their musings to one another.

"It is time to leave this place," said Carlos.

Stowe nodded his agreement.

"Get thee across the bridge and elicit all that you can from its occupants of the women caught between Robert's horses and his men," whispered Stowe.

"I will seek out Drake and converse with him to behest the release of our women. I shall tell him of their troubles."

The two men rose from their positions upon the cold stone floors. Both wished for cleaner, undecaying air and for information, which could lead to the recovery of their quarry. They walked, nodded on their agreements and started off in opposite directions. Stowe nodded at Carlos raised his eyebrow and dipped his head in the direction of the priests following them.

"Keep an eye to your back and a look out to your forward movements. There is evil making its way close by," whispered Stowe.

Drake's Proposal

Westminster Palace
June 1576

Elizabeth paced back and forth within her private chambers. She did not want to converse with anyone who did not report upon the situation of these invasive prisoners. She was tired of these games which played out their actions inside her realm. She was disgusted by the intrusions from foreign potentates and their emissaries. Having another potential explosive problem within her inner circle was intolerable. She needed to shut down this most troublesome development of the traveller.

Elizabeth grasped hold of her pearls and began rubbing them between her fingers. She willed herself not to seek out Robbie again, to speak in confidence with her favourite courtier despite the calm that she knew would prevail in her mind if she did so.

Her realm was not in danger despite what the men of her court had made themselves to believe. Her life was complex, but even so, she was still the master of it and not Cecil or Walsingham. Robbie did not, or most often did not, she thought, interfere in state matters. He was consistently her sounding board, listening and advising only when she became agitated. His advice was always calming, and he was consistent in his mannerisms towards her, never overstepping those delicate boundaries of feelings too much. She dared not let it be known that she enjoyed his company too much, but she needed his presence beside her nonetheless.

In her darkest hours within the Tower's prison she had been comforted by Robbie's words. He too had been imprisoned by the same gaoler, Elizabeth's sister, Bloody Queen Mary.

Both their father's had acted out foolishly in their selfish lives. Elizabeth and Robert had both watched in horror as Robert's father had been led out of the same prison they were in. Lord Dudley, Robbie's father, had walked to the scaffold reluctantly, presenting himself as best as he could, but his screams as he was dragged behind the cart still resounded inside Elizabeth's head. His innards had been pulled out of his belly and fried in front of him. What life that had remained, had then been dragged, wrenched up by his neck and hung for three days. His head had rotted for three years before it had been removed for another of her sister, Queen Mary's victims. Mary had retained the infamous title of the BLACK Queen of Death, she did not wish for the same for herself. A virgin WHITE Queen was more appealing. Elizabeth shuddered at the memory of times past.

Elizabeth braced herself for the next onslaught of intruders who would comment upon the recent events of this traveller. She had summoned a meeting of her councillors, those men whom she could trust to keep things safe from probing ears. Elizabeth sighed, picked up her pearls again and began the familiar rubbing of their glossy surface. Each bead was gently stroked, passing through her hands one at a time.

A knock on her chamber door indicated that the first one had arrived. She was startled to find instead that it was Drake. At least he had an apologetic deportment, thought Elizabeth.

"What is it this time, Master Drake? Have we not solved all of your issues? I do not want to discuss any further voyages at present. Do not speak to me of such matters. News, man, bring me good news," she shrieked at him.

Drake stood before his queen. He breathed in slowly, a long deep breath. He needed to put forth this idea that the traveller could help his queen. He already knew he would travel to far-off lands. The traveller had indicated so. But how? he thought. What new information could he impart? What would induce Elizabeth to finally let him pursue his goals of discovery along the south Pacific seashore sooner? He did not want to squelch the Irish again. The traveller, he thought, she is the key to this. What could the traveller tell Her Majesty?

"She has come, Your Grace, the one who imparts knowledge of King Phillip's plans. I told you before that she is not a spy. She does hold information, which would be of import to you. You must release her from the Tower's prison."

Elizabeth rounded on Drake,

"How dare you tell me what to do with my prisoners. I will decide their fate, not you or anyone else. How do you know of her existence? Speak. Tell all you know, NOW."

Drake dropped unto one knee and bowed.

"Your Majesty, I have come to this knowledge from the streets. It is everywhere. They say she is a witch, a foreteller of the future, who knows many things of which have yet to come."

Elizabeth looked up towards the ceiling of her chamber and slowly lowered her eyes down the length of the vibrant colours of the tapestry, which lined the one wall within her room. Its scenes were of horses and riders with their hounds in pursuit of deer and foxes. It always soothed her weary limbs and throbbing temples. Its familiarity eased her exploding brain. She found comfort from the memory of a recent chase. She loved the hunt, the smell of earth as its dirt flung up and past her horse's hooves. She loved the taste of the cool autumn air upon her breast and inside her lungs. The tapestry reminded her of the sweetness of the hay being gathered and stored within barns. It was the calming she needed to remember, to take her back to a time when she felt in control and exhilarated. She breathed in deeply before turning from her tapestry back towards Drake. Elizabeth faced Drake with the sternness of a vibrant, calculating queen, one who he dared not disobey.

Drake noted the stiffness of her shoulders, how the hands, which had gripped the pearls at her side now lay themselves lightly upon the fine linen of her bodice. She was thinking again, he thought. He would need to tread carefully. Elizabeth was an honourable queen, but one who he had to be wary of as well. Her temper resembled that of her father's, and the brightness of his red hair echoed out of her brows and the crown that she seldom wore. She is at her finest, as always, when provoked into action.

Elizabeth chose to disregard his last words. After all how could there be such talk on her streets yet. The woman hadn't been loose long enough. Her recapture had been swift.

She remembered then that the traveller had escaped and beaten Owen at what he had been most noted for. She raised an eyebrow. Perhaps it is Owen, then, that spreads these rumours. Someone certainly has.

Owen had broken more than a few noses of his own in his time. She smiled at the thought of a mere woman beating him at his own game. He would want revenge. His temper, thought Elizabeth, was never more controlled than her own. Elizabeth had seen him using his interrogation techniques before. Owen usually employed the use of tongs to snap his victim's nose. Less blood he had said. Elizabeth had witnessed these accounts herself. She did not want her men thinking of her as weak.

She was thankful that the same implements of torture used on her prisoners had not been used on her. It had occurred to her that Mary, her sister, had intended on torturing her during her imprisonment. King Phillip of Spain had rescued her from Mary's anguish over religion. Elizabeth had smiled as genuinely as possible in his presence. She knew then that he had intentions upon her body and not that of her sister. He had abhorred the thought of sleeping with his own wife. Elizabeth smiled at this memory.

Elizabeth's own flesh and family bloodline had shown its weakest link in that of her sister, Mary Tudor? Never. Mary was an Aragon through and through. No courage, no guts, no Gloriana. Mary embodied only the countenance of a weak woman needing a man to lead her.

Elizabeth would not be led by anyone, least of all a man. However, there are favourites to be had in this world, she thought. One needs favourites. They are very useful and pliable if led righteously.

Elizabeth smiled at the bowed form in front of her. She noted his formality of dress. He has changed his clothes to suit my vanity. He has changed tactics again, she thought. His humility before his queen showed some knowledge of craft. Drake's willingness to work for his prize was duly noted. Perhaps he could be of some use as yet.

He has outmaneuvered more than one adversary of late, including King Phillip of Spain. It might be useful, after all, thought Elizabeth, to engage Drake in the ferrying of her prisoners south of London, away from London's prying ears and eyes. Somewhere, Elizabeth herself could tolerate the oncoming hotter nights. A more intimate palace would suit her own needs, a palace such as that of Greenwich.

Here Elizabeth could even tolerate conducting the interrogation herself. This woman traveller has showed great courage in the face of trouble and was indeed worth conversing with. She surmised from the moment of first encounter that the traveller was quick-witted and showed no intention of harm towards herself or her women. This swiftness of the traveller's moves on the inner stairwell had impressed upon Elizabeth the usefulness of such an adversary. She had enjoyed her boldness, her lack of fear, even her confidence. And now Elizabeth would enjoy hearing of the traveller's escape from Owen. She would enjoy also reminding Walsingham's rogue Owen of this most fortunate ability of the traveller.

She let Drake kneel where he was purposely. Humility was good for a man's soul, especially towards his monarch. She would let him rise soon enough. She needed those knees of his to be supple and able to sail the seas for her again in search of badly needed treasures. Her store of funds was dwindling more than she liked at present.

Elizabeth needed to consult Cecil, her most loyal of councillors. His plans of action, of wait and see, of doing little to create great interest, were gaining impetus upon her actions of late. The usefulness of one's emissaries could only be relied upon if they were discreet, furtive and evasive. Discreet was the more challenging problem. The traveller was a problem, which Elizabeth could not afford to release upon London and her realm. She turned now towards Drake.

"A foreteller of the future? Indeed? Tell me more. This word upon my streets that plagues your mind so, Master Drake? Speak now." Elizabeth averted her eyes and looked down upon her thin hands and nails. They were clean at least, she thought.

"Your Majesty, there is a witch about, one who vanishes and reappears. She has created a furor of interest. There are priests about who wish to eliminate her presence."

"Do not be concerned with the follies of simple men. Their worries are frequently changing. This apparition will depart from simple minds and talk of it will disappear sooner than you think, good man."

"Not if those Catholic priests upon Bermondsey's shores have anything to say about it."

"What nonsense do you bring before me now? Catholic priests who dare rise up and stir sentiments against me? Now, now, dear man, this cannot be. That would be foolish indeed, wouldn't it?"

Drake chose then to look up and into the eyes of his monarch. Those penetrating dark eyes rimmed with red lashes revealed the amusement of her father's earlier years. She has chosen either to ignore or goad me, he thought. Drake smiled back, nodded his head in agreement and raised an eyebrow indicating agreement.

"Your Majesty, as always, you are ever so cleaver."

"Do not patronize me. My patience is wearing thin. Be done with this, unless you have more to impart."

He nodded again.

"It is just that the priests are plotting her capture."

Elizabeth stared down at Drake with a sneer.

"How come by you of such foolishness by these men?"

"I have overheard their speech. Their intentions are to eliminate the traveller and use her presence as an example of witchcraft and evil. They plan to stir up the masses and create turmoil, angst, even fear amongst your people. They must be stopped."

"Indeed they must. Thank you, Master Drake. You may go now."

"Your Majesty, May I – "

"You may not…I may, however, have a small task for you to perform. Stay at your lodgings until a messenger arrives. I will have need of your services soon upon the Thames. Now depart from my presence." She

343

glared at him with a slight grin, eager to have him gone. She would need to seek the company of Cecil immediately.

Francis Drake bowed his head with a nod. He was pleased with how things had passed. She recalls my skills upon the waters of this land, and she will use me to transport this traveller, he thought. Then I can control the one who bars my way from infamy. He rose without a word and backed away from Elizabeth, bending slightly at the waist, being careful not to exceed Her Majesty's height.

Walsingham slipped from underneath the tapestry, which hung along the hallway beside Elizabeth's chamber. Drake had known who had possession of the intruder, of this so-called traveller of realms. Walsingham's suspicions were right, as usual, he thought. The traveller has evaded Owen's capture.

"They are in the Tower. Her Majesty's favourite must have done this." He smiled to himself. "Her Majesty's Robbie will be running back here soon to gloat and brag and impress himself once more for his queen," smirked Walsingham.

He had forgotten his own rule for a moment of never speaking out loud publicly and slapped his thigh with delight.

"I will never let you become her favourite mariner." His grin was wide with delight. He floated across the floor like the dust that consistently lands without its sound echoing down the hall.

Developments of State

Westminster Palace, June 1576

Cecil read the short note from Elizabeth. He was reluctant to go back again to visit Her Majesty. Her missives always entailed great volumes of vellum. He was tired and hungry and now having to deal with Walsingham as well at the same time. This was always a challenge.

"What has he done now to impart such fury from her brow. All this fussing about the subjects who trample across her floors? I am weary but resigned to stamp out this new force which grows within her."

Cecil dipped his nib into the vial and shook off its ink. He gently rubbed off the droplets of ink which hung at its tip. Methodically, he placed his pen into the grove at the top of his desk where it would lay. He stroked its length, slowly caressing it lightly as he lay it down. He stoppered his ink well, placed the vellum whose smell he adored inside the leather folder they had come to him in. He adjusted his signet ring, placing its familiar marking upright towards his face. It was the one vain thing he adorned himself with in public. It was a habit worth keeping. Few could boast of the importance and rank this held. His ring would last centuries, unlike the many men who had come before him in the serving of a monarch.

Cecil recalled the days he had used it for Elizabeth's father. No other king had had so many wives, he thought. Dearest little Edward, recalled Cecil. Henry's only son had the misfortune of a weak body. It had been a joy to work with such an interesting mind, though. Such a pity, that this boy's mind had not been developed further before his untimely death. If indeed Edward had not been helped towards his demise. This was something Cecil had never got over fully. Was this boy King Edward, done in and by whom? Had he Cecil missed something amongst his courtiers? What a marvellous forward thinking mind Edward had, recalled Cecil. Elizabeth had taken an interest in the development of her younger brother's education, the student, Elizabeth, teaching the student more brilliantly than their tutor.

"And then there was Mary his eldest daughter," said Cecil with a sigh.

Cecil closed his eyes and shook his head slowly sideways.

"Such unfortunate passion wasted on religious fury."

As always, Cecil returned to his habits. He stroked the length of his pen once more and lifted the leather folder from his desk opening it as he did so. Its sweet musk scent wafted up to him. He opened his drawer with its key still attached to his waist and placed the briefs within. He locked its contents securely inside. Closing the drawer with the turning of his brass key. These documents would be forgotten until the routine of normal business in this realm started properly once again.

Cecil met Elizabeth already conversing with Robbie when he entered her chambers. They were deep in the rhythm of soothing sobering thoughts. Elizabeth noted Cecil's appearance first and released her hand gently held by Robbie. Robbie stiffened at this gesture of Elizabeth's but then smiled as he recognized Cecil, his friend.

Elizabeth smoothed down the rippling of her skirts at her waist. She got up from her chair. The gleaming pearls of worry flung from her hand. Robbie grasped hold of them and placed them back upon her skirts. She glared at his impertinence. Robert smiled back and grinned.

"Cecil there have been developments with the traveller," said Elizabeth. "We have business to attend. As of late there is a growing pestilence on my streets. Have you heard of its coming?"

Cecil nodded his head. "I too have heard of this rumour, Your Grace. But it is just that, no more. It is an evil wind whipped up to its potential fury, but it shall die down as others have. You must not let these trifles bar the business of your lands. Keep her locked up in the Tower. Rumours die off as quickly as they start."

Elizabeth stood silently and glared at the two men. She raised her eyebrows at them and indicated for Cecil to sit. Robbie had begun to rise from his chair. Elizabeth waved her hand at him with a flick and pointed at his hovering rear to descend back down.

"You have not foreseen what this trouble could foment. It is like a brewery. The more you drink within it the more likely you are to believe in its merits. Do not ignore the rot which begot from letting loose the rumours of a witch."

She turned her back upon them and paced in front of her fire. She smiled. How she loved a good argument. Invigorating, thought Elizabeth.

"We must remove this scar from my streets and sew up its tear with haste."

"No, it is too soon."

"NOW," shrieked Elizabeth back at Robbie.

"No." He smiled. "There is more to be found out. She is useful. She speaks of many things of which we must find out."

"What things," she snapped.

"Tell me, what are these things you speak of?"

Elizabeth turned away from her men and stared into the fire with a smile. She recalled how exhilarating as a child it was to argue and enrage her governesses. The only one who she did not ire was lovely sweet motherly Kat.

But these men were different from her governesses. These men had interesting minds, ones in which great things could be got from. How Elizabeth enjoyed the talk of talks, the impertinence of Robbie and the calmness of Cecil. This flowing of ideas was like the morning dew on a fresh spring day. It was new and full of promise. A budding rose about to burst forth with its engaging colours encased within closed petals. It reminded Elizabeth of a game of childhood. Holding one's breath in competition and not being the first one to relent. A win was a win no matter what way it was got.

"Perhaps," said Cecil, "we could remove this scar temporarily from view, to a place where it can be interrogated from prying contagions."

"How," she snapped.

"The Tower, Your Grace attracts many parties. They hang about for bits of gossip. Your guards are paid handsomely for displaying the unfortunate who find themselves amongst the lower classes. Do not bring her out in the sun's strong light."

"Surely the worst of my streets lot are not about foraging and making trouble at this ungodly night hours."

"That may be so," said Robbie, "but they will do their utmost not to be seen, and will scurry away at the sound of a mere hoof or two paced upon your cobbled streets."

"This traveller and her companion Edith must not be removed via the streets this time," said Robbie. "They must be ferried away from here."

"To where?" quipped Elizabeth.

"To one of your palaces not of London town. She must be removed to the forests beyond the city gates."

"To Greenwich, then?" said Cecil.

"No, to Hampton Court," quipped Elizabeth.

"Think not," said Robbie. "The tides are on their way out. She must go south and west of here. The tides are swift at present. It will be a challenge not to lose her in its swiftness."

"Then take her via a stronger ship," said Elizabeth with a smile. "Let not these wherrymen follow her path. Set sail with her downstream, whereupon she will be met with less prying eyes."

"To whom should we trust this cargo?"

"We must make use of your most skilled mariner then. Bring forth your privateer, Drake. His skills are most suitable to deception from others," said Cecil.

Robbie rose quickly. "Do not engage Walsingham into this fray, however. He has too many fingers amongst your servants," he gestured with his hands.

"No, I would not engage Walsingham at present, not for this," she said. "Use Master Drake. He has a ship worthy of its sail, and he has yet to sink its girth beneath the waves. At least we will know she has arrived and not escaped again." Elizabeth smiled at her two men.

Walsingham grinned at the knowledge that he had just gained. His ears were always available to the passage of men's and monarch's minds. His astuteness impressed even himself. He grinned. "It has begun. I shall have her before morning is out," he said aloud once more. His face broke into a wide smile, his head rose into the air. He took a deep satisfying breath.

"I will have you now traveller. Your time in this realm is up."

A Brazen Plan of Escape

Prize, Gain and Freedom
A bold man takes his prize
A wise man uses his for gain.
The prisoner battles both
To gain freedom
Methinks.

The Tower Prison, June 1576

The spirit of Drake rose from the Thames as the sun set upon English soil. Traitors Gate was easily accessible from the Thames. He had decided that the traveller had to make her escape before Walsingham, the Catholic priests or Robert Dudley could thwart his plans again. He checked that the coin he planned to give her was still in its satchel, along with the knife engraved by Elizabeth commemorating his capture of Spanish bullion from the Caribbean. I will give these things to her. The value alone of these articles should impress, he imagined.

"I must not be seen by my likeness. It will ruin everything," he said aloud. Drake had very little time left in this realm. His current predicament involved time here in London, and it measured less than the striking of an hour's passing. This irritated him to no end. He could bring others back and forth through time, but not himself for any measurable length.

Retrieving his journals and maps was impossible to accomplish on his own. Drake had mastered many things on his own without the need for others to help him, except this one task and the ability to retrieve his own journals from the grasp of Elizabethan England. After every former attempt at retrieval Drake recalled, he had lost more and more valuable time in which to accomplish this most urgent business. Unfortunately, others now would have to be used to do this for him. He hated the idea of relying on others, especially the unwilling variety.

The wherryman Drake had hired to ferry him across to Traitors Gate was too busy at present to bother with his customer's reasons for entering the Tower Prison. The wherryman's hands and mind were busy with the chore of navigating the choppy waters that spanned the shores of the Thames.

Drake stood as he always did when sailing salty seas. He liked to watch other men toil and attempt to maneuver the waves that slapped their wooden hulls. His disdain for inability enabled Drake to choose only the best of men. The overcoming of currents on treacherous waters was his constant delight. The challenge of the deep-sea and choppy shorelines invigorated his veins. He smelt the sea air, and delighted in it.

He shook his long hair loose from its tie behind his neck and stroked the beard he had grown. He wanted his appearance to frighten the soft souls he was about to encounter. The gems imbedded in his dagger should be enough inducement for any woman, he thought. How easy it will be then to persuade this wench to do as he bid.

Drake entered the prison and made his way along the ramparts and inner workings of the stone walls. He hummed along the way, whistling occasionally and entered the guardhouse with the forged letters of entrance. He waited patiently whilst the guard razed his sulking head from the cot where it had lain.

"I have come to interrogate your prisoners," said Drake.

"What writs do you bring to commence this speech?" said the guard, yawning. He yawned again and rubbed his eye against the knuckle of his index finger. Drake watched as the guard passed his weary eyes across the page of seals.

He does not read, thought Drake. He merely glances across as if in rote fashion. Others would not recognize this foible, but he, Master of the Seas, was intuitive enough to know when understandings commenced. This man was a puppet of someone else, a temporary watchman, assigned duties he had no business attending to. This is how mistakes take place, he mused. I might yet gain her escape more quickly than I thought.

He took back that which he had proffered in the face of his inferior. Indicating that his access to the women was accepted, the guard looked back at Drake and nodded his head in the direction of the women's stone cell. He loosed the keys from the peg upon the wall, and placed them inside Drake's proffered hand.

Drake listened for the footsteps to follow him down the corridor. Instead, they scurried off in the other direction. Hmm, he quietly mused.

"Perhaps this lad has more to his face than I thought possible. I had best be quick," he said aloud.

Drake banged on the wooden door of the cell. He knew this enclosure well. Its familiar odours wafted through the cracks in its joints. The dust of centuries of prisoners and their doubts, found their way up his nostrils.

He replaced the key back into his pocket after reclosing the lock on the inside of the prison's door. He walked swiftly over to the pallet which housed the huddled forms of the women crouched together on the floor.

"Get up, traveller. You stay there," he pointed to Edith. "I wish only to speak with this one." Edith remained rooted to her spot. She shivered at the cold draft that had entered their chamber. She could not see him clearly but recognized his commanding voice. His presence, however, alarmed her immensely, and she rocked involuntarily from side to side.

Kathleen had risen and looked down at the frightened form of Edith. She pitied the girl who shivered beside her feet. She had recognized his voice, with its booming commands and its aggressive assault of her thoughts, and it angered her. She looked directly into the eyes of the voice, which had loomed inside her head for so long. He was back from the garden to taunt her once more. What did he want now? she thought.

"You bastard," she said to his face. "What right have you to take my children?" Her fury reared itself uncontrollably. She brought her right hand up to smash his grinning cheeks. He caught the flinging wrist and brought the other one to his chest, shaking her in the process.

"Be quiet, woman," he hissed. "I have brought you your means of escape."

Kathleen stared into the eyes of her tormentor and searched for the signs of betrayal. She had observed the face of a liar before. Its vacant pupils and unknowing expression had passed itself off on her before, but she had learned through past mistakes how to avoid the liars of this world. She had no intention of relying on her escape from a man she could not trust. He had better give her something good to use. A weapon would be best. She searched his clothing with her eyes and caught the shape of his satchel hanging at his side.

"You had better not bring me false hope. I will do no man's false bidding."

She smiled up at him briefly kicking out at his shins as she did so. He loosed his hold of one wrist, and she wrenched the other one from his grip, backing away from him as she did so.

He let her go and cursed the viper before him. Such a snake, he thought, but her fury would be tamed with the knowledge he would impart. Drake watched her back up against the stone wall of the cell and the glance she made in Edith's direction. He noted the concern on the traveller's face as she viewed her cellmate's condition. The passion of women, he thought, is their undoing. She will commence this task I lay before her, he thought. The satisfaction of this knowledge brought a welling up of pride into the expanding chest beneath his cloak. He smiled, convinced of his intended plan's direction.

Kathleen inched towards the slit between the stone's outer walls and listened to the sounds, which wended their way inside her cell. The tide has turned, she thought. The chop of the waters turbulence echoed around her cell. She had forgotten to listen to the tide's change. She had intended to use its sway as means of keeping track of the days. Four days inside this ungodly century had been four to many. She longed for the familiar smell of unwashed happy boys on their way up the stairs to the tub. The bubbles and soap and endless dives beneath its surface...she could not recall more. The salt and cold wind that whipped across her face had torn the last visage of memory from her face.

"What means of escape have you planned for me and Edith?" she said.

Drake rolled the edge of his tongue across his lips and softly paddled his boots across the stone floor towards his prey.

"I will give you nothing, unless you make your bargain with me stick."

"What bargain do you speak of?"

Neither negotiator heard the slide of the door's hatch open. Edith watched it open and searched for the shape of a head, but she could not see one. They listen, she thought, but for what?

Drake eyed his prey, assessing the serpent's eyes for signs of treason.

"You have been given a task, and your children's lives are dependent on your obedience. Either you do as I ask, or I shall keep them here for my means. Do you understand the task before you now?"

"No, you have not said why I must do this bidding."

"You have been brought here to do as you are told, woman. Stop messing about with me," he hissed at her.

Drake removed the coin from his satchel and placed it inside the proffered hand.

"What can a mere golden coin do for my release?" she sneered. "Have you no weapons beneath your cloak?"

He shook his head and glanced in the direction of Edith. The pair of them noted her trembling had stopped. Drake and Kathleen locked eyes again.

"You have information that the queen wants. You must release this knowledge and convince her of the import of my voyage, and when I bring you back again in the correct era, you will retrieve my documents from Whitehall, including my maps and journal. "

Kathleen shook her head. "No." She shook her head. "No, you can't rewrite history. You must accept all that has come to pass. This is foolish. You can't alter history. That's impossible. What is done can't be undone. No, I won't do this. You must accept your fate."

Drake sighed slowly and released his foul breath. She shrunk away from its stench.

"Then your children will die here, as will you and that wretched woman who shakes beside our feet. Think on or I will release your children into the hands of Owen or those priests you fought off." He whirled away from her stricken face, his cloak rippling past her breast, casting up the dust of time into her lungs. She choked on the dryness which met her oncoming breath and gasped for the release it held in his wake. She sucked long and hard at the torment clinging to her lungs.

"Why are you doing this? What have I done to you? Why do you use my sons in this quest of yours?" She gasped.

"Because you are the one who can travel great distances and bring forth the glory of my ventures to fruition. Do not irk me on this matter. It has taken a long time to perfect this art of transference. It is not my fault that you are the chosen one." He grinned at the lie he had just imparted. He had chosen more than her to commence the time of travel through the Kraken's mouth, but this one had not been as willing as the others had. He was not about to allow the ignorance of one woman to thwart his path, and he never gave up on his quarry.

Kathleen continued to shake her head, but the breath which she was desperate to breathe had ceased to meet her lungs. She clutched her throat and slipped down the coldness of the stone upon her back. Her lasts remembrances were those of the smiling faces she longed to touch. Blackness gripped her thoughts as she fainted.

Drake leaned over the prone body of Kathleen and slipped the dagger behind her back and released his hold upon her lungs and watched and smiled as she gasped and coughed at the air, which raced the life back into her bones.

That would be enough of an inducement for now, he thought. He bent over the uncurling form of the traveller and whispered over her body.

"This is your chance for escape, do not let this hour pass you by. With each passing of the clock's hour, your success will fade. Do no bring this woman who lies beside you. Her fate is yet to be decided. And it is not yours to make."

Drake crossed the floor, looked out into the outer rooms holding fast its prisoners. He turned the key in its lock, not noticing the opening in the doors hatch. Nor did he notice the youth who had slipped into the darkness beneath the cot which lay against the wall in the outer chambers enclosure. He hooked the keys back upon their peg and wound his way back towards Traitors Gate.

Kathleen slowly sat herself up, confused by all that had passed. She reached behind her back to steady herself against the wall. Her hand passed across the hilt of the blade, which lay along the ground. She gripped it tightly and slowly brought it around to meet her face. Edith watched from the cot and shuddered. But a smile was beginning to emerge from Edith's face. The traveller had means of escape. She had promised to save her. She had heard every word and breath that Drake had uttered. A glimmer of hope and light had begun its trace across Edith's face.

"The traveller I am," whispered Kathleen, "but I did not seek out this task."

Kathleen turned the hilt of the blade over and over between her hands. She noted the few gems, which glimmered softly against the evening's fading darkness. Light was filtering through the windows slits now. Dawn was emerging brazenly before her. She would have little time to escape under the cover of darkness.

She released its blade from its hilt and ran her finger down its edge. She tasted the blood that flowed and trickled down her finger. She felt no sting, along her fingertip. Kathleen replaced the blade in its sheath and began to tear a strip of cloth from her skirts.

She wound the cloth around the hilt and tied it to her shin just below the knee. Lifting her head momentarily from her task she stared into the eyes of Edith and smiled back at the rocking form. Kathleen felt for the coin she had placed between her breasts. The un-conforming circle met her prying left hand. She would need to see its markings in the light of day to determine its real use. She lifted her head towards their prison's door when the hatch opening clicked closed into its place.

"Damn," Kathleen swore softly. She had made her second mistake. Getting caught had been her first, but a witness to her weaponry was even worse.

The small urchin Elway had stretched his arm up to close the door's hatch, listening carefully for the sounds within. He quickly ran out of the entrance and climbed the spiral staircase he had earlier descended. Elway heard the fast approach of the lone guard's return. He waited to hear more of what was to be said. He heard the wrenching of the hatch as it was opened and the slamming of it again. The guard had grumbled and complained of the intrusion of Drake upon his sleep. He hated the night's endless visitors when all he wanted was to sleep. Night watch was his least favourite duty.

"Night," he growled, "brings about more than the emergence of rats." He spat out his fury and lumbered towards his cot. "This had better not be one of those nights."

Elway streaked his way between the White wall's ramparts and made his way to the guard's gatehouse. He descended the stairs quietly and slipped inside their room. He could see the red and yellow uniform of Elizabeth's men-at-arms. He waited for the ritual of replacement to end. Soon, he thought, they would head back to their new posts. He would slip out between the iron gates and seek the men who waited for his return.

Walsingham would give him bread for his mother's kitchen, but Robbie would give him coins, and he would seek him out first.

Kathleen reviewed all of the night's transgressions. The magnitude of hiding on her the weapon she now fingered, implied her willingness to abide by Drake's rules. She wanted no more than to pierce his skin with its sharpened point. She looked over at the woman she had dragged into this mess. She felt suddenly guilty. Her mind churned and her heart beat loudly inside her chest. What would happen to the two of them if they were caught with this blade, gifted to Drake by Elizabeth, and now to her inside a prison cell? What was that stupid man thinking? She lifted the cut finger to her mouth and sucked on the drying blood. She had never liked the taste of blood and wiped its crust upon her sleeve.

"What am I to call you by?" whispered Edith across the floor.

Startled by this voice, Kathleen looked over at Edith.

"Kathleen," she said. "My name is Kathleen."

"Are you Irish?"

"No, my name is, but I am not." My distant roots are, thought Kathleen, but it had been a long time since the roots of her past had embraced the shores of Ireland without regret. She had almost been once to Ireland, but money had kept her on English and Welsh shores. Time had played a factor in that past visit as well. The unforgiving passage of time licked up her face as it gripped her cheeks.

"I am Irish," said Edith.

Kathleen looked up and smiled.

"Well, best not to tell anyone around here, eh? My name and your birthright just might get us burned at the stake."

Edith sighed slowly and lay back down. She closed her eyes, and the hope spilt out and ran down her cheeks.

Kathleen regretted her sharp tongue as soon as it had been said.

"I am sorry," she whispered across the floor. "I am sorry."

Kathleen recalled the last few days' events, the meeting of Drake in all his finery amongst the shrubs of Elizabeth's garden. She compared the two meetings. Their pompous host had demanded...she stopped. These men were different...these two men were different...she thought.

One knows about his voyage, the other seeks its voyages beginning. She had conversed with both of them, but how could this be? One had approached from the past, one from the future, and another from inside her head. This made absolutely no sense. Or did it? She would need to have all her wits about her to decipher which Drake was who. He thinks he has the upper hand. I am not beholden yet, thought Kathleen, to this plan of his.

Kathleen rose silently and crossed the floor to the prison's door. She placed her hands on the door's edges and pushed slowly. The door hesitated its release and then nudged forward. "It moves."

Edith opened her eyes then and viewed the moving block of wood, which had earlier barred them from release. Kathleen turned towards the sounds of Edith stirring. She grasped the door's edging and pulled it back shut. Shaking, Kathleen crossed the tiny room and sat upon the bed beside Edith.

"We will wait until the guard is snoring once more then we will leave, but before the night fades to light," she whispered gently against Edith's ear.

Intervention

Walsingham's study, June 1576

Walsingham waited for the return of Owen. He had heard now from Elway. The boy had been loosed of all he had gleaned. His reward had been a second loaf of bread.

"So Drake gave her no weapons? Perhaps he can be trusted, then?" he spoke softly to himself, but the coin, thought Walsingham, what of this coin. "Hmm." He clasped his hands behind his back and stared into the evening fire. Its embers, reminded him of his brother's fate. He shuddered at the thought of his twisted, corpse, only partially burned. Even the stake he had been tied to had not burned fully. The night raid he had led to retrieve his brother's body and the embers, which had smouldered at his feet, lay vividly in his mind.

The chosen one and a traveller, who wishes no task. This he needed to think upon more. But the queen's information, this he had to have.

"What is it that you know, Elizabeth? For that is my business to know what you think and plan," he spoke softly. He prodded the embers with the tong and placed another log upon the fire.

Walsingham needed to make haste. This recovery of the traveller, the fact that the interfering Robbie was about to transport her away annoyed and angered him.

"Robbie is a smug man, with over ambitious thoughts of gaining the crown. Placing the crown on an English head was perhaps advantageous. However, there are too many kingdoms across the English sea to allow Elizabeth to marry any homegrown man as of yet. And I have no intention of letting you, Robbie, gain that much power. I will rule this land, not you, oh, favoured one."

Walsingham had no wish to see the spectacle of Elizabeth's cousin Queen Mary of the Scots and her disastrous decisions repeat themselves on English soil. Mary Stuart needed still to be dispatched, and he, Walsingham, had plans afoot to embroil her in these intrigues, but not yet. Elizabeth was still against the removing of any kind of royal head, including that of King Phillip of Spain. Her fears of a bloody battle with that same monarch always made her nervous. He, Walsingham, would need more time to manipulate Mary, Queen of the Scots. He would need to play Mary against Elizabeth, convincing her into thinking she can seize Elizabeth's crown for Scotland. This was the only way he could convince Elizabeth to remove that royal head from its shoulders. "But I will," he said. "I will see to its rolling across the scaffold and lifting skywards to the entourage of willing witnesses." He smiled at the ingeniousness of his own brain.

Walsingham lifted his head at the sound of his chamber's doors. He recognized the footsteps that slipped past many but never him.

"Owen," he said, without turning and looking. "Sit down. We have plans to make. I am led to believe that the Tower's recent guest has plans of escape tonight?"

Owen lifted his eyebrow and grinned. "She will never escape. I will retrieve her for you gladly, though, we could feign an escape that would cover any unfortunate grumblings from our queen and her courtiers."

"You shall indeed do that, as Robbie, the queen's snivelling favourite, has been tasked with her removal to Greenwich via Drake's ship. I expect them to make a ruckus about her disappearance. But for now, we must find her a place of refuge." He turned then and grinned at Owen.

"What is it that you want her to impart?" smirked Owen.

"I want to know everything she speaks about our queen. She claims to be an unwilling traveller for Drake. He has imparted that she was the chosen one and has no choice. I want to know of what he speaks of and she denies knowing."

"Why not ask him? I can bring him in. He will talk."

"No, his value is on the seas. He has lined more than your pocket with the wealth he has seized. He outmaneuvers the Spanish and the French. He makes his enemies fear and admire him with his skills. No, I still need him. I do not trust the Spanish from invading our shores."

Owen nodded his head. "Vain bastard, though, eh, is he not?"

Walsingham smiled. "Yes, he spends a lot on his clothes to impress our queen. He is a but a mere peacock, sparing no expense to impress." He nodded his head in the direction of Elizabeth's chambers.

"This traveller is expendable. She is a mere woman, who knows too much. And I need to know what she knows."

"What are your plans for her after she speaks? A convenient death or a murder in the streets?" Owen barred his teeth with his crooked smile. He sat back and rubbed his palms together.

"I gather you would like to replace the bruises on your face with some on hers."

Owen winced at the thought that Walsingham had heard of his disgrace by that woman. He sneered and spat into the fire.

"She will pay for that. She will pay."

"I am sure she will, but not before she speaks. There are other inducements to speech than your fist. I want her whole, not bruised, not beaten. I want no blood spilt yet." He stared deeply into the face of Owen. He knew he could trust him to do as he was asked. Owen nodded his assent.

They locked eyes. Owen looked sad temporarily but brightened at the thought of a possible spillage of blood at a later date. He had to show patience once again. The spillage would come, as it always did. He enjoyed the sport of bloodletting. It intrigued him to no end how the body could be cut and its life bled from it. He liked to torment his victims, getting ever closer to them as death came upon them, telling them about the places they would go to and the demons they would meet. Their piety would do them no good now, he thought, nor would it the traveller. He smiled, and his grin grew as the breath he took filled his lungs.

Walsingham moved away from the fire and sat down in his chair.

"Robbie will move her before the night is over, and it is almost over. They plan on transporting her to Greenwich. You must be there first or intercept her route. Robbie must not know that you have been given orders from me. The traveller is to be captured escaping. See to it that she loses herself from him."

"I will do better than that. I will catch her in the act of escape from the Tower well before Robbie rounds up his men."

Owen left Walsingham in his study. He lifted the latch on the oaken door that led to the hallway. He headed towards the circular stairway hidden behind the false bureau along the corridor. "I will beat Robbie to the prize," he said aloud. "And I will send that traitorous wife of mine to the bottom of the Thames." She is of no use to me now, he thought. "Why did I have to be married to such a plain and pious woman, useless, except for the fetching of bread and trinkets for the queen?" He shook his head in disgust and spat at the wall. He gripped his scabbard clutched at his side and descended the spiral stairs at a pace.

Offence

Elizabeth's Privy Chambers
June 1576

Elizabeth paced her rooms as Robbie imparted the news from Her Majesty's prison.

"She has asked him for weapons? Did he give them to her?"

"No, he did not. But he gave her a golden coin, and she scolded him for its uselessness." His face lit up with a grin.

"What do you suppose he gave her this coin for, then?"

"Perhaps to bribe her way out of the prison?"

Elizabeth sneered at his reply,

"It is useless in this town amongst the poor. Are they not questioned when they possess such coins?"

Robbie nodded his head in agreement.

"Perhaps he felt to appease her woman's worth with such a prize."

Elizabeth stopped her pacing, momentarily.

"Perhaps," said Elizabeth. "I did not think this traveller would, however, be impressed by such a gift, as you have surely just stated?"

Robert sighed. He understood too well how Elizabeth viewed information. He needed to impart something of interest to Elizabeth without her realizing he would be the one releasing any new information to Her Majesty through his own interrogations.

"My informant has passed more important information, though," he sighed loudly in Her Majesty's direction.

Elizabeth clutched at her skirts and turned towards her chair.

"Sit, Robbie. We must make haste and plan. What else has been gleaned?"

"The traveller has talked of her need to escape, to return to the place where she has come from."

"Where is this place? What evil strikes at my shores now?"

"It is not evil which strikes your shores. This traveller has valuable information to impart, and she has travelled a great deal to release its worth."

"Hmm," replied Elizabeth. "We will see. I will decide if this information is worth its weight."

"She has admitted being the traveller against her will."

Elizabeth's red eyebrows lifted upwards. Her lips tightened their grip upon each other. She smirked.

"She plots, then?"

"I believe so." He smiled back. "To Greenwich, then?" replied Robbie.

Elizabeth nodded her agreement back.

"I want to be present at her speech. Do not lose her amongst the poor. And keep her away from Catholic priests. I want no eyes to recognize her face."

"Am I to beat her?" He said with disgust. The paleness of his face revealed his revulsion at such games.

"No." She smiled. "That is not what I meant."

He nodded. "Ah, yes, I shall see to it, then."

"You must depart before me. I will not follow until the morning has passed. I will put it about that you are laying out the grounds for my next hunt."

He rose slowly and pressed his hand inside hers. Hands squeezed together then loosened their hold. He bowed his departure, and she watched his form make its way across her rooms. Elizabeth sat back in her chair. His departure in the early hours of this morning, she thought, would inspire curiosity and bring about the arrival of others. There was always somebody alert in her palaces, especially from the turrets above.

"If she is not careful," said Elizabeth, "my deceitful sister and cousin, Catherine, will lose her head before too long. Spiteful little wretch," said Elizabeth.

Defence

Westminster Palace
Dawn, June 1576

Drake swore lightly under his breath as the hulk of Owen passed beneath him. He released his hold of the stone wall and leaned slightly forward. He could hear Owen's descent drifting downwards.

"Bloody hell. The wench shall be caught." He followed quickly, stopping every so often to listen further. "I had best be out of here myself, for someone else is sure to follow Owen," he said softly.

He recalled listening to Owen and Walsingham's speech. How the two of them had conspired to get at his traveller. Double-crossing bastards, he thought.

"I gave you both too much money after my voyage to Nova Albion. But that shall change now when this voyage of mine commences again. Time will be changed, my traveller, and you shall change its course."

Drake remembered the children and William and smiled. When John Stowe finds word of your negligence, traveller, he will write you out of history as well. Drake began his descent along the cold, spiral staircase. He smelt the dust, which hung in the air from Owen's pace. He would exit as Owen had, only this time he would make haste towards John Stowe and bring back the traveller's children. He would make it known to Edith that their lives were now firmly in his capable hands. If the traveller chooses not to obey, then they would all remain in Elizabeth's fiefdom and not that of the traveller, thought Drake.

"Surely that woman has loosed herself from that damnable prison by now. I made it clear enough that the door would not be locked without implicating myself. I made sure those guards had seen me leave without the prisoners."

Nova Albion's Approach

Robbie meets his match,
Owen meets his.
As a young woman speaks.

London 1576 for now

Edith followed Kathleen across the Tower's ramparts. They hugged the outer wall and kept their forms as low to the stone ground as possible. It was a long journey, having to walk up and down stairs on either side of the guard towers to avoid detection. Kathleen viewed the ravens huddled in their cages inside the Tower's expanse of green grasses. She wished not to wake their sleeping. As yet, she did not know how to escape fully, but she had viewed the fields beyond the prison's stone wall to the north side. Kathleen recalled that her most recent visit to London had not included the fully functioning moat, which now stood between them and the fields to the north and the stone of the White Tower.

How bloody deep is it? Could Edith swim? She doubted it, but I can, thought Kathleen. The next hurdle would be to convince Edith to jump into that frigid filthy moat and clamber up the other side to safety.

The two escaping women stopped momentarily, as a commotion at the main entrance to the prison erupted. Kathleen could just make out raised voices. Are there new prisoners arriving, or have they been found out? Kathleen waited patiently for the commotion to abate holding onto the trembling hand of Edith.

"Quickly, let's go whilst those men speak to one another. We have time to make a little noise ourselves here."

Edith nodded, and the pair ran across the grasses, past the armouries and up the final stairs on the north side of the Tower Prison walls.

Kathleen surveyed the scene before her. Fields lay on the other side of the moat. It was not that far across the moat, maybe twenty feet, but it was deep. Good for jumping into, she hoped. The town that stretched along the Thames to the west was maybe a mile away. If they could just get to that and hire a wherry, they would be able to cross the Thames later and gain their freedom.

"That golden coin may just become useful after all. I have to get my children, Edith," she said softly, "and you know where they are. We must escape first, and then you will take me to my children."

Kathleen looked at the quivering Edith staring into the moat below.

"We cannot escape," said Edith. "It is impossible."

"It is not. You must trust me. I can swim. I can get you across, but we must hurry. I'll jump first, then you must follow."

Edith shook her head.

"No, I cannot do that. I would rather be hung than the drowning," she croaked. "Witches drown. I am not a witch," she spoke, shaking her head back and forth.

Kathleen could see and smell the fear in the young woman's voice. Her pale skin greyed over, her pupils widened and her lips trembled at the thought of such a leap.

"You must trust me, Edith," she whispered.

Kathleen had not noticed the commotions cessation, but she heard the shouts of outrage at their escape.

Robbie looked across the open expanse of the White Tower's enclosure and espied the forms along the outer north walls of the ramparts.

"You men," he shouted, "up there. See to it that they are caught. Do not harm them."

Several guards streaked their way across the yard. Others went up the stairwells and ran across the ramparts. Robbie followed suit and took the nearest stone stairway up. Kathleen noted the distance. She had little time to waste. They had been spotted, "Damn, damn, this just got more difficult."

"Edith, they are coming for us. Get up here now and sit on this ledge." She pushed her up and then followed suit. The width of the stone wall was immense, nearly three feet across.

"Bring your bottom to the edge. Swing your legs over the side like this. Then I want you to lean forward and leap, pushing off the side of this wall with your feet."

Edith shook her head but moved her feet towards the edge.

An arrow shot past their heads, and Kathleen heard the curse of Robbie as he streaked closer to them.

"Stop," he shouted at the men, "do not harm them."

But it was too late. Edith in her panic and fear toppled forward and disappeared over the ledge. Kathleen did not wait. She heard the form of Edith splash its entrance into the deep waters below and pushed herself over the edge.

Emersion below the surface felt welcoming. All of her senses seemed to be humming. She viewed the struggling form of Edith before her. The water had been unexpectedly warm upon entry. Why? Her hearing was astounding, every word that Robbie spoke echoed around Edith and her.

"Damnation," he had said. "Do not harm them. Be quick. I want them found alive. Do not pierce their bodies with your arrows. Elizabeth, your queen, wants them alive and with speech. Go now, get them out of that moat."

Kathleen did not wait to hear any more, she knew she needed to act fast. These men meant to harm or worse kill them. The arrow that had shot past them was not the arrow of Robbie's men but of someone else's. She did not want to find out, though, who had ordered that. Desperate to get out of the water Kathleen grabbed hold of Edith's hair and pulled her to the surface.

"Edith," she shouted, "are you OK?"

Edith's spluttering and flaying arms was enough to convince Kathleen that she was unharmed.

"Be quite, I have you. You will not drown. Kick your feet out in front of you. I will carry you across the moat."

Edith did as she was told and pushed the two of them across the water faster than Kathleen expected. They hit the edge of the muddy bottom, just as another arrow whistled past their heads. The dawning light shone its light on the pair of them exposing them to the archer's bow.

"Stop your arrows at once," shouted Robbie repeatedly. "They can be got from the fields. Let us go at once."

Kathleen did not trust that the arrows would cease.

"Edith, trust me once again. We must get out of the morning light. Hold your breath and peg your nose, we must submerge and kick our way under the water to the shadow over there at the water's edge."

Edith looked towards the darkened area the traveller was pointing to. They submerged just as another arrow flew past their heads.

The two women disappeared below the water as the men above looked on. They could not see where they had gone. Robbie searched as best as he could.

"Damn it! Now we will have to retrieve carcasses," he cursed.

He raced down the stairs, across the yard and over towards the main entrance. He did not notice Owen's arrival in his quest to retrieve the women.

"Get my horse, man," he shouted at the guard. "Make haste, the prisoners have jumped into the moat."

Owen did not enter the Tower. He smiled at this news, and delighted in the fact that Robbie had lost his quarry, he turned his horse on its heel and streaked up the roadway towards the Tower's scaffold. He knew it well. He enjoyed a good hanging. They must be down near that end, he thought. The moat is shallower there, he remembered.

"No woman would jump from the north end," he said aloud. "They haven't the courage."

He turned the corner and drove his stag back up the stone pathway, which overlooked the prison's yard below, leading to the scaffold. He peered over the edge looking for signs of the struggling women.

"Their dresses will weigh them down. Oh, how sad," he said with a grin. Walsingham will not be pleased. "Stupid whores," he spat out.

His head ripped round at the sound of hooves speeding past the scaffold entrance grounds. He turned his horse and sped after them. He could just see the form of Robbie racing ahead of him. He sped off, chasing him, leaving a trail of dust and spittle along the pathway. Robbie could hear the man, Owen, behind him and hoped he was alone, but realized he needed another to help carry the women back to the docks anyway and then onwards to Greenwich. He expected that it was one of his men whom he had given orders to that was following.

Owen's horse was fast, and he soon caught up to Robbie.

"What chase are you on," he shouted at Robbie. "Who's lose from the Tower? Surely not your quarry from last night."

Robbie grumbled under his breath and reddened at the affront implied by Owen. He despised Walsingham's private Catholic minion. "Be off with you, Owen. I have no need of your help. My men are following."

Owen laughed aloud. "Your men are not following. I have told them not to come."

Robbie cursed under his breath and spat out his spittle towards Owen. He could see the women running ahead of them. They were fast, he thought. This traveller can swim well. What the hell else can she do?

The women ran across the fields towards the market town to the west, their wet clothes slowing them down. Kathleen heard the men shouting at them and encouraged Edith to run ahead. She stopped momentarily and retrieved the knife from beneath her skirt. Running on, Kathleen shouted out at Edith which way to turn, and directing orders as to how to fend off the men on horseback following them. She caught up with Edith quickly. If that bloody Drake has done as he promised, the Kraken will be showing up momentarily, and I need to be holding fast to Edith.

Kathleen could hear the voice of Drake emerging. Her throat tightened, and the wind whipped up at her back.

"Edith" she shouted, "we are almost there. I can feel it. He has come again. Our escape route opens."

Drake shouted at the women, "Run quicker. They are almost at your backs."

Kathleen could not see him, but she could feel the tingling up her spine. "Where are you?" She shouted.

"I am here, where I always am, beneath the waves of Nova Albion. You must find water. Run towards the river, which leads into the Thames. It is there that you shall find me. It is there that you shall find me." It echoed inside her head.

Edith looked over towards the traveller. "I can hear him," she shouted at Kathleen. "He speaks of the canal not the river. It is just over there. Come, I will show you."

"Just keep running," the voice echoed inside Kathleen's head.

Edith grabbed hold of the traveller's hand and pulled her towards the canal. Kathleen saw its murky waters splashing against the side of the canals sides. Something was frothing up from within its depths. Her face went taut, her spine arched, and her mouth went dry. She did not want to enter into that water. What lay below? Her memory brought back the enormous tentacles of torture crushing her sides and lungs.

The two women stumbled and fell forwards towards the canal. Kathleen felt her forearm grabbed hold of and she reached out to grasp Edith's other hand. She felt the jerking of her shoulder and the pain, which pierced her side as she collided against the horse.

"Edith" she shouted, "keep running, go on without me," she yelled into the swallowing abyss.

The gigantic tentacles sprang up from the canal and pulled her downward. She was gone. All of them were gone. The abyss that followed her shouting, raced past her face in a swirling mass of hooves, spit, shouts and rage. Her own vision blurred, and the breath from her chest broke forth as she retched involuntarily. Her feet left the sodden ground beneath her. Her head tumbled forward. She was moving forward, forward and not hitting the dirt. The movements of hooves, boots, wet clothing and her knife tumbled over and over, the swirling waters cascading down her back.

"This is what happens when you bring forth others into the void and mouth of the Kraken without my permission," snarled Drake. "You are on your own now. I cannot bring them all back. Get them out of my world, or I will eliminate your children," shouted Drake.

"I will eliminate your children, eliminate your children and eliminate your children." The sound echoed around inside her head. Kathleen tumbled over and over. She felt the hand of Edith lose its grip on hers. The sound of hooves hitting dirt and the suddenness of tentacles pushing at her spine bringing her head up. She found herself running and splashing through the muck along Wharf Street in Victoria, British Columbia, except that there were few buildings around. She knew she was home. It felt like home, but it was different, barren, no cars, no pavement and only a few people in a carriage ahead. She looked around slackening her pace.

A large fort loomed ahead, and she skidded to a slushy stop. Glancing back over her shoulder she stared right into the face of the horse bracing itself to avoid trampling over her. The horse reared up and its rider leaned back hanging onto the reins. He was furious, confused and bewildered. The shock on his face contorted. His mouth opened and closed. He craned his neck looking for familiar grounds switching back and forth across the small laneway.

"What have you done?" he shouted down at her "Where have you taken me?" demanded Robbie.

Kathleen stared at the spectacle before her. The two riders and their horses circled round Edith and herself with their weapons drawn. The riders, sneering at each other, paced up around the women.

"You must stop this. We must get out of here," Kathleen yelled up at the men before her.

"What have you done?" snapped Owen at Edith.

377

Robbie stopped his prancing around the women and brought his horse into control. He lent over the animal and placed the sharpness of his blade beside Kathleen's throat.

"For the third time, I ask of you, where have you brought us? What have you done?" said Robbie. "I want no more of your sorcery."

Kathleen edged herself away from the blade and stared up into the eyes of Robbie.

"I have done nothing. It is the Kraken's mouth which you have fallen into."

"Do not be smart with me," he growled. "Get us out of here, NOW."

"I can't, I don't know how." She snapped back her response.

Kathleen turned away from the waterfront and looked past Robbie, Edith and Owen. "Damn it all. This is all wrong."

"We can't stay here. That fort over there will be full of the queen's men, and they will be on the lookout for illegal Native traders."

"What nonsense do you speak. What traders be these Natives?" shouted Robbie at her.

"The queen owns no fort on foreign shores. We have castles, not these wooden pathetic structures, easily burned down. Speak now or I will remove your lying tongue," growled Owen.

Kathleen inhaled slowly. She needed to remember what queen was on the throne, and how did she know it was a queen? Her mind raced with the thoughts of sailors, sealing vessels, canoes, until she spotted the rigging of the small sloop held tight at the wharf below where they stood.

"This is not your queen's fort."

"Then whose queen's fort is it," snapped Owen in response.

Edith, Owen and Robbie stared with mouths open, both men angry. Edith was laughing hysterically. Owen reached down and grabbed Edith's hair and pulled it sharply up then slapped her across the face.

The anger that boiled up within Kathleen's breast, let itself lose. She reached over and furiously pulled Owen off his horse, dumping the stunned rider onto the ground. She kicked out at him and pounded her hands against his chest. The edge of her knife was just missing his chin as she did so.

"You bastard, you bloody little bastard. Leave her alone, or I'll remove your tongue," she said to him.

Robbie jumped off his horse and wrestled Kathleen into submission. He managed to pull her away from Owen, only to be assaulted himself. She pummelled his chest and began to weep with frustration.

Edith slapped her husband across the face and rose to defend herself from his blows. Owen stood and rounded on her.

"Owen," yelled Robbie, "leave her be. We must get these women and ourselves away from here." Owen held his arm back and above his shoulder, hesitating at the need to contact his fist with his wife's face. Owen lowered his arm and glared out at Robbie.

"This is my property to do with what I like. Do not interfere in husbandry responsibility," he said.

"Owen," breathed Kathleen. "Leave her be. She has nothing to do with this. She is a victim. It is my fault that she is here. Come, we must be gone from here."

Robbie pulled Kathleen's shoulder and spun her around to face him.

"What queen, do you speak of," demanded Robbie?

"Victoria, I think. Queen Victoria. She will reign longer than Elizabeth...Oh shit, I shouldn't have said that."

"Reign longer? By how much?" He pointed the blade once more beneath her chin.

"About twenty years longer, I think. I can't remember exactly, but she doesn't die until the 1900s, I think."

"What nonsense do you speak. It is only 1576."

"This is not 1576, but I would guess that it is close to 1875." She said looking around and surveying the landscape.

"Look, see over there, that way," she pointed away from her chest. "Over there, across the water. That, I think, is the Songhees tribe. See their houses and the tall poles in front of them? Those tall poles are called totems."

"Those are not houses," said Owen. "And the smoke rising from them has no chimney."

"They're not supposed to have chimneys. That's the way their houses are built, and this is not England. You are in my country now, subject to the rules of my land, not yours."

Owen sneered and pointed his finger at Kathleen.

"You have no lands to speak of. This is trickery. Now bring us back, or I will spill all your blood now, here, in this evil place. You are a witch, and witches need to be run through with my blade. Perhaps, though, you would prefer to die at the stake. That can be arranged as well. The choice is up to you."

"I am no witch. This is not sorcery. You have no powers here. This is my land, Queen Victoria's land, not Queen Elizabeth's anymore."

"What right do you have to take us here," said Robbie.

"I didn't bring you here, the Kraken did. Perhaps next time you follow me, you will think more on the matter."

"I have my orders to retrieve you, and you will get us out of here now," snapped Robbie.

"What is this place?" asked Owen.

"It once belonged to your queen, but she gave it up," said Kathleen.

"You lie," said Robbie. "Queen Elizabeth would never give up her lands to any other monarch."

Kathleen laughed then. "Elizabeth gave her rights up to this place long ago. She never acknowledged these lands got for her by your seamen. She feared reprisals from Phillip, the king of Spain. Once again, you are wrong."

"This does not change things at present," snapped Robbie. "You still have to get us out of here. I cannot guarantee your safety from Owen here for too much longer. I suggest you do something about this mess you have brought us all into."

"You are in Nova Albion now and out of your league. You are the ones in peril, not me. It is up to me whether I bring you back to your England, so be quiet," she spat back at Robbie and Owen.

"If you attempt to kill me or Edith, your lives will cease to be as you know them. I will not guarantee your survival, unless you help me find a way out of here. There is movement across the water. Men approach. We will listen to what they have to say. They will perhaps help to get you from this place, but you must attempt at least to be civil towards them. Do not offend them in any way," she warned.

Kathleen looked over at the forms moving along the shoreline. They were deep in conversation and kept looking towards her companions and her. Kathleen recognized them as the Native people who inhabited this region.

"Look over there, down below. Here is one of my people. He wears a headdress." The headdress trailed slightly down his back and held his hair tightly behind. Another Native stood and wore a tunic, which looked to be tied at the waist. The one wearing the tunic held a long spear and the hand of a young child. The young child was not dressed as they were. She wore a long pinafore to her ankles, and her hair was dark and loosely flowing. The little girl tugged at the Native wearing the tunic, and they entered the dugout canoe.

Robbie followed the traveller's gaze. "Who are these people who approach?"

Owen turned as did Edith, and they stared out across the water. Both furrowed their brows. Recognition was not evident in their stares.

"Robbie, we need to leave now," said Owen.

"I think not," he said, and turned towards Kathleen. "You know who these people are, don't you?"

She felt the coldness in her lungs again and sucked in her breath in a desperate attempt to keep hold of her breath, but it was not taken. Only the cold entered. She felt her throat and the vibrations which hummed inside. She could hear the wind again at her back and turned towards it.

Edith's eyes locked with hers. Edith felt it too, the wind, the tightness in her chest, the humming. Drake was coming again, after all.

"You will need to make your own pact with the shaman now. I cannot help you further. Be wise in your decisions," quipped Drake to Kathleen. "Remember what it is that I keep?" echoed around inside her head.

Robbie took hold of Kathleen's shoulder and shook her. "What it is that scares you so? Who is it that approaches?"

Kathleen pushed herself away from Robbie.

"I'll tell you more when I've spoken to them. Let me go, and I'll tell you more when I return."

"No. We will go together. No more games. I will question them myself." He took his horse's reins and handed them to Owen. "We will need these soon, I believe. Keep them at the ready," snapped Robbie to Owen. Take care of them. I will speak with those who approach."

Owen grunted his reluctance to obey Robbie, a man he despised. However, this scene was not one that was familiar to him. This presence of foreigners was troubling. He wanted nothing to do with sorcery and the devil which rose before them. This land was dark, with deep green forests everywhere. He could not imagine an escape route. He felt trapped for the first time in his life, dependent on a woman. The thought made him retch. Not one of his companions noticed. They were all too engrossed in this devil worship. He would see to all of their demises once back on England's shores. These wretched souls would pay for their sins, and he knew just where to remove this sin from outside London's walls.

The foursome moved towards the shoreline. The shaman waved the spear upwards and brought it back down. The canoe's paddler remained seated as the entourage left the canoe and approached the traveller and her escorts. The girl, the spear holder and the other Native with the headdress ascended the shoreline towards them. Edith backed away from the approaching Natives. Owen clasped the back of her dress and bent over towards her.

"Surely, after your jump from such a height earlier and your near drowning you are not now frightened?" He sneered into her ear.

Edith pulled away from her husband and spat into his face. She ducked just in time to miss the onslaught of his hand. Robbie caught Owen's fist, and the two men jostled momentarily.

Kathleen grinned and noticed the smile on Edith's face. She grows braver and stronger for now, thought Kathleen, but for how much longer will this adrenalin rush of boldness last? And can she continue it once they are back in Elizabethan England? The questions raced on in Kathleen's mind, but there were so many. Like why did she somehow know that it was a shaman approaching? And the girl looked familiar. How could this be?

"Emily," Kathleen blurted out as the little girl approached. "Your name is Emily, is it not?" The little girl nodded with a grin and then turned her eyes towards the horses.

"I like horses and animals," she said. "I like cats too. I have a cat." Emily smiled at Edith. "His name is --"

"Cicero," said Edith. "I know."

Both men turned at the statement made by Edith, and then they looked over at Kathleen. Owen glared at the women. Robbie looked back between the girl Emily, Edith and the traveller. His head whipped back around at the guttural sounds now emanating from the traveller, Kathleen's, throat. She spoke another language, and he listened intently for any recognizable words.

"You have come to help me, I think?" said Kathleen to the shaman.

The shaman nodded slowly, indicated with his hand towards his elder who extended his arm with a proffered seal fur.

"You have the knowledge of the Kraken within your bones. This is a sacred gift given to a few. It comes with much responsibility."

Kathleen nodded. She thought she understood the cost of this knowledge. Her children's lives depended on her returning to England to retrieve them.

"Drake wants me to help him. Do you know what he wants?"

The shaman nodded. He indicated with his head for the other man to approach with his gift.

"You must take this offering and gift it to your queen. In exchange, I will help you find your children. In return, however, you must help Drake, for he has taken our most valued treasures and not returned them."

"What has he taken?"

"My daughter and he holds her children inside the Kraken. She is weak now from white man's disease. She will die soon unless you help Drake."

Kathleen paled slightly and swore. "Bastard."

Robbie recognized the one word.

"What bastard do you swear at?" He spat and pointed the edge of his blade against her shoulder blade. "Do not play tricks on me."

Kathleen turned her head towards Robbie slightly and whispered over her shoulder.

"He speaks of the one who bars our passage back. That is all. Leave me be. I must talk with this shaman further."

Gently Robbie removed the knife from her back. He noticed the whiteness of Edith's face and traced her arm down to her waist where Owen held it. He had placed a rope around her other hand and was tying it to the other at her back.

"Let her go. We are on foreign shores now, Owen. We have no means of escape except via these women. That fort before you will be filled with soldiers. We need no commotion at present. Release her at once."

Robert brought his knife towards Owen's chest and pushed its point into his rough open shirt and doublet.

"We will both need to be wise at present. I do not believe this man before you will tolerate much more of us."

"He has no weapon," said Owen.

"He has no need of one. He brought us here. That is weaponing enough."

Owen slowly untied Edith.

"You will pay for your indiscretion, Edith. Do not forget whose house and home you live in," he sneered.

"Promise me," Kathleen said to the shaman. "You will help her as well." She indicated with a nod over shoulder. He nodded slowly his agreement. The shaman's people would never threaten their women with force like these white men who stood before him. How he hated the sight of these despicable lying men upon his shores.

Owen followed the motions of Kathleen's inclination towards Edith and the shaman's nodding response. Owen's cheeks purpled, and his teeth grinded slowly across each other.

"This will cost you more time within the Kraken," said the shaman, "but it can be done."

The traveller, Kathleen, nodded her response.

"You must get Drake to focus on the promise he has made to me."

"What promise did he make to you?"

The shaman raised his eyebrow in disbelief. "He has not told you?"

"NO."

Again, Robbie recognized this word and proffered a pointed blade gently into the traveller's back.

"What has he said to you that prompts such a definitive reply?"

Kathleen shook her head. "Leave it alone, Robbie. This is not your concern just yet."

The shaman watched this exchange and smiled. He understood white man's language. He would not be fooled by another white man's indiscretions.

"He has promised to return our heirs back to their homeland," replied the shaman.

Kathleen nodded her response.

"I will bring them back, if you promise to help me bring back mine."

"I have waited a long time for Drake's promise." He smiled. "My daughter and her sons are with him, are within my reach. I can feel their presence, however, Drake does not fulfill his promise, once again. He is a traitor, and he has used my world long enough."

Kathleen nodded her agreement once more.

"My daughter's children, however, are not with their mother. He has separated them from their mother as he has done to you with your sons. They too must be found," replied the shaman. "Repatriation is the only way to release the hold the Kraken has on Drake. It is the only way to stop Drake from manipulating time for his own gains."

"Drake has her children as well as mine?"

The shaman nodded his response with long slow dips with his head. Kathleen stared into his eyes for a long moment.

"That bastard." She spat once more on the ground. The shaman smiled softly, his grief revealing before her. His sunken eyes were searching her face, a few tears welling up. He brought his hand up and across his chest.

"There is an ache that will not go away. It cannot rest. It lingers like a trickster's affront. Nothing washes away this grief."

"Where has he got them?" Kathleen asked the shaman.

Kathleen's heart lurched at the recall of her own children's faces as they momentarily flashed before her eyes.

"How might I return them to you? asked Kathleen.

"The wind will guide you in all aspects. Voices will come to you. Listen to all that they impart. Do not be fooled as I was by this trickster, Drake. Your heart will suffer if you do not listen carefully to these voices calls." He bowed slightly and extended his hand in gesture.

Kathleen grasped hold of his hand and looked into his eyes. He winced as the blade he held cut into his palm. She looked down just as he did the same to hers. She winced and sucked in the air, which rushed into her lungs. The pain subsided as quickly as it had come. Their hands had clasped together, and their bloods mingled, faded and melted. The blood dust escaped from their hands and drifted up and swirled around them, slowly encompassing them in a cloud, and then it vanished.

The Kraken, she thought. The Kraken, he has her children. A voice echoed inside her head.

"Return the children of Drake and my daughter, and then they will be free from his grasp" Her eyes narrowed, and the moment of recognition flowed across her face in a wide smile.

"Repatriate and it will all be over."

He nodded back at her and smiled.

"I can feel his presence when he arrives. It is a cold chill that winds its way up my spine, but I cannot summon him into being yet."

"You cannot. It is my mistake. It is my creation, my responsibility. He has it in his control. I took Drake's soul when he died, and I placed him inside the belly of this sea beast, but he has learned to control the Kraken. I trusted him to honour his agreement with our nation, but he has refused. He uses the Kraken to fulfill his own needs. It is the one mistake I made with him."

"Can you not remove him?"

"No. But his control will end when repatriation is complete. You must find a way to gain his trust and convince him to release my daughter's children and yours."

Kathleen nodded her agreement.

"Can you help me find my children?"

The shaman nodded.

"Be careful with the agreements you make with this slippery one."

"How will we get back to where we have come from?" said Kathleen to the shaman.

"Klee Wyck will show you. She is another chosen one. She will help you. Go with her now, but be careful. Remember your words have different meanings to hers. She is but a child now before you, but her powers are those of an elder. She is wise beyond her years, and she has the nature of the trickster about her, so be aware."

"Trickster? But you said to trust her."

"You must listen very carefully to all that she says."

The other Native approached with the gift for Queen Elizabeth. The three Elizabethans, unfamiliar with the shaman's looks and speech backed away slowly with the horses. Robbie reached across Edith protectively with his arm and blade. The shaman presented Kathleen with the fur and bowed down at her. She took the offering and ran her hand across the softness of the seal's fur. She brought it up to her face and inhaled. She smelt the sea and the earth, mixed with smoke and the faint traces of salmon. Her eyes watered. She looked around at the shoreline and the surrounding greenness of the Douglas firs. Their immense height and breadth brought a sudden longing. She wanted to smell the bows that swayed in the wind around her deck. She longed for the comfort of her Diadora tree and its sweeping limbs feathering the moon's glow on a cool autumn night.

Tears welled up in her eyes and slowly ran down her cheek.

The shaman reached over and wiped them away. He nodded towards the other man and together they backed away from the small group, leaving the little girl behind whom he had called Klee Wyck.

"Do not be longing for what was," he said gently. "Your journey has a long stretch ahead. Focus on the now. Your past and future will not wither away, unless you wish for something that cannot come."

"But how do I get them back?" She indicated with a nod backwards at her three companions.

He nodded in the direction of the little girl now staring up at her.

Kathleen turned towards Klee Wyck and smiled.

"Hello Emily," she said in English. "My name is --"

"Kathleen," said Emily. "I know. You need me, don't you?" She smiled back.

Kathleen nodded. "Indeed I do."

"Come then, follow me," and she reached up to hold Kathleen's hand.

Owen burst forth and pushed Kathleen aside. He took hold of the little girl and shook her.

"You speak in riddles," he said. "Witch. You are all witches." He looked around at all the women. "Be done with you."

He drew out his blade and shoved its point through Emily and back out again.

Kathleen rammed her fists into the back of his head and brought her knees up beneath the back of his. She shoved him sideways, and he tumbled over. His blade fixed in his hand jarred into the dirt, and he swore as his wrist jarred free of its hold. Robbie leapt into action and restrained him. He slapped him hard across the face and rolled him over onto his face. Robbie placed his knee on Owen's back and held onto his arm wrenching it upwards.

"See to the little one," he said. "I fear we will be burying her," he said. "Most unfortunate. You are a fool of a man. Walsingham has no idea of your inclinations, does he? I shall see that he knows you make to kill children amongst your arts." He roared into Owen's ears.

Emily smiled at the dumbstruck faces of Edith and Kathleen.

"He missed you, then," spluttered Kathleen.

"No, he ran it through me, but I am not what you see. I am only here to help you. Be quick, for we must go." She turned and ran up towards the fort.

The women followed quickly behind Emily. They heard the fast approach of the men, as they ran to keep up. They followed the course of the fort's darkened form. Night was descending, not morning as it was during their retreat from London earlier. The earth's rotation had not yet caught up to that of London's. They trod quickly up and past the fort's long outer wall. Reaching the other side quickly, both women were now sweating, their faces hot with the weight of their clothing.

Emily stopped momentarily and pointed at the ship now moored to the dock before them. Women were walking down its gangplank and being escorted across the clearing into a building.

Kathleen looked closely at the familiar form of Edith as it trod past her in the distance. She shook her head and looked sideways at the shimmering, disappearing shadow of Edith. She gasped and looked back at the woman in the distance. Her head flipped back and forth between the two visions of Edith before her. Owen sucked in his breath and unsheathed his knife once again.

Kathleen pushed Edith out of the way and shoved her into Robbie. She looked back over her shoulder once more at the form disappearing at the dockside into the building. It vanished and was gone. It was just a flash, a stupid thought and another vision she could not understand. She looked over at the little girl grinning at her side.

Edith righted herself, and Robbie took in a long breath. Owen circled them and spat out his disgust.

"You are all witches. Your day will come. You shall pay for this. I will make sure there is a burning coming your way."

Robbie paled and looked over at Edith.

"What is it that she does?" he whispered. "This is treachery."

"No," said Emily. "It is a sign of what is to come. Do not be afraid of its coming."

Robbie looked directly into the eyes of the girl and raised his arched eyebrows. He cocked and tilted his head towards her.

"You are a powerful girl," he said quietly.

She giggled and nodded her assent with a large grin and laughed.

"Come, we must get you to the clearing and back to where you came from," said Emily. "Your queen awaits her answers, does she not?" She smiled up at the men.

Owen and Robbie exchanged cautious glances. Each sneered at the other and nodded in the direction of the little girl the shaman had called Klee Wyck.

Edith caught hold of Kathleen's hand and tugged.

"How is it that she lives when he pulled his blade out from her belly?"

"I do not know, Edith. I think we are all mistaken in what we thought we saw just now? Come, let us go."

"I do not want to go back," she said softly. "I like this place."

"That is a good thing, I think, Edith. There is a calling that awaits you here, I believe. It is merely a shadow of things to come. That is why you like it here, but for now, we must return to London and the year 1576. We have things to complete back there, you and I."

The outcropping of the little woods ahead of them loomed ever nearer as they walked quickly past the buildings next to the fort. Ahead, several houses and fields lay off in the distance. Emily led them past a bay and up the hill towards the woods.

The horses which had been forgotten in the milieu of twists and turns, followed behind their riders. Owen had regained his reins and Robbie let his be. His horse was eager to keep pace and did not spook easily.

"You will need to go on by yourselves now," said Emily. Emily had stopped walking and pointed in the direction of the woods ahead. I live down this way, along the path of bird carriage walk. I must go before my father calls, for he does not like me so much."

"I don't like children much either," snapped Owen. "Be off with you."

His horse's flanks twitched at the sound of his voice.

Kathleen glared at Owen and rolled her eyes away from him, raising her left brow with distaste. She looked over at the smiling girl staring back at Owen. Emily grins. This little girl, thought Kathleen, was not afraid of Owen.

Emily looked over at Kathleen and nodded her head towards the woods. I am not afraid of him, echoed inside Kathleen's head.

"You must take them back now. Be careful of the one who calls out against you. Listen to those who speak to you in whispers floating up and past your back. The wind is chilliest when accompanied by deceit."

Kathleen was reeling from all the happenings of one day. How could she be talking to a girl who should be covered from head to foot in blood? Yet no blood flowed out. That knife, she thought, it had gone in. And yet, had it? Was this all just some long nightmare that she was desperate to get over? No, she felt the chill again as it rose up her tingling spine. He comes to take us back.

"Leave that coin. Remove it from your breast. Let it slip out and push it into the hand of Klee Wyck," voiced Drake.

Kathleen plucked the coin from between her breasts and placed it firmly in the hand of Emily. The little girl got down and hugged her leg. She felt tiny hands put back against her shin the knife, which she had once held in defence against their pursuers, Owen and Robbie. Kathleen bent down and grasped hold of its hilt and pulled it back out. She nodded for Emily to leave. Slowly Kathleen stood and then quickly grasped hold of Edith's hand.

"Run, Edith!" she yelled at her. "Run like the wind."

The two women streaked off towards the woods. Kathleen felt the call of the wind pressing at their backs. She held onto the seal's fur as she and Edith ran towards the wood. Kathleen heard the men curse and rein in their horses. They mounted and took off after them. She knew what was coming. But how was she to escape, once the Kraken took them back and threw them out again into Queen Elizabeth's London?

Where is that blasted water we seek, and then she spotted the little pond within the woods. Grabbing Edith's hand she leapt off the edge of the rock ledge just as Robbie's hand grasped hold of the back of her dress. Whether Owen got hold of Robbie she could not care less. She hoped not, for he would be helpless in this part of Nova Albion amongst its sprits, Shaman's and little Klee Wyck's.

The Shaman's World

Nova Albion's Summer and Winter Camps
Shamanic Warriors
England's Unsettling Sun

John Stowe's study 1604

John Stowe reviewed his copy of Drake's manuscript. He had read and reread it many times now. Its importance in Drake's recognition was evident. If it were not found, then he would disappear inside history's vacant shelves, lost from the minds of contemporary scholars. He could not publish these documents, written in his own hand, without the originals found and presented to the present King James.

The problem was it pages had not been officially signed by Her Majesty Queen Elizabeth. Drake had been lost to the scourges of seafaring in the Caribbean. His manuscript had not been published with his monarch's approval. His exploits on foreign shores had been questioned. His only map of the Pacific Northwest had been published outside of England, and Queen Elizabeth had forbid its publication on England's shore.

If King James would not legitimatize it, then he would need to rescue the evidence to be exposed at a later date. This was what Drake had wanted the traveller to do for him.

John shook his head sideways. He knew the challenges that lay ahead. The exposure of this document would challenge everything that England had sworn against knowing. The fact that Drake had visited Nova Albion, that he had claimed rights for England upon its shores, that the English knew what these shores looked like and that the English had communicated with its Native inhabitants.

Commitments had been made to these feral people in exchange for valuable knowledge about the Spanish. This information alone would have had more than a Spanish fleet and the Armada bearing down upon England's shores. Rome and its papacy might even have launched a religious inquisition of its own against the English, if these documents before me had been published at the time of Elizabeth's reign.

Queen Elizabeth had been right, thought John, to avert this knowledge for a while, but it was time now for the past knowledge to bear fruit. It was time for recognition of past accomplishments to be awarded posthumously. It was time for England to gather up its muscles and descend upon feral shores and take what was rightfully theirs. The Spanish had been defeated. King Phillip II was, as was Good Queen Bess, dead. Spain was losing its hold of its dominions in the Caribbean. The threat of Catholicism landing its crushing hands upon English shores was gone.

Stowe needed now to put in place the means to this knowledge bearing its fruit. John needed to put William, his chosen fait accompli, back into Elizabethan England. He, John, would use Drake's resources, his Spirit Keepers, to transport this knowledge of Drake's accomplishments into the realm of known time. To do this John needed willing

Spirit Keepers of his own. Later on, he thought, I will have time to alter the fate of William Shakespeare's fame.

Stowe recalled how Drake had summoned up the powers of the Kraken. John had watched as Drake had thrown Elizabeth's most famous poet into the mouth of the Kraken, and spit him back out into John Stowe's world of 1604. The Rose Theatre and the Globe's infamy could only be preserved in history if William was to abide by Drake's commands. Young Will would deliver the documents of Drake's into the hands of the traveller. And he, John Stowe, would see to it that Will played his part. If Will did not abide by these commands, the world would never come to know of 'The King's Men' or its players or that of Master Shakespeare. Instead William would cease to exist at all. William's manuscripts would burn in the embers of his mind. His folios written of his hand would disintegrate.

"And once you have accomplished these tasks for Drake, and his documents are secured into the future, then I will eliminate your manuscripts myself," whispered Stowe. "These blasphemous plays are useless and will not survive the fate of time. My work, which is of more import than mere plays, will surface as the greatest achievement of the Elizabethan era. I will have no mere playwright trump my gifts to the future."

Stowe frowned. The issue of the traveller, however, loomed before him. How was he to trust her as much as Drake did? Would she release these documents into her world as Drake said she would? Or would he, Stowe, have to do this on his own? This menacing traveller would have to be used again in order to accomplish the task before him. She would need to be more cooperative. An inducement to acquiesce must be had. A pact would have to be extracted from her in regards to her children's safety. Stowe smiled at his own genius. "Mothers," he said and grinned.

Stowe had not yet sensed the coming of his flock gathering at his feet. They had slipped past his awareness. He had forgotten his place in time temporarily. The continuing of his storytelling was to commence.

Stowe stiffened at the sniffling at his back. He breathed deeply before he turned, loosened the tenseness that had gathered in his shoulder blades and unclenched his fists.

"Ahhh," sighed Stowe. "It is time once again, is it not, my lovelies?"

Stowe turned and greeted the upturned smiles of his flock and walked slowly back over to his desk. He scanned the melee of bodies wriggling before him. The anticipation inching its way across licking lips, bug eyes and squirming bodies lining up to listen.

He had been amused at the growing interest from his workers and their children about his tales of Nova Albion and its inhabitants.

Now it was time to use this interest to his advantage. William came in, leaned against the wall and scanned the room. His eyes cast down on the three traveller's children, Woody, Maddox and Kitt.

This was good, thought Stowe. William was finally willing to do as he was told.

The murmur of voices had quieted down. The traveller's children smiled up at Stowe. They had no knowledge of what would befall them if their mother did not obey the likes of men, thought Stowe. Such a pity. Such a loss. Such lovely healthy young boys.

"Now where did I leave off?" said Stowe.

Stowe looked down at the eager eyes before him. Several more adults wandered in and took their places along the sideboards and shelving strewn about his large study. Maps, books, vellum, writing implements lay about everywhere. His coffee tray and unfinished cheese and apple lay where it had been placed. Cicero lounged in his favourite basket perched above his desk to one side. Stowe leaned over towards the glistening coat and flickering whiskers of his favourite cat.

He petted the cat into motion. Cicero opened his eyes, stretched out lazily and gazed around the room. Cicero dangled his paw over the edge of the basket and flipped his head backwards towards the crowd of eager listeners exposing his belly for a vigorous rubbing by Stowe.

Stowe eyed the eager crowd at his feet. Maddox lay flopped out on his brothers. Their squirming giggles bringing smiles to the faces of the late wanderers into John's room.

"Now before I begin," he held out his flicked up hand, "you must remember that these tales I tell you are the result of Sir Francis Drake's encounters with the Native people of Nova Albion. He wishes to carry on his work for our late great queen, whilst he resides inside the belly of the Kraken. You are not to interfere in this process. If you are needed to assist in these endeavours, Drake, not I, will summon you. Is that clear? I cannot introduce you to Drake. What I can do, though, is tell you Drake's story. Is that clear?" said Stowe again.

Stowe looked around the hushed room into the eyes of his followers. He could discern the looks of disbelief and belief, its well-worn features, blossoming into raised eyebrows, glistening irises and the deepening of smiles or sneers. Whatever way his followers viewed his last statement, it did not matter to Stowe. For soon they too would all be swept up into something they had no means of escaping from.

"Well, now, how about that story?"

He ignored the whispering and mumblings of his flock. It would soon settle down, thought Stowe.

"Nova Albion has many divided cities. On the southeast shores lay the greatest of their dwellings. Enormous houses were built. Its timbers stretched over one hundred feet in length and sixty feet across. Many related families lived inside the same dwelling. A large painted entranceway was centred in the middle of the house, facing the rolling summer breezes racing up its shores. Many of these houses contained the spirits of their former occupants. Each house favoured a particular spirit animal. These animals roamed throughout the forests of Nova Albion calling out to its ancestors. The spirits were awakened by the stories told by Nova Albion's Native people."

Stowe leaned over his desk and stroked the neck of Cicero. The cat purred momentarily and then batted away Stowe's pressing hand in protest.

"This," he began, "was their summer camp." He continued. "When winters approach and bring along their chillier winds and the droplets of rainfall increased their abundance, these Native people moved their great house to their winter camps. They bundled up their possessions, dismantled their smaller houses and transported them in canoes and set up once again these long houses along the sheltered shores of their winter camps. Each family was responsible for the tear down and relocation of their own goods.

The totems fronting these large enclosures on the shores banks protected the spirits from mistakenly roaming into the sea and the mouth of the Kraken. Their looming large eyes, winged torsos, enlarged claws and whale tales drifted up and down these shallow shores chasing the spirit of the Kraken from entering their camp. The spirits of the dead lay in tombs high above the ground on platforms attached to the backs of their great totems. This roaming at will of the spirits of the dead is the only way these Natives of Nova Albion know how to prevent the Kraken from entering their villages and swallowing up its people."

Stowe sat back in his chair and surveyed his flock. All eyes were present. Maddox had sat up, and the brothers held hands. Edith was unusually quiet. Perhaps her memory was emerging, thought John. After all she had once been to this place called Nova Albion, albeit unwillingly.

"Drake had lived in the summer camp of these Native people for nearly seven weeks, whilst careening his ship," said John. "Drake's need to careen the Golden Hinde along Nova Albion's southern shores had enabled Drake and his men to engage in the celebrations and feasts of the people of the summer and winter camps."

Cicero rolled over and squinted his eyes at Stowe. He then curled his paws under his belly and placed his nose closest to Stowe's out-stretched hand.

"Now," said John, quietly.

"Let me tell you about the Songhees people of Nova Albion and their most feared enemy. The warriors of Nootka are known for their strength and deathly blows. The chieftain of the Songhees people had warned Drake that the Songhees people would not travel into Nootka warrior territories. These lands lay far to the north of the Songhees people, but their presence on this island invaded the bones of the newborn of Nova Albion's village. The Nootka were noted for their particularly handsome features. They claimed rights to the ownership of beautiful women. In their fiercest battles, the Nootka enemies would be slaughtered, including their children, the old and the ugly. The Nootka warriors will not recognize the beauty of white skin, fair or red haired or even freckled skin."

Stowe looked down at his flock and pointed to the sea of red and blonde urchins before him. He pointed towards Cicero the cat and its closed eyes. He stroked the long black tail, removing a few black hairs onto his hands.

"This is the colour of hair preference, black as coal, almond coloured skin and brown eyes. No blue eyes would be welcome in the lands of the Nootka warriors."

He held out his proffered hand for all to see.

"The blackest of black hair and only the brownest of eyes trimmed in dark lashes will survive the onslaught of these Nootka thieves."

He nodded his head at them, "Yes," he quipped. "They are not partial to the paleness of your skin, the blueness of some of your eyes, or the lightness of English hair. It is wise not to travel too far north into these murdering warrior's lands."

He sat back in his chair again and sighed.

"The women of the Songhees villages Drake observed smoked their salmon, which had been caught by their men. The Songhees fires produced little flame but lots of heat and smoke."

He raised his eyebrow at them.

"The Songhees salmon is laid across rows of sticks and twigs carefully woven together over their smoking pits. Drake and his men ate this salmon meat, oysters and clams found in abundance along their shores. Drake's men also ate the camas root cakes and dried salmon berries offered to the English as gifts from this nation of Songhees Natives. Drake had watched as the women of Nova Albion burrowed into the streams and dug out these bulbous camas roots with their feet, tossing the camas into their canoes. Later after boiling and drying, these women had shown Drake how to grind the root into flour and make the biscuits, which he and his men had bartered for. Drake's long journey homeward was about to commence, and the provisions and victuals that his men would need to cross the expanse of the mighty Pacific had entailed more than one form of bargaining. Drake had bartered for the passage of three Natives on his return to England and had promised to return these Native people back to Nova Albion.

"Drake had, however, dismissed the elders of the village and their shamanic power. The honour of trust that the Songhees chieftain had given to Drake had been disregarded. The chief's suggestions that the breaking of this sacred trust would bring consequences had merely amused Drake and his men." There was no need, thought Stowe, to enlighten his flock with this sort of news. These feral people would simply have to give way to the commands of smarter men.

"Drake," began Stowe, "had decided the items wanted by their chief were not necessary to the benefit of inferior beings. The Spirit Keepers who roamed these shores told the chief of Drake's deceit. Their wise chief had listened carefully and decided that one must trust first before any conditions are put on their guests."

"The village's elders had discussed their chief's advice. He was a good leader, and they respected him for this, but the shaman's premonitions had worried the elders, and they asked the village shaman to place a bounty on Drake's soul. A chieftain like Drake with all his magical tools and grand canoe must obey the laws given by mother Earth. Drake, they agreed, would be tossed into the mouth of the Kraken and kept there until he had returned the heirs of their lands back to their rightful place of birth. If he did not fulfill this vow, then upon his death he would be returned to the spirit world to roam there for eternity until he undid the wrongs he had done to the houses of Raven, Bear, Whale and Otter."

Stowe looked over the bug-eyed children leaning closer to his desk and locked eyes with William. William grinned and nodded in Stowe's direction. At last, he thought, this wilful young teenager was listening. Perhaps one day his poetic verse would outlive his life here on earth. For now all this was held in balance whilst William took heed of his advice and brought back the traveller's children into Elizabeth's London. William, unfortunately, would now have to remain in London with the offspring of the traveller, enabling him to write his blasphemous tales of times past, but that too could be reversed, he mused.

However, first, William would have to be diverted from learning the art of storytelling. Stowe would see to this teenager's capture and forge on him a new guild to be associated with. The recording of London's history had been easy, but storytelling was Stowe's real gift. He enjoyed ever so much the reactions of his listeners to the tales he told them. And he, John Stowe, would see to it that the upstart playwright obeyed his orders as well and erased all knowledge of William Shakespeare from the history of London's tomes that had been written by him.

"Now," said Stowe, "we must remember the necks of the betrayers to our realm. Do you recall the execution of our good king's mother? The bewitching Queen Mary Stuart of Scotland? She was a plotter to treason. She paid the price for the ordering of her husband's murder. The Scots chased her out of Scotland for it. They chased her all the way into England and into Elizabeth's prison, whereupon she tried to take hold of Elizabeth's crown and place it upon her own thorny head. Queen Mary Stuart of the Scots met her end with the swift chop of the executioner's axe."

Stowe slammed his fist down hard on the desk and peered menacingly over its edges. He sneered and curled his lip upwards and roared loudly. He reached up with one hand to his throat and clasped hold of his voice box silencing his raging groan. With one last slam of his other hand onto the desk his head dropped suddenly down, and he collapsed his chest and head down onto his desk with a thud.

Gasps, cries of distress and the littlest fingers pinched over little mouths. Eyelashes pinched together and the moistened tears loosened their hold, trickling down the smallest of faces.

Stowe leapt up from his desk with a roar and laughed.

"Ah my lovelies, that is the fate of the traveller too if she disobeys the likes of men such as Sir Francis Drake." He spat on the floor.

"Now," he said, "Drake's spirit is calling out to the people of this realm to listen carefully to all that has taken place before now. The sailors before him who landed on shores never seen before have been honoured with their discovery. Drake's discoveries must also be remembered and recorded for prosperity."

"Jacques Cartier conquered the Natives of Kanata in 1534," Stowe roared out at them.

"Sir Hugh Willoughby and Richard Chancellor found the White Sea in 1553."

"Martin Frobisher founded his bay in 1576," he snapped.

"John Dee led an expedition to the Northern Passage of Nova Albion in 1577 but failed to find its western end."

"John Davis discovered Newfoundland on his voyage of 1585-1587."

Reaching upward with his arms spread and waving them about before them.

"Why then, I ask you, has the master of all mariners, Sir Francis Drake, not been accredited with the discovery of the Pacific western end of this passage across this northern route to Asia and the very coast it emerges from?"

Stowe looked down upon the children at his feet. He glanced around the room.

"I will tell you why," he said, shaking his fore finger at them. "It is all because of the Spanish and their inquisitional King Phillip of Spain. But he is dead now, gone off to his grave, never to be heard from again," he spat out at them. " So the ghosts of our most recent past have come back to claim their inheritance. The voices of reason have descended upon our gracious King James' lips. Infamy will reign and roar its vicious head until wrongs of our past have been righted by the just."

Stowe settled back into his chair quietly, took up his pen and looked across at his flock and smiled.

"The jaws and teeth of the Kraken have awoken. Its mouth is hungry and will not cease in its searching of souls until the sweetness of victory, infamy and trust have been restored. She will swallow whole all those who oppose her in her vengeance for the truth. Be careful, my little ones. Remember to close your eyes tightly at night and pray to your God. His is a merciful Lord. You may trust in all that he prescribes."

He flicked his hands upwards and shooed at them to leave.

"Be off with you for now, my lovelies. If you are good and righteous, I will continue the tale of the traveller and her sons tomorrow. Before you let the sleep of time wrap you in its arms, remember that the sun will soon always shine upon England's shores."

Confer, Deceive and Measure

Greenwich Palace

June 1576

Walsingham strode quickly back along the hallways leading up from Elizabeth's prison at Greenwich. "Witch" he spat out. "The traveller is a witch." He ignored the glances made in his direction. At present Walsingham was not bothered by the stares or glares of his fellow men.

"This woman has too much hold on my mind. I will rid the venom spewing out of her silky voice."

Walsingham was reminded once again of the traveller's resemblance to the disappearing Huguenot woman in Paris. Remembrance of the whole incident, his brother's burning at the stake, the slaughter of thousands of innocents brought bile into his mouth.

"How could she have lived through that slaughter? She cannot have," he spluttered. Walsingham's body shook involuntarily and his anger mounted at his own body's weaknesses.

He shook his head and strode even faster towards his chambers at Greenwich. Perhaps it was time to eat, thought Walsingham with disgust.

"Eating is just another inconvenience on my time. I must eat to live. It is a fleeting enjoyment, and I've already wasted enough valuable time with the drooping of my eyelids en route. The need for sleep evades my body most days. Time is wasted on such frivolous actions. If only I did not have to sleep, so much more could be accomplished."

Walsingham strode into his chambers and shut the door behind with a thud. He signalled towards the urchin Luke sitting by his fire.

"Get to the kitchens and find me some bread, cheese and mead," he gestured towards the inside door and its passages.

"And be quick about it, or you shall have none of it yourself."

Luke quickly leapt up and scurried out of the room he shared with Walsingham whenever they were ashore in Greenwich. The mute boy was useful. Walsingham had noted how well he observed his surroundings. This lad would not take much training, he had thought. But his communications through script had been a challenge. The series of scrawled codes had been developed over time.

Walsingham paced back and forth between his desk, the fireplace and his window. He heard the boy's light patter and found his way to his chair. He sat down and thought about how he would devise his plot to execute the traveller. Slaughtering with a knife had evidently not been very successful. He shook his head. How could the traveller be the same Huguenot woman? He had watched her die, just as he had his brother. He had stoked his brother's flames to hasten his death. And he had watched from the window this very same woman and the child she carried being clubbed and stabbed to death. He would device a kinder and less painful form of death. He despised torture, even if at times it was necessary. Poisoning was so much swifter and easily accomplished.

Walsingham's one regret had been his mistake at surmising the possibility that any of his siblings would be branded as traitors and had been horrified at the outcome of his brother's trial. Perhaps there was some truth in it somehow, but there couldn't have been. He shook his head. "No, not him."

"This is nonsense," he blurted out. His siblings were all dead, cut down all of them one after the other. He would be dead now too if it were not for Owen.

Walsingham looked up into the eyes of the urchin he had saved from Catholic beatings. The small boy had quick eyes and a bright future if he behaved himself. He smiled then and gestured to the boy to sit and eat food with him.

The two ate slowly, as Walsingham had instructed him to do. Never eat more than you need. Eat quietly, Walsingham remembered telling him. Always look for the items, which most excite the interests of your adversaries. Keep a mental note of their habits, in particular their weaknesses, he had scolded. The two ate more cheese and bread. They each lifted their tankards in the same manner. Teaching a child to remember and mimic someone had proved more than once the identity of an individual. It was these small gestures and the memories they brought to mind, which had endeared the lad and brought him into Walsingham's retinue.

"I have a new job for you at some time today. Owen, my man from London, will arrive with boys your age in tow. You will accompany them to their chamber and remain with them until I recall you back to me. Is that clear?"

The silent boy nodded his assent and splayed his right hand slowly rocking it up and down before Walsingham.

"Yes," he indicated, "watch them closely. I want all their movements recorded. They may yet be useful to us both."

Luke looked up and smiled. He nodded his head and took one more smallish piece of cheese. Walsingham pushed the plate towards him. "Take the rest to your sister and be back here within the hour."

Luke nodded, rose from his seat and gathered up the rest of their meal pushing it into the pouch pulled from beneath his jacket.

Elizabeth will need to be convinced of this execution order for the traveller, thought Walsingham.

"Nothing from Edith is of any use. She might still be useful if..."

Walsingham heard the footsteps approaching and silently returned in haste to his desk. He picked up his quill and removed the former notes he had made from view, slipping them beneath the desk into a slight opening he had fashioned onto the frame of his drawer. This nook had been very useful in concealing items from anyone curious enough to linger too closely. Even Her Majesty at times was not to view these documents until their completion and intentions were fully developed. Walsingham could tell by the state of her approach that Elizabeth was intent on gleaning information. She will want control of his prisoner. Interrogation was his prerogative. This was far too delicate a manner for Her Majesty. Presenting a prisoner before, during or after interrogation would only dissuade her from letting him get to his work. He wanted this one to be pumped and ready to give him more without the interference of his queen.

Elizabeth opened his door with a flourish of demonstrative expletives towards her entourage.

"Leave us alone. Don't follow too closely at my heels. I will send for you when I am done here. Now stop all of this fussing and close the bloody door."

She turned towards her guards, flapping her hands in agitation towards them. Her dark angry eyes, flashing venomous stares back out at them.

"Yes, Your Majesty. Very well. We shall wait here for you."

"No, NO, NO. Be gone. I will return to my chambers on my own."

"Yes, Your Majesty," the five armed men breathlessly replied, bowing down as deeply as their assorted swords, shields and clothing would allow.

"BE OFF WITH YOU, THEN," she bellowed out at them.

Walsingham rose from his seat and stood erect in his posture, waiting for the onslaught to conclude.

Elizabeth turned after the door had closed and smiled sweetly at Walsingham.

"How are you, Walsingham? I see you got here before me," she said raising an eyebrow at him.

"Your Majesty," he said with a formal bow. "It is always nice to see you. Do come sit by the fire. And yes, I thought it wise to come here as quickly as possible. We must not delay in our proceedings with regard to this most troublesome traveller."

"I wish you would not make more of this than is necessary. How is it that you come to view this mere woman as being so detrimental to my safety?"

"It is merely a precaution, Your Majesty. She has escaped before now. We must be careful with a woman who beguiles and entrances young men into careless regard for your safety."

"I have yet to be harmed by anyone, as you can see. So how is it that you perceive such dangers when I myself have met with her? Lower your hand in protest. Do not raise your eyebrows in my direction."

"Yes," Elizabeth nodded back at Walsingham. "I too have met this woman. I also let her go. She means no harm in my realm or towards me."

Walsingham nodded his agreement.

"Perhaps," he said. "Perhaps. However..."

"However?" she tilted her head towards him raising an arched flash of red brow towards him. She breathed in deeply, lowered her chin towards the ground in a circular motion, and raised it again towards him in a challenging retort.

"Do go on." She smiled sweetly at him.

"Let us see first what it is that the traveller says. Let us see how she defends herself."

"I did not know she had anything to defend herself from as of yet."

"It seems she is capable of elusive and magical import."

"SPECIFICS!"

"AH, well…she took Robert out of your realm and returned him back again against his will."

"The return or the taking?" She smiled.

"Both."

"Explain fully," she snapped back at him.

"She transported herself, Edith, Owen and Robbie to a place called Nova Albion."

"And?"

Walsingham paced the room. Not looking at Elizabeth, he continued on.

"She transported them to an island outside of the known realm, to a place where a small village exists, next to the inhabitants of a shaman and feral people. Owen witnessed this. He was transported as well. He ran his blade through the entrails of a child."

"HE DID WHAT?"

"She lived through it."

"Impossible."

"I have seen the blood myself. This has been confirmed by both Edith, Owen's wife and Robert."

Elizabeth looked at him then and squinted at Walsingham. He plays games again with me, she thought.

"I do not... Am I to believe that there are more than a few whom are listening to this discourse you are engaging in at present? We could move into my chambers where quieter matters can be discussed," she retorted.

"You have misjudged me, I am sorry. Your Majesty, I have already swept the room for unnecessary eavesdropping interlopers. None exists. I am here to tell you, Elizabeth, that this woman, this traveller, whom you are sure to be of no import and harmless, is in fact quite the opposite."

Elizabeth raised her eyebrows and glared at Walsingham.

"You speak in riddles Walsingham. This is not like you. What do you hide from me? Speak now on the truth of this traveller.

"This traveller is the devil or as near to it as is possible. She can transport others into her realm."

Elizabeth clenched her jaw tightly together and ground her teeth back and forth. Elizabeth supposed that she had placed too great a burden on Walsingham's shoulders. His nerves were shot, or he was losing his ability to reason. Elizabeth concluded that what Walsingham needed was to take leave, for his countenance and his abilities to return.

"Walsingham. It is time I think for you to leave the running of my affairs into the capable hands of Cecil for a month. You must be exhausted after your hasty journey. Uh"... she raised a hand in his direction. "That is enough."

"NO," he replied. "I do not need...you do not need...to dismiss me like this. Summon up Robbie yourself. Speak with him. He will confess to these claims of travel beyond your shores. It did, after all, come from his lips first."

Elizabeth whirled around and faced him. Her cheeks were glowing with fury. She breathed in deeply.

"Am I to believe that Robbie has spoken with you on this matter?"

"Ah, not as such. I have heard this through Owen. He too was transported as was his wife Edith."

"What have you heard about what this traveller wants, then?"

"She is on a journey of sorts. Claiming to be searching for her lost children."

"That I have heard before now. What of it?"

"She also claims to be from the realm of Queen Elizabeth II, Your Majesty."

Elizabeth stood erect and still. She stared into the eyes of Walsingham. He flinched not a muscle. His erect, defiant, knowledge-able stance, familiar and yet foreboding, radiated back at her. She had seen this before. The truth in his presence of mind had been revealing and correct even impossibly right before now. Elizabeth surmised this traveller and her last encounter with herself, had been no accident. What indeed did this traveller possess that enabled her to appear and disappear so quickly?

"Perhaps, there is another explanation, than the one to which you have come to?" suggested Elizabeth.

"No, I think not. She is a danger to you and all who come into contact with her. The traveller must be dispatched."

Elizabeth nodded her consent. She paced the room thinking. She did not like to be watched when she was doing so. Another Queen Elizabeth. She was not familiar with any other reigning queen on the continent. She recalled the familiar handwriting of her own dear letters to Robbie. They had appeared on the vellum from the journal the traveller had made her escape with. The words, which had once appeared upon the pages, now loomed back up at her.

Execution of Traitors…

Birth

Death

Ascension to throne…

Heirs

Casket let…

Voyagers. Magellan, Sir Hugh Willoughby…lost at sea, Richard…
Chancellor, John Dee and Humphrey Gilbert endorse Northwest
Passage route…

Discoveries…

Accumulated wealth from voyages undertaken for Elizabeth…

Spanish Invasions…

Deceivers…

Favourites. Robert Dudley, Robert…

Tower Prisoners. Robert Dudley, Elizabeth I, Lady Jane Grey.

Popes edict dated…

Elizabeth stopped her pacing.

"Elizabeth II." She looked deeply into Walsingham's eyes.

"What other Elizabeth are we talking about?" retorted Elizabeth.

Walsingham smiled back at her. He strode over to Her Majesty and
bowed his assent of her acknowledgement.

"Exactly," he said after rising from his bow.

"We must extract from her all that she knows and then execute her.
A woman with that much knowledge is a danger to anyone's realm. I
cannot have her bandying about that there is another Queen Elizabeth
to come into your realm."

"Why?"

"Because, Your Grace, if the Lords and gentleman are alerted to
the presence of another queen reigning after you, they will revolt."

"I take offence to such talk as this. Walsingham, explain yourself."

"Your Majesty, men will want to know whom the father is or how
to become that father. There is already great consternation afoot at
your lack of a foreseeable male heir. If any mention of another queen,

regardless of her name, were to be proffered about, speculations will be hard to contain. Moreover, the possibility of a princess ascending the throne will only dig up further discourse."

Elizabeth sat down beside the fire. She motioned with her hand for Walsingham to approach her.

"Stay standing. Do not sit down. I just want to make it clear to you before you leave that I have no intention of inciting riots with regards to my successor. Nevertheless, I will have you know that I have no intention of another queen replacing me. See to it that the one who resides northward does not displace me. That is your main concern at present. The former Queen Mary of the Scots has been most foolish in this regard."

She turned her head away from him and waved the back of her hand at him as if to shoo him away.

"And there will never be another Catholic heir residing upon England's lands. See to that as well."

"She has talked of the plague's return and of London burning, the loss of our bridge being destroyed and even the Spanish invading our shores. What of these, then? Are we to ignore these declarations by this traveller?"

Elizabeth turned towards Walsingham.

"No, these are serious claims. I wish to speak with her before I sign any writ of execution, and I will not have her harmed beforehand. Is that clear? No bruising, beating or blood. I want to walk into her prison and have a frank conversation without the terrors of intimidation radiating from her pretty little head."

Walsingham strode out of his own chambers with a smile and a grin. He would return shortly to execute his next maneuver.

Walsingham quietly left his room.

"It begins," he said with a smirk.

Visitation

Kathleen had watched how quickly Edith had been taken from their prison, struggling and screaming at the guards. It was only when she had assured Edith that the voice would return to save them that the terrified woman had quieted down again. The look of terror on Edith's face had never really left completely. The visible twitch in her left eye and the shaking of her body only slowed its pace slightly.

"Look for his signs. They are there. Become familiar with them. It will be all right. Trust in this." She had repeated over and over.

Edith had nodded her head in acknowledgement and trembled silently before being led out. She had stolen one last look at the traveller, hoping that all would be as she had said.

The vision of the terrified Edith cemented her own predicament. And now Kathleen had to believe also in Drake's plan. If she were to find her children and retrieve some vestige of his former trip, some article of acknowledgement, then this whole crisis would be forgotten. She and her children could return to their realm and their Queen Elizabeth. Professor Kathleen O'Malley had no desire to remain in Elizabeth I's realm any longer. It was a horrible, stinky, vicious place.

416

The drowned and condemned dead that had littered the piers was revolting. It had made her skin clammy. The decapitated heads lining London Bridge's pikes had made her vomit more than once along this last journey to Greenwich.

Robbie had sworn he would put an end to her misery quickly if she did not comply with Her Majesty's wishes.

"How can you people be so evil as to think so little of humanity, of human forms, of dignity?" she said to him. "This cruelty and animalistic behaviour exhibited towards others is appalling." Kathleen wanted no more to be of this realm. She wanted only to save her children and return them to a place far less cruel, less polluted, less poisoned by its religiosity.

Another visitor was approaching, one of importance, she could tell. The retinue of feet and voices echoed around the outside of her prison walls. She crept up to the looking door and removed the wedge she had placed between its hinges. It had allowed her to hear entire conversations about the comings and goings of prisoner visitation. Her Majesty was to enter her guarded little room. What an honour to meet the queen, however fleeting it would be, she thought. What will Elizabeth want and expect?

Elizabeth strode in with Robert Dudley. He placed a chair for Her Majesty to sit on. Elizabeth waved him away and indicated for the traveller to sit down instead. Hesitating, Kathleen looked around the room and backed herself up against the wall.

"Sit down," Elizabeth commanded. "I have no quarrel with you at present. Unless of course you play games and do not tell the truth."

The cold dark eyes of Elizabeth I stared, into her own. Kathleen felt herself swallow and gently removed herself from the wall.

"I'd rather stand," she said bowing slightly in Elizabeth's direction.

"I cannot judge your face whilst you are standing above me. You are a tallish woman for your race. And if you did not yet know it, you are to be below me when we speak."

"Oh, I didn't know. Please accept my apologies, Your Majesty."

Elizabeth walked around the seated traveller. She held her pearls gently in her hand.

"They say you see into the future and have knowledge which may be of use to my realm. Is this true?"

Kathleen swallowed again and dropped her lids closed. She breathed deeply several times before reopening them to face the stormy face of the stooped queen before her.

"I cannot reveal the future to you as such. That is impossible."

"I think not. You have revealed the comings which are due to this land. You have revealed to Robert and Owen and Edith that which is due to me. What are these shores you imply I have forfeited? What of that do you have to say in reply?"

Kathleen dropped her head towards the queen and nodded.

"What they have seen is in the future and therefore not harmful to yourself or this realm."

"Explain the presence of the Spanish upon my shores. You have seen something of this as well. What is it?"

Robert removed his blade from its sheath, slid his hand down the sharpness of its edge and blew his breath out towards the traveller.

"I can't explain what it is, but I do know that we can't prevent what's coming. And I can't alter the history that will be played out."

"Then perhaps we have no further use for you?"

"We may not be able to change it, but I can prepare you for what lays ahead."

Elizabeth stopped in her retreat from the chamber.

"Such as?"

"You must let Drake go on his voyage."

"I need him here, not off venturing into some unknown Catholic territories."

"You only need him here to quell the Irish revolt which is troubling your realm at present. That is all. That will pass as well. You have no real need to worry about the Irish at present. Drake will see to their troublesome aspects, but he will return unharmed. Your realm is not in danger from the Irish."

Elizabeth and Robbie locked eyes and both turned their heads in the traveller's direction.

"What do you know of the Irish and their revolt against me?"

Kathleen turned away from them and closed her eyes in contemplation. Could she use these supposed powers of seeing to her advantage, she thought? If they thought that she could see what was to come, perhaps, then, Edith and my children could be spared.

Elizabeth stared intently at the form rocking back and forth before them. Could this indeed be a foreteller? Was such a person to be believed? Who else had seen the foreteller? she wondered.

Kathleen stopped her rocking and opened her eyes.

"Francis Drake," she said. "He must go on this voyage, but first he must prove his worth and loyalty to you. Send him off to Ireland and let him rescue the religion of your father from the Catholics. Once he has returned, you will find that Walsingham has been planning to let him go on this great voyage for some time. He is one of its principle backers."

Elizabeth stretched her neck increasingly higher and took in a large breath.

"Are you suggesting that my secretary is deceiving me?"

"No, Your Majesty, he is not. He is only just formulating his opinions on the options of using Drake as your principle navigator and defender of your English seas."

"And what of London burning? What of that vision will you impart?"

"I can't say when it will occur, only that it will not happen during your reign"

"And what of Queen Mary's head and the Spanish?"

"You will need Drake to defend your shores from the Spanish, but first he must go on his voyage, gain more knowledge of the Spanish and their territories if he is to defend your shores adequately. There will be traitors to come in your realm, though. You must wait and watch for their coming."

"What of this other Queen Elizabeth II," snapped Elizabeth I? "Who is she?"

"She is the queen of my realm," replied Kathleen.

"What is your real name," said Elizabeth?

"Professor Kathleen O'Malley. I work at the University of Victoria in…"

"Enough," snapped Robbie. "You are Irish, aren't you?"

"No, I am not. O'Malley is my late husband's name. Obviously I should have changed it back to my maiden name years ago."

Elizabeth smiled. "How long will be my reign? And why will your queen reign longer than I?"

Kathleen swallowed hard. She couldn't tell Elizabeth too much, she would need to simplify what she told her.

"Your reign will continue into the next century, Your Majesty. You have many more years before you. There is another queen who will reign longer than you and my Queen Elizabeth at present. It is her realm where Robert Dudley, your Master of the Horses went with myself, Edith and Owen. She is called Victoria. It is she who is the master of these shores of Nova Albion where Drake wishes to go and make contact with the Natives."

"I wish to speak with these other queens, especially with this other Elizabeth."

"You can't. I can't do that for you. It is impossible. I have no connections with these women. I don't know how to bring you to them."

"Well, if Robbie here has visited their realm, why can't I?"

"He wasn't supposed to. That was a mistake." I will not do that, thought Kathleen. Never! I need to distract her.

"You will never have children, Your Majesty," whispered the traveller.

She stared back into the eyes of Elizabeth. The two women locked eyes. Robbie intervened on Elizabeth's behalf, placing his blade inches from Kathleen's throat.

"That is enough, Robbie. I have heard all that I need to at present." Elizabeth turned to leave.

"And our pact, what of it?" stated Kathleen.

Elizabeth, turned back again towards the traveller.

"What pact, do you so speak of?" Elizabeth sneered.

"The one I will make to return to your realm when it needs me to protect you from the dangers yet to be revealed."

"I do not need help from the likes of you."

"Oh, but you will, Elizabeth, you will. We have unfinished business you and I," replied the traveller.

Robbie pushed open the door and held it from swinging out to quickly. He replaced it back with a thud after Elizabeth glided through. Kathleen could just see the tail end of Elizabeth's skirts ascending the stairs as the door slammed into its place.

Evidence

Walsingham sat in his chair, waiting for the irate queen to return from the prison's cellars. Elizabeth would be outraged by the effrontery of the woman's replies to her questioning. He had managed to conceal himself quietly behind the cellar tapestry whilst the guard kept watch. He knew Elizabeth would confer with Robert before re-entering his chambers again. Walsingham so liked to be in charge. Now he would see to this traveller's execution order being writ. The first part of his plan was indeed coming into fruition. Death, retrieval, death, next the rescinding of that order of execution. He smiled and rose from his chair.

As expected, Elizabeth strode into Walsingham's chambers with Robert Dudley in tow. She was agitated, flustered and even breathless. The exercise had done her complexion much good. Elizabeth's rooms were a great distance from his. He would need to complement her appearance and distract Her Majesty from her current conundrum.

"Your Majesty," he bowed, "how good to see you looking so well."

"I am not well, as you can see, Walsingham."

"Your cheeks are rosy, flush with evident exercise coursing through your veins. It does your complexion much good to see you like this."

Elizabeth noted the smile and pleasure upon seeing herself viewed by Walsingham so favourably. She nodded her head. Swishing her skirts past him she stood next to him by the fire. She rubbed her pearls softly and breathed less and less quickly.

"You flatter again. What is it that you conceal from me?" she said lifting her head up and staring into his eyes.

"I conceal nothing. Perhaps I was wrong to have judged this traveller so quickly. Perhaps there is more need for her abilities just yet?"

Elizabeth nodded. "Go on."

"She could be useful in the capture of invaders upon our shores?"

Elizabeth moved away from Walsingham and past Robbie, winking at him as she did so. Robbie knew this to be their sign of intimate conversation. His queen needed to converse outside of state ears and contemplate the matters at hand. Robert moved slightly away from the pair and sat down at Walsingham's desk. He watched as the two circled each other with glances, nods and gestures. Walsingham indicating Elizabeth should sit and converse with gestures. Elizabeth nodded her head side to side in reply. They continued their tête-à-tête.

"What is it that she, this traveller, knows about invaders to my shores, do you think?" She looked up then into Walsingham's eyes. She wanted to read every thought that crossed his brows and discern if he knew more than he had let on.

"I think she must be referring to the recent Irish uprising. We need to quell that. She must know something of it."

"Hmm, and what of the Spanish 'invasion' that is supposed to be on its way? What of that, then?"

"This is exactly why we must keep her safe. She must be gleaned of all she knows, and she must be kept away from prying eyes."

Elizabeth nodded her approval and signalled Robbie she was leaving. She turned just before exiting Walsingham's rooms.

"See to it that she is fed, watered and cared for properly. I will not have women treated poorly in my prison. If she is as knowledgeable as you say, then I want her coherent, unbruised and unsullied." She stared back at him until he had acknowledged her. Walsingham nodded his assent.

"As you wish, Your Majesty." And he bowed Elizabeth and her interfering Robert Dudley out of his study.

This is not the end of our discussions, he thought. That traveller will soon be gleaned of any useful information she hides beneath that silky head of hers. He raised his head and body up, reached for his quill and wrote a short note to Owen.

See to it that all visitors to our Quarry are watched thoroughly. I want evidence of treachery, even if you have to make it up.

Edith's Chore

Greenwich Palace, June 1576

Edith winced at the wind and rain, which greeted her as she was brought up and out of the prison's cellar enclosure. It was a warm rain, but because of the time spent indoors with little fresh air, it was a shock to her system. Edith hated enclosed spaces and the dark. Owen used this knowledge of her fear often in his punishment of Edith. Owen was always scolding her for burning too many candles at night to keep the devil from invading their rooms.

She arched her back as the wind whistled up her spine. Was he approaching again? Was this the sign? She waited in anticipation for its approach but heard nothing at first, seeking out an image in the grounds before her.

Edith had never been to Greenwich before, so her surroundings were not familiar to her. She hoped her captors would not put her back on that ship they had travelled down here in. The retching over its port side had been especially embarrassing. She hated being so weak minded. Owen had told her often enough how weak women were, and Owen despised weakness. But this was not weakness. This was fear at the thought of her demise and that of the traveller's children at the hands of Owen and his Catholic priests. They had shown no mercy to the helpless urchins, who so frequented Elizabeth's yard of late.

Edith heard Drake's voice before the tingling in her spine snapped her into attention.

"You will be needed soon to save the traveller and yourself. Be prepared to do all that you can to save her children too."

Was she really to see those children again? To come upon their lovely glowing smiles, the cheekiness of their retorts. Edith smiled then. A glow and happiness flowed through her veins. The traveller is right, then. We will be saved.

"The traveller has spoken a truth," she whispered. Edith turned towards her captors and relaxed her shoulders, walking gently now with knowledge that all would be well.

"Be on your guard for the signs of evil. It is never far away. Trust only those who favour the children," said Drake.

Owen looked towards his wife and noted the countenance of her smiling face. I'll wipe that look off your face, he thought, disgusted at the look of Edith as she stood there defiantly grinning at some void. Her face was a mask of evil to him, a witch in the making. He would see to her burning and soon.

Edith looked around for another sign from the voice and received a slap on the face from Owen.

"Do as you are told, woman. Stop your smiling or I will see to its removal permanently."

Edith turned away from the hand of her husband and his clenched teeth. Edith vowed then only to listen to the voice, her conscience and the traveller. She would listen for the signs of the children's arrival and vowed to herself to save them from Owen's cruel blows.

"I have a job for you." He said leaning down towards her. "You are to take charge of that traveller's children for now. Be careful in your watch of them. See to it that they mind their own business. I have no problem with cutting their throats or yours. However, if you do as you are told, your neck might just remain in its place for a while yet."

Captive

Greenwich Palace

June 1576

Kathleen surveyed the rooms she had been moved to. They were spacious, warm and comfortable. She paced around them hoping that this was a good sign. She tried to open the locked door many times. It would not move. Its hinges were deep inside the door, either that or on the other side, she thought. Kathleen pried open a window and could see the grass below and thought she had seen Edith walking across it in haste. This was a good sign. Perhaps Elizabeth had good intentions towards her after all.

Walsingham had been and gone again, demanding that she reveal whom she had been conversing with in London. Where had she really come from and lastly why did she want Francis Drake to go on his voyage. Was there a reason she wanted him to sail away from England's shores? Who commanded these requests? Was it Phillip of Spain?"

Kathleen had told Walsingham, "NO," she had replied she could not converse with a Catholic king.

Walsingham had demanded her full attention. His implications were that whatever she called herself, traveller or Kathleen, he would never let her escape from him. He was not as clumsy as Robert Dudley. He would be watching over her with due diligence. And she had better start telling the truth. Elizabeth would only keep her neck upon its shoulders as long as she told them the truth of what lay in that journal of hers. Kathleen had stared back at him with closed lips and open eyes. She had watched him pace the room, studied his smile, his countenance, his breathing. He was controlled in all he did. Walsingham's purpose was meaningful to him only. This was a man with definite ulterior motives. All this pretense was a guise. Walsingham had no intention of letting her go. He spoke of nothing new. His actions were that of a man not really looking for anything. His intent was to look good in the eyes of someone else, to play a part of something, but Kathleen could not decipher yet what that was.

Elizabeth, however, had left Kathleen's former prison in a huff, although no consequences had come of that other than her removal from the confines of the prison below Greenwich Palace to the sumptuous rooms above ground. Elizabeth was willing to keep her fed, watered and comfortable to gain information. It will take a lot of concentration to persuade Elizabeth to let her go and not let on what the future held for Elizabeth and her courtiers.

Revealing history to them was not part of their future. They would have to live that part of their lives on their own. It would only get in the way of their destinies. That was not part of releasing Drake's heirs from their predicament nor was it part of the bargaining that would guarantee the safekeeping of her children.

However, she had one advantage over Walsingham. She had emissaries capable of releasing her from her captor's grasp. As of yet, though, they had not shown themselves. What was the manner of her escape to be? What plans had been put into place this time? she thought. Who was to visit me next? Foe or adversary?

"What do Walsingham, Elizabeth, Owen or Robert want from me now that I'm locked up in this place? And how am I ever to get out with all those people down below? This is becoming more complicated each moment I'm here. Where are you, Shaman? Why do you not speak?"

Kathleen looked back out the window, across the immense yard, its stables and the people milling about in the distance.

"Oh, Maddox, Woody, Kit, where are you?"

Predictions, Execution Orders and Revocation

Elizabeth's chambers, Greenwich Palace
June 1576

Elizabeth paced her rooms. Her second visit with the traveller had been illuminating at least. Elizabeth had wanted to believe all that the traveller had revealed. There was to be another Queen Elizabeth. She herself would not die in this century. Elizabeth was annoyed that the traveller had not revealed anything more on that subject, but the traveller had said that there would be two – no, three great queens known in history, Elizabeth, herself would be known as well as the other Queen Elizabeth. The other great queen would reign the longest of all known monarchs, Queen Victoria. All would be English, all would be independent of their husbands, and all would bear heirs to the throne, except her.

That was promising she thought. I won't have to bear the pains of child labour. She smiled at this thought. Her image as the Virgin Queen would remain intact, despite Walsingham's protestations at her refusal to marry. Never would she let another reign over her. Never. Marriage may have its perks, but management of herself by another would never take place ever again. But another Queen Elizabeth on England's shores? That was interesting. She had a namesake. Someone in history was to name their heir to the throne after her. She smiled at the thought of it. However, it still irked Elizabeth that this other queen would reign longer. In fact both of those other queens would live and reign longer. When in fact would she die? That question had been posed to this traveller as well. All she had replied was that she would outlive all before her now and live well into the next century.

Elizabeth's mind now wandered back to the revelation of traitors to come forth during her reign. Elizabeth bristled at the fact that this was a prediction that she did want to know about. How obtuse. How could the traveller know this information when it took Walsingham all his time ferreting these intrigues out? Elizabeth had signed the traveller's execution order on this effrontery alone, but as always, Elizabeth had misgivings now. She would call Robbie at once to send a letter to Walsingham not to go ahead with the execution of this traveller. And if Robbie could not be got, then she would seek out Walsingham herself.

There was this niggling thought in her mind. If Robbie had been transported forwards in time, then so too could she. She was not willing just yet to let go of this idea. Its usefulness was interesting, very interesting, indeed.

Edith's Dilemma

Edith hustled the traveller's children into the barn and back out again. They had lingered only momentarily inside, waiting for the men who followed them to walk past the doorway and down the footpath that led to the shore. A bend in the path would obscure the men's vision for a good two or three minutes of walking, Edith had timed it so. Wanting to test her escape routes out of the yard, she played hide and seek from these men with the children often throughout the day. Day and night had passed twice now and still no further sign had been given from Drake.

Edith had been given the traveller's rose journal. William had accompanied the traveller's children back from where they had been hidden. Edith had placed the journal beneath her skirts. Owen had found the journal and had been attempting to read its pages, but he was not as proficient at reading it and had thrown it away from himself in disgust, mumbling at the indignity of a woman knowing how to read and write. His frustration at not being able to read had been taken out on her often enough.

It was the one thing Edith knew she could do better than Owen. Her mother had been able to read, despite the teachings of the church against this. Her father had insisted that his wife and children would learn to read in case of his demise. Somebody would need to record and continue on with the running of his business. He had no sons to pass any of this on to, having lost his only son to the Kraken. He did not want to leave his wife and children begging on the streets of London. There was far too much disease and unkindness in this world without that too befalling his kin.

Edith had noted the form of the young man, William, lurking about the gardens of late. He had introduced himself once and given her the traveller's journal stating that in time Edith would need to place it into the hands of one of the traveller's children. She didn't understand how she knew him. Was this William a guardian of these young boys? wondered Edith. He had spoken to her once after she had been reading the traveller's journal. William had let it be known that it would be best for the traveller and the children if she not let others see the vellum. A slight chill had entered her spine at the journal's mention.

"These are fine children," he had said and then wandered away smiling at her as he left.

"Make sure the traveller holds onto it when you return it to her, and make sure there is plenty of water nearby when you give it to her," were his final words Edith recalled.

Her spine tingled, and the hair along her neck and back rose in anticipation. Maddox turned towards Edith and smiled.

"He comes now I think, doesn't he?"

Edith was surprised by the revelation that Maddox could feel the voices penetration as well.

"Shhh. We do not want anyone else to know about this, do we?" said Edith.

Maddox nodded and smiled back at her.

"We have to go home now. I can feel it. Will you come with us?" said Maddox.

Edith shook her head and closed her eyes. The memory of that place loomed inside her thoughts. She had liked it there. Its shores were clean and unpolluted. The air was fresh and the landscape green. The snow-capped mountain she had seen popped into view suddenly taking her breath from her lungs. Edith shook her head and opened her eyes. Woody stared back into her eyes.

"You can play with us at home. My mum has room for you to stay."

Edith quietly shook her head sideways. She smiled at them, all three of them and their lovely blue eyes. She wished for this to be true, but Edith knew deep down in her heart that it was not quite time yet to leave this realm. Edith didn't understand why. She just knew.

"We must return to the cottage," said Edith. "Those men will be angry again at our hide and seeking. Let us see to the dinner which waits our arrival. We will tell the men when they catch up with us, that we were hungry again. Aren't you boys always hungry?" She smiled down at them, but sadness filled her heart as soon as they ran off in the direction of their aching bellies and the dining hall. She would not listen to William. She so desperately wanted to go with the traveller's boys. Her heart leapt at the possibility of surviving another voyage forwards in time, despite everything in her mind telling her that this was not the time to do so.

Execute, Rescind, Execute

Walsingham intercepted the letter written to Elizabeth's beloved and read its contents. She had instructed Robbie to go with haste and place in Walsingham's hands the enclosed order of her rescinding of the traveller's execution. Carefully Walsingham replaced the order and the note inside the folio that it had come in.

Walsingham deliberated on the matter before him. He smiled. Elizabeth had rescinded the order to execute the traveller. Once again, she had played out her courtly maneuver. Walsingham knew this ploy all too well. He had anticipated its event. He smiled again.

Robert Dudley will soon be hurrying towards Her Majesty. The proffered folio containing Elizabeth's rescinding order would have missed its target. Walsingham wafted the offending document across the embers of his fireplace. The urge to destroy it completely amused him, but he thought that would render it entirely useless.

A misplaced document showing up in unexpected places had better consequences. But where was he to place it most effectively? Who needed to be sorted and displaced the most right now? Catherine could use with a good lashing by her sister and cousin the queen but to what benefit, he wondered.

"No, she is not here, another miscreant, perhaps Owen," he mused aloud. "I still have need of him, despite his flagrant disregard to order. But I can see the time coming soon enough where his Catholic leanings may well need to be squashed, if he is to remain with his head firmly attached to its body. His acts of violence, however, will definitely need to be limited. There is too much talk of his glee and enjoyment at such events."

Walsingham recalled his youthful days spent with Owen and how much he had enjoyed his company. He wondered why he needed so much to save Owen from his Catholic leanings. Owen needed to give up these fervent Catholic beliefs. Hadn't he, Walsingham, provided Owen with protection via marriage to his wife Edith? Surely he had not forgotten this saving grace. The Church of England had already branded him as a heretical monster full of hate and rage towards them.

Walsingham despised the Catholic service, its occupants and its ability to twist the word of God into unholy, sanctimonious doctrine.

He would think on about the matter of Owen later. What to do now with this letter of Elizabeth's? A note to Robert had been sent suggesting Elizabeth had need of him directly. "Humph." He smiled. How much longer would Elizabeth forgive her Robbie, if he keeps making such blatant errors?

Walsingham instructed the urchin before him to lay the folio containing Elizabeth's document on Robert Dudley's desk. He smiled then as he watched the small boy disappear into the hallway. He clasped his hands together at his fingertips and bounced them off each other.

"Execute, Rescind, Execute." Walsingham's lips opened and broke into a full smile. He put his head back and laughed out loud. "Oh, you stupid man." He laughed again. "Let me see you get out of this one."

Walsingham was giddy with his plan. How he loved to redden the face of those who coveted his queen more than they ought to. He got up, walked quickly over to his passageway and descended down the spiral staircase. An executioner was to be waiting for him to give the command to chop. This time, he thought, this Huguenot woman's head would roll, not rot or disappear before his eyes.

The Missive

To The Palace Gardens
June 1576

Robbie travelled just as far out of the village as possible. He knew when he was being played. Walsingham's orders to retrieve a missive from Cecil at great haste had alarmed and worried him at first. However, he had learned to detect when he was to be temporarily removed from Her Majesty's presence. Robbie had sent off instead one of his men in pursuit of the missive with instructions to return forthwith. Stopped by no one and quickly retracing his steps, Robert returned as quickly as his horse would carry him. He would go back to his room near Elizabeth and change out of his riding gear.

"Something is amiss. That man is planning again. But what?"

Robbie rode on as quickly as he could. He reined his horse in suddenly.

"The traveller," roared Robbie. "He is after the traveller. DAMN that man. He is after the traveller. He means to remove her from her placement." Robbie changed course and headed straight towards the palace, which enclosed her.

"He means to do away with her, and he will use her means of escaping again as his reasoning for immediate execution."

The idea that Elizabeth would now be without counsel was appalling. He understood the working of her spy maker, Walsingham. His espionage was intriguing until it wrapped its wings around others, including his own person. Robert returned as quickly as he possibly could, concealing his horse in a nearby stable outside of the palace's main gates. He walked back into Greenwich Palace through the woods and back into Her Majesty's lodgings quickly.

Elizabeth looked up in surprise when Robbie strode into her chambers without the letter in hand.

"I see you do not take my instructions seriously, Robbie. Why?"

"I have received no instructions."

Elizabeth's faced paled.

"What is it?" he said, racing over to her side.

"I have sent you an order to rescind the execution of our traveller. There is still more to glean from her. Let us go quickly before it is too late." The two of them left then via Elizabeth's private chambers into the hallway and ran as quickly as they could towards the traveller's rooms and prison below. They would need to move quickly. The traveller was located right next to the Thames. Its swiftly flowing currents would be an easy place to dislodge a body. Nothing ever surfaced from beneath its murky waters once entered down here in Greenwich.

Greenwich's Thames was famous for ridding the city of its unwanted, tainted, foreigners. What a perfect place for releasing the traveller into the abyss of London's missing souls.

The Axe Man Cometh

The Thames Riverbank, Greenwich, June 1576

Kathleen stood up and moved across the room as the commotion outside of her chambers gathered noise. She could hear the voices of Edith and Owen arguing about her children. Walsingham's booming voice commanded them to quiet their tongues. The door to her chambers opened and in entered the entourage of men. Walsingham placed in her hands the execution writ of his queen. She was to die now in front of all those who had seen her. Her body would be burned forthwith outside of the church grounds. As with any sorcerer, she would be denied the burial of even a commoner.

"Seize her now," demanded Walsingham. "Take her down to the river. From there she can be caught once released again. You will give her ample opportunity to run."

Walsingham's guards took hold of Kathleen and shoved her out into the daylight. She could see the block placed next to the embankment. Its guardian watched over it with his axe.

Walsingham's men grabbed hold of the traveller's face.

"This is what it feels like to be a traitor. Do enjoy the experience," he said.

Kathleen gasped as her children emerged in the distance with Edith and another young man.

Walsingham turned in the direction towards where the traveller had been looking. He did not recognize the little entourage and smiled.

"Excellent," he quipped, "we will have witnesses to her escape." He grinned. This was getting better and better, he thought.

Walsingham turned and walked away from his men. He knew what would take place, and he had no need to watch any further. His best advantage was now to remove himself from this little foray. The traveller would be dispatched within minutes. And he would be nowhere near the remains. His instructions were to dump the body as quickly as the deed was done into the swiftly flowing movements of the water below. And if the axe man were as good as he had claimed, her head would be lobbed off and sent forwards into the Thames as well. Little bloodshed would be seen or discovered. The trick was to set up the rest of her escape. And to that he now intended on putting in place the tools she might have used to proffer her escape.

Kathleen could feel the tingling sensation momentarily rising up her back. She watched as the water below her frothed and broiled before her. The Kraken comes, but how was she to reach it? Why was it here now? Her children. He promised to save her children. Why were they not closer? She looked around her once more, desperately searching for sight of her children again. She watched as an executioner lifted his axe ominously before her. Horrified she watched as two men followed suit and placed the block on the ground in front of the axe man. Two men then grabbed at her arms and shoved her towards the ground. Kathleen kicked out at their feet and was rewarded with a slap in the face from the axe man, but she was also free of her captors. She got up quickly running directly at the executioner, knocking him off his feet.

Kathleen looked around quickly searching for her children. Edith emerged and pushed them forwards as she had been instructed to do by William. Her blackened eyes watering, weeping as she did so. Edith bent over and retrieved the rose journal from her skirts, placing it in Kitt's outstretched arms. Together the children took hold of their mother's hands and skirt. Maddox turned suddenly and gripped hold of Edith's trembling hand.

Edith screamed as the axe swung upwards and then descended downwards.

The axe came down narrowly missing its mark.

Maddox flinched as the axe rose up again.

The man holding it roared at them.

"Seize them, stop them now."

Kathleen grabbed hold of her children, pushing them away from the crazed man wielding his axe out at them. Edith screamed again. And then they heard the cries of Elizabeth.

"STOP," cried out Elizabeth.

Kathleen froze and spun around, Woody and Kitt pulled their mother towards the river. A large orange and purple bulbous head emerged from the river, its tentacles snaking along the riverbank towards them. She shoved her children even closer to the mass emerging fully from its watery depths.

Kathleen felt the enormous tentacle wrap itself around her waist just as the blade made contact with her neck.

Desperately she gripped hard onto the little hands at her fingertips. Her spine left its forward facing position and flew upwards in an arch. She felt the blood rush up past her face and the whirling of her feet as they lifted off the ground. Her grip on her children's hands loosened, then tightened then loosened again. She could see blood everywhere. She could feel nothing temporarily. Then a searing pain reached her head and blindness welcomed her. The pain in her chest exploded as she gulped into her lungs the salty taste of her blood and the bile of her gut rose up into her mouth.

Her body travelled upwards then flung itself down again. She felt herself swirlling into nothingness, and then blackness reached her. She no longer moved, merely floated upwards. Was this heaven?

She hadn't noticed all the assorted bodies floating around her. Edith's hand had gripped hold of Kitt's. William was attempting to drag Edith backwards clinging desperately to her other outstretched arm.

No one seemed to notice the axe man thrashing temporarily beside them. Held fast by one long tentacle shaking him into silence. His body flung upwards and then sideways. In one swift motion the axe was flung back towards the shore.

On pain of Death

Greenwich, Thames Riverbank
June 1576

"STOP, STOP," roared Elizabeth as the axe came down near the neck of the traveller. Kathleen's body had risen from the ground encased in a singularly enormous thrashing tentacle. Her body had been flung up high above the forms desperately attempting to grasp hold of her. The traveller's children had equally been thrust upwards and then sent plummeting into the swirlling mass of orange and purple tentacles writhing along the Thames embankment. They disappeared below the surface. Edith and a young man had been taken as well. Their bodies had been swung out and away from the children's grasp taken hold of by another set of tentacles and sent plummeting as well into the swirlling mass of foaming waters.

A silence enveloped everyone as the blood surrounding the block seeped into the ground and disappeared into its cracks.

Walsingham watched from his perch above in the palace as the splattered bits of wood and blood vanished before the men and Elizabeth below. A chill blew in from the opened window and forcing air into his lungs.

"Come back. Come back here now, all of you," shouted Elizabeth. Walsingham heard Her Majesty screeching at the remaining witnesses to this orchestrated debacle.

The queen turned towards Owen, Robbie and the men left behind, who had recently held fast to the traveller. Walsingham looked on as the queen spoke her warning.

"I want no word of this…this occurrence leaving your lips. It is on pain of death that you will swear to me now before you leave here. Do not cross me or I will see to it that your heads roll." The frightened guardsmen looked terrified. They had never seen their monarch so irate.

"I solemnly swear, Your Majesty, that I will not repeat this occurrence on pain of death," each man repeated to their queen before exiting her presence as quickly as they could.

Robbie had signalled for the terrified men to leave by removing his blade from its sheathing. Elizabeth stood shaking. She was horrified by the apparition, which had emerged from the Thames. Robbie reached over and held Elizabeth's shaking hand.

"You need to remove yourself from this place, Elizabeth," he whispered cautiously into her ear. There is dark magic about. You need to see the safety of your rooms and quickly. Let us make haste from these offending waters and their intriguing beasts."

Elizabeth nodded her head and took the proffered hand of Robbie. He led her away from the shore walking backwards as he steadied the queen. He instructed her not to look over her shoulder, lest she saw another beast emerge from those vile ungodly waters.

Elizabeth needed to make sense of this unnatural occurrence. What was this apparition of a beast that had emerged into Elizabeth's world and vanished again, claiming the traveller and her children as its prize? Elizabeth wanted answers, and she wanted them now.

But a more niggling thought was forming within Elizabeth. This formidable traveller, whence next was she to emerge in Elizabeth's realm. Elizabeth vowed, "You will never again leave my shores."

Separation and Anxiety

Nova Albion's Shores
June 2002

Kathleen held on to her son Maddox's hand as long as she could. The swirling mass of blood encircling them had dissipated somewhat, but her grip was loosening. He was trying to get away from her. Why? she thought. What is he doing?

Her vision was clearing. She could see the forms of Edith and William, her sons, Maddox, Woody and Kitt tumbling before her. Every inch of her body was resisting that of Maddox's hand. He was loosening his grip on her. He was fading away, struggling to go.

"Let him go now," yelled Drake. "You cannot save him now. He is mine."

"No, you shall never have them. They are mine. You have no right to take them again. LEAVE THEM ALONE. Leave my children alone," she shouted out at him. But where was he?

"Maddox, take your brothers home, but first, remember what agreements you have made with me. Repeat them back so that your mother may know what has come to pass between us."

Kathleen listened as Maddox, Woody and Kitt made promises to return to Drake when he needed them. He told them how skillful they were at climbing his ships masts into the crow's nest. He was proud of their swimming abilities and prowess on his ship, the Golden Hinde. Drake congratulated them on their choice of returning to his ship when they were ten years older when they would be considered men, men capable of long voyages across the Atlantic and perhaps even to the shores of Nova Albion before the coming of the white man's menacing embrace.

"You have no right to make these bargains with my children," she shouted out to Drake. "These are my children. They are underage, and therefore you cannot make bargains with them. It is against the law in my country to make these ridiculous pacts with underage children. I will see to you going to prison, you despicable man."

She heard him laugh then, a cunning, deep tone emanated from below. A vision of a man loomed in front of her face. His pointed beard swished back and forth in the swirlling waters around them, And then his voice faded.

She watched as the forms of William and Edith were thrown back away from her boys and her. Their spiralling forms swirlling and kicking in protest. Kitt waved his goodbye to Edith and William.

"I hope you will come and play with us again. I like playing with you," he said in a jovial tone.

Kathleen was horrified.

She heard William's reply.

"Yes, we have much to discuss the next time you visit. Please come into my playhouse. We will play with my swords once again."

And then the two forms disappeared completely from view. Kathleen stared out into the mass of waters, hoping that this was some kind of ridiculous nightmare. It had to be.

Maddox's voice brought a chilling sensation into her heart.

"Bye Mum, we have to go now." And he pulled his hand from out of his mother's loosened fist.

Kathleen gasped and her mouth filled with salty, seaweedy water. She gagged and spluttered. Her boys were leaving her behind. They didn't love her anymore, raced through her head.

"Stop your whining, woman. You have more chores to attend to ahead. Get thee to the surface. There are others yet who still need your services."

Recollections

Drake's Premonition and Boots
Caddy Bay, Victoria, British Columbia, Canada
June 2002

Kathleen felt her lungs fill with blood and then rush out again. She could taste the blood in her mouth, and she could feel it running down her breasts, across her stomach and around her feet. Her body was wrapped in a ribbon of it, every orifice engulfed in the wetness of it. It was salty, cold and sopping. The weight of the dress pulled her deep down, her feet brushing past the entangling ribbons of crimson.

She felt the movement of the seal as it pushed and prodded at her head upwards from its limp state. She opened her eyes and could just make out the light emanating down through the swirlling mass of kelp, plankton and the curious seals rolling beneath the waves.

More seals began pushing at her stomach and back, prodding her body and swimming up her dress's skirt. They pushed her upwards, sideways, slipping her past the encasing ropes fastened tightly to the ocean's floor. Kathleen felt the rush of warmth as the sun's rays shone on the approaching surface. And then they were gone, disappearing as quickly as they had come, but she was yet to break to the surface. She struggled with the weight of her dress and pulled as hard as she could with her arms and kicked out with her feet willing herself to the surface.

Splashing around madly, she took in great gulps of air, sucking it in past her teeth. Kathleen could see the form of something gliding beside her. Its head bobbed up and down beneath the surface. It was large with dark tuffs of fur splashing in and out of the water's surface. She momentarily forgot to breath then until the salt from the sea entered her mouth, and she spat it out, sucking more of it in and coughing, spitting and gasping for air as best she could.

A lone voice was calling out to her.

"Grab hold of him. Bring Nuno over here where I can help you. Quickly get him to shore."

A carved wooden paddle emerged over the break of the wave as it rolled over and past her. Kathleen grabbed at it, missing it at first, her fingers numb from the cold, its wooden handle just beyond her reach. Kathleen turned her head at the sound of the splash towards her left and was startled to see the familiar rose journal floating alongside of the paddles broad end. She reached out for her journal and grasped hold of the paddle instead. With a quick movement, she scooped the journal onto the end of the board and moved as quickly as she could towards the journal, sliding along the paddle as she did.

Kathleen heard another voice again. Why was someone calling out to her? What she needed was help. Surely that man could see that? She turned towards the beach and could see a man approaching, waist deep in the water pointing at something behind her. Kathleen slowly looked behind, terrified of what may lay beneath the water. Was it the beast? she thought. Am I to be eaten after all that has happened?

Turning her head slightly, Kathleen stared at the gasping man struggling in the waters beside her. His head slipped below the surface. Clinging to the paddle, Kathleen stretched down beneath the water and searched beneath the surface, her outstretched hand seeking that of the disappearing man, his black hair slipping between her fingers grip. She dropped her head below the surface and stretched down even farther, grabbing the black hair of the limp drowning man.

Kathleen grabbed hold of his chin and pulled him back up towards the surface, flipping his limp head back across the paddle. Releasing the paddle, Kathleen swam around the man and grasped hold of his chest and squeezed, thrusting her fists into his sternum as she did so. The black-haired man gasped and threw up an enormous amount of bile and vomit into the water.

Kathleen heard the shouts again of the man on shore encouraging her to swim towards him, yelling at her to hold onto Nuno as best as she could. The yelling man now entered the water fully and began to swim out towards her. It's about bloody time, she thought.

They met twenty feet from the shoreline and safety.

"Come, we must get him to shore. He is not yet out of danger."

"Neither am I," she hastily replied.

"You will be fine, but Nuno, I am not sure if he made it through completely. He will be terrified. I would appreciate it if you would help me get him to shore. I would hate to have to go back there again. He has been most stubborn. It has cost us both much."

Baffled, Kathleen ignored the man talking nonsense swimming beside her. She could make no sense of his ramblings. They were all in great danger. The shore had not been reached yet. She was cold, shivering, breathing hard and faint.

The two of them stumbled onto the beach, dragging the delirious man with them. Kathleen tripped and dropped hold of the man she was carrying. The two men then tumbled down into the sand, and the incoherent man mumbled and coughed up blood. Blood seemed to be dripping out of his nose and mouth, and then he coughed up even more blood, spitting it out onto the sand. Then the man who had entered the water to help, rolled the black-haired man he had called Nuno onto his side and thumped him hard across this back.

Nuno took in great gulps of air, screamed loudly and then fainted.

Kathleen looked up at her fellow rescuer and stared into his eyes. Where had she seen him before, she thought. His features were Spanish, his eyes almond coloured, his hair black, curling at his neck. His voice was soft and familiar, but how she thought, how could this be? Kathleen stared at him. He looked back at her searching her face.

"You do not yet recognize me. I had hoped that you would remember me by now."

Kathleen rolled away from the men and stood up suddenly, backing away as quickly as she could.

"Do not be frightened. I come as a friend," replied Carlos. "We have work yet to be done together. Quickly now, help me save him before it is too late. He will not be familiar yet with this place this time, but he will if he survives this passage of time. Please, come help me now," he begged. "He will not last much longer without help."

Kathleen felt a sudden coldness creep up her spine, her eyes widened in alarm. She hesitated, rocking sideways from the coldness that had crawled up her spine in haste. She felt a sudden need to run away, but the coldness of the chill running up her back rooted her to the spot. A tingling sensation coursed through her nerves. Her knees buckled, and she plopped back down onto the sand bottom first. Her neck tensed, her voice left her as she attempted to scream in protest. Kathleen gripped her throat, something was stuck inside, and she could no longer breathe.

"Do as you are told, or I shall end your life now," snapped out Drake.

Just then, Kathleen saw the image of the shaman, momentarily as his spear reached its climax and was thrust into the ground beside her. The shimmering image vanished, and her throat opened up as she gasped for air. Kathleen breathed in deeply.

"Leave her alone. You have played enough games within my world. You cannot harm her as long as she remains on Songhees shores," replied the shaman to Drake.

The apparition vanished as soon as these words had been spoken.

"Very well, then. But I have not finished yet with this travelling professor or her children."

Kathleen whirled her head around, searching for the voices that had spoken.

"Who are you? What do you want with my children? Why are you talking to me like this?"

"Kathleen, I am Carlos. Drake cannot be seen in this world. He resides, as you will come to remember, in the spirit world. Do not look for him here."

Kathleen lay back down on the sand and closed her eyes. She was confused, shivering and sopping. Her eyes filled with tears, and she rolled over covering her hands across her face. Her body shook with her sobbing.

Carlos left Nuno where he lay and scooped up Kathleen. Grabbing her shoulders he shook her lightly.

"We must get Nuno out of here. He will be more frightened than you are right now. Please gather yourself together. I need your help with him."

Kathleen opened her eyes and took in a long breath, nodding her assent.

"OK, but you must explain all of this to me. I don't understand any of it. I don't understand this. Where am I?"

Gasping suddenly. "My children, my children, where are they?"

"They are at home. They are waiting for you. Come," he said gently. "We must go now quickly before Nuno dies."

Kathleen shook her head in protest, feeling the stiffness in her neck. Reaching back she held her neck in her hand and felt the crusted blood suddenly soften. Bringing her hand forward she watched as the blood disappeared into the palm of her hand. The faintness released its hold of her and Kathleen began to feel her focus and strength return. Looking up she stared deeply into the eyes of Carlos.

"Boots. You wore those boots. You followed me. It was you who followed me along Bermondsey's shore, wasn't it. Answer me. It was you, wasn't it?"

Carlos smiled, nodded his head and stared back.

"It begins. You recognize me. There is more yet to come. We are not done yet, you and I."

Kathleen looked down then at the struggling man Carlos had called Nuno.

"Who is he," she said pointing at Nuno.

Carlos raised an amused eyebrow at Kathleen, bent his head over Nuno as the younger man struggled to focus and lift himself up.

"This," he said, without looking back at Kathleen. "This is Nuno, Master Francis Drake's cartographer. He makes and charts his maps. He must be saved. His life has much to reveal to us yet."

"No, that is impossible. He comes from another time, another era. Sir Francis Drake is dead. How could they possible have known one another?"

Carlos shook his head from side to side and then smiled at Kathleen.

"That is true, but life has a way of catching up, don't you think, of bringing our pasts up to meet the present day. Making us wish we had not done something or could do something better if we had the opportunity to do it over again."

"No. One cannot wish for these things. What has been done needs to stay that way. We cannot undo or change the past. We can only make what we do now in the present better for ourselves and others."

"Exactly, but you must think on this more. I think you will agree that interpretation is an amusing thing, is it not?"

Kathleen studied Carlos' face. She did not like what he might be suggesting.

"He will die soon if you do not help me," said Carlos.

Kathleen looked into Carlos's eyes. She traced his body, his hands and his face with her eyes. Nuno watched her do this.

Gently Kathleen reached out to feel if Nuno was really there. He flinched and stretched back away from her. His skin had been cold, clammy and wet. She rubbed the sand off of her fingers and hands and looked into the palms of her hands, focusing on the solitary line running across her palm. Most people's hands had two lines running through them, one of which was supposed to be their lifeline. Where was her lifeline? Why did she only have one line across her right palm?

Kathleen closed her eyes, wishing she would just wake up somewhere else, somewhere that made a lot more sense than sitting on this beach, sopping wet with two strange yet familiar men.

Carlos took hold of her hand and shook it.

"We must go quickly or...Nuno is dying. Please, let us move him away from here. I will explain all of this to you later"

Kathleen opened her eyes, swallowed the saliva that was in her mouth, pinched herself and took in a deep breath.

"Why? Why is he dying, and how do you know this?

"Inquisitional tongs have penetrated his body. His tongue has been torn open from this torture as well. He needs medical help now. We must help him before it is too late, and I vowed to help him survive. It is my duty now to make that happen."

Kathleen opened and closed her mouth. She did not know how to respond to this statement. However, looking at the writhing body of Nuno, she felt a compelling need to help him. Whatever had transpired, whatever nonsense Carlos had said, it didn't preclude her from helping this obviously injured man. She would have to help, just to get out of here and to relieve her conscience from the responsibility of leaving these men here on the beach at Caddy Bay.

"I will help you -- help him on one condition, that you tell me all that you know about Nuno. And that you will tell me what the hell is going on here?"

Carlos nodded his response. Rising together they took hold of Nuno and steadied him. It was a short distance off the beach, but the journey seemed to take forever. Kathleen noted the grass and its greenness, the patches that were longer in height than others. The bits of sand patches scattered throughout their pulling of Nuno up the stairs and along the pathway.

Kathleen's thoughts wandered, as she recognized four rusted bottle caps en route, a twist tie, a plastic bag filled with dog poo, disgusting, she thought, some string, a red plastic shovel. Some kid will be upset about losing that, and his mother will be searching bags and the car and everything she thought she had brought along with them to the beach.

Carlos was mumbling something at her, and Kathleen looked up at him.

"We are here now. I will bring him inside. You must go now. Find your children. They are waiting for you to come home."

Kathleen stared at the little yellow house a little ways down the street from Pepper's Food Market. She espied the pharmacy and the awnings of the businesses across the street, unable to read their headings from where she stood. She remembered the lovely bookstore and smiled.

Carlos reached out for Kathleen's hand placing a bag between her fingers. He pushed at her back, urging her to go. "Go to them. Your children await your return."

Kathleen looked into the bag, her dress and the one she had felt clinging to her sides in the water, lay inside it, sopping and bloody. Turning back towards Carlos, she saw him disappear inside the yellow walled cottage. Her running tights felt damp and cool. Her hair was crumpled and her skin still plumbed and wrinkled from the salty sea. People were beginning to stare and walk away from her, she thought. Did she really look that dishevelled and odd, she wondered.

"I need to get out of here and back home," she said a loud.

Once home, Kathleen placed the bag of wet bloody clothing in the garden shed and bolted the door shut. She threw her journal against the inside wall of the shed in disgust.

"I don't ever want to lay my eyes on you again," she said as the journal thumped against the wall and slid down to the ground.

Kathleen looked down at her clothing and noted the sand and seaweed stuck to her leggings and torn shirt. Her leggings were at different levels along her legs, one ended above her knee the other below. The knife she had carried was strapped to her left leg on the outside of her calf. Reaching down, Kathleen pulled the blade out from its sheath and turned it over and over again. She stared at the blade and the jewels encrusted on its handle. Her teeth felt suddenly dirty, like two weeks' worth of not brushing them. She spat in disgust.

Reaching back with her other hand Kathleen grasped the back of her neck and felt a warm sticky mess. She brought her hand back around and stared at the pinkish hue of the jell congealing in her palm. Bending over to smell her fingertips Kathleen caught the faint traces of iron linger and disappear. She swallowed again, and the last of the congealed blood disappeared down her throat. She coughed and gagged then at the wedge of goo, which slipped up past her tongue and out of her mouth.

Kathleen's back stiffened and chilled, as she felt the tingling of her spine. She arched her back and tucked her hips in shaking her shoulders from side to side.

"Remember that taste, me lady. Remember that taste." And he laughed. "This is not over yet. Your children's pledge of allegiance earlier will be more cause for alarm in your little world. I won't forget what they have promised me. I doubt you will either," he snapped.

Flinging the knife out towards the side of the shed, Kathleen raced away from her garden and its raised boxes, slamming the kitchen door as she ran past the table and into her bedroom.

Stripping off her clothing as fast as she could, Kathleen stepped over the sill of the shower and closed the door. She would rid herself of these smells and memories. What she needed after that was her bed, her favourite pillow and the quietness of a good long nap. But first, she would call the school and see that her children hade made it there today.

Restful sleep did not come, though. Instead, she lay there, her mind racing, going over the events she imagined had occurred. Kathleen could see Elizabeth I and her dark irises, ringed by red lashes boring down at her.

She felt clammy again then cold. Each memory she recalled found herself flinging her body around in another direction of discomfort. She reached up and slapped Owen's face. She watched in horror as his face bloodied and bruising loomed over her. His nose was broken, and she found herself pulling at it, listening to the crunch as the cartilage moved back into its proper place. But his nose had reappeared crooked and bleeding. Another vision appeared just as suddenly. The priests from Bermondsey's shoreline rose up from their hard stone floor and chased Edith and herself out of a church doorway.

Kitt, Maddox and Woody came into view. Kathleen could smell them, and they ran over and hugged her legs. They were smiling up at her. She felt herself grin and giggle. Then they lurched backwards away, and she felt herself leaping forward to grasp hold of their tiny hands as they disappeared from view.

She jerked up suddenly as the mouth of an enormous octopus wrapped its tentacles around her waist and started pushing her body towards its cavernous mouth. Kathleen felt the air leave her lungs again and the emptiness, which seeped in afterwards. Her mouth dried, moistened and dried again. Her lips parted.

"Run.

Hit him.

No, No, No, No…

Never.

What allegiance?"

She felt then the brush of Queen Elizabeth's I's skirts as she moved past her. Kathleen reached out to touch the fabric of Elizabeth's gown and was slapped across the face. Her face stung from the blow of the enormous hand that had come out of the blackness.

"Never, ever, touch Her Majesty…"

Kathleen felt the cold of steal as it entered the back of her neck. She saw the whole axe's curved blade as it passed through her and the blood, which blotted and pooled on the five inches just above its steel tip. The axe disappeared from view momentarily and then came back at her, being swung maniacally. Kathleen ducked out of its way this time and saw the waves as they rolled over the oars being pulled by the wherryman. She viewed the hard stone arches which supported the beams overhanging the edges of Tower Bridge as she was swept under and up on top of its surface. She clung there momentarily, until she found herself running past buildings squeaking beams along the squashed, cramped laneway that spanned the breadth of Tower Bridge. Edith appeared, nudged up beside her, with horses enclosing them together inside a cage. The horses' hooves trampled the soil sending up dust into the air, enclosing them in further.

Kathleen felt the cold of the water as her head sunk below its surface once more. Gasping for air, she threw her bed covers away and rolled off her bed onto the floor with a thump.

Huddling there, Kathleen pulled her knees up to her chest and rocked back and forth. She tucked her head into her knees and breathed in deeply, sucking the air into her lungs with large gasping gulps.

She looked up as the warmth of a breeze rolled across her back encircling her in its blanket. The image of the shaman walking into Cadboro Bay emerged, and she watched him climb into his cedar canoe. Emily stood on the beach and waved back at her. Smiling, the little girl climbed into the canoe and sat quietly, as the tiny boat left the shores landing, and the shaman's companion rowed them out into the sea. The waves around the trio in the canoe rose up and enclosed the canoe. When the waves crested and abated, the sea flattened, and the tail of an orca slipped beneath the seas surface. Not a ripple moved, ebbed or flowed. The flatness peaked in the distance, its furthermost point lifted up into the sky. At the edge of the world it rolled over and towards Kathleen. Wave after wave after wave, its rolling edges moving closer and closer.

Pirate Talk

Feltham Road, Victoria, BC
June 2002

Kathleen couldn't remember teaching that afternoon at the university. Her mind said she must have played hooky. She had shirked her responsibilities for the first time ever. Whatever would the faculty think of her now? Surely she must have taught her students. Her briefcase was still in her hand. She had just clearly walked back from campus. Is my life that boring? Am I hallucinating about other things whilst teaching? So much so that I cannot remember what I was doing an hour ago?

She shook her head. "This has been an impossible day. I can't have seen or done those things that keep popping in and out of my thoughts." Placing her case down on the landing, she crossed the hallway towards the children's bedrooms. No sound came from the hallway. Where were they? she wondered.

It was only now three o'clock. They would be home soon. Woody would gather his brothers up from Torquay Elementary School and bring them home. He always did this. It was part of his chores. Convincing Kitt to follow him home at times took an enormous effort.

Grade one and all those friends were increasingly more challenging to pry Kitt away from these days. Summer holidays were approaching soon, and the promise of good behaviour meant that all the boys could expect a long time up at grandma's house in Pender Harbour, which lay vacant most of the year, if they did as they were told. Chocolate chip cookies, grandma's hugs, oodles of ice cream and the lakes to swim in again were usually enough incentive to persuade Kitt back on track.

"They'll be hungry as usual," she said to herself. "I'd better get some snacks ready." Fruit and fruit juice popsicles freshly made this morning…she thought, but she stopped as an image flashed before her. An image of a shivering Edith shimmered before her. A frightened woman was lying on a cot inside their stone prison cell. Then it disappeared slowly, descending down towards the basement, where she now needed to go.

Kathleen hesitated and then shook her head. "This is ridiculous. I'm obviously in need of a break from teaching." May and June's spring term was nearly over, and she had taken leave for the entire summer term as well. "I'm just anxious to go away from Victoria for a wee while," she said to herself.

Kathleen heard her kids from afar. Their laughter was infectious. She only wished there were more children on the street for them to play with. Ferrying her children from play place to place felt more like a taxi service these days but not tonight, she thought. This was her night with them, no friends. Thursday was pizza night and movie time. Cuddles and popcorn would only last for a few more years, she thought. "Six, eight and ten are fast becoming twelve, fourteen and sixteen," she said aloud without realizing it, and then she would have a big challenge keeping them indoors at all, especially at night.

But for now she intended on enjoying their company as much as possible. Her spine tingled, and she felt an icy chill run up its length.

"Twelve works for me," said Drake.

"What? What do you mean?"

"Just that. I could use them when your eldest reaches twelve. What do you say to that?"

"You can't have them at all. I won't allow that ever."

He laughed then with a riotous maniacal and deeply reverberatingly growl. "You have no say in the matter now, my lady. They have already promised me their hand…in adventure. You will never know…when they leave your shores for mine."

"I will know. I know when you approach. I will hear your call, and I will prevent them from ever going out my doors again…Understand that you disgusting vermin-ridden monster…you will never have access to my children again," she spat out in fury at him.

His chilling laughing reverberated around the stairwell, echoing downward towards her children, now coming in from the outside, returning to her, not him. Kathleen ran down the stairs as quickly as she could. She felt the wind sucked out of her lungs and then put back again.

"You have no choice, my lady. I will be back for them before you know they have even gone. And when I do, humph," he pondered, "who knows when they'll return." His laughter faded into the ceiling as she caught up with Woody entering last behind Maddox.

"Mum, who were you just laughing with," said Kitt?

Kathleen froze. "I wasn't talking to anyone just now. That's the radio on upstairs," she spluttered her reply, thinking it was most unconvincing.

"Iced juice lollies?" She smiled and spoke out to her three lovelies.

"YA," was the triumphant reply from the boys. She smiled again, more confidently. She was happy to have distracted them. Had they really been able to hear that maniac Drake laughing and taunting her?

She dismissed the thought immediately, wanting nothing more than to spend some of her precious time with her boys.

No homework tonight, she thought. Great. The boys had chosen their treats and were now playing outside. She could hear their shouts of piracy from the kitchen as she cut up the fruit. "Time for another distraction from this sort of play," she said. It was time to talk of canoe rides on Garden Bay Lake and swimming at Sakinaw Lake and Catherine Lake. Perhaps they could even go caving this summer up island at Horne Lake. They had always wanted to do that.

Kathleen broke up what she thought she heard was of Drake's promise to her sons. They were arguing over who got to go with him first.

"None of you will be going anywhere with any imaginary pirate. Do you understand? Never," she shouted at them, regretting the sharpness of her tongue the moment the words passed her lips.

Kitt was crying now. "I'm sorry, darling. I've had a very difficult day. Come here. Let us play something else."

She spied the handle of the knife Woody was brandishing. Its jewel encrusted base glittering in the sunlight.

"Where did you get that, Woody," she whispered, feeling the blood drain from her face as she did so?

"It was out by the shed. It's perfect. Can I have it?"

"I found it first, so it's mine," piped up Maddox. "Give it back."

"It's mine," said Kathleen. "I'll take that, please."

"But you threw it away, and besides Edith owns it, not you."

"I don't know what you're talking about, Woody, but it does not belong to anyone I know called Edith."

"Of course you know Edith, Mum. She was with you…"

"She doesn't want to remember," said Kitt, as he walked up beside his mum. "Do you, Mum? You don't want to remember them."

Kathleen looked down at Kitt and stared into his lovely blue eyes, wishing that everything he had just said had not come out of his lovely little lips. She twisted her lips into a desperately fake smile.

"That's right, darling. I don't want to play with those people any more. Not tonight, anyway. Not tonight."

Carlos' Ramblings

Victoria, BC
August 2002

It had been six weeks of a wonderful holiday with her boys in Pender Harbour this summer, but still niggling on her mind was the statement made by her youngest all those weeks ago.

"You don't want to remember them, do you, Mum, do you?" Kitt had spoken the words that had crumbled her heart. She was still refusing to believe that Drake had somehow managed to make contact with her children. She didn't want to remember those terrible days spent inside Elizabethan London.

That couldn't have happened. Or could it have? Doubts were creeping into her thoughts lately at an alarming rate. It was just school jitters again. The start of a new term at the university always made her nervous. That's all it was, she kept telling herself. But the images kept appearing, not as frightening or menacingly as before, but they were still there, persistent, jabbing at her heart, pinching her nerves at the base of her neck.

She would have to approach him again and find out what had really happened to her. Demand that he explain himself to her. Carlos had said he would explain, but he hadn't. Well, she hadn't pursued him for an answer yet, but she would now!

The holidays for her were over. Life -- no, work beckoned. Another school year would soon begin for the boys. Another term of first year university students would be arriving on campus. Her busy little ants would be crawling all over the campus any day now. Scurrying to get the lay of the land and their respective classroom locations. Fascinating time really, she thought. All that potential, all that piss and vinegar wending its way across campus.

Soon enough, the separation of those who would persevere would become apparent. She would do her best to persuade those who really didn't know what they wanted yet to gain some perspective. There would be lots of time this year and the next to figure out what they liked most. A little bit of everything, a smattering of interests was best spread out over a couple of years. Drop this course and pick up another. It's okay not to have all the answers. Time would in itself reveal to them what they liked, what they were good at, what could work for them.

Professor Kathleen O'Malley's thoughts wandered now back to the other problem eating away at her soul. Had she really gone back in time? Had she really been in Elizabeth I's Elizabethan realm? What the hell would her students or the faculty think of her if she mentioned this? She couldn't. The only person she could talk to about this was Carlos. For some stupid reason, he believed, even encouraged her to believe in the possibility of the unbelievable.

She had made the call finally, unwillingly, but desperately needing to sort this nonsense out. And unfortunately, the time and place of this meeting had come.

Kathleen stood outside of the café, tea in hand, waiting for his arrival. She thought of her children and shivers ran down her spine. Why, she thought, why her children? Why not somebody else's?

"Because," said Carlos, "they have never been to all the places you have. And neither have their children."

Kathleen spun around. "How do you do that," she snapped at him.

Carlos brought his fingers up to his lips, "Shhh, there are too many people about, and one of them might just be a student." He smiled, then, a great big toothy grin.

She was not amused. She looked around her. There were lots of possible students lurking about. She nodded her head.

"Where, then? Where can we talk freely?" she asked.

"I can see you are angry. I too am angry with him, but let us walk further down the beach. Over to where this all started for you in June. I will begin to reveal to you all that you must do and still have to do to be rid of him for good."

Kathleen raised her left eyebrow skyward and walked towards Cadboro Bay Beach.

When they sat themselves down next to the Cadborosaurus nestled amongst the sand, he began his tirade of anger against Sir Francis Drake.

"He had no need to use your children in such a manner," spat out Carlos. "He has overstepped his bounds now, and I will personally see to his end of rule over these seas."

"I don't understand. I don't understand any of this…"

Carlos held up his hand. "I can well imagine your frustrations and dismay. Your anger must be at the boiling point. I would be if he had taken my children as hostages to enable this quest of his."

"I don't understand any of this. What are you talking about?"

Carlos gave Kathleen an enormous look of surprise. "Surely you have figured this out by now? You have had all summer to think it over."

"Explain now," she said to him. "Explain to me everything which you are proposing has just happened to my sons and me in June," she snapped raising her hands in the air in disgust.

Carlos stared for a long minute at Kathleen, and then he began nodding his head in earnest.

"So you are in denial." He heaved an enormous sigh and took in a large breath of air. "You have pushed this memory to the far side of your right brain, where logic lodges its complaint of disbelief." He raised his hand in protest. "I too have been in your shoes."

Kathleen raised her left eyebrow skyward. "What is that supposed to mean exactly," she quipped back at him.

"It means that…I too have been forced back in time, repeatedly. I was his first successful unwilling applicant on this quest of redemption he is on." He raised his hand again. "Please, just listen. I will explain more. Drake is a very powerful and persuasive man at present. He is long dead, yes, now, as you very well know. You teach all about him in your history classes at the university up the hill from here. However, you understandably cannot tell your students all that you know about Elizabethan life. There are certain details which when spoken about must be emphasized as theory. You do not have specifics for the details of which you have recently encountered inside Elizabeth's prisons and streets, do you?"

Kathleen shook her head. She couldn't tell her students those details. That would make her look, well, loony. Nodding her head she indicated for him to proceed.

"For a long time now, Drake has been trying to locate his documents hidden by Elizabeth. These documents pertain to his famous voyage of discovery around the world, and more importantly the very existence and placement of Nova Albion. He was never allowed to publish his true explorations to the Elizabethan world."

"They don't exist…gone…destroyed by who knows what in history," she said.

"Ah, but that is not so. I know where they are, but I cannot get access to them."

"Why," she snapped at him.

"Because I am a spy, at least to the court of Elizabethan courtiers. I cannot just waltz in and take documents from any king or queen. I…"

"Of course you can't. That's ridiculous. Nobody can," she said firmly to him.

"But they can. You can. You have seen Elizabeth. You have spoken to her. You have been released by her. Only you can retrieve those documents. It is you who can begin the demise of Drake, and I will help you in this quest."

Kathleen stared back at Carlos. "This is madness. I am not going anywhere near that place again."

"But you must. You have to go back again. You have a duty to perform. You made the pledge of allegiance to him. He has your soul just where he wants it."

Kathleen began to breathe deeply, panting almost in her panic. "I don't want to go back there again," she pleaded with Carlos.

"If you don't, then I won't be able to stop him from taking your children again." He sighed. "We won't be able to save Nuno de Silva from his fate with inquisitionist tongs. You saw his mouth when we pulled him from this bay earlier in June. You saw his mouth."

Kathleen's own mouth dropped open. "What are you saying? Are you out of your mind? I'm not going anywhere near any inquisitional hearing. Do you know what they will do to a woman? Are you crazy?"

Kathleen stood up as if to go. She looked out across the bay. An image rose from the depths of the water. The shaman stood tall and erect inside his long canoe. A little girl sat below him. She was waving her hand out towards her. And then the image disappeared.

Carlos placed his hand inside hers. "Please," he begged, "this is the only way to stop him from manipulating your world and theirs." He pointed towards the now empty bay.

"I didn't see anything out there, nothing."

"Of course you did. You are not letting yourself believe. You must believe."

"WHY," she yelled back at him.

"Sit, please," he said.

"I didn't ask for any of this to happen. I'm not willing. Do you understand that," she yelled back at him.

"Of course you didn't." He motioned for her to sit back down. "I didn't either. I just wanted to end my nightmare, but you came along, and you saved me."

"What are you talking about now? I haven't saved you from anything. What nonsense are you spouting on about now?" she demanded.

"You and I have a past. You saved me from Drake's men. You stopped Drake from having me skewered at the end of a sword. You convinced him of my value, and to that I owe you my allegiance."

Kathleen sat down and put her head inside her hands. "This is ridiculous. I can't have saved you. I can't have."

"I understand that this is overwhelming. I do," he said. "But you must start to believe and believe soon."

"Why, why, why, why, WHY," she blurted out.

"Because if you don't, he will take your children again. He has made a pact with them already, one that you cannot undo. Their fate is sealed if you do not comply with his wishes."

"There has to be another solution. There simply must be."

"There is," he spoke softly. "You must close the portal before he takes them again. You must return to the shaman all of his heirs taken by Drake. When you do, that portal now available to Drake will close. He will never again be allowed into the sacred world of the spirit people of Nova Albion."

Kathleen looked directly into the eyes of Carlos. "Show me where that portal lies. I will close it as soon as I can."

"In time," he said. "First, though, you must understand its properties. And you must believe in all that has transpired. There is more than the portal's closure at stake here. Edith needs still to be rescued, and John Stowe needs to be reined in. He has devised a plan to erase all traces of William Shakespeare, and he has begun to do so. He must be stopped."

Kathleen turned away from Carlos. She didn't want to hear any more of this. Her life was just fine as it was. She had no need to contemplate the fate of William Shakespeare, Sir Francis Drake or John Stowe. However, inside her heart a niggling pang began its beat. Her pulse raced. Her breathing quickened, her hands began trembling and became sweaty.

"I will never let him take my children again," she whispered softly. "Nobody can take them away from me again." She looked back into the eyes of Carlos. He was smiling, trembling and breathing heavily.

"I will remind you of that statement every time you waver from the truth."

Kathleen cringed. "I thought you were here to help me?" she said to him.

"I am, and I will help you. That is enough for today. It will get easier once you take seriously the call of the Kraken. Listen for it when it appears. Believe." Carlos rose and started walking away from her. He turned back and smiled. It was a sweet, welcoming smile, however, it troubled her. Somehow this conversation had not been nice. She watched him move across the sand and back up the stairs. She watched him until his figure disappeared from view. How was she to recognize this call of the Kraken? she wondered. And how was she to prevent Drake from taking her children without her knowledge?

Tribute to a not forgotten Mum
Mary Elizabeth Milner (Nee-Hammond)
May 23rd, 1933- Jan 3rd, 2017

Mum was born in London, England, near Le-Bow bell's ringing tones. One of those cockney's with the funny English accent. Drop all those H's in your pronunciation and you'll pretty much get it.

She was a great, squishy, cuddly, kind, generous lovely mum. Always telling jokes, smiling and being kind. She liked kids, cooking, tennis, cats (tussypats), squirrels and birds. And of course her family, her brood of three kids, the grandchildren and Dad.

She travelled lots, read books, played cards, gardened, cooked fabulous meals and listened to her music collection, which was immense.

I can smile now in remembrance of her. The memories are great and I treasure each one as it pops into my head. You are truly missed. The book is out now. The procrastination is over. The long await is dusted and bound and being read. Thank you mum for the encouragement and unconditional love.

Here, to a stiff Gin, a raised glass, and lots of bubbly. I will love you for ever and ever and always.

Kagee Kate.